Under a Dark Cloud

Louisa Scarr studied Psychology at the University of Southampton and has lived in and around the city ever since. She works as a freelance copywriter and editor, and when she's not writing, she can be found pounding the streets in running shoes or swimming in muddy lakes.

Also by Louisa Scarr

Butler & West

Last Place You Look
Under a Dark Cloud

LOUISA SCARR

UNDER A DARK CLOUD

First published in the United Kingdom in 2021 by

Canelo
31 Helen Road
Oxford OX2 0DF
United Kingdom

A CIP catalogue record for this book is available from the British Library.

Print ISBN 978 1 80032 348 3
Ebook ISBN 978 1 80032 347 6

Look for more great books at www.canelo.co

Printed and bound in Great Britain by Clays Ltd, Elcograf S.p.A.

1

For Marie and Alec.

Your enthusiasm is infectious.

Prologue

The smell sticks in his nose, cloying and alien. It hangs in the air; he feels it down the back of his throat. It's something he's never experienced before. Instinctively, it makes his heart race.

He opens his eyes. His vision is blurry. All he can see is a grey tinge of moonlight and he gropes around to try and find his glasses. He's aware his hands feel dirty, a layer of something sticky on his skin.

He's seeing double. He blinks and pushes his fingers into his eyes, until a kaleidoscope of colour dances on his retinas. The fuzziness persists. But even through the darkened haze he can see his hands are stained a deep red. The stuff is everywhere, under his nails, all down his arms. Some of it has started to dry, and he rubs at his palm with a finger.

He glances down at his T-shirt; it's stained and filthy. He can sense damp patches under his arms and down his back. He feels cold, his body starting to shiver.

He squints to force his eyes to focus. He is sitting on a hard, rough floor, slumped against a metal cabinet. He is in a large vehicle – what appears to be the back of a truck or a van.

His mind feels like pieces of a wet jigsaw: soggy and fragmented, unable to fit together. He can't remember what he did to get himself here.

He puts his hands either side of him to push himself up, recoiling as he touches a puddle of something wet. He looks frantically around the small space. He can just make out the indistinct edges of cupboards, the side of a table. Papers scattered across the floor, some soaking in patches of the same stuff he is sitting in.

And then he knows what it is. It's blood. Blood is everywhere. Pools of it across the floor. Spatters across the cupboards and ceiling and windows. Covering his jeans and T-shirt and skin. He tastes it in his mouth: metal and rust. The smell of it in his nose. It is hideous, and bile rises in his stomach.

He starts to panic, his heart racing, adrenaline jolting his body into action. But then he freezes. He sees it now. Something in front of him, lying in the middle of the floor, half hidden under the table. Something more horrifying than the blood.

He jumps away, the back of his head hitting a corner of a cupboard, sharp and painful. He pulls his knees up to his chest, wrapping his arms around them, his body locked in fear.

He pushes his eyes tightly shut. His hands ball into fists. He starts to rock.

And then a noise fills the inside of the van. It is loud and terrifying, and after a moment he realises it's coming from his own mouth. It echoes off the walls, making his throat raw, draining the air from his lungs.

He is screaming. And he knows there is nothing he can do to make himself stop.

Part 1

1

Wednesday

At first: a buzz. A fractious whine, intermittent, next to him. He wakes with a jerk, his hand groping on his bedside table. He picks up his phone and holds it to his ear.

'Butler,' he grunts.

He opens his eyes and glances across to the clock, bright digits shining in the hazy glow of morning: 5.42 a.m.

'DS Robin Butler? This is DC Grey from Thames Valley Police. I'm sorry to wake you.'

The voice sounds nervous and young.

Robin clears his throat, leaning back against the pillow. 'How can I help, DC Grey?' he mutters, scratching his chest absent-mindedly.

'I'm sorry,' the voice apologises again. 'I was told to call you. I'm sorry it's so early.' He is stuttering to get the words out, and Robin grits his teeth.

'Get to the point, Detective Constable.'

'Yes, sorry. It's about your friend. Dr Finn Mason?'

Robin frowns, struggling to digest the information. 'What about Finn?' he asks.

'He's involved in an incident,' Grey continues. 'And he's asking for you. Normally, we wouldn't call, but because you're a detective—'

Robin sits up in bed. 'What sort of incident?' he snaps. 'Is he okay?'

Grey hesitates. 'Yes, yes, he's fine,' he says at last. 'Well, not exactly fine. We're not sure yet. We're struggling to work out what's going on. Perhaps you could come up here.'

'Is he injured?'

'We don't think so, no. But…' He pauses again. 'He's locked in a van and he's refusing to come out.'

Robin switches on the light next to him. His brain is only half awake, and Grey's confusing waffle isn't helping. He didn't sleep well last night, thanks to the massive storm raging outside the house until the early hours of the morning. 'Why is he locked in a van?'

'He… um… Just come up here and my DI can explain.'

'Text me the location. I'll be with you as soon as I can.'

Robin hangs up, then stares at his phone as the information comes through. The Oracle multistorey car park, in the middle of Reading. Top floor.

Light is starting to trickle in through the curtains. Robin lies back on his pillow for a moment, stretching out in the middle of the bed, enjoying the last luxury of warmth. He can't understand what's going on. What is Finn doing in a van on top of a multistorey car park? And why is it a matter for a detective inspector?

He hauls himself out of bed, has a quick shave and a shower, and dresses in the first clothes to hand: jeans and a shirt. He dries his short hair roughly with a towel and smooths it down with his fingers.

As Robin goes downstairs, he considers when he last spoke to his best friend: they had met up to celebrate Finn's birthday in February; he had been talking about a big project he was working on, some weather instrument.

Robin hadn't understood the details, but Finn had been excited. Robin remembers the conditions last night: the rain hurling itself against the window; the wind so strong it felt like it could rip every tile from his roof. The forecasters had told people to stay inside, but Robin knew that was the sort of storm Finn lived for. He hadn't been out in that, surely?

He looks out of his window now, the weather calm again. His road is littered with twigs and leaves and rubbish, the pavements wet and puddled. The quiet is bizarre in contrast to last night. He had lain in bed in the darkness, listening to the rolls of thunder booming, other-worldly, across the night sky, hoping a tree wouldn't come through his ceiling. But hours passed and the storm abated; Robin wonders now what new one has begun for Finn.

He puts the kettle on, spooning a generous helping of instant coffee into his travel mug. Caffeine is always the priority; he can grab breakfast later.

As the kettle boils, he stands in the doorway to his living room. His furniture is stacked against one wall, a stepladder leaning against another. Strips of wallpaper dangle from where he was removing it at the weekend. It looks a mess, and he wonders when he's going to have time to finish. Still, small steps. He feels a grudging swell of pride that he's actually even started.

Robin makes his coffee then leaves the house, glancing upwards to his roof as he climbs into his faithful Volvo V60. All tiles intact, that's something, he thinks as he starts the engine, taking a swig of his coffee then resting it in the cup holder. The roads are clear as he heads out, but the residual mess shows the extent of the storm. Broken roof slates lie scattered across the tarmac; fences lean drunkenly against fallen trees; puddles rise into giant waves as his car charges through them. The wind has brought down a power line on one of the main roads and it holds up his progress, waiting patiently for the uniform to wave him through, the yellow-and-blue police car creating a temporary cordon.

As he eventually turns onto the deserted M3, he dials a number and it rings over the hands-free speaker. It goes to voicemail. DCI Neal Baker's rough London tones fill the car, and he hangs up before leaving a message. There's still time, he thinks, glancing at the clock. Nobody's expecting him at work yet and besides, he's not sure what explanation to give. Personal matter or police business? It's unclear.

He debates calling his DC, Freya West, but leaves it for the moment. He doesn't want to wake her; she won't care where he is for at least another few hours. He's noticed she's been looking a bit worn around the edges of late and remembers her mentioning a bout of insomnia. He dismisses the niggle. He'll speak to her later.

Robin knows where he's going: north on the M3, then up the A33, past Basingstoke, towards Reading. Radio 2 plays, more of a distraction than anything else. Robin can't imagine what Finn has got himself into.

Finn is studious and sensible and – most of all – law-abiding. There's no way he's got himself into trouble with the police; it isn't him. They grew up together, living two doors apart. His mum, Josie Mason, has known Robin since he was a baby, but it's been a while since he last saw her. Nearly six years ago – Robin knows exactly when.

Finn is everything Robin isn't – considered, clever, intellectual. It had been Finn talking Robin out of scrapes when they were teenagers: Robin's impetuous nature

8

getting him into trouble. And now the tables are turned? Robin can't believe it.

His phone rings and Robin answers it. His DCI's voice comes through on the overhead speaker, rough and to the point.

'Butler? Craig called me, she said you were on your way.'

'Craig?' Robin echoes. 'Guv, do you know what's going on?'

'DI Jo Craig, Major Crimes at TVP, in charge of the situation there in Reading. I know her, she's good.' Robin takes Baker at his word: his boss – a no-nonsense ex-Met beat cop – isn't one for tolerating incompetency. 'And no, not much. What I do know is that you're right to be going. It sounds like a mess, and they need someone who knows him personally. To get him out of there.'

'Why's he locked in a van?' Robin's shouting to be heard over the road noise. 'What's he doing in a car park? And why is it a matter for Major Crimes?'

There's a pause. Then Baker speaks again, but he's distorted by the poor reception and Robin only hears snippets. 'It's not just that he's locked… Robin. There's… him.'

'Sorry, boss. You're breaking up. What did you say?'

This time, his DCI's voice comes through loud and clear.

'It's not just him in the van,' Baker says. Robin catches the edge in his tone. Something far more serious is going on.

DCI Baker continues: 'There's a dead body in there, too.'

2

8.10 a.m. and DC Freya West slides into a seat next to DC Mina Desai, at the edge of the main incident room.

'My first day back and you're ten minutes late?' Mina hisses.

'Shush, I brought you coffee,' she says, handing one of the takeaway cups to her friend. 'Power went out last night, my alarm didn't go off.'

It's not been a great start to the day. Already Freya's annoyed. Waking with a jolt to a blank bedside clock; no power to boil the kettle; worrying about food spoiling in her silent freezer, until the power flickered back into life just before she left the house. She senses an excited undercurrent from the other detectives; a level of chatter and laughter that can only result from something as out of the ordinary as the huge gales and pouring rain last night. They are all as wound up as kids.

She glances round the room again: where *is* Butler? She'd brought the second coffee for Robin, but as he is nowhere to be seen, and Mina looks like she'll fall asleep any second, she figures the latter is more deserving.

Mina takes it with a grateful smile and clutches it tightly in her hands. 'Where's your boss?' Mina asks, and Freya shrugs.

'Must have a day off,' she whispers back. But she knows that's not true. They'd worked together yesterday as usual, finishing off the paperwork for a GBH, and he hadn't mentioned being off today. It's odd. Freya looks at her phone again: no message. She briefly wonders whether he's hung-over and has overslept, as he tended to do in the past, but things haven't been like that for a while. He's been more together lately – clean-shaven, shirts ironed. Sometimes he even gets a haircut. She sends a quick text: *Where are you?* as Mina tugs on her arm.

'Is that the new guy?' she says, nodding towards a man sitting at the edge of the group.

Freya glances across. The male detectives are, as usual, wearing an identikit version of the same outfit: pale-blue shirt, boring tie, smart trousers, lanyard slung round their necks. Freya thinks they must all shop in the same place – Next or Marks & Spencer – creatures of simple habit, not known for their dress sense. The new guy is wearing something similar, although he pulls it off better than the rest: slightly more fitted, slightly more fashionable. 'That's him,' she replies. 'Josh Smith. Transferred from up north somewhere.'

'Hot,' Mina comments with a sideways look at Freya.

'Maybe.' Freya feigns nonchalance, like she hasn't noticed, but yes, he is. And he knows it, too. Ever since he arrived six months ago, just before Christmas, the women at the station have been all abuzz. Relaxed smiles and hair-tossing. It's a bit too obvious for Freya. Not that she has the brain space for any sort of flirting nowadays.

In front of them, DCI Neal Baker clears his throat and the whole room hushes in reverence. 'Good morning, everyone,' he begins. 'A warm welcome to Mina Desai, on her first day back after maternity leave.'

Freya glances at Mina, whose face has gone red. She leans over, her mouth next to Freya's ear.

'To be honest,' Mina whispers, 'if I can get through the day without breast milk leaking through my top, it'll be a win.'

Baker continues: 'As you've probably guessed, the storm last night has pulled up more than your usual number of crazies. Reports of supposed criminal damage have gone through the roof and domestics have escalated, with everyone stuck inside. Response and Patrol are doing all they can to get on top of the problems on the roads with trees down and flooding, so some of the more serious B and Es are going to fall to us.' A groan ripples round the room. Breaking and entering – hardly a favourite for detectives who assumed their days of taking dull statements from annoyed homeowners were over. 'Now, we're already low on DSs and DIs, and with Butler out dealing with a personal issue this morning, Smith, West and Desai, I want you reporting to me, with Smith in charge for the time being as acting DS. The rest of you, please report to your supervising officers, who will point you in the direction of your newest priorities.'

Conversation starts up, as the other detectives begin their day. Freya stares at her phone again. Nothing. What could possibly have happened for Robin to take an unplanned day off? The man has no personal life. His parents and sister are dead. His love life non-existent. It worries her.

Mina leans across to Freya. 'So, it looks like the hot guy's in charge. Ooh, here he comes.'

Freya hurriedly puts her mobile in her pocket as Josh stands in front of them. He looks smug.

'Josh,' he says, holding his hand out to Mina. 'You must be Mina.' She shakes his hand, and Freya notices a flirty smile on her face. Then he turns to Freya. 'And you're Freya. Where's your charming boss this morning?'

She knows he's being sarcastic; Robin's reputation around the team is hardly one of jollity and fun, despite the Little Miss Sunshine mug that resides on his desk. Her hackles go up in response. 'How should I know? I'm just thrilled you're in charge this morning,' she replies, returning the sentiment.

But he takes her comment on the chin and smiles, showing a row of even white teeth. 'Now, that's no way to speak to your new boss,' he jokes, then stops dead, as he feels Baker behind him.

Baker gives a stern eye to Smith. 'Josh,' he says, 'I know you were a DS in Newcastle and you had to take a step down to come here, but don't bugger this up.' Baker's an intimidating figure: over six foot and nearly as wide, with a shaved head and a salt-and-pepper goatee. He glares at Josh. 'You do, and I'll put you back in uniform on one of those shitty bikes that no one will use.'

Josh nods, his face serious.

'Now, I wasn't kidding about the storm. It's shaken loose some weird and wonderfuls, but this probably takes the biscuit.' Baker hands a thin file to Josh and they all crowd round. 'Body found in a chest freezer in the car park at Riverside Country Park, near the airport.'

'A freezer?' Freya repeats, looking up.

'Yes, a freezer. Staff report it had been there since the weekend, but they assumed it had been dumped by someone fly-tipping who wanted rid of it. An employee knocked it over when trying to move it this morning. Found a nasty present inside. SOCO are on the scene, pathologist on her way. Go down and see what you think.' Baker looks at the three of them. 'Probably too much

13

resource for one dead body, I know, but West, we'll have you back with Butler as soon as he returns. And Desai, I figured you'd appreciate the company on your first day back. Ease you in gently.' He pauses, waiting for a response. 'Okay?' he prompts.

'Yes, guv,' they chorus.

Baker heads to the next group of detectives and Josh watches him leave. Then he reaches over and taps Freya on the head with the file.

'Let's go,' he says, then turns, picking up his jacket and walking away.

'What was that?' Freya whispers to Mina, touching the top of her head and tucking a stray strand of her long blonde hair behind her ear.

'He obviously likes you,' she laughs. 'That's his way of showing it.'

'What? Like some little schoolboy?' Freya grumbles.

'Who cares when he has a bum as nice as that. I like the Geordie accent.'

'I can barely understand him. And you're married,' Freya retorts.

'I can still appreciate talent when I see it. Plus, my hormones are all over the place. Giddy not to have a baby attached to my tits.'

'Yeah, well, keep it in check, will you, Mina?'

But her friend's already out the door, her black curls bouncing as she practically skips after their new boss.

Freya stomps after them. As she goes, she pulls her phone out again. Her mood is soured by the lack of contact from Butler. It's unlike him.

They've been partnered together for nine months now and have developed an easy shorthand. Two coffees bought every day, taking turns through the week. Him saving a seat for her in briefings – not that anyone else chose to sit near him anyway. She knows how he works. No niceties, no fake smiles. But she understands him, and he her. Both have experienced unimaginable loss; they went through a lot in that first month working together.

It wasn't an auspicious start. Their first case was an accidental death: a man found dead in a hotel room, hanging from the back of the door in an apparent sex act gone wrong. But the man was Freya's boyfriend Jonathan, a fact she kept quiet so she could stay on the investigation and make sure she got him the justice he deserved. And then Robin had found out. It hadn't ended well.

Freya thought Robin had got over that initial deception. She thought he trusted her. There were far greater secrets between them now, after all.

Freya shakes her head. She isn't going to think about that now. Focus on the new case.

But she expects more from Robin. A text at least, telling her what's going on. Why isn't he here today? Why has he left her to work with this guy? This new bloke, with his ridiculously symmetrical face and bright blue eyes?

Freya lets out an audible sigh. 'He's going to be such an insufferable twat,' she moans to herself, and follows Josh and Mina out to the car park.

3

After twenty years in the police force, Robin hates being on the back foot. He's used to arriving at a crime scene with sparse details, quickly working out the accused, the victim, what happened. But today: late, stressed, under another constabulary's orders? It puts him on edge. Especially when it's all to do with his best friend.

He's been driving for over an hour, radio tuned in to the news, negotiating the many roundabouts of the A33 and the infamous IDR road network of Reading. He turns off and slows as he approaches the multistorey car park. The entrance is blocked off, a uniformed officer posted at the gates. Robin spots a crowd of people, some with cameras, and he wonders why the press are so interested this early in the morning.

The PC crouches down to Robin's window, as he pulls his car up next to him.

'DS Robin Butler,' he says, showing his warrant card. The PC nods.

'Park on level six. Then use the stairs to get to the top.'

He does as he's told, parking his battered Volvo next to the two patrol vehicles and one unmarked white Skoda. He notices a first-responder ambulance car as he climbs the stairs to the top, dodging the puddles pooling on the concrete.

It's still only half eight in the morning and the temperature is cool for May. The storm last night has taken the muggy, oppressive heat with it, leaving a fresher wind that tugs at his jacket as he opens the heavy metal door and walks out onto the top level.

It's indistinguishable from any other car park in the UK. White painted lines, a raised metal barrier round the edge. Robin can hear traffic on the road below, normal commuters, going to work on a Wednesday morning.

There are people everywhere. More blue-and-yellow patrol cars are parked, creating a cordon, and crime scene tape has been stretched between them. In the centre is a large silver van, sideways on, with the BBC logo emblazoned across it. It looks like a long-base Transit: driver's cab at the front, one square clear window on the side, large double doors at the back. Odd-looking technical equipment, including a large, white satellite dish, is secured to the roof. It seems big, too big for its surroundings, and Robin wonders briefly how they got it up there. Everything is quiet.

Robin makes his way towards the crowd of uniformed officers and detectives in plain clothes. As he approaches, the whole group hushes, and a short, boyish-looking detective taps the arm of a woman standing next to a fold-out table in the centre. She looks over from their makeshift operations centre; Robin attempts a smile but it comes out as a grimace.

'You must be DS Butler,' the woman says. She's tall, with long, poker-straight hair tied back in a severe pony-tail at the nape of her neck.

Robin nods. 'DI Craig?'

'Hoping you can shed some light on this mess,' she replies bluntly.

Robin hadn't expected pleasantries. It isn't common for a detective to be welcomed onto another constabulary's crime scene, and he can only assume they've tried a number of possibilities before calling him.

'What's going on?' he asks.

Craig looks towards the van.

'We believe there are two people in there – your friend Finn and his colleague Dr Simon Sharp. From what we've been told,' she says, gesturing towards a group of nerdy-looking men on the far side of the car park, 'they were parked here last night to record the storm.'

'Just the two of them?'

Craig shakes her head. 'No, there was a cameraman, but he left the van early to pick up extra equipment. The storm swept in quicker than expected, leaving Mason and Sharp in the vehicle. Since then, nobody's been able to gain access.'

'And why were the police called?' Robin asks.

'Cameraman came back around about half three, once the storm abated. Couldn't get in. All doors are locked tight from the inside and his key didn't work. He was debating calling a locksmith but then he heard screaming.' Craig looks away from Robin, towards the van. 'Someone was hysterical. At that point he tried to bash the back door in, but no luck, so he looked in through the windows. He couldn't see much, but he noticed what he thought was blood, so he called us. That was around four this morning. The rest of his team showed up shortly after.'

Robin nods slowly, trying to remain calm. He can see small dents on the metal door, but nothing that has made any impact. He looks around for a moment, then sees what he's looking for: a large metal cylindrical object on the floor next to one of the police cars. He points towards it.

'Have you tried the battering ram?' he asks.

Craig screws her face up. 'Not yet. Not until we know what we're dealing with. We made an initial approach, got as much intelligence as we could...' She pauses. 'But then he started shouting about killing himself.'

Robin recoils. Finn — threatening suicide? What *is* going on? Craig bends down towards the laptop on the table and pulls up some photographs. 'This is all we could see.'

Robin squints at the photos. They are blurry, obviously taken at speed through the plastic window. But there is no doubt what they're showing.

The first is the floor of the van. And it's a mass of red. Running through the grooves in the flooring, pooling at the edges. It seems to be blood. And there is a lot of it.

The next photo is a leg, lying at an unnatural angle, under a table. Jeans stained with red. A socked foot. A shoe missing.

And the last. Robin takes a quick intake of breath. It's Finn. His face is up against the window, contorted in anger or fear or... or what? Whatever it was, it wasn't good.

'And that's definitely your friend, Finlay Mason?'

'Finn, yes,' Robin confirms.

'Has he been in trouble before?' Craig asks.

Robin straightens up and stares at her. 'No.'

'Ever tried to kill himself?'

Robin shakes his head. 'I don't know. Up until today I would have said no, but given the circumstances...' He trails off, feeling deflated.

He thought he knew Finn, but the reality is that over the years their relationship has become more distant. They haven't seen each other much lately. They aren't kids any more; this isn't rural Devon.

Work gets in the way. They have busy, all-consuming jobs. Finn's work is his passion, and Robin? Well, Robin's life had dissolved following the events six years ago, and it hadn't left him as great company. Even if he had dragged himself out for a quiet drink at the pub, what would he have talked about? The death of his sister and her twin boys, killed in a hit-and-run by a drunk driver? The subsequent downward spiral in his mental health? It was hardly light conversation over a game of pool.

But since everything that happened all those months ago with Freya, he'd tried to pull his life back, starting with making an effort to see his best friend. Still, he'd only seen him once recently – months ago, in February, for Finn's birthday.

'I can't believe that Finn would be violent. To himself or anyone else,' Robin finishes.

Craig frowns. 'Well, let's get him out and we can deal with it from there. We've requested a warrant for his medical records and called his next of kin. She's on her way.'

'His mother?'

Craig looks for confirmation to the skinny younger guy in a navy suit to her side. He nods. 'Yes,' she says. She points to the man again. 'DC Grey. I believe you've spoken already?'

Robin doesn't offer a greeting. 'Was she okay?' he directs to Grey, knowing how confusing his own phone call was from this guy.

'We only spoke briefly,' Grey replies.

Robin nods. He stares at the van.

'We'd like to exhaust all other options before we bash our way in there,' Craig repeats. She looks at Robin. 'And right now, that means you.'

–

Robin walks slowly up to the van. Craig's words ring in his head: get him talking, try to find out what's going on, empathise, listen, make sure he feels like he's in control. Yeah, yeah, I know, he thinks. This isn't his first negotiation. But, fuck. It's a lot to take in.

He pauses by the back doors of the van and glances back to Craig. The team are silent; he feels the weight of their expectation on him. He knocks on the metal panel. The noise is tinny and echoes in the looming concrete of the car park.

'Finn? It's Robin,' he shouts. 'Can you hear me?'

He listens but there's no response from inside. He tries again.

'Finn? Are you okay?' This time he hears a barely audible whimper. 'Finn?' he shouts. 'Talk to me – we can help you.'

'Go away.'

It's quiet, but it's something. A fragment of communication.

'Finn, please. You called me here for a reason. I'm not going to leave you. Tell me what's going on.'

'He's dead. I know he's dead.'

'Who's dead, Finn?'

'Go away!' This time the voice is louder, shouting. 'There's something wrong with me. I can't… I don't… I don't want you here. I'm going to kill myself now, unless you get away from me.'

Robin backs off. 'Okay, okay, I'm going to move. But I'm still outside, Finn. I'm still here. Just don't do anything to yourself, please.'

Robin retreats from the van, then turns and goes back to Craig.

'Fuck,' he says under his breath. Craig's face is stern. 'Sorry.'

She shakes her head. 'We were hoping because he asked for you...' She takes a swig from the coffee cup next to her, thinking. 'We need to get more information, a bit more intelligence before we make definite plans. I want to know how likely a suicide attempt is. I want this guy's medical history.' She directs the instruction to Grey, standing next to her. 'Go and find out where this warrant is.'

She turns to Robin. 'Do you have access to his flat? A key or something?'

Robin shakes his head. 'No, but I think his mum does. I can go as soon as she arrives. I know the place,' he says. A bit of a mistruth, but Robin's desperate to get to the bottom of what's going on. 'It wouldn't take me long to notice anything amiss,' he adds.

Craig hesitates for a second, then nods.

'I'll call her myself now,' Robin says, and Craig continues barking orders at her team.

Robin pulls his phone out of his pocket and moves away from Craig. He wants privacy to call Finn's mum, but he also needs space. Up until today, as far as Robin knew, the worst thing Finn had done was accrue interest on his credit card.

Robin feels guilty at the sight of Freya's text. He replies quickly, then looks for the number for Finn's mum. After a pause, his call is answered.

'Josie? It's Robin. Robin Butler.'

'Robin?' He can hear car noise in the background. 'Are you with Finn? Is he okay? What's going on?'

'Finn's fine. Well…' Robin's unclear how to explain. 'I'm sorry, Josie, I don't know much. Finn was working last night—'

'In the storm?'

'Yes, and something happened. He's locked himself in a van. Are you on your way?'

'Sandra's driving. We'll be about half an hour.'

Robin is relieved. He knows that Sandra and Josie have been inseparable for years. It used to be the three women together – Sandra, Josie and Mary, Robin's mother. The last thing he wants is an emotional Josie driving three hours from Devon by herself. Enough people he loves have died in car accidents already.

'Is he okay?' Josie pleads.

Robin pauses. Growing up, her house was an extension of his own. Every day after school, he and Finn would come home to find Josie drinking tea in her kitchen, with either Mary or Sandra, or both, keeping her company. And as much as Robin is used to delivering bad news, it's different when it's someone you know.

'We're not sure, Josie, I'm sorry. We can't get to him at the moment.'

'What do you mean, you can't get to him?'

He can understand her confusion. It's such an incomprehensible situation to explain. Robin tries again, as simply and calmly as he can. A locked door. Finn upset and refusing to come out. A dead body. He doesn't mention the suicide threat or the sheer amount of blood. 'We just need you here as soon as possible. Listen, Josie. Is there anything we should know about Finn? Has anything odd like this happened before?'

There is a long pause, and Robin takes the phone away from his ear and looks at it, wondering if reception has cut out.

'Josie?' he repeats. 'Are you there?'

'Yes, yes, Robin. Um, no, of course not.' Robin hears a sniff down the phone. 'Listen, Robin, you look after him until we get there. Love? You keep him safe?'

'I'll do all I can,' Robin says softly.

He hangs up and looks back over to the van. He isn't lying. He will do all he can. But right now, he wonders whether that'll be enough.

–

Robin walks back to DI Craig.

'She's on her way, won't be long.'

Craig nods, then makes another call on her phone. He knows what'll be going through her head: how to get Finn out without making matters worse. Whether to bash down the door, hit and hope that they can get to Finn before he does anything. Send in a dog, or PCs armed with Tasers. But zapping a potentially mentally ill man with 50,000 volts doesn't make for a great sound bite on the evening news.

A shout diverts their attention. A woman's voice, on the edge of the cordon, screaming at the top of her lungs. A policeman is holding her by the arm to stop her pushing past, and she is shouting something about police brutality.

Robin turns away, recoiling from the woman. He hadn't forgotten about her, only hoped she wasn't on the scene any more. The shouting continues and Robin groans. Craig looks at him.

'Who's that?'

Robin wrinkles his nose in disgust. 'Sophie. Finn's girlfriend.'

Craig gestures to the policeman to let her through, and Robin grits his teeth.

Fucking Sophie. That's all they need.

4

'So, what's going on with Butler?' Mina asks, leaning forward from the back seat of the unmarked pool car, as Freya drives the three of them to their new crime scene. 'I was looking forward to seeing him today.'

'I forgot you know him from training,' Freya replies.

Josh pulls a face. 'You actually *want* to have a conversation with him?' he comments.

But Mina smiles. 'Butler comes across as a grouchy sod, but once you get to know him, he's a good bloke. Solid, loyal. Trustworthy.'

'You make him sound like a Labrador,' Freya laughs.

'More like one of those big mastiffs. Looks like they'll take your hand off, but all they want is to be petted.'

Josh scoffs. 'I'd like to see you pet Robin Butler. So, what's the gossip?' he pushes Freya. 'What's he up to today?'

'I'm not sure,' Freya replies. Robin's return text was brief: *Not coming in, Finn in trouble.* Freya hasn't met Finn but has seen photos – a studious bloke with thick glasses and a perpetually serious expression, much like Robin's. 'Something about a problem with a friend of his.'

'Let me look. If it's police stuff there might be something online...' Mina ducks away into the back seat, her eyes on her phone. 'What's his mate's name?'

'Finn Mason,' Freya replies.

'Here it is,' Mina says. 'Oh, no.'

'What?' Freya asks, and Josh swivels round in the passenger seat to look.

Mina starts reading. 'Information is unconfirmed, but reports state that Dr Simon Sharp and his colleague Dr Finn Mason have been trapped following the storm last night. Dr Sharp, who rose to fame in the BBC series *Storm Chasers*, is reported dead under suspicious circumstances.'

'Shit,' Josh says. 'That doesn't sound good at all.'

They both stare at Freya. Her eyes stay fixed on the road.

'What are you looking at me for? I don't know anything.' Freya shakes her head. 'And you know what the papers are like. Let's wait to see what Robin says.'

'Who is this Simon Sharp guy, anyway?' Mina asks.

'You must know, he was on TV constantly over Christmas,' Josh replies.

'I've seen nothing except *Peppa* bloody *Pig* and *PAW Patrol* for the last year, Josh,' Mina exclaims. 'Especially not some nerdy weather guy.'

'Oh no, he wasn't nerdy,' Josh says. 'More Bear Grylls than Michael Fish.'

Freya pulls up in the car park and turns the engine off, as Josh loads a photo on his phone.

'Super macho, very alpha male,' he continues. They all look at the picture. Dark floppy hair, strong jaw, excellent stubble. Freya gets a slight glimmer of recognition. Josh looks at them both, expecting a response. 'You must have heard of him?' Josh's voice rises in surprise. 'There was this episode last year. Him and his crew got stranded for three days in the middle of the Mojave Desert. Survived by bashing up cacti and drinking their own piss. Made all the headlines.'

Mina shrugs again.

'Anyway. He's dead? Wonder what happened.' Josh puts the phone in his pocket and opens the car door. 'Come on, let's go and see about this freezer.'

—

The crime scene is in full flow by the time they arrive, ducking under the blue and white tape of the outer cordon and approaching the freezer. The woman in charge indicates for them to move to the side, then lowers her face mask.

Freya can see that Dr Steph Harper is already sweating, her face pink, the white plastic suit not ideal in the May morning sunshine.

'Nice of you guys to make it, at last. Freya,' she says with a quick acknowledging nod. 'Good to have you back, Mina. How are those kids of yours?'

'Feral,' Mina replies with a smile. 'But happy.'

'Best way,' Harper laughs.

'What do we have?' Josh asks impatiently, and Steph gives him a look.

'Who put the new guy in charge?'

'Shortage of officers,' Mina replies.

'Must be.'

Josh shifts from foot to foot. 'If you two have finished…' he says, and Steph rolls her eyes.

'Unidentified male,' she starts. 'Found this morning at half six, when one of the staff tried to move the freezer and tipped it over. Gave the old guy quite a shock.'

'I bet,' Josh says. The four of them look over to where three white suits are loading the corpse into a black bag. Freya can see a socked foot and a leg. The chest freezer is still on its side behind them: a big old thing, it's no wonder it hadn't been shifted. The too-small, wheeled pallet truck responsible for the mess sits behind in the mud, clearly unsuitable for the job.

'I estimate the body to be between fifty and sixty years of age. No obvious injuries or cause of death. Pretty fresh, by the look of things. Dead no longer than eight hours, rigor present, still warm.' Steph runs the back of her hand across her hot face, wincing. 'We'll finish up here with the body, then SOCO can take the whole freezer back for processing. Can't be done soon enough, as far as I'm concerned.'

'Anything else of interest around the freezer?'

Steph shakes her head. 'SOCO said no usable footwear marks in the mud. The storm made a complete mess. Mud, rubbish everywhere.'

'And any idea who the freezer belonged to?' Josh asks.

'That's your job, Detective,' Steph says. 'Clear serial number if you want to get it.' Freya watches as Josh leaves and goes through the inner cordon to the freezer, putting on shoe covers and gloves as he goes. Steph moves further away and pulls the hood down from her head, the gloves off her hands. She runs her fingers through her brown hair, tying a few sweaty strands back where they've come loose.

'How are you, Freya?' Steph asks. Freya's pleased to see her. It's been a while since she's spoken to Dr Harper, as Steph hasn't been allocated to any cases she and Robin have been working on for a while. Freya suspects it was deliberate, following Steph's break-up with Robin last year. 'Surprised to see you without Butler,' she adds, face flushing slightly as she mentions Robin's name.

'He's off today. Had to go to Reading to help one of his mates out.'

Steph nods. Freya can see she wants to ask and pauses, waiting.

'And how is he?'

Freya gives a small smile. 'He's good.'

'Same old grumpy Robin?'

'Sort of. He's taken up running.'

Steph steps back in mock surprise. 'Butler?'

'I know.' Freya laughs. 'Something you said must have rubbed off on him. Are you still doing those insane triath-lons?'

'Of course,' Steph replies, then shakes her head, smiling. 'Well, I never. Robin Butler in shorts. Say hello from me when you see him.' She stops, blushing. 'Actu-ally, don't.' Steph looks over to Mina. 'Give that gorgeous baby a kiss from me,' she shouts across to her, then heads off after the body.

Freya watches her go. She'd always liked the idea of her boss and the forensic pathologist together, but for some reason it hadn't worked out. Freya isn't sure why, when it's clear there are still feelings and Butler is still single. But Josh interrupts her thoughts with a wave, and she walks over to where he and Mina are waiting.

'Freya, you come with me to interview the witness, and Mina, can you have a wider look at the location?' Josh is obviously taking his new role seriously, more than a hint of officiousness to his voice.

'What am I looking for, Sarge?' Mina asks.

'Anything that looks out of place, that might show how the body got here.'

She raises her hand in a mock salute, then heads off away from the crime scene. Freya and Josh walk silently along the track towards the train shed that doubles as the visitor centre.

'You and Mina know each other well?' Josh asks.

'Yeah, she's great,' Freya replies with a smile. 'We started as DCs together, must be... oh... five, six years ago,' Freya finishes, thinking back. They were the only two new female detectives that year, bonded together out of necessity, darkly laughing over coffee and cake at the many misogynistic comments directed their way. Over the years, it had turned into real friendship, but Freya's only too aware of how she's let it slip while Mina's been off. 'Have you been to the model railway before?' she says, changing the subject as guilt threatens.

'Narrow gauge, not model,' Josh replies, then looks slightly embarrassed. 'Once, with my nephews. Only in England could it be acceptable to spend your Sunday pootling around on a tiny train.'

They pass through a dark passageway into the main station. Two perfectly proportioned steam trains wait on the tracks, carriages behind them. Freya looks at them while Josh goes off to ask at the gift shop. It's a different world to Freya. Places to go on a Saturday afternoon to amuse the kids. Fresh air, bright sunshine, gaudy metal playparks.

Josh comes back, pointing towards the café on the far side.

They walk over and slide open the door, heading towards the older gentleman sat at one of the tables. He has a mug and a fry-up in front of him. He is wearing baggy oil-stained overalls and looks up as Freya and Josh approach.

'Are you the police?' he asks and they nod, both showing their warrant cards.

'DS Josh Smith and DC Freya West,' Josh says. Freya glances his way with a small smile: didn't take you long to assimilate the new promotion, did it? Conveniently forgetting the fact it's only temporary. Oh, to have that confidence, she thinks ruefully.

The man points towards the bench opposite him, gesturing for them to sit down. He introduces himself. 'Barry Headley. Do you want anything? They do a mean sausage sandwich.'

Freya's mouth waters but she shakes her head, following Josh's lead.

'I'm surprised you have your appetite, after what you saw this morning,' Josh starts.

'Yeah, well. Need something to boost up the blood sugar. It was quite a shock.'

'I can imagine. Do you mind telling us about it?'

The old man takes a swig from his coffee. 'Got here about sixish, needed to work on the Silver Jubilee – that's the green Pacific-type loco out there. Her pistons have been a bit out of line, keeps on misfiring, you know how it is.'

They both nod in pretend understanding.

'Are you always in at that time?' Freya asks.

Barry nods. 'I don't sleep so well these days. So I might as well be doing something useful.' Freya smiles and he carries on. 'Well, when I pulled the car in, I saw that the bloody freezer was still there. It made me angry that the council hadn't done anything about it, so I thought I'd try and shift it myself. Should have waited for Connor, did nothing but knock it over, and that's when it fell out. It didn't look like a body. Like an overstuffed pillow. Until I saw the head.'

'And you didn't touch it? Try to take a pulse?'

The man shakes his head, grimacing. 'No, it was obvious he was dead. Called you guys straight away.'

'And had you checked the freezer before? When it was first dumped?' Freya glances at her notepad quickly. 'At the weekend?'

'Yeah, Sunday night. Found it first thing Monday morning. No, we assumed it was empty.' He stops and looks at Freya. 'What a horrible thought, that that body was there all along.'

The three of them turn as the door opens, and Mina comes inside. She joins them at the table and introduces herself to Barry.

'The bus shelter at the end of the road,' Mina asks. 'Have you noticed anyone hanging around there?'

'Not unless you mean the people catching the bus?'

Mina shakes her head. 'No. It's full of beer cans and bottles. The cheap stuff, you know. And cigarette butts. Feels like the sort of mess teenagers would leave behind.'

'There are a few kids sometimes. I can ask Connor when he gets in,' the man says, checking his watch. 'He was here last night.'

'Connor?' Josh asks.

'Connor Vardy,' he replies. 'Good kid. Bad start in life, helps me out with the trains. Has a real skill with engines – he's doing some sort of apprenticeship with the college. Sad, really. When a kid has so much potential but no self-belief.'

'If you could ask him, that would be great,' Josh says, passing him his contact details. 'Get him to call us.'

The three of them say their goodbyes – Freya still thinking wistfully of that sausage sandwich – and walk back to the car.

Mina points to the bus shelter, now cordoned off, as they go.

'I told SOCO to collect what they can,' she says, climbing into the back seat. 'Take photos and the like.'

'Good work,' Josh says.

'Thanks, boss,' Mina replies.

Freya glances back at her. She's smirking. It's definitely going to take a while to get used to their new supervising officer. And Freya misses Robin.

It's clear that Josh is trying hard, saying the right things and asking the right questions, but he's missing the air of competence that Butler exudes. With Robin, Freya's always sure they're on the right track. And they have one of the best case-closure records in the Major Crimes team, a fact she's proud of.

But Josh? Well, he's certainly nicer to look at, she thinks, watching him joke with Mina. But in terms of finding out how the cold, dead body of this man ended up in a freezer, in a deserted lay-by? He's got a long way to go yet.

5

Sophie screams in frustration as she attempts to get past the policeman, who body-blocks her again. She'd managed to sprint past the man at the bottom of the car park, ducking up the back stairs to get to the top, but now she can see the van, the bastards won't let her through.

The first thing she had done this morning was phone Finn. And when he hadn't answered, she'd known something was wrong. That night she'd slept badly, the storm howling outside her flat, her dreams uncharacteristically dark. She'd been looking for Finn, frantically calling out his name, and when she woke, she knew. The unconscious is a powerful tool; she's learnt to listen to what her brain is telling her.

She'd seen the news reports. Vague, speculative accounts of Dr Sharp's death. So she headed straight to the car park, where she knew Finn had been spending the night. But now they won't let her get to him. She sees heads turn, then a man walks towards them. He holds up his hand and the policeman backs off.

Sophie's lip curls. Robin, Finn's best mate.

But Robin being there has stopped her in her tracks. Not because she is cowed by him, but because his presence only confirms her worst fears – something has happened to Finn.

'Nice to see you, Sophie,' Robin says, even though she knows from the look on his face that it is anything but. The feeling is mutual.

'What's happened? What's going on? Is Finn okay?'

Robin glances back to the van, then to the woman approaching extending her hand. Her expression is dark and serious; she stands up straight with an air of authority. Clearly the person in charge.

'DI Jo Craig,' she says. Sophie shakes her hand. Her grip is light but reassuring. 'There's a problem involving Finn. He's refusing to come out of the van. What can you tell us about last night?'

'He's what?' Sophie stutters. 'Well, let me get over there. He'll come out if I talk to him. He's probably just tired and confused. He gets like that when he hasn't had enough sleep.'

'It's more complicated than that, Sophie,' Robin says quietly.

Sophie looks from Robin to the police detective. There's something they're not telling her. 'It's Simon, isn't it?' she says. 'He's dead?'

'What do you know about last night?' DI Craig repeats.

Sophie shakes her head. 'Finn and Simon left about nine p.m. with Justin, the cameraman. They were due to be out until dawn, filming the storm. Finn has been developing a new dual polarisation Doppler and Dr Sharp wanted to use it for his TV series, so he got Finn on board.'

'A what? Sorry?'

'It's a high-resolution radar. Storm chasers have been using them for years, but this is next-generation, the first of its kind. Finn was excited. He's wanted to see it in action for ages, but funding's been a problem. Not once Dr Sharp came along.'

She remembers Finn coming back from the university six months ago, bubbling with excitement. He'd received an email from an old friend – that TV weather guy, have you seen him on the BBC? – and he wanted to get together. Discuss some new project he had in the pipeline. Sophie was pleased for Finn, but excitement had slowly turned into nerves, then anxiety. Finn has put everything into getting ready for this storm.

She knew she couldn't trust them – she *knew*. Finn had told her the stories from the lab; all those egos, competing for attention. People think all scientists are quiet – nerds, harmless, unobtrusive – but they can be sneaky and under-hand. And now look what's happened.

'So they were out here to film the storm and use this equipment thing?' Robin continues, and Sophie nods. Robin turns to DI Craig. 'So what on earth happened?' he whispers to her.

Sophie feels the panic swell in her chest again. 'What has happened?' she pleads, her voice rising. She looks desperately to Robin, then to DI Craig and back again. 'Please tell me.'

She sees Robin steel himself before he speaks. 'We understand that Simon Sharp is dead, yes. And Finn's refusing to come out of the van, saying he'll kill himself if we come close.'

'What?' Sophie can't believe what she's hearing. 'But that's absurd! Finn would never kill himself, he's not like that. You know that, Robin!' She looks at her boyfriend's so-called best mate. Robin is just standing there, completely calm. 'How can you not care what's going on? How can you be so robotic?' she screams. 'Do you not have feelings?'

Robin's expression hardens. 'I'm as worried as you are,' he says in Sophie's face. 'But I know that getting hysterical isn't going to help anyone. I want to get to the bottom of this as quickly as possible, and screaming and shouting won't get us anywhere.' Robin stops and looks at her closely. 'Are you high, Sophie?' he asks.

Sophie rapidly backs away.

'You are. Fuck!' Robin throws his hands up in exasperation. 'You've turned up to a crime scene stoned out of your head. We should search and arrest you now.'

'I have a licence from the Home Office, you know that!'

'To grow it for medical tests, you stupid cow. Not to smoke it yourself!'

'Is that all you're concerned about?' Sophie screams back. 'You cops, you're all the same. The man I love is in danger and all you care about is some pot.'

DI Craig puts her arm in between them, and Robin turns quickly, walking a few metres away from Sophie, his back to her.

'You can stay,' Craig says softly, looking at Sophie. 'But don't get in our way. And don't smoke anything else while you're here.'

She walks up to Robin and whispers something in his ear. He pulls his phone out of his pocket, looks at it, then nods.

Robin turns and goes back over to Sophie. 'Finn's mum is here and I'm going to go with her to his flat. We need to look for anything that can help us work out what's going on.'

'You can't do that,' Sophie exclaims. 'That's an invasion of privacy. Police can't break into anywhere they want!'

Robin looks at her, a withering expression on his face. 'I'm not going as police, I'm going as his friend. And Josie has a key, so we're not breaking in.' He pauses. 'Would you prefer that Finn stays here, Sophie? Locked in a van with a dead body, threatening to kill himself?'

Sophie reels at the stark reality. But she shakes her head quickly, stunned. 'I'm coming with you,' she stutters.

'You can come if you want, but if you get in my way, I will arrest you, like I should have done three months ago.' Robin's voice is dispassionate, his emotions back under check. Sophie doesn't know how he does it, but she feels sad for Robin. She'd rather be herself, emotional and reactive and feeling, experiencing the world as it happens, than be that cold.

'Do you understand me?' Robin adds.

Sophie bites her lip, nodding slowly.

'Fine, then let's go.'

6

Robin feels warm arms round him, pulling him tight. He enjoys the closeness for a second, remembering the familiar scent of lavender talcum powder, then pulls away, kissing his best friend's mum on the cheek.

Josie looks tired, but her presence is the tonic Robin needs. She puts two hands either side of Robin's face and looks at him closely, a kind smile radiating towards him.

'Let me look at you, Robin,' Josie says. 'It's been too long.' She pulls him first in one direction, then the other. Robin is used to being examined in this way by Josie and lets her prod him in the tummy. 'You're looking good.'

'That's your way of saying I've lost weight,' he replies, good-naturedly.

'Well. You had spare,' Josie says, and Robin snorts. 'I'm sorry we haven't seen you since… since Georgia died,' she continues. 'I tried to call—'

'Let's talk later,' Robin interrupts, awkwardly.

He pulls away from Josie and receives a second embrace from Sandra, standing next to them. He towers over her, his six foot compared to her barely five.

It's been nearly six years since he saw them last, at Georgia's funeral. Josie's still tall and slender, her build the same as her son's, her grey hair now short and cropped. In contrast, Sandra's got rounder, her rosy cheeks surrounded by a halo of ash-blonde curls. It's his fault he hasn't seen them. He'd ignored Josie's calls, not wanting to talk about what happened, how Georgia died; entombed in his cocoon of misery.

'You'll sort this, won't you, Robin?' Sandra says quietly, and he nods, despite his reservations.

Robin points to Sophie, who is receiving a hug from Josie.

'Sandra, this is Sophie, Finn's girlfriend,' Robin says, doing a quick introduction.

The women all smile at each other, but then expressions turn serious, as Craig comes over. Robin waits impatiently as she spends precious moments outlining the situation to the older women. Sharp's death, Finn locked in the van, the confusion and lack of clarity over what's going on.

'…so any clues to his mental state would be invaluable right now,' Craig concludes, explaining their need to visit Finn's flat.

'And I'm sorry to be pushy, but we need to go,' Robin adds. He's desperate to get there and see what they can find that might help them piece together this mess.

They all nod grimly and make their way down the stairs to Robin's car on the lower floor. They climb in: Robin driving, Josie in the front, and Sandra and Sophie in the back.

–

They drive in uncharacteristic silence. Normally, with Josie and Sandra, the air would be filled with chatter. Personal questions about his life, his job, prospective girl-friends. Enquiring whether he is eating okay, getting enough sleep. Then when those topics of conversation ran out, they would move on to TV, to books, to whatever Josie had seen lately, out for her daily walk round the village.

Josie and Sandra always have an endless supply of conversation, even though they see each other every day, still living next door on the same street, in the tiny Devon village where Robin and Finn grew up. Finn's dad left when he was a baby, and the three households almost existed as one: the Butlers, Sandra and the Masons. He remembers the giggles from the three of them when Robin's mum was still alive and how they would shush as he and Finn came into the kitchen – talk not right for the ears of small people. He always wondered what they might have been gossiping about, curious to be allowed into the exclusive inner sanctum of girl talk.

But it seems today circumstances are too serious for such frivolities.

As he drives, Robin glances in the rear-view mirror at Sophie. She is staring out of the window, lost in her own thoughts, chewing on a fingernail with chipped pink nail polish. She is wearing a patchwork flowing dress, knee-high brown boots and what seems to be a green army coat over the top.

Robin takes a deep breath, suppressing his irritation. If he was being honest, he had considered phoning Sophie when he heard the news about Finn, but he couldn't bear the thought of having to spend time with the woman.

He first met her three months ago, out with Finn to celebrate his birthday. Just the three of them.

It hadn't started well. She'd wafted in, scented delicately with a soft perfume, but also something else: the sweet, earthy smell of pot he easily recognised. But surely not. Surely nobody would be so stupid as to turn up for dinner with a police detective – albeit one off duty – stinking of marijuana?

The conversation was fine at first. Finn telling them about his latest project, the details of which neither of them understood. Sophie talked about her doctorate at the university – research into the effectiveness of cannabinoids in the treatment of cancer. Worthy work indeed, Robin thought, although there was then no doubt in his mind that she was sampling her own product.

But then— Robin grits his teeth just remembering the conversation.

'…it's not that I've got anything against investing in defence, but it seems to me the money could be better spent,' Sophie had said. 'When people are depending on food banks to survive and NHS waiting lists are at crisis point, I think there are bigger priorities.'

'We can always do with more coppers on the front line,' Robin replied.

'I'm not sure that's where the money is best spent—'

Robin frowned. 'You mean, making sure our streets are safe?'

'If that's what you call it,' Sophie said, taking a large gulp of wine. 'All I see are police trying to get in the way. For example,' she continued, waving a hand as if plucking a thought out of the air, 'peaceful protests. Why shouldn't we protest about climate change? Why shouldn't we march for what we believe in?'

'No one's stopping you marching, but police need to be there to ensure everyone is safe. And if you weren't protesting, maybe police resources could be better used elsewhere,' Robin argued. He'd kept a smile on his face, but his tolerance was straining at the seams.

'Nobody requested you to turn up. Nobody asked the police to stop the climate rebellion protest.'

'Police go where we're needed the most,' Robin replied. 'And if someone's spraying red paint at a public building, then that's the priority. We don't go where you ask us to go.'

'Well, why not?' Sophie had added, ignoring the warning hand from Finn on her arm. 'Our taxes pay your wages, after all.'

'What?' Robin said incredulously. 'You pay tax? On your PhD salary?'

'Time for a break,' Finn interrupted, quickly. 'Now.'

And he'd taken Sophie's arm and pulled her away from the table.

Robin sat, alone, his mouth still open in surprise. Then he'd finished the last of the wine from his glass and signalled to the waiter to request the bill. Enough was enough.

He'd paid and left the restaurant, looking around for Finn so he could say goodbye. He'd glanced round the corner, and there Sophie and Finn were, passing a cigarette between them. Except it wasn't a cigarette.

Even from that distance, Robin could detect the strong smell of weed. He continued watching them, unsure of what to do.

Then Finn turned and caught his eye. And Robin knew the expression on his face; he'd seen it a million times as a child. Finn could not hide when he was lying or when he'd done something wrong. It was the same expression he had when Josie had caught them stealing biscuits before dinner or sneaking in late after curfew.

'Robin…' Finn had started, and Robin walked up to them, taking the spliff out of his hand and stubbing it out underfoot on the pavement.

'Hey…' Sophie said, objecting.

'I should arrest you,' Robin growled. He faced Finn, turning his back deliberately on Sophie. 'I don't care what you do in your own time, Finn, but smoking pot in front of me is plain stupid. And it puts me in a really awkward position.' He'd shaken his head. 'I'm leaving. I'll call you later.'

Robin had walked away, ignoring their indiscretion. But he hadn't called. And Finn hadn't called him. A pause in their contact that was unusual. They'd argued in the past but made up without even so much as a mumbled apology. This time there'd been nothing. And Robin had no doubt in his mind as to why.

So he had no wish to see her again. Yet, here she is, sulking in the back of his car.

They turn into the car park for Finn's block of flats and pull into the numbered space. Robin knows that Finn's Ford Focus is currently parked at the multistorey, a few floors down from the van – left for the morning, when he would have planned to go home after the storm and get some sleep. Things haven't turned out that way, though, and the empty parking space just reminds Robin of it.

The four of them get out of the car, and Robin opens his boot. He takes out plastic gloves and shoe covers, and turns to face them.

'We're not here in a police capacity, but we should treat this visit as if it were—' he begins.

Josie interrupts him. 'What do you mean, Robin?'

'We need to disturb as little as possible. We need to wear these,' he says, holding out the gloves. They all stare

45

at them, blinking. 'We're looking for anything that will give us an idea of Finn's state of mind, that will help us persuade him out of there. Outside of that, we should try to avoid contaminating potential evidence.'

The moment the words are out of Robin's mouth, he sees Josie's face fall and regrets his official terminology. He'd said it automatically, so used to telling officers under his command what to do. He'd forgotten this is family.

Next to him, Sophie scoffs. 'I know Finn's state of mind,' she says, sulkily. 'I don't need to go snooping around his flat.'

'Fine, then stay here.'

Josie slowly reaches out and takes the gloves from Robin, her face grey. She hands a pair to Sandra. After a moment, Sophie sighs and does the same.

They walk up the concrete steps to Finn's flat. Robin puts the key in the lock and turns.

The smell is the first thing he notices. It's musty, with an undercurrent of burnt toast and stale sweat. The hallway is dark, so Robin gropes around for a light and switches it on.

And gasps.

It looks like the flat has been ransacked. A narrow hallway leads to a small living room that includes the kitchen, with a bedroom and bathroom off to one side. Clothes and belongings are strewn on the floor; the kitchen overflows with dirty dishes and a full bin, over which hopeful flies hover. A line of black dirt on the carpet shows the usual walkways.

Josie and Sandra stand in the doorway, their hands over their mouths. Robin turns to Sophie.

'When were you here last?' he asks.

'I... I...' Sophie stutters. Her eyes are wide; she's clearly as shocked as they are by the state of Finn's flat.

'When, Sophie?' Robin asks again.

'Not for a while, a few months maybe. Finn always comes to mine, he says his place is poky, and...' She shakes her head. 'I didn't know.'

Robin slowly continues his way inside, looking downwards, trying to avoid treading on the mess strewn on the ground. He goes into the kitchen and opens the fridge. There's little food inside, just two cans of beer and some nearly empty bottles of condiments – tomato ketchup, mustard, mayo – and a few plastic bottles of water. Robin frowns.

'Did he eat at yours, too?' he directs over his shoulder to Sophie.

'Sometimes. I'd cook for him, but for the last few weeks he's been spending more and more time at the university, getting everything ready for Simon's visit.'

'Hmm.' Robin can't make it add up. His intelligent, sensitive, previously house-proud friend is living in this... this pit? What's he missing? What's going on?

He turns round and gently escorts Sophie over to the sofa. She lets him guide her, still shocked. Robin pushes the clothes and newspapers aside and sits her down.

'Sophie?' he says gently. He waits until she has stopped gawping at the flat and looks at him. 'How has Finn been?' he asks. 'In the last month or so. The truth, please.'

Sophie opens and closes her mouth a few times, then rubs her eyes. Robin can see she is on the edge of tears.

'He...' she starts. 'He hasn't been himself. Finn's always been quiet, but lately he's completely retreated. Would barely talk to me. When I asked him about it, he said he was worried about work – about Simon's visit and the

BBC filming. He said there was a lot riding on this going well. He's been struggling to get funding for the next bit of research, and this would have solved all their problems.'

She sniffs. 'But I didn't think things had got this bad. Or maybe… I just…' She tails off again. 'He's lost a bit of weight. I knew he wasn't eating properly. I'd bring him food to his lab, but most of it went untouched.'

Robin sighs. They need to finish their search, then get out of there. It's bad enough when you're a police officer, used to seeing this sort of shit, even if he's struggling to attribute it to his best friend. But it must be impossible for Finn's mother.

'You guys can wait in the car, if you like,' he says gently. 'I'll finish up.'

But Josie shakes her head. 'No. I'm here now. I need to know what I'm facing. When Finn gets out of that van.'

Robin nods. 'Shout if you find anything,' he says, although he doesn't know what they're looking for.

He goes into the bedroom and it's much the same in there, if not worse. The bed sheets are yellowing and stained, and there are clothes discarded across the carpet. Empty mugs and crockery lie on their side on the floor. There are a few books on the bedside table: science fiction authors that Robin remembers Finn loving in their youth. It makes him feel sad. How did Finn get from that to this?

Something must have gone seriously wrong in his head to let his home get to this state. And Robin hadn't noticed. Hell, he'd not been around enough lately to notice.

But Sophie had. She is his girlfriend, for crying out loud. He turns on his heel, a flare of anger, about to confront her again, but when he steps into the living room, Josie and Sandra are standing next to the window, their backs bent, something in Josie's hand.

48

Robin goes over to join them, looking over their shoulders. 'What have you found?' he asks, and Josie turns, a puzzled look on her face.

She holds a small plastic bag between two fingers.

Robin looks at it, his stomach sinking. It contains a few tiny blue squares of what looks to be paper, plus some even smaller pieces, tiny triangles, cut from the original.

'What is it, Robin?' Josie asks.

He glares at Sophie. She's taken a step back from them, her face pale.

'It's LSD, Josie,' Robin says. 'Finn was taking acid.'

7

'Did you know?' Robin fires at Sophie. 'Were you aware what Finn was doing?'

He is trying hard to stay calm, for Josie's sake as much as anything, but is struggling to keep his voice level. And when Sophie nods slowly, his hands clench into fists by his sides.

'He wasn't doing it to get high,' Sophie gabbles, crying now. 'He was microdosing.'

'It's an illegal class A drug, Sophie.'

'He's been stressed. The infighting, the squabbles he has to deal with in his team. It's too much for Finn. And this helped – with his anxiety, his depression.'

'What's she talking about?' Josie asks Robin. 'I don't understand any of this. I know people took LSD in the Sixties, but that was then. They were hippies. What's Finlay doing with it?'

Robin takes a deep breath. 'From what Sophie's saying, Finn was taking tiny amounts of it, Josie. It's been known to help with some kinds of mental illness.' He turns back to Sophie. 'But there's no scientific evidence to back it up. It's unpredictable. There could have been anything in this.'

'He said it was helping. He said it calmed him down.'

Robin holds the small plastic bag up to Sophie's face. 'And where did you get it from?' Sophie pushes her lips together and shakes her head. 'This is no time for protecting your dealer, Sophie!' Robin shouts. 'We need to know what was in here. We need to know what he took.'

'I don't know!' Sophie cries out. 'He got it from someone at uni.' Tears are streaming down her face and Robin turns away, exasperated.

'I need to phone Craig,' he growls and walks out of the flat, into the bleak concrete corridor.

The phone rings and Robin waits. Craig answers without pleasantries.

'Have you found anything?'

'The flat's a mess. It looks like Finn hasn't been functioning properly for a while.' Robin looks at the bag in his gloved hand. 'And a small quantity of LSD.'

'LSD? Seriously?' Craig exclaims.

'Yes, apparently he was microdosing to cope with his anxiety and depression—'

'But he could have got the amount wrong,' Craig finishes for him. 'Would explain a lot. One of our DCs managed to get close to the door and plant a listening device, but all we're getting is garbled nonsense.'

'You're thinking Finn's at the tail end of a bad trip?'

'Maybe, yes.' There's a long pause, and Robin fills in the gaps. A bad hallucination, and who knows what Finn imagined. God knows what he might have done to Simon Sharp. 'Bring it back,' Craig says at last, 'and we'll get it rushed to the lab for testing. See what nasties might have been included.'

Robin signs off the call and rejoins the others in the flat. The three of them are still in the living room. Sandra has her arm around an ashen-faced Josie, who is holding a notebook in her hand. On the sofa, Sophie is crying quietly. They all look up when Robin comes back in.

'No change,' he says, and they look away, disappointed. He points to the notebook. 'What have you got there?'

Josie flicks through the pages. 'Oh. No. Sorry. This was on the side, one of Finn's weather record books.' She looks at it, almost reverently. 'I have boxes of these at home. I'm surprised he still does this.'

She holds it out to Robin, and he runs his finger down the page. *Temp. Dew point. Humidity. Wind speed. Rainfall. Air pressure.* And their corresponding numbers. He glances towards the window; outside he can see an array of strange-looking instruments attached to the wall on a pole. He remembers Finn doing this as a kid, excitedly showing Robin his first weather station, Robin baffled by his enthusiasm. The technology has obviously improved since then, even if his method of record-keeping hasn't, and Robin feels a sudden wave of sadness.

He returns the notebook to Josie. 'We need to be getting back,' he says, quietly.

–

They drive in silence, Sophie staring out of the passenger-side window, Josie and Sandra in the back.

Sophie turns to Robin. 'I want to go in there,' she says. 'I can persuade him to come out, I know I can.'

Robin glances her way as he negotiates a roundabout. His anger has subsided, and tiredness and hunger are starting to take over.

He sighs. 'It's not as simple as that, Sophie. He's not in his right mind. You don't know what you're going to face if you go in there.'

'He'd never do anything to hurt me.'

'I would have said he'd never do anything to hurt anyone, but here we are: Finn locked in a van with a dead body. There's blood everywhere,' he says quietly, trying to keep the women in the back from hearing this fact, one Craig had held off from telling them earlier.

'There's blood?' Sophie says, her face draining of colour.

Robin nods. 'And I'm guessing you've never seen a dead body before, right? Let alone one that's been murdered?' Sophie looks like she's going to be sick. 'It's a messy crime scene, Sophie. It's not like it'll just be you and Finn having a cosy chat.'

She shakes her head. 'I can't believe Finn killed him.'

'Nor can I,' Robin says quietly.

Sophie goes back to staring out of the window.

As he drives, Robin thinks about the van. What would he do, if he was in charge of the case? He glances at the time. It's one p.m. now, and Finn's been in there with a dead body for at least seven hours. With no food, on little sleep. Robin knows there's no way they'll let it get to nightfall.

The longer it goes on, the worse it's going to be. Robin knows Craig will be trying to get eyes into the van so they can see what's going on. He knows she will be trying to talk to Finn. Keeping lines of communication open in a negotiation means the offender might let you into what they are thinking. And then be persuaded into leaving peacefully. An offender. He's still struggling to see Finn in that way.

In the past, they've called a dog unit. He's had people lock themselves in buildings, and the mere threat of a large toothy Alsatian being sent in has been enough to get the most hardened skinhead out with their hands in the air. But not with Finn. Not with him in this state.

Professional detachment has helped him this far, but in the face of what they've seen in the flat, he is scared for his friend.

Finn was his closest ally growing up. His sister Georgia was two years older and had her own gaggle of giggling girls to hang out with. He and Finn played together every day. Elaborate games of make-believe. Of cops and robbers, of scientists and laboratories — their disparate interests clear from an early age, but each happy to play the part created by the other. Finn got Robin through school, helping him out with homework, science and maths a mystery to the practical Robin. And Robin was there for Finn. Bullies stayed well clear from the skinny glasses-wearing nerd, knowing that his mate Butler wasn't afraid to throw around a fist or two.

They stayed close, even when they both went away to uni. Finn got a first in physics, then a doctorate. He landed plaudits and gained respect from his peers; Josie always spoke about him with pride. Robin scraped a lower second, then joined the force. But despite feeling in his shadow, he's always been proud of his friend.

He finds it hard to reconcile his calm, nerdy, slightly naive mate with this bloody crime scene. He needs to get in there, talk to him, find out what's going on. There is no way Finn killed someone. No way.

But as they drive into the car park, his feelings of dread intensify. The small crowd of press is bigger and clamours to see into the car as they pass; a large ambulance waits on the ground floor. And where before first responders were standing around waiting, almost bored, now there is activity. People are milling round computers, talking in frantic, hushed whispers. A DC runs up to the car, ushering him towards Craig.

'Over the last half hour he's got louder,' she says. 'I tried to talk to him but he started shouting.'

'Saying what?' Robin asks. They walk closer to the van.

'I haven't been able to make it out. But the nearer I got, the more pissed off he seemed.'

They stop about five metres from the van. It's silent again now; the car park goes quiet as everyone waits. Then Finn appears at the window.

Robin involuntarily gasps. Finn's face is gaunt, cheekbones protruding sharply. He isn't wearing his glasses and he screws up his face, squinting out. His hair is in disarray, and Robin can see traces of something dark across his chin and face. Blood, he assumes.

He feels a nudge from Craig next to him.

'Finn,' Robin shouts. 'Are you okay?'

'Robin?' Finn's face rumples with confusion, as if he hadn't realised that Robin was there. He glances back into the van.

'I'm here, Finn. Your mum, too.' Robin hears footsteps behind him, as Josie walks up to his side.

Finn looks back out to the car park. 'Mum...' he says, but he stops as he begins to cry. His voice is softer now; Robin can just make out what he is saying. And it makes his blood run cold.

'Mum. He's dead,' Finn sobs. 'It's my fault. It's all my fault.'

8

Shock reverberates across the car park. A ripple of chatter, buzzing around the detectives and first responders alike. 'Did he...?' 'What did he...?'

Craig is staring at the van. Then, as Finn disappears from view again, she turns to Robin.

'We need to get him out. Now.'

Robin is still stunned by Finn's words. 'There's no way he killed Sharp. Something else must have happened.'

'Well, we're not going to find out standing around here. I'm tempted to do a smash-and-grab and hope for the best.'

Robin turns on her angrily. 'Hope for the best, DI Craig?' he replies. He gestures for them to move away, far enough so Josie can't hear the exchange. 'What? Pray that he doesn't kill himself in front of his mother? Or injures a police officer in the process? Please say your tactics are more sophisticated than that?'

'Listen, DS Butler,' she says, reverting to formalities to emphasise her senior rank. 'Despite what you say, it looks like we have a murder on our hands. You know as well as I do that his confession doesn't mean shit under PACE without a caution. What am I supposed to do? Bellow one from here?'

Robin stares at the now-silent van. She's right. The Police and Criminal Evidence Act, Code C, requires that a caution be given before any questions are asked about an offence, along with a million other requisites, to make it hold up in court. But he hasn't got any solutions either.

He can see everyone getting ready: first responders are standing by with big green bags, two PCs kitted out with stab vests. One steps forward, holding a yellow and black Taser.

'You're not going to use that, surely?' Robin snaps.

'My DCS is going nuts,' Craig replies. 'He wants him out, negative press coverage or not. We're hoping the red dot on his chest will persuade him. But if you want to try before we do, this is your last chance.'

Robin snatches the black stab vest that Craig is holding and puts it on.

'And don't go messing up my crime scene.' He's handed a full white suit, gloves and shoe covers. He pulls them on obediently.

'But if he's a threat to himself, or others, we won't hesitate to go in with the Taser.' Craig's face is grim as she continues, 'And caution him the moment you get in there.'

'Roger, boss,' Robin mutters, sarcastically, and gets a warning look in return.

Robin takes a step forward towards the van. Everyone is silent. He glances back and catches Josie's eye. She's standing with Sandra's arm round her, her face drawn. Sophie is next to them, looking stunned.

He turns back. The easiest way in is through the main double doors at the back, so he heads towards them. He can feel his hands shaking slightly; he's not sure whether it's anticipation or the fact that he hasn't eaten all day. He takes a long breath in, then reaches forward and knocks on the door.

The loud metallic bang bounces around the car park.

'Finn? It's me, it's Robin.' There is no noise from inside, so he tries the handle. It's still locked. 'Finn, please. Let me in. I can help you.'

He hears movement from inside. The sound of someone shuffling closer to the door.

'You can't help me.' Whispered, close to where Robin is standing.

'You trust me, don't you?' Robin says. 'Finn? You know me, I wouldn't lie to you.'

Robin hears the almost imperceptible sound of metal against metal. He stops and listens. The lock being pulled open.

He glances back towards Craig. She makes a sign with her hands, urging him to go in. Robin reaches forward and pulls at the handle; this time it moves. The door clicks open.

He pulls it towards him and pokes his head inside. The first thing he notices is the smell – the unmistakable odour of a dead body heating up in a warm van all day. The second thing is the blood. It's all over the floor, smeared up the walls, across the window.

'Finn?' he says quietly. 'Can I come in?'

There's a pause. He tries to look inside but can't see him. Then he hears a voice.

'Just you,' it croaks.

He pushes the door open further and carefully steps up into the van. He has to stoop to get inside. It feels claustrophobic, anxiety-inducing, and that's even before Robin considers what's in front of him. On the metal floor is a prone figure. Stained with dark red, it is almost unrecognisable as a person. It looks like it has been dipped in blood, clothes ingrained, skin stained. Robin looks down at the body, following the torso up to the head. Wide-open eyes, blank.

His neck is in pieces, sinew and muscle visible. Eyes stare upwards. Glazed. A large gash runs horizontally from his throat to the right-hand side of his face; Robin can see the white of the jawbone and the tendons in his neck.

A pool of blood lies under a small table. How much is actually left in him? Robin wonders. Not much.

'Finn?' Robin whispers. 'Where are you?'

'I'm here,' he says.

He leaves the door open, moving further inside the van, past the body, and there he is. He's sitting in the furthest corner, his legs pulled up to his chest, his arms wrapped around them. His face is covered in blood, his clothes saturated with it.

Robin crouches down in front of him, his eyes level with his friend's.

'Are you hurt, Finn?'

'I... I don't know,' he starts. 'I don't feel right, I...' He stops again. His gaze flicks to the legs under the table, then back to Robin. Robin notices his eyes seem strange – Finn's eyeballs are constantly twitching side to side and he looks slightly cross-eyed.

'Why'd you lock the door?' Robin asks gently.

'I was scared. I...' He looks to the dead body again. 'I don't understand what's going on.'

Robin kneels down, knowing that blood will be soaking into the white suit, his presence contaminating the scene. But there's nothing he can do about that; he needs to get to Finn. He holds his hand out, slowly, as if approaching a nervous dog. Then, when Finn doesn't recoil, takes his hand in his.

It is cold and covered in blood; his fingernails, some of which are broken, are stained underneath. He wonders what other marks he might have on his body – indicators of a struggle, Dr Sharp fighting back as he was murdered.

Robin can't think about that now.

'Finn,' he asks quietly. 'Would you like to come with me? To get out of this van?'

Finn looks at him again, his mouth opening and closing redundantly.

'It's my fault,' Finn repeats.

Robin knows what he should be saying now. Cautioning him, following protocol. Procedures every copper knows by heart.

Instead, he puts his finger against his lips.

'Shush,' he says quietly. And Finn stops, his eyes still flickering. 'Finn, listen to me.' It goes against all of his police training, but this is his best friend. Family. 'Don't say another word, you hear me? Don't say anything else until I say so.'

Finn nods slowly.

'Now, let's get out of here.'

Robin stands up again, as much as is possible in the confined space. Holding onto Finn's hand, he pulls him to his feet. Finn is wobbly and uncertain, standing with his legs wide apart, struggling to get his balance. Robin moves so his arm is supporting his friend's weight, and he realises just how skinny Finn is. It takes little effort on Robin's part to support him, and they start moving towards the exit, one shuffling step at a time.

At last, they reach the open door and they both blink in the light. Hands rush forward to meet them, paramedics in green helping Finn down the step and into a carry chair.

Robin watches him go, as Josie and Sophie run to join him. Craig walks up to his side.

'Did he say anything in there?' she asks, and Robin shakes his head.

'He's confused. There's definitely something wrong,' Robin replies. 'This isn't Finn. He wouldn't do something like this.'

Craig looks at him, her gaze resolute.

'You know as well as I do that people do strange things. Even the people we love,' she says, after a pause. 'Did you caution him?'

'No.' Robin expected the scowl he receives in return. 'He wouldn't understand it anyway, boss. He's completely out of it.'

'And the body?'

'Definitely dead. And starting to stink the place up.'

Craig grimaces. 'Pathologist en route. Hopefully, he'll be able to tell us more.' She looks at Robin. 'And we'll need a formal statement from you. Once you've got cleaned up. I want that suit for forensics.'

Robin looks down at the white coverall. It's streaked with blood, red soaked into the material.

They stand in silence as the SOCOs descend on the van in a cloud of white.

'I want to be involved,' Robin says at last.

Craig sighs, her gaze locked on the paramedics as they wheel Finn away to the waiting ambulance, one of the uniforms accompanying them as an escort. 'You know full well that's not possible. You're personally involved.'

'He didn't do this,' Robin protests again, weakly.

'He was locked in a van with the victim,' Craig begins. 'Nobody else could get inside. Multiple witnesses heard him say it was his fault. We'll follow procedure, of course, but it's not looking good, wouldn't you agree, DS Butler?'

She uses his police title deliberately, highlighting the fact that, as a cop, he shouldn't doubt the evidence either.

'I won't touch anything,' Robin says. 'I won't say anything. Consider me a silent bystander. You can have one of your DCs with me at all times.'

Craig closes her eyes for a moment in frustration. 'Christ, Butler. You're making my life difficult, you know that?' She rolls her eyes. 'Fine. Come along, see for yourself. But if I hear you have so much as sniffed at a witness, then you're out, okay?'

'Fine.'

'Now, I need to update my DCS on how this shitshow is going. If it's okay with you,' she finishes sarcastically and leaves, her mobile phone clutched in her hand.

Robin watches her go, then turns back to the silver van. It's easy to identify the crime scene manager, already giving orders, locking down the scene, preserving the evidence. Robin's glad that DI Craig has given him permission to come along, but the sinking feeling in his stomach is telling him something he knows intuitively as a cop.

Craig's right.

In terms of murder charges, this is one of the most open-and-shut cases he's seen.

9

When they get back to the police station, Josh seems to adapt well to his new responsibilities as acting DS.

'Freya, if you could follow up on the serial number on the freezer,' he says, passing her the piece of paper. 'Mina—'

'Is going to pump,' Mina interrupts, pointing to her boobs. Josh's face goes red.

'And I'm going to get some lunch,' Freya adds, walking away before her acting boss can make his objections.

Freya heads up to the top floor to buy a sandwich, then back down to the parking level to sit in her car. She has no wish to eat in the canteen, with all the bustle and people wanting to make conversation. In the past, she enjoyed her lunch breaks. Sitting with the other DCs, laughing along with the banter, but for a while now she hasn't felt a part of it. She knows the moment it stopped: when Jonathan died. When the murder of the man she loved dragged her into a world of deception and hate. And guilt.

It's something she can't talk about, and something her colleagues wouldn't understand. Her conscientious, hard-working teammates, with their 2.4 children and long-suffering spouses.

Only Robin knows the full extent of what she's been through. And without him here today, she feels strange. For eight months he's been her buffer. They never speak about the events of last October, but she knows implicitly that he has her back. A connection that goes beyond colleagues, or DS and DC.

Sitting in her car, she checks her phone. No response from Robin. She presses his number and listens to it ring, then cut to voicemail.

> This is Robin Butler. Sorry I can't take your call, please leave a message.

She listens to the recording, enjoying hearing his voice. The hesitation, the uncomfortable edge she's come to know so well. He was there on that dark Friday night last year. He's been through loss himself – the death of his parents, followed by the tragic killing of his sister and her children at the hands of a drunk driver. So why doesn't she tell him how she's feeling?

The dark, lonely nights staring at the ceiling. Scratchy eyes in the morning, her body weary and aching. She hasn't slept well for a while now. She can't concentrate, the guilt overwhelming her.

She alone made the fateful decision that night. Someone died because of something she did. That knowledge won't go away. The self-hatred, the fear that someone will realise. She works every hour she can get her hands on just so she doesn't have to sit in an empty house.

Nobody understands that better than Robin.

But now he isn't here. Caught up in everything with Finn.

She picks up her phone and googles *Finn Mason* and *Dr Simon Sharp* but there aren't any more updates following the one that Mina found in the morning. She finishes her sandwich and throws the wrapper in the footwell, leaning her head back as tiredness overtakes her. She'll just close her eyes for a moment, get a coffee on the way back in...

Her phone rings, jerking her out of her doze. She glances at the clock. Shit! She's been asleep for an hour.

'Where are you, Freya?' Josh shouts down the phone.

'Nice, Josh, nice,' she mumbles in response. 'Heading back now, no need to yell.'

Freya hangs up as Josh starts talking again. She sighs. Smith has a few things to learn about motivational leadership, that's for sure.

–

Freya has been on hold for twenty minutes, waiting to get through to the customer helpline for Hotpoint. Having the serial number is one thing, but speaking to someone about it is another.

She rests the phone against her ear and leans over to see what Mina's doing next to her. She has a black-and-white video file open on her screen and is watching it, her eyes half glazed.

'Anything?' she asks.

Mina sighs. 'Nothing that stands out.' She points to the screen. 'This is the CCTV from Riverside, and it's well off the beaten path. You wouldn't need to pass here to get to the freezer, so it's unlikely there'll be anything useful.' She picks up her coffee cup and takes the last swig. 'This storm was a blazer last night, though, that's for sure. Look at it.'

Freya squints at the screen. Trees blow wildly in the wind and the rain pours, forming lakes where the road should have been.

'Who would want to be out in that?' Freya comments.

Mina nods, then sighs, throwing her head back in barely disguised boredom. She picks up her empty cup. 'Want another?' she asks.

Freya nods.

'Please,' she says, then turns her attention quickly back to her phone. 'Yes, hello, hello,' she says, as the call is answered. 'This is DC West, from Hampshire Police. We need information on a chest freezer.'

The woman at the other end of the phone doesn't seem too worried about data protection and gives the inform-ation willingly. Luckily, eleven years ago the new owner had been conscientious enough to register its warranty. Freya takes the number and dials. The phone is answered on the tenth ring by a woman, her voice reedy and frail.

'Yes?'

'This is DC Freya West, calling from Hampshire Police. Is this Vera Woodley?'

'Are you one of those cold–callers I've been told not to talk to?'

'No, no, I'm phoning from Hampshire Police. I need to talk to you about your freezer.'

'My freezer?'

'Yes, a Hotpoint chest freezer. That you bought in 2010?'

Freya is almost shouting down the phone. Mina places a cup of coffee in front of her and looks on with interest.

'Don't have a chest freezer, sorry, love.'

'But you bought one in 2010? Do you remember that?'

'Don't have a chest freezer any more. Are you trying to sell me one?'

'No, I'm phoning from Hampshire Police.' Freya rolls her eyes at Mina, who laughs quietly.

'I don't want another freezer, sorry,' the old woman says and hangs up.

Freya puts the phone down and gives an exasperated sigh.

'Looks like you're going to have to go down there,' Josh says, appearing behind them.

'I'm not sure she'll be any better face to face.'

'Well, it will have to wait,' Josh says. 'Connor Vardy has arrived at Riverside. And he's waiting to talk to you two.'

10

Freya and Mina arrive at the railway station and stand on the platform; in the distance a small narrow-gauge train chugs its way round the track.

'We've brought the kids here a few times,' Mina says, watching the plume of grey smoke. 'I'm not going to see it as such an innocent place again.'

Freya shakes her head. 'I'm not sure I'm going to be able to look at my freezer in the same way,' she agrees. 'I have that exact same one, you know.'

'Why do you own a chest freezer?'

'Mum thought it would be useful for storing leftovers,' Freya says. 'As a lonely single girl, and all that.'

'Yeah, for all that cooking you do,' Mina replies with a snort.

Freya laughs, then puts an arm round her friend. 'I'm glad you're back,' she says, and Mina returns her grin. 'It wasn't the same without you.'

'I missed you, too, honey.'

Freya hesitates, an apology on the tip of her tongue for not visiting Mina more over this past year. But how could she explain? I had a boyfriend. But he was married. And then he died. Freya can predict the questions, but she doesn't feel ready to offer the truth; and Mina would see right through a lie.

The small train wheezes its way to the platform, distracting Freya from her dilemma. They both step forward as Barry Headley approaches with Connor, guiding him with a stern hand on his back. Connor Vardy is skinny and tall, and looks years younger than eighteen, with short, cropped hair and a perpetual stoop. He's less than keen, hanging back as the four of them walk towards the café again.

'Connor?' Mina begins. 'I'm Detective Constable Desai, and this is DC West...'

'I don't know anything about that freezer,' Connor says quickly. He has a black smudge on his cheek that looks like a bruise; Freya wonders where it came from.

'You're not in trouble, Connor,' Mina adds gently. 'But Barry says you might know something about the group of teenagers that hang around at the bus stop.'

'I don't know them.' So there are kids that hang around there, Freya thinks. The four of them sit down at the same table as before. She gets the feeling that if the old guy weren't there, Connor would make a run for it.

'That's fine, Connor, just tell us what you know.'

Mina takes charge of the interview, her gentle manner better suited to calming the twitching lad. Freya admires how she docsn't talk down to him, but lets him guide the conversation, nodding and smiling in encouragement. She may have been off for nearly a year, but the patience and grace she has honed since becoming a mother put her in a perfect position for getting a witness statement from the boy.

Freya realises that Josh has stayed away for that exact same reason.

'You don't want some tall, scary policeman dominating the conversation,' he said, while Freya suspected he
fancied putting his feet up for an hour, drinking tea.

After a while, Connor relaxes into the conversation,
taking a sip from his can of Coke. This time, Freya and
Mina have agreed to mugs of strong coffee, and Freya cups
hers in her hands, as if extracting the caffeine through the
chipped ceramic.

Connor attends Eastleigh College down the road. He
tells them about his apprenticeship attached to a local
company, and how in his time off he comes to tinker with
the engines.

'He does more than tinker,' Headley adds with pride.
'He fixed that engine on the track. Got her up and
running in weeks.'

Connor looks embarrassed. 'The locos make sense to
me – the way they run. But they take the piss, say I'm
playing with my toy trains.'

'And these are the boys that hang around at the bus
shelter, right?' Mina asks.

'Yes. I don't talk to them.'

'But they talk to you?'

Connor nods. 'I walk that way home. They want me
to buy them alcohol. They've been banned from all the
local offies and pubs.'

'But you don't,' Headley says, and Connor mumbles
'No,' staring at his hands.

You bloody do, Freya thinks, but she lets it go.

'And when did you notice the freezer?'

'It was definitely there Monday morning.'

'Did you touch it? Look inside?'

'No, I assumed it was rubbish. Didn't pay it much
attention.'

'What time did you leave here last night?' Mina asks.

'Just after dark. About nineish.'

'And did you see the other boys?'

Connor nods again. 'They were at the bus stop. I think they do football at the sports ground.'

'But you didn't speak to them?'

'No.'

'And you didn't see them by the freezer?'

Connor shakes his head.

'And do you know their names?' Mina pushes.

Connor puts a grease-stained finger in his mouth and chews on the nail.

'Connor, we won't say the information came from you.'

'They don't know anything about the freezer.'

'We just need to ask, Connor. It's important we find out what happened to that man,' Mina adds gently. 'It could be someone's grandad or father. And they deserve to know.'

At that comment Connor looks up sharply, meeting Mina's gaze. She pushes her notebook across to him. He looks at it for a second, then picks up the pen. 'I don't know them,' he says again, scribbling in an almost unintelligible handwriting.

'That's fine, whatever you can give us.'

He pushes the notebook back then looks to Headley, who nods. He scuttles out of the café.

'He's a good kid,' the old man says. 'Just had a shit start in life.'

'He obviously looks up to you,' Mina replies.

'I do what I can.'

Mina calls Josh as they walk back to the car, and Freya tries Robin again. This time he answers.

'How are you doing? What's going on?' she asks him.

There's a long pause. 'It's a fucking mess,' he says at last. Freya can hear the stress in his voice. 'Finn's on his way to the hospital now, but he keeps on saying it was his fault.'

'His fault what? That Simon Sharp's dead?'

'What else?' Robin sighs. Freya can imagine him standing there, gaze fixed on the ground, phone clamped to his ear with one hand, running the other through his short greying hair. 'The van's a bloodbath, Freya,' he says quietly. 'It's everywhere. All up the walls, all over Finn.'

Freya hesitates. 'Do you think he did it?'

Another pause. 'I can't imagine...' His voice breaks.

'Do you want me to come up there?' she asks. 'I can help you look into it?'

'No, no, it's fine,' Robin says quickly. 'They're barely letting me near it. Anyway, what have they got you working on?'

'Dead body in a freezer,' she says.

'What?'

'Found this morning. Bloke tipped over a dumped freezer, corpse fell out.'

There's another silence, then she can hear Robin laughing. She smiles, the noise welcome after her worry for her boss.

'I'm sorry,' he says. 'Just after the day I've had. My imagination went a bit bonkers.' He snorts again then manages to contain his laughter. 'Who's in charge?'

'Josh Smith.'

'Who?'

'The new DC? The one from Newcastle?'

'The one who sounds like he's in *Byker Grove*?' Robin starts laughing again. 'Oh, good grief.'

Mina comes up and stands next to her. 'Is that Butler?' she mouths and Freya nods.

'Mina is here, she says hello.'

'Oh shit, it's her first day,' Robin replies. 'Say hello from me.'

'He says hello,' she directs to Mina. 'When will you be back?' Freya asks.

'I don't know. I've got to find somewhere to stay tonight, then go and see Finn in the hospital.' He pauses. 'You okay?'

'Yes, of course,' she says, but her voice sounds squeaky and forced. 'I hope Finn's all right.'

'Yeah, me too. I'll call you later,' he finishes, then hangs up.

'Josh has confirmed Connor's story,' Mina says as they get in the car. 'CCTV from Riverside has him leaving at 21:04.'

'That's something, at least.'

Freya puts the phone in her pocket and notices Mina staring at her.

'You two always speak when Robin's on holiday?' Mina asks.

'I was worried about Finn.'

'Hmm,' Mina replies, but doesn't say any more on the subject.

—

Josh wants them to check in with the uniforms doing the house-to-house, so they pull into the main railway station car park on the way back – the one with full-sized trains. Two uniforms are there, half-heartedly canvassing staff.

Freya recognises one from her days on Response and Patrol.

'West,' PC Uberti nods to her. 'Look at you, all out of uniform. Getting us to do your grunt work.'

Freya ignores the jibe. 'Anything of interest?' she asks, and Uberti shakes his head. 'Nothing. The place was deserted last night; most went home early because none of the trains were running in the storm. You might want to speak to the station manager, though. When we showed him a picture of the vic, he got a bit cagey. Perhaps a prodding from you highly trained detectives might shake something loose.'

Freya gives him a sarcastic look in return, then catches Mina's eye and indicates the main office. They go over and knock at the door.

It is opened by a short man in an ill-fitting polyester suit. His name badge tells Freya that he's called Norman, and from the look on his face, he is not pleased to see them.

'I've spoken to your colleagues,' he says, when Freya and Mina show their ID. 'This bloody storm has caused a nightmare on the rails. I have a hundred things to do.'

'They mentioned you saw our victim last night?'

'Briefly. He was always hanging around. Homeless. Begging, and suchlike. Leaving his sleeping bag and shit in the doorway. Threw it out three days ago.'

'You threw away his belongings?' Mina says.

'He'd left it there, stinking up the place, so yes, I binned it.'

Mina exchanges a look with Freya. 'And do you know anything about him? His name, for instance?'

74

'We've never chatted,' Norman says, a disgusted look on his face. 'Don't you keep records on this stuff? I called the police about a fortnight ago. You guys moved him on.'

'We'll follow it up,' Mina replies, coldly. 'Can we see your CCTV?'

Norman sighs and gestures for them to come inside the office. He points them towards an ancient monitor and keyboard, images playing out in front of them, flicking from one scene to the next every few seconds. He clicks quickly, and the screen changes to a directory of files.

'Knock yourself out,' he says. 'Now, if you would be so kind…'

He leaves, the door slamming loudly behind him.

'What a charmer,' Mina says, as her phone starts ringing. She holds it up so Freya can see the screen. Josh again. Mina rolls her eyes and answers it.

As Mina speaks to Josh, Freya cracks on, looking through the various CCTV files. There are three cameras – one each for the two platforms, and one showing the outside, looking away from the station building. She selects yesterday's date, then scrolls through the video, the timestamp clicking round as the day progresses.

Mina sits down next to her.

'He's pissed we're taking so long,' she says.

'What did he expect?' Freya replies. 'Here, this is last night.'

They both squint at the screen. As with the CCTV from Riverside, they can see the wind gathering speed, rain starting to pour as the storm takes hold. Mina points.

'What do you think? That guy there?'

It's the first image they've seen of the victim alive. He's the only one out in the storm, walking slowly, arms wrapped around his body. It's clear he's wearing just a few thin clothes, with no coat to protect him from the rain. He sits down in the doorway of the station building, taking shelter.

Then Freya watches as Norman charges out through the double doors and strides up to him, arms waving wildly. He points away from the building. The man gets up slowly and Norman stands with his hands on his hips, watching him shuffling off into the night.

'What a dick,' Mina whispers. 'Where was this guy supposed to go, in weather like that?'

Freya frowns as the man disappears out of shot.

'That's exactly what we need to find out,' she replies.

11

Finn looks very small in his hospital bed. Robin watches him through the glass panel in the door of his single room, as Josie sits next to him. He looks more himself – wearing a spare pair of glasses, cleaned up and less bloody – and Robin has an abrupt thought that everything is normal, that this is a normal visit to see his friend, in normal circumstances.

But then the uniform standing guard next to him hands back his warrant card. 'You're cleared to go in,' he says, giving him a long look.

He's given his statement to Craig's team of what happened when he went into the van, then nipped to the shopping centre, picking up extra clothes to tide him over for a few days. And he came here via the McDonald's drive-in, ravenously destroying a burger in a few bites.

Finn and Josie look up as he comes into the room.

'Hi, Finn,' Robin says. 'How are you feeling?'

'Terrible,' Finn replies. He manages a small smile. His face looks pale, a fine layer of sweat on his forehead. 'Is Simon holding the fort?'

Josie holds tight to her son's hand. 'Let's concentrate on getting you better, sweetheart,' she says with a warning glance in Robin's direction. 'We'll worry about Simon later.'

Robin sits in the chair next to his bed. 'Do you remember what happened last night?' he asks.

Finn furrows his brow. 'I was filming the storm. Then things get a bit muddled.' He reaches up and rubs his eyes behind his glasses; Robin notices his hands are shaking. 'Where is Simon, anyway?' Finn continues. 'We need to talk. There must be loads of data to go through.'

Robin puts his hand on his friend's arm. 'Soon, Finn.' He indicates to Josie. 'We'll be back in a sec. I need to talk to your mum.'

Robin takes Josie's hand and ushers her out into the corridor.

'That's all he's been saying,' she whispers to Robin. 'He seems so confused. He keeps talking about Simon.'

'What do the doctors say?'

'They're still running their tests. They've done an initial CT and bloods, but they say they need to take him for an MRI. They mentioned memory loss. Something about a psycho... a psychotic episode, triggered by stress? They asked if we have schizophrenia in the family.'

'And do you?' Robin asks.

'No! And they asked about drugs, so I told them about the LSD and the marijuana.'

'Good.' Robin frowns.

'Could the drugs have caused this? What they're saying he did to Dr Sharp?'

'I don't know, Josie, I'm sorry. I'll try to find out what I can. Is Sandra still around?'

'Yes, she's gone to find somewhere to stay tonight.' Josie reaches forward and takes Robin's hand. Her own is cold, shaking. 'He's all I have,' she says, her voice trembling. She looks back through the window, towards her son. 'I know he's a grown man and over six foot, but he's still my baby. I couldn't… I can't… If anything happens to him…'

Robin feels the weight of the responsibility. The pressure makes his shoulders tense, his head hurt.

He covers her hands with both of his, squeezing tight. 'I know, Josie. I know.'

—

Day revolves into evening. Lights are turned on, curtains closed. Nurses tend to Finn. He gets worse, at one point throwing up in a bowl. He tries to sleep, but he's restless and irritable. A doctor comes in, talks about doing more tests, but can't offer any more in terms of prognosis. He mumbles something about the psychiatrist coming by in the morning.

Josie tells Robin to leave.

'I'll stay,' she says. 'This chair's comfy enough for me.' He tries to persuade her to come with him, but he knows his attempts are futile. Sandra has reserved him a room in the local Travelodge, and he heads there.

He checks into the hotel, slumping down on the bed as soon as he gets inside his room. He rubs his eyes. He needs to get some sleep. But first he needs to know what's going on.

Robin calls DI Craig's number, but gets no response. He tries again, leaving a voicemail. Eventually, she calls back: brief and to the point.

'Forensics are still going over the van, Butler,' she says. 'The body's been taken away. Have they done his MHA?'

Mental Health Assessment. Standard procedure for anyone threatening suicide. Finn needs to be cleared prior to being deemed fit to detain or even be interviewed by the police. 'He has bigger problems than that, Craig,' Robin replies. 'His memory's gone.'

'What's he saying?'

'Nothing coherent. He just seems out of it. Sometimes he can't understand what we're saying, or he acts like he doesn't hear us at all.'

Finn asked a few more times about Simon Sharp, but Josie and Robin continued to be evasive. At one point Finn dropped back even further in his mind, talking about needing to leave, to get ready for the storm. None of it made sense.

'Have they found a murder weapon?' Robin asks.

A pause. He knows Craig is reluctant to share. 'Yes,' she says at last. 'A penknife, a posh one. Seems to be Sharp's – has his initials engraved on the side. The main blade was out. It's with forensics now.'

Robin sighs and ends the call. He knows it's only a matter of time before the results come back. There'll be biologicals, fingerprints – something – tying Finn to that murder. He remembers the bloody crime scene. Simon Sharp's body lying on the floor, his neck slashed to pieces. Whatever had gone on in there had been violent and nasty.

He calls Baker next, aware that he's been missing his calls all day. His DCI answers instantly, his tone direct.

'What's the update, Butler?'

'Sorry to call you so late, guv,' Robin begins.

'Cut the crap, Robin,' Baker interrupts. 'You know I'm still working. When are you coming back?'

Robin imagines his boss sitting at home in his study, files in front of him on his impressive polished wooden desk. He's been to Neal Baker's house many times, both on a personal basis and in a professional capacity. He's met his wife, knows his kids. And Robin also knows that

Baker's gruff style doesn't mean he doesn't care, far from it.

'I need a few more days yet,' Robin says. 'It's not looking good.'

'Craig filled me in.' Baker pauses, and Robin can imagine him running his hand across his shiny bald head. 'Do you think he did it?'

'I... I don't know. The evidence says he did.'

'But?'

'I just can't believe it. Finn's not that sort of man. He can't even kill spiders.'

There's another long pause. 'Listen, Robin,' Baker says, his voice low. 'I've known you long enough to know that your instincts are good. If there's something off, then follow it. I've persuaded Craig to keep you informed. But ask yourself this – are your personal feelings getting in the way of your professional judgement?'

Robin sits up, leaning against the headboard. Are they? There's a reason you don't work on cases too close to home – emotions interfere. Is this what's happening here?

Baker takes the pause as confirmation. 'And you know that any evidence you find will be inadmissible because of your relationship with Finn. Make sure one of their team is with you at all times.'

'Yes, guv.'

'Anyway, Butler, that wasn't the only reason I called. We need to talk about West.'

Robin frowns. 'Freya? What about her?'

'This isn't the right time, and when you're back we'll have a proper conversation, but I've noticed her overtime is off the scale.'

'She mentioned she'd picked up some extra paperwork on the side.'

'This is more than that, Robin. She hasn't had a day off in four weeks. It's got to the point I said I couldn't pay her for the extra hours and she said that was fine, she'd come in anyway. What's going on?'

'I... I don't know, boss.' Robin's confused.

'Is she trying to get a promotion and thinks this is the way to do it? Because it's too much. There's dedication and then there's burnout. And I think she's heading for the latter.'

'I'll talk to her,' Robin confirms, and the call's over.

He looks at the phone in his hand, his thumb hovering over Freya's number. Fuck, he should have known what she was doing; he shouldn't need to have Baker telling him. But Freya can be secretive; he knows that from the Jonathan Miller murder, if nothing else. But what is she up to?

He touches the green symbol and calls Freya. It rings for a bit, then cuts to voicemail. He hangs up without leaving a message. He glances at the clock, just gone half nine, and wonders where she is. Must be at home, asleep. She can't still be at work. Even given what Baker said, that's beyond devotion to the job.

Before Robin started working with Freya, he preferred to tackle cases alone. Constables would filter through his working day, some forced to work with him when the caseload got too much, but none he could stand. They all knew about him, knew his history. The death of his sister, his time off work after. And his manner since had hardly been approachable. He knew the whispers that had gone around the station. *Lost it. Gone nuts. Stay clear.*

But Freya hadn't cared about any of that. She took the piss, ignored his blunt manner. And, better still, she got the job done. Between the two of them, they tackled case after case, starting with the death of Jonathan Miller, a man who turned out to be Freya's lover – a fact she kept from him for the majority of the investigation.

He knows Jonathan's murder hit her hard. Not to mention the subsequent death of Amy Miller, his wife, three weeks later.

He picks up his phone again, then puts it back down. He'll call her tomorrow. She has a life of her own, he tells himself, leave her alone. He just wishes he had someone else to speak to.

The only other person Robin can call is Liam, his brother-in-law. He's been missing his calls all week. But Robin knows Liam will be in bed well before this point: always up at the break of dawn for an early-morning workout. He's reconnected with Liam over the last few months, sharing nights of football and pizza in front of the TV, trips to the pub – even the occasional run together, although Liam's athleticism well exceeds his own. And Robin likes it. It keeps him close to the memories of his sister and his nephews; the two of them sharing stories over a beer, grief starting to evolve into something else. Something Robin can cope with.

Contemplating Liam now, thoughts of Trevor Stevens enter his head. The man who killed his sister. Who criss-crossed his life, resulting in actions and consequences that Robin had never even imagined possible.

Robin thinks about everything that happened after his sister died. And if he could behave in that way, what was Finn capable of?

What circumstances could have driven Finn to murder?

12

Sophie wearily puts her key in the door and pushes it open. She goes into her flat and closes the door behind her, dumping her bag and coat on the floor then standing in the hallway for a moment, unsure what to do.

She is exhausted. Her body is grimy with sweat, her clothes sticking to her skin. She feels empty — not just because she hasn't eaten all day, but emotionally, her mind drained.

Even though they haven't said anything, Sophie feels the judgement from Robin and Josie. Why hadn't she known about the state of Finn's flat? Why hadn't she tried to stop him taking the LSD? Why hadn't she encouraged him to eat better, to look after himself? She had tried to speak to Finn, tried to get him to open up. But he'd been so stressed, so busy. She hadn't wanted to pile on more pressure. And he is a grown man, she tells herself. Finn is a forty-three-year-old adult, an intelligent man, who can make his own decisions. But still. That feeling of guilt remains.

She can't believe what has happened. She went to bed last night excited about what the future might hold. Finn was on the edge of making a huge breakthrough in his field. If the new technology had worked, he would have made a name for himself. He could have worked anywhere in the world, in the most prestigious universities, talking about and teaching what he loved. And she would have gone with him. She would have never left his side.

Finn is different to her usual boyfriends. In the past, she caught the eye of flashier types: men with nice cars and even nicer homes, who would barely listen when she mentioned what she did for a living. They didn't challenge her – she knew she was smarter than them, and as long as they didn't realise it, she could do and say what she liked.

But on one faculty night out, Finn had turned to her and simply said: 'You're wrong.'

'Pardon?' Sophie had replied.

'What you just said, about the coffee? That's actually true.'

She'd been talking about a story she'd read on Twitter, which claimed that scientists who work with cockroaches often become allergic to pre-ground coffee. She'd scoffed at the people that believed it, prompting superior laughter from all around her. But not from Finn.

'Many scientists develop allergies to the things they study,' he'd explained. 'And the cockroaches that infect large piles of coffee beans are too expensive to remove, so they just grind them up into the coffee.' He'd stared at her, with those dark eyes of his, a small smile touching the edges of his mouth. 'But that's America for you, Ms Hall,' he'd finished.

Sophie knew that some people found him strange. His manner, that blunt challenge, his clinical approach to information and knowledge. But she thought he was fascinating. She could tell there was more to him than that self-imposed distance. That the air of arrogance was simply shyness and a lack of confidence.

She'd actively sought him out. Looking for him in the canteen at lunchtime, tracking down his lecture timetable. She did her research this time. She'd asked around, found out what he was like.

Nobody who knew him had a bad word to say. Witty. Serious. Clever. And best of all: single. She'd asked one of his PhD students why – he'd looked blank. 'Just never seems interested,' was the response.

Sophie wasn't used to waiting around for something. She'd had maybe half a dozen conversations with Finn, and he was polite and interested – but he hadn't asked her out.

So one day she went to his office when she knew he would be there. His door was open, and she felt her heart jump slightly as she knocked then poked her head round.

'Finn?' she'd said, and he'd looked up from his desk. He'd stared at her over the top of his glasses.

'Sophie...' he'd replied, pointing towards the chair next to him. 'What brings you to the exciting world of meteorology?'

'I...' Sophie hesitated. She'd never done this before – ask someone out. Men always came to her. With flowers and overblown conviction. 'I was wondering if you'd like to go out sometime? With me?'

'Out where?' he'd replied, initially confused. Then the penny dropped and his mouth parted in surprise. 'On a date?' he'd asked.

Sophie wondered if she'd got it wrong. Perhaps he wasn't interested in her. Perhaps he was gay.

'Yes,' she'd replied. 'On a date.'

He'd grinned – an expression that opened up his whole face – and she realised she had never seen him smile like that before. Then it was gone again, and he'd looked almost embarrassed.

'I'd like that,' he'd said quietly. 'Very much.'

They kept it simple. To the cinema. No need to talk to each other if they couldn't think of anything to say. But they chattered through the adverts, then through the trailers, finally being shushed by the older couple behind them.

Remembering that first date brings fresh tears to Sophie's eyes. That was over eighteen months ago, and she'd never regretted a day. There is nobody like Finn. Nobody as clever or as determined. Nobody who looks at her the way he does. To him she is more than some silly hippy chick, researching pot and cancer. When he looks at her, he sees *her*.

And they never stop talking. About politics. About their work. He challenges her to think about what she is saying. When she first met Robin, she was nervous. She drank too fast and said too much, and she knew why Robin hated her. But after, Finn just said, 'Opinions should be based on fact.'

She'd turned on him, eyes blazing. Determined to take her bad mood out on someone.

'What do you mean?' she'd shouted.

'Your opinions on the police force. You don't know Robin. You don't know how hard he works. What motivates him,' Finn had answered quietly. 'You were rude, and it made you look foolish.' And he'd walked away, leaving her fuming.

But he was right. She should have apologised, she knew. She resolved to make it up to him, but good grief, Robin Butler could hold a grudge. In his eyes she wasn't good enough for Finn. And the events of today only proved it.

She can't believe what they're saying about Finn. She's never seen him lose his temper, not even raise his voice. So the idea that he could kill someone? It's ridiculous.

The papers are painting him as some sort of evil genius: Finn the villain and Dr Sharp his innocent victim. But Sophie knows that tensions were running high, and the team were starting to crack. It's no wonder Finn had to turn to drugs.

She catches a glimpse of the small suitcase in the corner of her living room. The plan for the rest of this week was for Finn to get some sleep, analyse the data, get his students set up to do the rest, then go away for a few days. They were going to Rome. To see the sights, to hold hands walking around the ruins of the Colosseum, to eat pizza and gnocchi and drink red wine. Finn had packed his case in advance and left it here, ready for their departure that coming weekend. Sophie knows the police are now searching his dirty flat, but what about this suitcase? What else has he been hiding?

She goes over and kneels on the floor, pulling it onto its side and unzipping it. Slowly, she takes the contents out. She goes through his toiletries, opening the bottles and sniffing the contents. Shower gel. Shaving cream. Some sort of hair product. Toothpaste. Deodorant. That's all. Nothing sinister.

On the top is a sweatshirt, his favourite, that he wears far too often. Worn grey cotton, with the words UNIVERSITY OF READING emblazoned on the front. Sophie has often berated him for it, taking the piss and threatening to give it to charity, but now she picks it up, burying her face in the soft material. It smells of him, and she feels a wave of loss. She misses him. She wants to hug him, to hold on and push her cheek into the dip next to his collarbone, where she fits the best.

She goes to put the sweatshirt on, but in doing so, something falls out and rolls under her sofa. She crouches down and pokes her head under, pushing her arm until her fingers come in contact with the object.

She pulls it out.

It's a small grey velvet box. She opens it slowly.

Inside is a simple platinum ring, the diamond in its centre sparkling in the overhead light. It isn't big or flashy – a single stone – but the light catches the edge of the diamond and it shines. She pulls it out, turning it over in her palm, her brain struggling to catch up.

Then she starts to shake.

Finn bought this. He'd chosen a ring. An engagement ring.

On their trip to Rome, he'd been intending to propose.

The weight of how this week should have turned out presses down on her chest; Sophie feels like she can't breathe. She imagines them excitedly sitting on the Spanish Steps, watching the sun go down, planning their wedding. The rest of their lives together.

She misses his hand in hers. His dark, kind eyes watching her intently behind his glasses, stylish by luck rather than choice. A man who has no idea how funny he is, who gives a small self-conscious smile whenever she laughs.

She wants to go to bed tonight with his long limbs wrapped round her, the feel of his slow breathing against the back of her neck.

Instead, Finn is in hospital. Ill. Confused. And the prime suspect in a murder investigation.

Sophie slowly replaces the ring in the box and shuts the lid. She tries to pull herself together. He needs you, she tells herself sternly. And she needs him. Back here, with her. And what Sophie wants, Sophie gets.

But the pep talk isn't working. The worry for Finn, the guilt that she hadn't known about his awful flat, takes over. Her body crumples and she puts her face in her hands.

Alone, in the darkness, in her empty home, she starts to cry.

13

The pub is noisy, filling up with jostling punters now it's past half nine, windows already steamed with condensation. Freya sees Robin's name flash up on her phone, but she doesn't answer it. She glances to the bar. Josh is standing there, waiting to be served. The background music, multiple conversing voices – everything is loud. There's no way she could hear a call from Robin in this.

'Here you go,' Josh says, putting the glass of wine in front of her. 'Cheers.'

He holds out his pint and she clinks her glass against it.

'How was your first day in charge?' she asks him. Josh suggested a drink at the end of the long day and, desperate not to return to her lonely house, she found herself saying yes even before Mina agreed. But then Mina turned down the offer, and now Freya finds herself alone at the pub with her latest skipper.

Josh laughs. 'Excruciating. Was I a nightmare?'

Freya scratches her nose for a second, not sure how to reply. Josh laughs again, taking her pause as confirmation. 'Oh god, I'm sorry. I never know how to play it. Too chummy and no one gets anything done, but too harsh and everyone thinks you're a wanker.'

'Baker said you were a DS in Newcastle?'

'Yeah, and nobody liked me there either.' He smiles and takes a long pull on his pint. 'Did you get any further with the CCTV?'

Freya shakes her head. 'Nothing more than the few images outside the station. Where did you go this afternoon?'

'I went to see the woman you were speaking to. About the freezer?'

'Oh, no,' Freya laughs.

'Yeah. She was just as hard work in person. But I worked my irresistible charm and got there in the end.'

'And?'

'She'd sold it. Couldn't remember who to. Dead end,' he finishes. 'So, tell me about you, Freya West? What's your story?'

'Not much to tell.'

'I don't believe that. Are you from around here?'

'Grew up in Salisbury, then went to university in Southampton and stayed.'

'What did you study?'

'Law.'

'Really?' Josh sips his pint, smiling. 'And you didn't want to be a solicitor?'

'I worked as a paralegal for a few months, then realised that it was the policing side I was interested in.'

'So you joined the force?'

'Exactly.'

'Married? Single?'

Freya laughs. 'I feel like I'm being interviewed!'

'You're avoiding the question, Ms West,' Josh says, leaning across the table and adopting a mock-detective style. 'You don't fool me with your beautiful blonde hair and innocent blue eyes. What are you trying to hide? Hmm?'

'Single,' Freya grins. 'Married to the job. Happy now?'

Josh smiles back. 'Definitely.'

Freya's caught off guard by his flirting. She feels herself getting flustered, her face going red. She's used to banter around the station. Direct insults, fine. But this is new.

'So why did you move down south?' she asks, keen to change the subject.

'For love,' Josh replies. Freya raises her eyebrows in surprise. 'What?' he enquires in response.

'You don't seem the type, that's all,' Freya says.

'What? To uproot my whole life, move hundreds of miles down the country, for a woman I hardly knew?'

'When you put it like that, yes.'

'How do I seem then?' His words are confrontational, but his manner is light, accompanied by a smile.

Freya's cheeks flush again, and she regrets getting into this line of conversation. 'Just...' She points to the pint in his hand, already half gone. 'A bit of a lad.'

He reluctantly smiles. 'That's not wrong. What she said, too.'

'So what happened?'

'I met Elise when she was in Newcastle on a hen do. We hit it off. Fell in love.' He winces a bit as he says the words. 'And the long-distance thing was shit, so after six months of to and fro across the country, I applied for a transfer and ended up down here, just before Christmas. But there weren't any vacancies for a DS, so now I'm a DC.'

'So you got a demotion, and you got dumped.' Freya smiles over the top of her wine glass.

Josh laughs quietly. 'Absolutely. I'm surprised you haven't heard the story. Everyone round the station knows it.'

'I've been busy.' Distracted, more like, Freya thinks. 'So why didn't you go back?'

'With my tail between my legs? No way! Besides, I like it here. My sister and her family live in Oxford, and the weather's nicer, even in winter. Plus, I'd already met some good people by then.'

'So here you are.'

'Here I am.'

At that point, Josh's phone rings and he answers it, shouting over the din of the pub. He hangs up and looks at Freya.

'Some friends are out. I said they could meet us here. That okay with you?'

'Course.'

'Want another?' Freya nods and Josh heads off to the bar. She watches him go. He's not the man she thought he was. He was right; she'd heard the rumours, but she'd also heard that the reason the infamous Elise dumped him was because he slept with someone else within a month of arriving here. Yes, she had thought he was a bit of a wanker. But the self-awareness, the friendly charm, disarms her slightly.

The door to the bar opens and three men burst through. Jostling each other, they spot Josh at the bar and greet him with boisterous cheers, then manly handshakes. So yes, laddish, Freya thinks again. Josh points to her and their table, and one of the group heads over with a big smile.

'Adam,' he says. He's big and brutish, wearing an English rugby shirt. 'And you are?'

'Freya,' she replies, shaking his hand. He grabs a spare chair from behind them, picking it up with ease and sitting down next to her.

'How do you know our Smudge?'

'Smudge?' Freya asks, but before Adam can reply, Josh is next to the table again, placing her drink in front of her. His other two friends are right behind him, and they greet her as they loudly find chairs and sit down. There's not even close to enough room, and Freya finds herself shoulder to shoulder between Josh and Adam. Not an unpleasant situation.

'I'm sorry,' Josh whispers to her, as the other men catch up, shouting across the table, expletives and banter flowing freely. 'I forget what we're like when we get together.'

'It's fine. Smudge,' she adds deliberately.

He laughs. 'Football thing. That's how I know these guys, from five-a-side.'

'You have time for a life? I'm jealous.'

'Not always. But when I can. It's a laugh. Better than sitting at home alone every night.'

Freya says nothing. I'm sure it is, she thinks ruefully. She knows that only too well.

Adam leans across Freya. 'You didn't tell us about the lovely Freya,' he says. 'Shame on you.'

'Freya's a colleague,' Josh retorts. 'Nothing like that. Not yet, at least,' he adds, with a wink to Freya.

'Another copper, eh? All the better then,' Adam replies.

'You're married!'

'Details, details,' Adam laughs.

Freya sits back, enjoying her wine and listening to the guys taking the piss out of each other. Being in the force, she's used to large groups of rowdy guys and relaxes in their undemanding company. Josh seems to enjoy himself with them, laughing loudly at a joke, and every now and again glancing her way. He meets her eye and smiles. At one point he mouths *you okay?* and she nods. A gentlemanly gesture, and Freya finds herself warming to him.

But it's getting late. She finishes her wine and stands up. She waves a hand over the gathering.

'Nice to meet you all,' she shouts over the din.

Josh stands. 'I'll walk you back.'

'I was going to get a taxi.'

'Then I'll walk you to it.'

They fight their way through the bodies in the pub, out into the cool spring air. After the heat inside it's a relief, and Freya takes a few deep breaths.

They start to walk down the road. Freya feels tongue-tied, not sure what to say. It's been nine months since Jonathan died, and she hasn't thought for a second about anyone else. But tonight? Tonight has been nice.

They stop at the taxi rank, and Freya holds her arm out for the one approaching.

'Well…' Freya begins.

'See you tomorrow, Freya,' Josh says. And he leans forward, placing a kiss on her cheek.

'See you tomorrow, Sarge,' she replies.

He laughs and holds up a hand as he walks away.

The taxi pulls up next to her, and she opens the door. But for a moment she allows herself to look behind her, at Josh's departing back. Mina was right, she thinks. He does have a nice arse.

14

Thursday

Freya must have fallen asleep, because the alarm jolts her awake.

She'd arrived home from the pub tired, slightly groggy from the few glasses of wine, heading for bed without delay.

All day she'd felt knackered. Eyes itching, downing caffeine to keep herself alert. But once she was in bed, she couldn't have been more awake. Her body felt twitchy and tense. Wound up to the max.

Her brain refused to switch off. She knew that the moment she closed her eyes, she would remember. She would hear Amy Miller's voice, see her lying unconscious on the sofa. Her mind conjured up images of her dead on her kitchen floor, blood pooling from where she'd banged her head. She squeezed her eyes closed. She needed to sleep. She needed to forget. But how could she?

In the dim light of the morning, she lies in bed, forcing her eyes open. She knows if she closes them again, surrenders to the exhaustion, she'll fall back to sleep. But one more hour surely couldn't hurt…

Her phone buzzes, making the decision for her. A message from Josh.

> Morning! Pick me up at 08.30 – we're going to Eastleigh College.

Then another text with his address.

Christ, how is he so awake? He must have drunk way more than Freya did last night. She hauls herself to a sitting position, resting for a moment on the edge of the bed. She sighs.

'On my way, Sarge,' she mumbles to thin air.

–

The smell of disinfectant and cheap teenage aftershave is distinctly reminiscent of Freya's old college. It reminds her of detentions and disappointment. Expectations not met. Efforts unrecognised. And sitting in the corridor outside of the principal's office doesn't help.

'Bloody awful, isn't it?' Josh whispers, echoing Freya's thoughts.

She doesn't miss being eighteen. The constant uncertainty, all those bloody hormones.

'How was your college experience?' Freya asks.

'I played a lot of sport,' Josh replies. 'So spent most of my time caught up in that. Rugby, football, cricket – the lot.'

'Ah.' Freya slowly nods in understanding. One of the in-crowd. A popular boy, getting the prettiest girls, spending evenings at the pub when still underage. She'd been on the outskirts of that. The one with the cheap cider in the park, looking on from afar. Wishing, wondering how to be that cool. That feeling still haunts her, even now.

A woman bursts out of the office, distracting her from her thoughts.

'Sorry to keep you waiting. Come through, please.'

The college principal holds the door open and they go into her office. A bland space, impersonal except for the sign on the door. The woman is well groomed, precise hair in a chignon at the nape of her neck, wearing a suit over a crisply ironed shirt. She takes the chair behind her desk, gesturing towards the two in front of her. Freya and Josh sit down; Freya notices they are slightly lower than the principal. She wonders if it's deliberate, to exert her authority over these kids in any way she can.

'We'd like to talk to you about Connor Vardy,' Josh begins. 'And a few of his friends.' He looks at his notepad. 'Tyler Garratt, Mark Black and Lee Cernis?'

She nods. 'I know them,' she says slowly. 'I wouldn't describe them as Connor's friends, though.'

'How so?'

'Tyler, Mark and Lee – yes. Thick as thieves, those three, and just as devious. I'm surprised they're not known to the police already, but I would guess they're too clever to be caught.'

'What sort of things do they get up to?'

'I don't know any of this for sure,' she says, glancing towards the door. 'But I've heard the teachers talk. Drinking, drug use, vandalism.'

'And Connor?' Freya asks.

'Nothing like that. He's a good kid. He missed college for a while when his grandfather died, played up in class, that sort of thing. But since he's been working at Riverside, we've seen a change in him. I'd be worried if you said he was hanging around with those three.'

'What's his family life been like?'

99

'Not good. His mother was in and out of prison. When she died, he moved in with his grandfather. He's always been a key influence in his life. Can I ask why the interest?'

'Their names came up in conjunction to a case we're working,' Josh says, cryptically. 'Thought it would be helpful to get some background before we take their witness statements.'

'And you want to use a room here?' the principal asks.

Josh nods. 'Please. If you wouldn't mind.'

The three of them stand up to make arrangements. Freya turns back to the principal. 'We appreciate your help. But if you don't mind me asking,' she says, 'why are you being so helpful? It's just, we don't normally get this level of information from teachers. They're usually more protective of their students.'

The principal smiles grimly. 'I am protective of my students – but those three? They're on their own. And between you and me, the sooner I have an excuse to expel them from my college, the better. Now. Shall we go and fetch them from the common room?'

–

Freya watches the three boys through the window. Men, really, all over eighteen, so no need for a responsible adult to be present when they speak to them. They are exactly the sort of kids she despises. Cocky little shits, baggy jeans, caps on, laughing with each other in the corridor. These are boys who think themselves smarter than their teachers, above the law. Entitled to do whatever they like.

Freya knows they are the kids that tripped her up in corridors, that pulled her hair and made comments about her legs, her boobs. But I'm an adult now, she tells herself sternly. Those days are over.

They've already interviewed Tyler and Mark. Separately, but both giving identikit answers, even down to the phrasing. No, they weren't out on Tuesday night. They were all in Mark's garage, playing on his Xbox. *Call of Duty*, if you must ask. Yes, they know Connor from college, but no, they don't hang out with him. Freezer? What freezer?

Mark Black seems to be the leader of the three – right now the other two are looking at him as he tells a story. He has a level of arrogance far above the others. Mark and Tyler laugh, and Freya watches as Lee gauges their reactions before joining in. Lee Cernis is the weak link, that's for sure.

'Let's get this over and done with,' Josh says.

They call Lee into the room. As he gets up, he looks back to the other boys. Mark Black mimes a gun with his hand, pointing it at Lee, in full view of Freya and Josh. He doesn't give a shit, and it makes Freya's blood boil.

Josh gives Lee the standard warnings, explains that his witness statement is a legal document and that he might have to be called to give evidence should anything go to a trial. Josh tells him he's free to leave at any time and the statement is voluntary. Like the other two, Lee nods.

But unlike the other two, Lee is nervous, pulling at his eyebrow and staring at the tabletop. Josh asks the same questions and he gives the same answers, Freya writing them on the MG11 form.

Josh looks over to her and nods. She puts the pen down and leans forward in her chair.

'Lee,' she starts. 'I know you want us to believe you're like the other two out there, but that's simply not true, is it?' Lee continues to look down. 'See, we've done a bit of background on you all, and what I can't understand is why you hang around with them.'

Lee pauses the abuse of his eyebrow for a moment.

Freya pulls out her notebook and looks at the details. 'Let's see. Your mother is a teacher, your father is a plumber. You live in a nice part of town. You got good GCSEs, you studied hard. And yet, you hang around with those two.'

'They're my mates,' he mumbles.

'Apparently so. But the fact remains, you have a lot more to lose. You have a brain, you could go on to have a good job, a good life. Why are you prepared to throw that away?'

'We didn't do anything.'

Freya notices that away from the other boys, Lee's speech is more precise, his grammar better. *We didn't do anything*, rather than *we didn't do nuffin'*, which is what they got from the others.

'What happened on Tuesday night, Lee?' Freya asks again.

'We were playing Xbox. Nothing happened.'

'You didn't see Connor Vardy?'

'No.'

'You haven't been near Riverside?'

'No.'

'You didn't see the freezer?'

'I told you. We were at Mark's. We were playing Xbox.'

'Where nobody saw you, not even Mark's dad?'

'Mark saw me. Tyler saw me.'

Freya glances across at Josh, who shakes his head. Freya sighs, then pushes the completed MG11 form across to Lee.

'Fine. Sign this and you can go.'

Lee gives Freya's handwriting a cursory glance, scribbles at the bottom of the page, then walks out. The other two stand up, clapping him on the back as they lope away, jeering.

Josh makes an exasperated noise. 'Bloody kids.'

'I know they're a group of tossers, but perhaps they didn't have anything to do with that body,' Freya suggests. 'Perhaps they just hung around in the bus shelter for a bit, then did go home to play on the Xbox.'

Josh scowls. 'Perhaps, but I'd love to wipe those satisfied expressions off their smug little faces.'

They head towards the reception area, ready to drive to the station. But as they go, Freya catches a glimpse of the back of someone – someone who looks strangely familiar. Long dark hair, slim frame, tall. As she passes, the woman turns her head and Freya knows who it is. Olivia Cross. Amy Miller's sister. Her clothes seem more expensive, her hair glossy and styled, but she's definitely the prostitute and stripper that Freya remembers from nine months before.

Their eyes meet, a moment of recognition. Then Olivia smiles.

'Detective West,' she says.

Then she turns to face her and Freya's breath catches. Although from the back she looked as slim as before, Freya can now see the massive bump. She's pregnant. Very pregnant.

Olivia rests her hands on her tummy. 'What a surprise to see you,' she continues.

'Olivia. How are you?' Freya asks, forcing a smile onto her face. Next to her, Josh pauses, sensing something interesting going on.

'I'm good. Been busy,' she laughs, gesturing to her belly.

'I can see. Congratulations. How far along are you?'

'Thirty-five weeks. Due soon.'

'How exciting,' Freya says, but her head is mentally working out the maths. Thirty-five weeks. So – eight, nine months? Which would take it back to...

'Detective Sergeant Joshua Smith,' Josh says next to her, holding out his hand.

Olivia shakes it, then looks at Freya. 'Are you not working with Robin any more?'

Robin? Freya thinks. Informal. 'No, I am. Just here doing a few interviews. And you?' she asks, curious.

'Handing in final coursework. I've been doing a diploma in beauty therapy. Need a career that's a bit more respectable,' she adds with a stroke of her belly. 'For when this one comes along.'

'Of course. Nice to see you,' Freya finishes, suddenly desperate to get away.

'You too. Tell Robin hello from me.'

They walk away quickly. Josh whispers, 'Who was that?'

'Sister of Amy Miller,' Freya replies. 'Olivia Cross.'

'Amy Miller? As in the Jonathan Miller case?' Freya nods, and they both climb into her car. 'I heard about that one. Before my time, but everyone was talking about it.' Josh continues, 'The psycho wife who died?'

'That's her,' Freya says, feeling her body grow hot.

'Didn't the sister end up with all the money?'

'Yeah. Next of kin, so all the life insurance and inheritance went to her.' Freya feels a trickle of sweat run down her spine, and stares resolutely at the road as she drives.

'So who's the father?'

'I don't know.'

'She seems to know Robin Butler well.'

'Hmm...' Freya says.

Josh senses her reluctance and moves on to what he found out about the freezer first thing that morning, even before Freya was awake. With some determination, he'd managed to get hold of the old lady's daughter, who explained that they gave it away six months ago on Gumtree. Two blokes, no idea about names. She gave Josh a mobile phone number but it wasn't registered, and the account on Gumtree is now closed down.

Freya's glad of his change of subject, her mind full of Olivia and this surprise baby. The maths isn't good. So Olivia got pregnant around the time they were investigating Jonathan's murder. When Robin was close to Olivia. How close? she wonders. She knows there was a lot Robin didn't tell her around that time. Get-togethers, just Olivia and Robin, one of which culminated in him getting beaten up outside her strip club. A rumour of a complaint, that Olivia had stayed the night at Robin's. But what had happened? Not *that*, surely?

'So we're nowhere,' Josh finishes.

'CCTV?' Freya asks, keen to keep him talking.

'Mina is on it now.'

—

Back in the office, Mina is slumped in front of her screen. She has a half-empty mug of coffee in one hand, which Josh swaps for a full one without a word.

'Anything?' he asks.

'Nah.'

'Anything back from the lab?'

'Nah.'

'You called them?'

Mina looks up at him. 'What do you think?'

Josh slumps in front of his own computer.

'So where are we?' he asks the two of them.

Freya ticks it off on her fingers. 'We have a dead body in a freezer, with a time of death in the early hours of Wednesday morning, and an uncertain cause of death. We have kids playing in the bus shelter' – Mina looks up with interest – 'who were apparently never there because they were playing on their Xbox,' she adds for her benefit. Freya continues: 'We have the freezer and clothing down at the lab, an appliance we can't trace—'

'A shitload of CCTV with nothing on it,' Mina finishes for her.

'And a body with no ID,' Josh says. 'We think he was homeless, right?'

'That's our theory.'

'So, Freya, you get on that. Start phoning homeless shelters, work out who this guy is. And I'll nag the lab. Mina,' – she looks up hopefully – 'you carry on with the CCTV,' he says. 'And see if you can find any footage of the people that dumped the freezer. Sunday night, early Monday morning. Must have been a big van or a truck, for a freezer that bulky.'

'Yes, skipper,' she sighs.

Freya sits down at her desk and boots up her computer. She picks up her mobile, holding it in her hand. She hasn't heard from Robin that morning, and for the first time, she dreads his call. Does he know about the baby? Freya wonders.

And, more to the point, if he doesn't, should she tell him?

106

15

DC Grey calls first thing, his voice reedy and apologetic.

'I spoke to the university, Sarge. They said if we want to know what Dr Mason and Dr Sharp were working on, we should go down there. Easier to show, than tell. DI Craig said you could come with me. If you want to.'

Robin agrees, keen to be involved, although he suspects Craig's main motive is to keep him away from whatever interviews they are doing back at the station. He waits for Grey outside the Travelodge, not looking forward to getting into a car with the kid.

While he waits, he phones Josie. No change from the hospital.

'He's had a terrible night,' she says. 'Couldn't sleep, headache, shaking. And he's still confused.' Robin can hear the tension in her voice. 'One moment he's talking about needing to see Simon, the next he's saying how big the storm was last night and how well their filming had gone. It's like he's making stuff up.'

'And what do the doctors say?' Robin asks.

'Not a lot. They're going to do the MRI this morning.'

'Good. I'll be there as soon as possible.'

'Take your time, Robin,' Josie replies quietly. 'I'd rather you were out there finding out what happened.'

Robin hangs up, his mind full. He has no idea where to start, but perhaps Finn's lab will hold some answers.

DC Grey is so quiet in the car, it makes Robin nervous so he makes an attempt at conversation. It isn't that he's exactly chatty himself, but the complete silence is disconcerting.

Despite Robin's protest, Craig insisted on them taking Grey's car, and having someone else drive him puts him on edge. Especially DC Grey: he's serious, face forward, concentrating intently on the road. It seems to Robin that he's only just passed his driving test, leaning forward slightly as he drives, and the broken exchange distracts Robin for a moment, if nothing else. It soon transpires that DC Grey had been a civilian analyst for the force for a couple of years, eventually training and transferring into uniform, before becoming a detective. From the look of him, he can't be much older than his late twenties, with a chin that barely needs shaving and delicate, almost androgynous, features.

'What's your first name?' Robin asks, trying to conjure up some familiarity.

'Kennedy.'

'What, sorry?'

Grey chances a look at Robin. 'Kennedy.'

'That's your first name?'

'Yes.'

'Anyone call you Ken?'

'No.'

They lapse back into silence. Grey it is, then.

'What's DI Craig like to work for?'

'Good.' They pull up in the car park of the university, and Grey looks across at Robin. 'She's smart, Sarge. I know she'll do what's right.'

To secure a conviction, or what's right for Finn? Robin's not sure.

The two of them head towards Finn's lab, with Robin leading the way. He had a tour years ago, when Finn was doing his PhD, and knows he hasn't moved locations since.

A tall, well-built man waits in the doorway, standing up straight when he sees them approaching. He looks older than DC Grey and holds out his hand when they're near.

'Ian Calloway,' he says. 'One of Dr Mason's PhD students.'

Grey introduces himself, showing his ID. 'And this is… Robin Butler.'

Robin glances at Grey, then shakes hands with Calloway. So that's how it's going to be, he thinks. No police credentials at all? But he stays quiet, accepting his fate.

'We haven't got much time,' Grey continues. 'Could you show us what Dr Mason was working on? Some sort of equipment they were trialling?'

'Yes,' Ian says as they walk. He escorts them through the electronic security doors into the lab. 'It's a dual polarisation Doppler. Basically, a high-resolution radar that scans the atmosphere and tells us what's up there. The party trick of this guy is that it can measure wind speed and direction, as well as tell the difference between hail and rain and other debris.' He stops next to two large white satellite dishes attached to an array of electronics. 'This is one of our prototypes. Bistatic, operating at 94 gigahertz. We've used it before, but only in experimental settings. We were all excited to see it play out in a real storm, especially one of Tuesday's magnitude.'

'But Doppler radar has been around for some time,' Grey points out. 'What makes this one special?'

'The level of resolution. And the algorithm Dr Mason developed means the data returning can be translated into a much more detailed backscatter image.'

'And why is that important?' Robin says, still baffled. He knows he's supposed to be a silent observer, but his police inquisitiveness is ingrained.

Calloway takes the question in his stride. 'The greater the detail, the better we can know what's coming. Rain, hail, snow, ice. Tornadoes.' He smiles. 'It saves lives. But not just that – it has incredible commercial applications, too. Hail destroys millions of dollars' worth of crops every year. It decimates solar panels. Being able to forecast this stuff means companies can save a huge amount of money. Insurance companies will love it.' He pauses. 'Do you know when we'll get the equipment back from the van?'

'It's going to take some time, I'm sorry,' Grey replies. 'How did the BBC fit into all of this?'

'Dr Sharp's an alumnus here, he did his doctorate alongside Finn. He's quite a celebrity, so when he got in touch, we were all excited.' Ian sits back on one of the stools, warming to his explanation. 'He particularly mentioned the Doppler, saying they wanted to try something new, showcase new technology, and asked whether Dr Mason would work with them.'

'Sophie said Finn was reluctant at first?'

'Yes, we couldn't understand it. But once Finn realised what it could mean for our funding, he quickly came around. You saw that van?' Robin and Grey both nod. 'Custom-made, specially adapted so it could fit up into the car park. Finn would have sat there in his Ford Focus, given half the chance, but Sharp only wanted the best. Needed to look good on TV.' Calloway grins happily. 'And we didn't complain.'

Mystery solved, Robin thinks. Although it still must have been close, barely squeaking through the maximum headroom of the multistorey.

'And the storm was a loaded–gun scenario, right?' Grey asks, and Robin looks from the DC to Calloway, confused.

'That's right,' Ian confirms. 'You know your storms.' Grey smiles back.

'Explain?' Robin asks, bluntly.

Calloway turns to him. 'How much do you know about thunderstorms?'

'Nothing.'

'Okay, so...' He turns to the whiteboard behind him, and draws a crude outline of the British Isles and the north of Europe. 'From the beginning. The storm was caused by the Spanish Plume effect.' He draws a series of arrows, moving up from the main body of Europe. 'Hot, dry air moves north from Spain towards the UK. Since the Spanish interior is over 700 metres above sea level, this hot air acts like a lid, trapping the build-up of warm, moist air near the surface.' He looks at Grey. 'The loaded gun,' he adds with a smile. 'As it moves north, the elevated plume of hot air rises, begins to cool and forms cloud. This makes it unstable, creating storms that are made bigger by feeding off the warm, moist air trapped below.' He draws another diagram with yet more arrows and what Robin assumes is a cloud. He feels sorry for the poor students in Calloway's lectures if this is the quality of the teaching; he's certainly none the wiser.

Calloway continues: 'It means the warm, moist air near the surface needs to get strongly heated by the sun. It will then break the cap and release its energy as powerful thunderstorms.'

'And this is common in the UK?' Robin asks.

'Once every two to three years? And we can only predict a few days ahead, so once we realised, it was all go.'

Robin accepts defeat on the technical explanation. Desperate to move onto simpler ground, he asks, 'Could you show us his office?'

'Sure.' With a last caress of the satellite dish, Ian walks out of the lab and up the stairs at the back. They arrive at a row of standard-looking offices that wouldn't seem out of place in a corporate headquarters, albeit a shabby one. He stops at the end, at a small, poky room with *Dr F. Mason* written on a piece of paper, crudely Blu-Tacked to the glass.

Ian pulls a key out of his pocket and opens the door. Robin walks inside.

'Dr Mason's a senior staff member, right?' DC Grey asks, the two of them standing in the doorway. Calloway nods. 'So why the small office?'

Ian laughs. 'It's the same one he was allocated when he first became a lecturer. He never moved.'

'And you're his PhD student?'

'One of. Dr Mason has four. But I'm the one who works most closely with him on the radar.'

The office is as messy as Finn's flat. Paper litters the floor, and the bin is full and overflowing. A row of stained coffee cups runs the length of the windowsill, next to a brown spider plant.

'So why weren't you there the night of the storm?' Robin asks. He gets a look from Grey. Well, if you're not going to ask, he thinks, with a glare back.

Ian flushes. 'He wanted me here. Man on the ground. To watch the data as it came in.' Robin sees his demeanour change – the red cheeks, the hesitation – but he doesn't push. Not yet.

'And how did Dr Mason seem in the last few weeks?'

'He was working hard. I know he was here all hours of the day and night. We can only predict the storms a few days ahead, so once we realised, it was all go. There was a lot of pressure to get everything ready before it hit.'

'And in himself? Did he seem okay?'

Ian screws up his face. 'Depends how well you know Finn. Some of the others were worried about him, saying he wasn't eating or sleeping, but I've been on his team a while now and he gets like this. There's nothing more important than his work. He's incredibly driven.'

Robin knew that side of him. He was the same when he was studying for his A levels. 'To the point of making himself ill?' he asks.

'Maybe.'

Robin moves further inside, leaving Grey addressing technical questions to Calloway in the corridor. He runs his fingers across the top of a dusty bookshelf; to Robin, it seems like the office of an academic. The paper, the books, the notes – they all show someone hard at work on something way outside of Robin's comprehension.

He feels his throat narrow. Just days ago, Finn was here. Working hard, getting ready for what should have been the making of his career. And instead, he is in hospital, while the police investigate him for the murder of a colleague. And a celebrity at that. Robin briefly saw the papers this morning: it was front-page news, even in the nationals. He knows they'll be reporting what happened, facts or no facts.

He catches sight of the corner of a photograph, pinned on the wall, behind a stack of files. He pulls it out.

It's one taken at Finn's PhD graduation ceremony, standing straight in his hat and gown, Robin next to him, his arm around him. He was so proud that day. Of everything Finn had achieved.

He leans forward to put the photograph back, but as he does so, his nose catches the edge of something. A particular smell. Stark. Medicinal. Subtle, but there nonetheless.

He bends down again, sniffing around the desk. The cups smell of coffee and something unpleasant. The empty water bottles…

He picks up the one closest to him, empty but its cap off. He sniffs, then recoils. The unmistakable smell of alcohol, strong stuff at that. He looks at the dregs in the bottom, then, against his better judgement, puts it to his mouth and tips the few drips in.

It's vodka.

He picks up the bottle next to it, takes the cap off and sniffs. The same. Then the next, and the next. They all smell of alcohol.

'Butler?' Grey appears at the door. 'DI Craig's been on the phone. We need to be getting back.'

Robin points to the bottles. 'Fetch some evidence bags,' he says, Baker's instructions forgotten. This is too important. 'Get these labelled up to take away.'

Grey looks annoyed, but nods.

'And then,' Robin says to himself, 'we're going back to his flat.'

16

The mood is sombre the moment they step into the mortuary. Freya was waiting for the homeless shelters to get back to her, and Mina had reached her limit with the CCTV, so when the call came in, Josh sent them down there. He had an ulterior motive: it was just after lunch, and nobody wants to view a post-mortem on a full stomach.

Dr Steph Harper greets them with a wave as they arrive. She is already head-to-toe in protective gear, dictating notes to her assistant as she makes her way round the body on the table. Freya feels cheered at seeing Steph again – her straightforward and logical thinking is always a welcome balm, especially with Freya's now-scrambled brain.

Freya and Mina stand at a distance as she starts her post-mortem. The body is skinny, hip bones protruding, arms with little fat or muscle. Freya looks up to his head to distract from where Dr Harper is starting to make the Y-incision, running the scalpel down the length of the chest, opening up the ribcage with a loud whine of the saw.

The man has long matted hair and a full unkempt beard. It's clear he wasn't looking after himself.

Steph turns to them both, scalpel in hand, body open on the table. 'You guys ready?' she asks, and they nod. 'Let's crack on.'

Hours later, Steph concludes her autopsy and leaves her assistant to finish up. She pulls off her protective glasses and scrubs, then gestures to Freya and Mina to follow her out.

Steph's tiny cupboard of an office is clean and tidy, with neat files of paperwork lined up on the desk. A small fridge sits on one side with a kettle on top, and she flicks it on.

'So, show me some photos of those babies of yours!' Steph smiles as she sits down, and they lean over Mina's phone for a minute, as she and Steph go through the snapshots, cooing over the chubby dark-haired baby and Mina's older toddler. It makes Freya think about Olivia Cross again. That bump, and who the father might be.

'Anyway,' Steph sighs, back to business. 'I'm not sure how much of that you understood, but essentially we're looking at a malnourished male, in poor health. Your victim had infected sores on many parts of his body, obviously been there for a while. Little chance of healing without proper medical attention. Plus, a nasty infestation of lice.'

Freya scratches involuntarily. 'Homeless?' she asks.

'That would be my guess. We'll have to wait on the tox screen, but from the cirrhosis of his liver, I would guess alcohol abuse. There are no signs of injection marks, and hep B and C are negative, so I'd probably rule out drugs. Age between fifty and sixty – hard to tell for sure with someone in this state.'

'Any idea of cause of death?'

'A number of possibilities. He had a blurred, brownish tinge around his knees and elbows, and some sludging of the blood in the small vessels of many of his organs. Both of these would indicate hypothermia.'

'But it was warm that night?' Mina asks.

'It wouldn't have taken much. If he was wet from the rain, plus his low body mass?' Steph shrugs. 'I wouldn't rule it out. But given he was found inside a chest freezer, hypoxia is the most likely possibility, especially considering the clear cyanosis of the skin of his face. It wouldn't have taken long to suffocate in that freezer.'

They're all quiet for a moment, considering this man's last moments.

'Any signs of foul play?' Freya asks.

'A few,' Steph replies. 'He had scratches on his forearms, two broken fingers and a number of torn fingernails, although it's hard to tell whether they are related to cause of death or just his way of life. I've taken scrapings from under his fingernails and from inside his mouth.' Steph acknowledges Freya's blank look. 'In case he bit someone, or similar. No evidence of sexual assault,' she adds.

'Time of death?' Mina asks. 'You mentioned no more than eight hours yesterday.'

Steph nods. 'Being in a contained space like a freezer can slow down decay because it prevents carrion insect infestation. The overwhelming majority of soft-tissue destruction is due to feeding by insect larvae,' she explains. 'But in John Doe's case, when we got there in the morning, his body was still comparatively warm and stiff.'

'So he died some time Tuesday night?' Freya asks. 'The night of the storm.'

'Yes. I'd estimate between eleven p.m. and three a.m.'

Freya and Mina thank her, then walk, dispirited, to their car. They know the freezer has been shipped to the lab, where the techies will examine it for trace and fingerprints. Freya hopes something will point them one way or the other, give them a direction to take the investigation.

But which is better? she thinks, as Mina starts the engine. It's tragic, whichever way they look at it. Suffocated, desperate for oxygen. Or soaking wet, freezing to death. Alone. Scared. Nobody should end their life like that.

And, worse, they have no idea who he was.

Freya gazes out of the car window as they drive back to the police station. Did he have family? Children? A wife? People that loved him? She thinks of her own situation, and tears threaten behind her eyes. She'd never have imagined her own life like this. Single, at thirty-six. Living alone. Clock ticking.

She's always wanted kids. Two – a boy and a girl, like Mina. A husband who puts the bins out and mows the lawn. Taking the maximum time off when the baby arrives, maybe going back to work part-time. She's more traditional than she likes to admit.

She'd thought it could be possible with Jonathan. But now? Not now.

Who would marry her? She's a state. She doesn't sleep. She's working too hard. Jittery from caffeine. Hasn't done any exercise or eaten anything green in months.

Next to her, Mina is still quiet. Like Freya, shocked into uncharacteristic silence when faced with the stark finality of the slab. Freya stares out of the window as familiar neighbourhoods flash by and resolves anew to sort herself out. To get Amy Miller and what happened out of her head.

But how? she thinks. How?

When, despite the sunshine and the scent of summer in the air, everything feels so dark.

17

It doesn't make sense. But it's an explanation of sorts.

Robin stands, back in Finn's flat, the fridge open in front of him. He has one of the bottles of water in his hand, cap off. He takes a quick sniff. It's vodka. The bottle is full of vodka. He takes the next plastic bottle out and does the same – the alcohol fumes are stark and biting.

Grey is next to him, evidence bags in hand, waiting. Robin is grateful for his silence, as he struggles to digest what he's found.

'Bag it all up,' he says to Grey, then leaves the kitchen and goes out of the flat. He's looking for where the bins are kept, and eventually finds a small, gated door into a fenced-off outbuilding round the back of the flats.

He slides the latch open and starts moving bags around inside. And then, there it is. A box of glass recycling, full to the brim, containing five huge empty vodka bottles.

He wants to imagine this is from the whole block of flats, but he knows he'd be deluding himself. The sign on the wall says that the bins are taken away every Friday. This is from less than a week ago. And all the same brand of vodka.

Robin takes a quick succession of photos on his phone, then shuts the door in disgust. He slowly climbs the stairs back to the flat in silence.

So, Finn is a drinker, and a serious one at that. How had he not noticed? They've been out for dinner, out to bars and clubs over the years and, sure, Finn had been drinking, but so had he. He hadn't noticed his friend had been particularly the worse for wear. No more than him on some occasions, although that was hardly a recommend-ation. And the last time they went out, none of them had drunk much at all. He'd been driving and had one glass, Sophie and Finn sharing the rest of the bottle of wine.

But he knows alcoholics can be sneaky. His own sister was killed by a drunk driver, and that man claimed to be going to AA, while still downing bottles of Jack Daniel's.

His phone rings, and he answers it. It's Craig.

'Bring my DC back now. He has work to do.'

Robin scowls, but he does as he's told.

–

Robin squints at the tiny video screen. He's annoyed he isn't allowed inside, although he grudgingly understands why. Sitting behind the table in the interview room are Craig and DC Grey, and opposite them, Justin White, cameraman for the BBC.

They've already completed the first interview with the producer. A posh, officious man with nothing interesting to say. He hadn't been near the van because it was too small, and only essential staff were meant to be there. Personally, Robin thought he hadn't been present because he was scared of the storm, but it didn't matter – he didn't know anything. He maintained that the whole team had been on the best of terms in the run-up to the shoot, overplaying it so it sounded like the production of the BBC's *Storm Chasers* was some sort of weather-obsessed Disneyland.

But Justin White is a different matter. He is constantly shifting his position in the chair, glancing around him.

'You're not under arrest,' Craig is clarifying for the third time. 'And as my colleague said, you are here on a voluntary basis and free to leave.'

'But you're recording me?'

'Yes, and we'll give you a copy of the video when you go. Now, can you tell us why you weren't in the van?'

Justin White's a good-looking man like Simon was, but rugged, while Dr Sharp was clean-cut. Long hair on top, tied back in a short ponytail, shaved underneath. Stubble. Checked lumberjack shirt and artfully ripped jeans.

He picks up the plastic cup of tea in front of him and takes a gulp.

'We have cameras all over, filming the outside. I hold a Panasonic VariCam with an 85 mm portrait lens to take the close-ups of Simon.' He pauses again and Craig fidgets in her seat. Robin can tell she is trying hard to stay patient. 'We got everything sorted, the equipment up and running on the top of the van, then did some initial footage.'

'Such as?'

'Simon's set-up on film, some shots of Dr Mason explaining the equipment. But then at about midnight I had a problem with my camera.'

'What sort of problem?'

'Nothing big, just a firmware issue. I think it needs an update. But I didn't want to risk it failing as the storm reached its climax, so I went down to get the backup out of my car. But it wasn't there.' His hands fiddle with the plastic cup. 'I was sure I'd packed it along with everything else, but I must have forgotten. I tried to phone Ian back at the lab to bring it, but my mobile couldn't get reception, so I left to go and pick it up.'

'Leaving Sharp and Mason alone in the van.'

White nods.

'And what time was this?'

'About half twelve, I think. The storm was starting to build momentum.'

Robin knows that time fits with the footage they've already been given by the BBC team. Someone is going through it all now, wading through hours of video of the car park, viewed from the outside of the van.

'Then what?'

White pauses, rubbing at his eyes.

'Do you want to take a minute?' DC Grey asks gently, receiving a glare from Craig.

'No, no, I'm fine. Just want to get this over and done with. It took me about half an hour to get to the lab, then back again. But by the time I returned to the car park, everything was really hairy. The storm had escalated, it was bigger than any of us had imagined. I parked a level down and tried to get up to the top, but the wind was too violent.'

'You couldn't get to the van?' Craig asks.

'Have you ever tried walking in a downdraught from a supercell, DI Craig?' Justin White turns bolshy, and Robin can see the side of the man that regularly drives into tornadoes with only a camera to protect him. 'You're talking wind speeds of up to a hundred miles an hour. Pouring rain. There was no way I was getting up to the top level of that car park. Sharp had a Sony FS5 – he regularly recorded storms himself. And there was a camera top-left capturing the interior of the van. I knew that even without me there we could get the footage we needed.'

'There were two more cameras in the van?' Craig glances at Grey.

'Yes. Haven't you found the footage?'

Craig gestures to Grey and he gets up quickly, leaving the room.

Robin meets him in the corridor. 'This could be what we need, couldn't it?' he says to Grey, who nods.

'I'll put a call in to the SOCO team, see if they can find them.' Grey pauses. 'And White's not lying about the mobile reception. BT confirmed today that the main mast near the car park was down from midnight until three a.m. Unfortunate,' he adds, before hurrying off.

'You could say that,' Robin mutters.

He goes back to watching the screen. Craig is continuing the interview and has put a photograph in front of White.

'Can you tell me what this is?' she asks.

White picks it up, looking closely at the image. 'It's Simon's penknife,' he replies.

'And you know that for sure?'

'Yes.' His finger points to the photo. 'There's an engraving on it – see? *SS*. It was a gift from one of his old professors, or something.'

'Why would Simon Sharp have a penknife with him?'

'He always did. He carried it everywhere he went. Said it was good to be prepared. Even if it was just for the corkscrew.' White laughs, then it's overtaken by a sob. 'Guess it didn't save him this time.'

'No,' Craig replies simply.

'Was that… was that what he was killed with?'

'We believe it was the murder weapon, yes,' Craig replies.

Shit, Robin thinks.

Craig moves on.

'What was Dr Sharp like?' Craig asks.

'Have you watched the series?' Justin replies. Craig nods. 'Just like that. Simon is – was – exactly the man you see on TV. So smart. Always two steps ahead. And the bravest sod you'll ever meet.'

'He seemed... determined,' Craig suggests.

White nods. 'Oh, he was. But that was the way the show was set up – whatever Simon says, goes. If he wanted us to drive into the middle of an EF5 tornado, we would. If he wanted to film in the aftermath of flash flooding, we were there. But nobody ever minded. We would have followed Simon to the ends of the earth, and frequently did.'

'And how would you describe the relationship between Sharp and Dr Mason?' Craig asks.

'Colleagues. Friends.'

'Colleagues or friends?' Craig interjects.

'Friends, I guess. Simon was excited to be working on this project. I know he'd been frustrated.'

'Why?'

'In the beginning, when *Storm Chasers* started out, it was all about the science. Simon got a chance to talk about what was going on, about the weather changes and the meteorological tech that means we can do what we do. But as time went on, the powers that be wanted more action and less talk.' He frowns. 'Better ratings. I know Simon missed it. He moaned once: "I'm not a scientist any more, I'm an entertainer."'

'And this was his chance to get back to the science?'

'Yeah. Dr Mason is the best at what he does, but he's not exactly...'

'Charismatic?'

White nods. 'He needed Simon as a frontman. And Simon needed his new Doppler. But...' He scowls. 'They didn't always work well together.'

'How so?' Craig asks, and Robin leans forward, closer to the monitor, desperate to be in the room.

'They worked in different ways. Dr Mason liked things to be ordered and controlled. Simon was more... haphazard, I guess. He worked off the cuff and I know that annoyed Finn.'

'Did they ever argue?'

'No. Oh...'

'What, Mr White?'

'I... I don't know why I haven't remembered it before. I came in late, about a week ago, and they were both in Dr Mason's office. They were arguing. Or rather, I could hear Simon shouting, and Finn was sitting at his desk. He looked upset.'

'What were they shouting about?'

'I think it was to do with the Doppler that Finn was working on. Finn said something, but I couldn't hear what. Then Sharp shouted at him.'

White starts to cry now, angrily wiping at his eyes with the edge of his shirtsleeve.

Craig leans across the table towards him. 'What did he shout, Mr White?' she pushes.

'He said... he said, "Only over my dead body..." then Finn stormed out. As he went, he was muttering something under his breath, but I didn't think anything of it at the time.'

Craig stares sternly at White.

'What was Finn Mason saying?' she pushes.

Justin White looks up at Craig. There are tears in his eyes.

'Finn said, "That can be arranged."'

18

Freya, Josh and Mina don't get much further that day. Still no ID on their victim, nothing back from the lab. And she hasn't heard from Robin since he tried to call her the night before.

He's been on her mind. Ever since she saw Olivia at the college, she's been debating what to do. He needs to know. Even though she's certain he has nothing to do with it.

She's cooking dinner – pasta, *again* – when she hears a knock on the door. She opens it, and Robin's there.

'You're back,' she says, surprised. Then: 'Come in, come in.'

He frowns apologetically. 'Sorry to come round unannounced. I just…' But Freya knows what he's saying. He's had a bad day and he doesn't want to go home to an empty house. She felt exactly the same. Last night she went to the pub with Josh to avoid it.

'Do you want something to eat?'

'God, yes. Please. All I've had is vending-machine shit for two days.'

'And how's Finn?'

Robin slumps into one of her kitchen chairs. He runs his hands across his face. 'Not good. No change.'

'What do the doctors say?' She goes to the fridge and takes the bottle of wine out of the door, pouring him a glass without asking.

He takes it with a grateful smile. 'They don't know. Waiting for the MRI results to come back. The psychiatrist is still talking about psychotic breaks. Basically, they haven't got a bloody clue, but they don't want to say that.'

He goes on to tell her about finding the vodka in his flat and office, her mouth dropping open in surprise.

'You didn't suspect?' she asks.

'Not a clue,' Robin replies, the guilt clear on his face. 'So now they're dealing with the withdrawal symptoms from the alcohol addiction, too. The shakes, the headaches, the vomiting. He's even had a few hallucinations.'

'And he can't remember what happened?'

'No. And he can't form new memories either. He doesn't remember what we tell him or even what sodding day it is.'

Freya stands next to the cooker, watching him. He looks knackered, black rings under his eyes, his face drawn. Over the last few months, she's watched her boss look better and better – losing weight after taking up running, colour returning to his cheeks from being outdoors in the spring sunshine. Eating more healthily, drinking less. But tonight he looks back to square one.

'Sorry, how are you?' he asks, looking up with a wan smile.

'I'm fine, don't worry about me.'

'Smith okay to work for?'

She smiles. 'Yeah. Nicer than you.'

'That's not hard.'

'Better-looking, too.'

'Again – low bar.'

The beeper goes off and she drains the pasta into the sink. She enjoys this easy banter. Unlike with others in the office, his manner with her is relaxed and self-deprecating, and she likes being around him. She's missed him these past couple of days.

She stirs pesto sauce into the pasta and plonks a bowl in front of him. It's hardly *MasterChef*, but she knows he won't mind. She lets him eat a few mouthfuls in silence, steeling herself.

'Robin,' she says, and he looks up, chewing. 'I bumped into Olivia Cross today.'

'Liv? Where?'

'At Eastleigh College, when we were doing the witness statements for those boys. She's studying for a beauty therapy course.'

'Really? Good on her.'

Freya pauses. His tone seems light. 'Have you seen her since... you know?'

She can't bring herself to say the actual words. *Since Amy Miller died. Since we covered up our involvement in her death.*

'No, not at all.'

'It's just...'

He clocks her tone and looks at her. His forehead furrows. 'What?'

'She's pregnant.'

He stops, fork hovering above his bowl. 'Okay...' The word is long and drawn-out; he knows she's waiting to say more.

'Nine months pregnant. So the baby would have been conceived—'

'Around last October.'

'But that's nothing to do with you, is it, Robin?' Freya blurts out. 'I mean, you never slept with her?' Her boss is still silent. 'Robin?' she asks again, a bad feeling coming over her.

'That first night, when I met her at the bar?'

'Yes…?' Freya says slowly.

'I got drunk. I mean, really drunk. And she had to take me home. She stayed the night.'

'Robin!'

He holds his hands up in defence. 'She said that it was all innocent. That I puked, and she stayed to make sure I didn't choke on my own vomit, but…' His face is pale. 'I don't know. Anything could have happened.'

'You would have known! Surely?'

He shakes his head slowly. 'I'd have thought so, yes. But I can't remember anything.' He stops. 'No. No, I would have remembered if I'd slept with her. There is no way it's mine.'

But Freya knows what he's thinking. The dates. They tally. Exactly.

They eat another few mouthfuls in silence. Freya feels awful for making his day even worse than it was already.

'Should I have kept quiet?' she asks, softly.

Robin shakes his head, finishing his dinner and resting his cutlery on the bowl.

'What are you going to do?'

'I don't know. I'm sure it's not mine.' But he sounds uncertain, like he's trying to convince himself. Freya picks up his bowl and tidies everything away to avoid having to continue the conversation.

Robin's phone beeps. She looks back and sees that he's reading a message.

'Simon Sharp's autopsy has been completed. Results back tomorrow.' He looks up at Freya. 'You ever watched this *Storm Chasers* programme?'

She shakes her head.

'Want to take a look?'

–

They carry their drinks into the living room. Freya is still finishing off the white, while Robin has moved on to a cup of tea, his car parked in the street outside.

Freya logs onto iPlayer and does a search. She's glad of the distraction, to be able to move on to easier topics of conversation. She finds *Storm Chasers* – two series, ten episodes each – and loads up the first.

They slump back on the sofa. Freya quickly sees the reason why the programme reached its levels of popularity. It's fast and exciting, the team driving across huge, wide, desolate American landscapes. One large shiny four-by-four, and a larger van, equipment poking out of the top. There are three main men – all in tight T-shirts, caps, sunglasses and shorts. They clutch laptops, patterned coloured graphs on the screen, as they charge down long roads.

And then they see it. A huge cone-shaped grey cloud, swirling, moving fast across the field next to them. Rain peppers the windscreen. The men exclaim loudly, clutching cameras. The tornado sucks up everything in its wake, yet they drive towards it, windscreen wipers on full blast. Dramatic music plays; Freya finds herself holding her breath as the men shout, 'Go, go, go,' driving faster into the chaos.

And Dr Simon Sharp is as much of an attraction as the storm. Chiselled jawline, wide Hollywood smile. He bounces excitedly in his seat as they approach the tornado. Shouting to be heard above the noise, he explains in detail what they're seeing, explaining complicated scientific terms in a way that even Freya can understand. She's completely caught up in the drama.

Sharp gets out of the car, his T-shirt blown tight against his broad chest as he points at the tornado. It's moving away now, blue sky visible in the background, but his childlike wonder at the storm is something to behold. His enthusiasm is infectious.

Neither of them says a word throughout the thirty-minute episode, Robin as transfixed as she is. The team of three – Sharp, the cameraman and another guy with a laptop – seem tight. They joke happily between themselves, dispensing handshakes and slaps on the back as they track down twister after twister.

'That's Justin White,' Robin says, pointing at the cameraman. 'They interviewed him today.'

'Any motive?' Freya asks.

'Doesn't seem like it. And he was nowhere near the van when it all happened.'

'So he says.'

'Waiting for the footage to confirm,' Robin agrees. 'I don't recognise the other guy, though – they must have had a change in the team.'

The reason for the switch soon becomes clear. The series is addictive, and they watch without pause. Then tragedy strikes.

A disclaimer appears at the beginning of an episode: *This contains scenes of a distressing nature. Viewer discretion is advised.* It starts out much the same as the others: a crop-filled field in America, rain and wind buffeting the car in which Simon Sharp and another guy sit, being filmed.

And suddenly there's a huge bang, and the footage shifts to darkness. There's shouting, panicked cries, and then the camera comes back up.

A voice shouts, 'Keep filming, keep filming!' and Freya and Robin can see the problem. The four-by-four has been hit by something, the windscreen smashed. Sharp has a bloody cut on his forehead and is bending over a prostrate man on the concrete. A small crowd has gathered around them.

'He can't breathe,' a voice behind the camera shouts. 'Call 911.'

'I can't open his mouth! His jaw must be broken,' Sharp says. The unconscious man is pale, his lips turning blue. Blood pours from his nose; his chin looks twisted and deformed. 'He needs an emergency crike.'

Freya watches, her hand over her mouth, as Sharp takes a penknife out of his pocket and opens out one of the blades.

'You can't do that here!' someone exclaims, and Sharp looks into the camera, eyes intense.

'If I don't try, he's not going to make it,' and with that, he leans over the man, pushes his chin back, tent-atively runs his fingers down the windpipe, then cuts. A trickle of blood runs down the injured man's neck, as Sharp's muscles visibly tense. He removes the penknife, then pushes his finger into the bloody hole. 'Pass me that,' he says, pointing towards a biro in a man's pocket. He removes the ink, then thrusts the body of the pen into the hole. Even on the screen, it's hard to watch, and Freya feels her heart racing. People cheer as the injured man's chest starts to move again. Sharp turns to the camera, a relieved expression on his face, blood streaked across his cheek.

It's almost Oscar-worthy, pulled from the pages of a screenplay.

'Quite the alpha male, isn't he?' Freya remarks.

'Just makes me wonder,' Robin says, the perpetual crease on his forehead. 'How did a guy like this get overpowered by someone like Finn? I mean, look at him.' He points to the screen, and Freya knows exactly what he's referring to. Sharp is fit: a wide chest, impressive arms.

'Not your average scientist,' Freya agrees.

'Exactly. Finn is tall but built like a matchstick. If those two got physical, there's no doubt who would come out on top. And it's the guy currently in the mortuary.'

He falls back into silence. Freya doesn't know Finn, but she can imagine that Simon Sharp wouldn't have had to work hard to defend himself. Unless Dr Mason took him unawares, Freya thinks, but doesn't say it.

They watch a few more episodes. But Freya's struggling to get the image of the broken man on the concrete out of her head. She keeps on imagining Amy Miller. How she died. She'd seen the final crime scene photos: the blood on the kitchen floor.

The familiar guilt returns. The fluttering panic in her chest, the knowledge of what she did. Freya forces herself to take a long breath in. She focuses on Robin next to her. His solid presence.

It's been getting bad for a while now. And she doesn't know what to do about it. Somehow she feels her boss has been putting his life back together while hers has been falling apart. And there's nobody she can talk to about it but him.

'Robin?' she whispers. In her head she rehearses the words. *I need to tell you how I am, how I'm feeling. I need you to help me.*

She looks over. But her boss is asleep. His head is tilted to one side, his body slumped against the cushion.

He can't have slept well last night. She can't imagine what he's had to deal with.

She can wait. Her problems can wait.

Freya knows she needs to go to bed, get some sleep, same as Robin. But she clicks on to another episode of *Storm Chasers*. She watches the men as they charge around, driving fast after the tornadoes. Actively running towards danger. The episode Josh mentioned in the car comes on, the team stranded in the middle of the Mojave Desert — big grins on dry, cracked lips when the helicopter comes to rescue them.

She curls her legs up on the sofa. Next to her, Robin mumbles slightly in his sleep. Her eyes feel tired and scratchy, her body exhausted. But she doesn't close her eyes. She doesn't go to bed.

She doesn't dare.

Because when she sleeps, the nightmares come.

19

Christ, again? Olivia wakes in the night, her bladder close to bursting. She feels a small foot move and silently curses the baby in her tummy.

She rolls awkwardly out of the bed, then waddles to the toilet. This is becoming an unwelcome habit. The ultimate irony: depriving her of sleep when she needs it the most.

In the dark, she sits and pees, her bare feet cold on the tiled floor. The baby shifts and kicks, awake. Liv places a reassuring hand against a protruding foot; who'd have thought this is where she'd be now? Fat as a house, arse still steadily expanding from all the extra Ben & Jerry's she's been consuming – but happy.

She gets back into bed, lying on her side, tucking one pillow under her bump, another between her legs. It's the only way she can get comfortable now. But she still can't sleep.

The surprise meeting with DC West thrums in her head. It was strange seeing her after all this time. She looked the same: the long blonde hair, tied up in a tidy bun. The steely blue eyes. She'd known. Liv watched her doing the maths in her head, taking her back to that terrible October when her sister had died, freeing the way for Liv to have this life now.

She'd cast off her old job. Nobody wanted to sleep with a pregnant hooker, and the ones who did were too disgusting to consider: that wasn't a fetish she was prepared to explore. For a while she'd worked a few waitressing shifts at the strip club, but the moment the probate cleared and that inheritance hit her bank account, she'd quit.

Free. Free to work out what she wanted to do. Free from her psycho sister. And free to bring up this little baby the way she wants. But her thoughts keep on coming back to Robin Butler.

Amy had always been mean, joking nastily that Liv was no Julia Roberts. Robin wasn't going to turn up and sweep her off her feet. But he's always been in her thoughts – a low-level hum, distracting her when she wants it the least. She's always had a soft spot for him – that frown, the silent, haunted expression.

But he is no innocent. Liv knows that Robin has his secrets, too.

Thoughts of sleep evaporated, Liv reaches up and switches the light on. She swings her legs round to a sit, the baby bouncing happily on her bladder again, then leans uncomfortably to open the bottom drawer in her bedside table. She takes it all the way out, then pulls at the piece of Sellotape holding something tight at the back. A black memory stick.

She holds it in her hand for a moment. When Amy first gave it to her, she'd been confused as to what it was. What had her sister found? A scratchy CCTV file of Robin in a petrol station, talking to a man she recognised as Trevor Stevens. The man that killed Robin's sister. Who then died, moments after this footage was captured, in a fireball of a car accident, merely a mile down the road. Robin's encounter with Trevor Stevens minutes before his death has never been mentioned, but Liv knows that this memory stick could open up a can of worms.

She fastens it back into place and returns the drawer into its hole. Now is not the time to dig this up again, she resolves, one hand on her bump as the baby kicks.

She has done without Robin in her life this far; she doesn't need him now.

She groans, feeling the physical pressure on her bladder. Then she stands up wearily and walks to the toilet again.

20

Friday

Robin races up the A33, cursing himself for leaving Reading last night. But he hadn't wanted to spend another night in that dratted Travelodge. He'd been desperate for his own bed, then, ironically, waking up at five a.m. on Freya's sofa, with a crick in his neck. It's not the first time he's slept there, and he guesses it won't be the last.

He left before he saw Freya, hurrying back to his house for a shower and change before hitting the road. He's already tried to call Craig, but she's not responding to his voicemail.

He puts the radio on to distract himself, but it doesn't work. The news is playing out, and the top story is the death of prominent TV presenter and personality Dr Simon Sharp.

'Cause of death is as yet unconfirmed, although sources report Dr Sharp died in suspicious circumstances, related to the storm on Tuesday night. As yet, no arrests have been made, but pressure is mounting on the Chief Constable of Thames Valley Police to make a statement.'

Robin swears under his breath and switches it off.

In the silence, his mind turns to the news that Freya imparted last night. So, Olivia Cross is pregnant. When Freya told him, his head instantly went back to that night in October last year. When he'd woken up, head fuzzy, stomach rolling. He tried to remember how Liv had been towards him. She said nothing happened, but had she been lying? Had they slept together? All he can remember is the woolly fug of his hangover.

He knows he needs to go and see her. To find out properly.

But what if it is his? The thought that he could be a father so unexpectedly makes his brain hurt. He's not ready for that — for the responsibility, the expectations, the lack of sleep. But it doesn't freak him out as it had in the past.

He's had another text from Liam that morning, his brother-in-law up for his usual early-morning bike ride. He remembers his words, all those years ago, after the twins were born.

'Things change for the better, Robin,' Liam had said, eyes half closed from tiredness, three days' worth of stubble on his chin. 'We have different priorities now. Nothing else matters but these little guys.'

And look how that turned out, Robin thinks with a sting.

He shakes his head. He can't think about this now. First the A33, then back to the Royal Berkshire Hospital.

He calls Craig again.

'Butler, I can't constantly be updating you on the case,' she snaps when she answers.

'Please, tell me what's going on. I know the pressure you're under—'

'You bloody well do not,' she interrupts. 'You ever been SIO on a celebrity's murder? I've never known press interest like it.'

'Please, DI Craig.'

She sighs. 'Are you at the hospital?'

'ETA ten minutes.'

'Meet me in the café at eight.'

—

When Robin gets there, DI Jo Craig is already sat at a side table, two coffees and two slices of toast and scrambled eggs in front of her.

She pushes one of the mugs across to him. 'I thought you'd want this. And you'll have to put up with me talking with my mouth full, I've been here since half six.'

'Thank you,' he replies, 'for both the coffee and agreeing to meet me.'

'I'm only showing you this to get you off my back.' She pushes a file across the table. 'And I hope you've eaten already, because it doesn't make for pretty reading.' Robin opens it. Colour photos of Simon Sharp's autopsy greet him: jagged wound edges on his neck, the inner workings of blood vessels and tendons exposed.

'That's what killed him,' Craig says, eggs balanced on her fork. 'Exsanguination following a knife wound to the neck. Full-thickness lacerations on the right-hand side, severing the carotid, most likely inflicted by the penknife we found at the scene. Massive blood loss in minutes.'

'What about these?' Robin asks, pointing to smaller slashes at the front of his neck.

'Penetrating stab wounds, not deep. We're guessing hesitation marks.' She puts another forkful in her mouth and continues, her speech muffled. 'Bruising on his upper arms, here—' She pulls out one of the photos and points for Robin. 'And some larger ones on his lower flank.'

'These look like fingertip bruises,' Robin observes.

'That's what I thought. Like someone' – she looks at him pointedly – 'was holding Sharp tightly by his upper arms.'

'Any other defensive injuries?'

'Apart from the bruising, no. Stomach contents approximate some kind of sandwich, consumed just before his death.' Craig pushes the rest of her breakfast aside, appetite obviously lost. 'We're still waiting on approval for a full examination of Dr Mason.'

'To look for any corresponding injuries?'

'Right. Although we have his clothes at the lab. Results back today.' She pauses as her mobile starts to ring. 'That might be them now.'

Robin waits as she answers the call, drinking his now cold coffee. From what he saw in the van, the PM results are pretty much as he expected, but to have it confirmed in such stark terms is sobering. He flicks through the remainder of the photos. It's hard to reconcile the charming man he watched on the television last night, full of life and enthusiasm, with the cold dead body on the slab. His skin in the photos isn't golden and tanned in the American sunshine, but dove grey and rubbery. His bright blue eyes are glassy and dulled. Death has stripped everything from him.

Craig hangs up and Robin looks at her hopefully.

'That was Grey,' she confirms. 'Finn's doctor is coming down to talk to us.'

Robin frowns. That can't be good.

Craig continues, 'Grey confirmed that all the blood on Mason's and Sharp's clothes comes from the victim. No other sources.'

'Have you found the cameras yet? The ones from inside the van.'

'No reports yet, sorry.'

'And the tests on the knife?'

'Still waiting.' She looks up, then waves as a tall figure comes into the canteen. He collects a coffee and joins them at the table.

'I can't be long,' he says. He extends a hand to Robin. 'Dr Blackstone. We haven't met.'

'DS Robin Butler.' Robin shakes it. His hand is cold and bony. Everything about the doctor is grey: grey hair, brushed back from the temples, grey suit. He reminds Robin of an actor in an old black-and-white film: he has a proper old-school air about him.

'Finn's best friend,' Craig clarifies. 'Not here in an official capacity, but you can talk freely in front of him.'

The doctor nods sternly. 'I've done as you asked, DI Craig, and my assessment today is the same as when Finn came in on Wednesday.' Robin looks from Blackstone to Craig, confused. 'Finn Mason is not fit to be interviewed by the police.'

Robin scoffs. 'Of course he's not.'

Craig glares at Robin but stays silent.

The doctor continues, 'Yes, he has the ability to understand the nature and purpose of the interview and to appreciate the significance of being questioned by the police.' He takes a sip of his coffee, regarding them with dark, heavy-lidded eyes. 'But his current mental and physical state means that there is no way he can be accurate or tell you the truth.'

Craig glances to Robin. 'Is he faking?' she asks.

'Piss off!'

But the doctor ignores Robin's outburst. 'No, I very much doubt it. Initial results from the MRI on Finn's brain shows swelling in the prefrontal cortex, which would tie up with his memory problems. He can't remember what happened, even if he has the correct functional ability to tell you.' Blackstone finishes his coffee with a flourish. 'The craving for alcohol alone affects his reliability and makes him mentally vulnerable. So no, detective, you can't interview him.'

With a final nod, he leaves them alone.

Robin turns to Craig. 'Really?' he asks, disbelieving. 'You honestly thought the doctor would say yes?'

She sighs. 'No, of course not. But the medical opinion gets my chief off my back.' Her phone starts ringing. She pushes her chair away from the table and stands up.

'Here he is now. If you'll excuse me, Robin, I need to speak to my DCS before he has a coronary.' She looks at him sympathetically. 'Go and be with your friend, Butler. Step away from being a copper for a change.'

Robin watches her go. He finishes his coffee, then, his stomach growling, he picks up the leftover slice of her toast and eats it quickly. He hasn't had time for breakfast either.

He does as he's told and walks up the stairs to the ward where Finn is being treated. He moves slowly, in no rush, keen to digest the information about the case.

It simply isn't possible for him to stop being a copper. It's built into his bones; nearly twenty years of police work has it hardwired into him. And he knows it isn't looking good for Finn.

He has motive: the argument with Sharp in the days before the storm. Means: the penknife found in the van. And the opportunity: he was the only other person there. Post-mortem confirms Sharp's death was most likely an unlawful killing, and Finn's own confession in the van gave the likely culprit.

What else could Robin possibly do?

The policeman guarding the room allows Robin through as he shows his warrant card. Finn's asleep, but Josie's still by his bedside, holding tightly to his hand. She looks up when she sees Robin come in.

'Josie,' he says gently. 'Have you had any sleep?' She looks exhausted.

'Not a lot,' she admits.

'Any change?'

'No. His confusion is getting worse, if anything. I'm so glad you're here, Robin.' Josie looks back to Finn. 'Do you mind staying with him for a bit? It's just… I've been here all night. I need a break.'

'Of course, you go. I won't leave him.'

Robin watches Josie stumble off down the corridor. He studies Finn's face. Next to him the monitors beep; a clear bag of something drips steadily into his arm. Finn looks so helpless, Robin finds it impossible to believe he's a murderer.

Finn stirs and opens his eyes. Robin notices the same slightly cross-eyed look, the twitch of his eyeballs as he tries to focus. His upper eyelids droop slightly, making him look half asleep.

'Where's Mum?' he croaks.

'Gone to get some tea, mate,' Robin says. 'She won't be long.'

Finn sits himself up then pauses, staring into the middle distance. His fingers play with the edge of the blanket on the bed. This man here has nothing in common with Robin's quick, vibrant friend. This man is dulled, his mind absent.

'How are you feeling?' Robin asks after a pause.

Finn stares at him, squinting to focus without his glasses on. 'Terrible,' he replies. 'Do you know what's going on, Robin? Mum said…' His voice trails off, as if he's lost track of what he was going to say.

They hear movement in the corridor, and Robin sees Craig's face peer through the window in the door.

Robin gets up. 'I'll be back in a moment, Finn.'

He goes outside, where Craig is arguing with Josie.

'I don't want you in there,' Josie is saying, trying to block Craig's entrance into the room. 'You're only going to confuse him.'

'Mrs Mason…' Craig stops, her arms folded.

A bad feeling runs through Robin's body. He knows exactly why she's there.

He looks at the detective inspector. Her face is solemn but resolute. 'You don't need to do this now, DI Craig,' he says quietly. 'Finn's not going anywhere. The clock won't start until he's in custody, you know that.'

Craig shakes her head. 'DS Butler, do not interfere.'

'Give it more time. Look for different evidence. Finn can't have done this. He can't have.'

The look on Craig's face is pitying, and Robin hates her for it. 'You know as well as I do, we have more than probable cause already. Even if the confession is inadmissible—'

'Which it is.'

'There was no one else there. The van was locked. The cause of death is clear.' She stops. 'There's nothing to show any other involvement in Dr Sharp's death, except Finn's.'

'But what about the drinking? What about the LSD?' Robin tries. He told both Craig and Josie yesterday about their discovery in the lab and in his flat, the clear liquid now confirmed as vodka. Josie was confused; Craig was indifferent.

'You know as well as I do,' Craig replies, 'that intoxication – voluntary or otherwise – is a weak defence. And anyway, that'll be for his lawyer to decide.'

'So why do it now?'

She stops, looking down at the floor. Robin can tell she's as unhappy about it as he is. 'I'm getting pressure from above, Robin. You know how it is.' She's appealing to his knowledge of working cases like this. 'The press are having a field day. My detective chief super wants an arrest.'

'So, it's PR, DI Craig. No more than that,' Robin growls.

'No, Butler. We have our man. I know it.' She points through the glass at Finn. 'Even he knows it. And it's time you faced facts. Your best mate committed murder.'

She pushes past him and opens the door into Finn's room. Josie goes to protest, but Robin puts his arms round her shoulders.

'I'm sorry, Josie,' he says, and she turns, clutching his hand.

In the hospital room, DI Craig stands next to Finn's bed. He looks up at her.

'Dr Finn Mason?' Craig says, and he nods. He looks at Craig, then to Robin and Josie, his face puzzled. 'I am arresting you on suspicion of the murder of Dr Simon Sharp on Wednesday the nineteenth of May.' Finn's mouth drops open. Still in Robin's arms, Josie makes a small noise, halfway between a gasp and a sob. 'You do not have to say anything. But it may harm your defence if you do not mention when questioned something you later rely on in court. Anything you do say may be given in evidence.' Craig stops. 'Do you understand?'

Finn blinks. 'Simon's dead?' he says.

Josie starts to cry, and Robin wraps his arms around her, holding her tight.

His best friend – his oldest friend, the one person who knows him better than any other, who he spent his entire childhood with, who he would trust with his life – has just been arrested for murder.

And Robin hasn't a clue what he's going to do about it.

Part 2

21

Freya watches the press conference on her monitor, open-mouthed. A detective chief superintendent she doesn't know is standing on the podium in front of a large blue backdrop, reading from a statement. Lights and cameras flash; the room is full to bursting with journalists and photographers.

'While I am not at liberty to share the identity of the man at this time, I am pleased to confirm that someone has been arrested in relation to the murder of Dr Simon Sharp and is currently helping us with our enquiries.'

'Helping, my arse,' Mina observes next to her. 'No doubt in their minds, they've got their man.'

The coverage has cut to a video of Simon Sharp: a hastily knocked-together montage, his handsome face smiling out of the screen in slow motion, while sad music plays. Freya scowls. Finn has no chance of a fair trial if this is how the media are pitching it.

She checks her mobile again. No reply from Robin; he must be distraught.

'Any progress?' Josh asks, coming up behind them.

Freya flicks her screen back to the search. There aren't many homeless shelters in the area and she has contacted them all, sending round photographs of their John Doe and his identifying marks.

'Nothing so far,' she directs back.

'Can we put an appeal out on the news?' Mina asks.

'Awful way to find out your loved one is dead,' Josh replies. He sits down in the seat next to them, stretching his arms above his head; Freya gets a nice waft of something manly, an aftershave she likes. 'But better than never finding out at all,' he adds, and she has to agree with him. 'Let's wait to hear first.'

Freya flicks to one of the photographs of the victim's tattoos, and as she does so, Josh leans forward.

'Go back,' he says.

She moves away from the rose surrounded with thorns on his upper arm, to his hand, where five small dots laid out like a dice mark the space between his thumb and first finger.

'You've tried searching the PNC for his tattoos?' Josh asks.

Freya nods. 'No matches.'

'How about contacting the prisons directly?' He taps the image on the screen. 'These dots often represent time inside. Start with Winchester, see where you end up.'

Freya's annoyed with herself. She should have realised that; she's really not operating on all cylinders at the moment. 'Yes, Sarge,' she says.

'Mina – keep going with the CCTV. I want those boys' movements on tape.'

'Yes, Sarge,' Mina replies, with a grin.

'I'll go and see the parents and check if they confirm their stories.' He gets up, then turns round, taking in their smirking faces. 'And enough of the sarcasm,' he grumbles.

'Yes, Sarge,' they chorus in unison.

–

The day progresses slowly, work monotonous for all. Freya makes call after call to HMP Winchester, shunted round from department to department.

'You need the probation service,' the voice at the other end says. 'If he's been released.'

'But that's where I started!' Freya cries out in frustration.

'Sorry.' She can almost hear the indifference at the other end of the phone. 'Can't help.'

'Ugh,' Freya says, putting the phone down. She turns to Mina, who's sat resting her head on her hand, staring at the screen. 'Coffee?'

'Please.' Mina sits up and rubs her eyes. 'You're going to be glad to get back to Butler, after working for Sergeant Smudge here,' she remarks. Freya had told her about their night out on Wednesday, and the nickname given by his friends.

'I like working for Butler,' Freya replies, taking her mug. 'You don't get stuck doing this shit, for a start. Anyway, you know him. You were in training together.'

'Yeah, but that was *before*,' Mina replies. Freya knows she's referring to his sister's death and how Robin had changed, retreating into silence and an ever-worsening bad temper.

'He's much better now,' Freya replies.

'Must be your influence,' Mina says, with a raise of an eyebrow.

'Really, Mina,' Freya laughs. 'Stop trying to matchmake. Especially with Robin Butler. I'm happy being single.'

She takes their mugs off to the kitchen, and as the kettle boils, she thinks about what she's just said. She isn't, not really. She doesn't mind being alone; she has plenty of friends to go out with at the weekend if she chooses, and work keeps her busy, but she misses that closeness. The sharing of secrets, the warm body to keep her company on the sofa.

But if it was down to that, then it would be Robin. They have their fair share of secrets between them, and more often than not it was him she would be sitting watching television with. No; she missed a strong arm around her at night. Legs wrapped together. Full body hugs and snogging.

She looks out into the incident room, at the rows of desks and detectives. Josh has arrived back and is laughing with one of the DCs as he takes his coat off. She watches him: the wide grin, the laid-back manner. It's raining outside, and he ruffles his dark hair with his hand, trying to get the water out of it. Josh Smith is attractive; she'll give him that. But does she want to go out with someone from this world?

Being female in the police force is hard enough. It has moved on from the blatant discrimination of the past, but some of the sexism remains. And sleeping with a colleague comes with stigma. Shagging your way to the top. Slut, tart, police bike. Slurs that are never applied to the men.

She gets another mug out of the cupboard and makes him a coffee, too, then awkwardly carries the three hot drinks back to their desks, plonking them down and shaking her burning fingers.

She gets a broad smile from Josh and finds herself grinning in response.

No, she tells herself, stop thinking of him like that. Just no.

'Anything from the parents?' she asks.

Josh pulls a face. 'Bloody awful. Tyler Garratt and Mark Black, much as you'd expect. Rough as… well, you know. Didn't give a shit. Said they have no idea where their kids had been.'

'Weren't they all supposed to have been at Mark's?' Mina asks.

'Yeah, but Black's dad said they would have been in the garage, and they don't go in there.'

'And Lee Cernis?'

Josh sighs. 'Oh, bless them, not a clue. I spoke to his mum, and she was lovely. But thinks the sun shines out of Tyler's and Mark's arses, and is more than happy with Lee hanging around with them.' He pulls his notebook out and flicks through the pages. 'Says Lee was out from six p.m. Didn't hear him come home, but she knows it was late. He was there in the morning at breakfast and he told her he got in about two a.m.'

'On a school night?' Mina remarks.

'I asked that. But he's eighteen. Free to come and go as he pleases, as long as she knows if he's going to be there for dinner.'

Mina scowls. 'I'm going to be locking my kids up until they're at least twenty-five,' she mutters.

Freya gives her a sympathetic smile. Her desk phone starts ringing so she answers it and speaks briefly to the voice at the other end.

'Thank you, thank you very much,' she finishes. 'Yes, please email anything you have through.'

She puts her phone down and faces the other two with a smile.

'That was the Society of Saint James, one of the homeless charities in town. One of their volunteers identified our vic.' Freya sits back in her seat, feeling a swell of satisfaction. 'His name was Duncan Thorpe.'

22

Finn's arrest creates a ripple of emotion around the hospital room. Finn alternates between confusion and disbelief; Josie continues to cry; Sophie has arrived and is redundantly trying to comfort her boyfriend.

Robin can only feel anger.

He turns to DI Craig, pointing at the door. 'Can I speak to you for a moment...' he says, trying to keep his voice level. 'Please?'

He sees her taking in the chaos and, knowing her presence won't be helping, she nods. In the corridor, she confronts Robin.

'Don't tell me you wouldn't have done the same if this was your case.'

'He's not going anywhere. You can't interview him. You certainly can't take him into custody. What's the point?'

Craig stares back into the room. 'He's got two perfectly functioning legs. Yes, he's confused, but there's no medical reason why we can't arrest him. We've had uniforms on the door, but you know as well as I do that we've had no power to stop him from walking out of the hospital. Now he's under arrest, we can keep him here. Legally. We should have done so the moment he got out of that van – god knows why I didn't.'

'Have you got enough to charge him?' Robin asks.

She pauses. 'Not yet.'

Robin's aware of what she's not telling him: their evidence is still patchy. But now he's been arrested, the police have the power to properly search his flat and workplace, even go through his computer. And who knows what they'll find.

DC Grey is standing awkwardly a few metres away in the corridor. 'Grey,' Craig shouts, finding a suitable conduit for her frustration. 'Have you chased the lab yet?'

'No, no, I...' and he scuttles off, mobile in hand.

'Listen,' Craig says sternly. 'I can't have you interfering like this. I am a DI, you are a DS. This is my case, my patch. You can't be questioning my decisions in front of my team.'

Even through his anger, Robin knows she's right. He would have had stern words long before Craig did, if someone had been undermining him in front of West. She outranks him, and his behaviour has been perilously close to insubordination. 'You're right, boss. I apologise,' Robin replies, contrite, pushing his personal feelings aside. 'Are you asking me to leave?'

'No. I'm simply saying that you need to decide whose side you're on. Either you want to get to the bottom of this case and have access to our investigation or you're family, and you stay the hell away from me.'

Robin stops. He wants to clear Finn's name. And the only way to do that is to play ball.

'I want to find out what happened.'

Craig looks at him, trying to read his face for sincerity. 'Fine,' she says at last. 'But if we find something that shows Finn is guilty of murder and this case goes to trial, you may be called to testify against your friend. You're aware of that, right?'

Robin nods, silent. He'll deal with that problem when the time comes. *If* the time comes.

Craig shakes her head in disbelief. 'Then come with me and shut the fuck up. We have an appointment with a blood–spatter expert.' She starts walking, and he follows. 'I must be crazy,' she mutters as they go.

–

The van is still cordoned off as a crime scene, SOCOs swarming round. Craig and Robin both show their IDs and are signed in by the scene guard; he hands them white suits, then points towards the silver vehicle.

'She's inside,' he says, ominously.

They put on their PPE and head over. Both back doors of the van are open, and Craig bangs on the side by way of introduction. A short, stout woman pokes her head out.

'DI Craig and DS Butler,' Craig says. 'You must be Hodgson?'

'Susie,' she says. 'Come inside. If you can. Don't touch anything.'

Craig leads the way and Robin follows. The three of them crowd into the van. It's larger than Robin remembers from Wednesday, but just as shocking. The body has been removed, but the mess remains – blood over almost every surface, dried on the floor, spatters up the walls. How someone can make sense of this, Robin's not sure, but that's exactly what Susie does for a living.

Craig and Robin go to stand at the cleaner end of the vehicle, next to the driver's cab, bending down slightly to fit in the decreasing headroom. Every inch of the tiny space has been utilised to its full extent. The area near them, where Finn had been sitting on Wednesday, is crowded with computers and other technical equipment. A small, seated area is at the far end, with a table and two low stools. Robin remembers Sharp's body lying under that table.

'So,' the crime scene investigator begins. 'You want the headlines?'

Craig nods. 'Please.'

'We took the body away yesterday, but you can see the void where it was situated.' Susie points to the patch of clean floor, and the clean line of dark red. 'The rest is a complete mess. We know the victim died from a wound to his neck, but even without that knowledge I could have made a pretty good guess that was what happened.'

'How?' Robin asks.

'Volume and distribution of the blood. It's a huge amount.' She gestures round the van. 'Especially to come from one person. And up the walls, across the ceiling. Most of it is smeared and smudged. The pair obviously moved around and spread it everywhere. I've seen their clothes – both soaked in it. And we have contact stains all over. I'm not surprised, given the space in here.'

She points to a long smudge up the wall. 'Handprints, possible finger swipes with some ridge detail – don't know whose yet – plus marks from fabric where they might have fallen against the wall. Footwear marks in blood, here,' Robin looks at the clear tread pattern, 'and here. Your victim was wearing size ten boots, so these are probably his. Yours,' she adds, pointing to Robin. 'Here. You didn't contaminate the scene too much, thankfully. And here's another mark from you. Your knee, right? I read your statement.' Robin nods, remembering the nauseating feeling that he was wading in someone's blood.

Susie carries on, pointing to the floor under the foot-plates. 'And your offender,' she says. 'Trainers, here.'

Robin and Craig look at the distribution of the marks. Sharp's are grouped closest to where his body fell, while Finn's are all over the place. It looks like he was moving backwards and forwards across the van, each time walking through the blood.

'And these?' Craig asks, pointing up the window.

'How much do you know about projected blood stains?' Susie says. They both look blank. 'You used to call it arterial spray.'

'Start from the beginning.'

'So, when an artery is damaged, the blood is emitted in a jet, if you like, which will hit any nearby surface or simply fall to the floor. These spots of blood on the floor are arterial rain.' Robin winces at the term, although given what he's seeing, it's appropriate. 'They project out by some distance. You can also see the separate spurts on the walls, landing dependent on how the victim is moving. Following?'

Craig and Robin nod obediently.

'So, I can estimate it started here,' she points to the wall, 'then he turned to his left, distributing the blood in the pattern you can see here.'

Robin stares at the wall. He can see five distinct arcs of blood drops – some intact circles, others dripping down, running together.

'Then he must have fallen, smearing and smudging as he went. The majority of the blood is pooled under the table, where the body was.'

She stares at the large dark red stain, her eyes narrowed. 'I estimated about five litres in here. He bled out, right?'

'That's what the pathologist said, yes.'

'Thought so. That's most of his blood volume, right there, on the floor.'

'Christ,' Craig says under her breath. She inhales slowly, deeply, then faces the CSI again. 'Any sign of anything else? Cast-off or impact spatter?'

Robin knows what she's asking. Looking for the telltale signs of a weapon being brandished, or someone being beaten.

'No, nothing. And that would tie up with the body, right?'

'Right,' Robin says, with a glare at Craig. Why is she looking for something that isn't there? Aren't things bad enough as it is? 'And whose blood is this?'

'DNA not back from the lab, but given the analysis on the victim's clothes, my guess is this all belongs to Simon Sharp.'

They thank the investigator and walk silently away from the van. Out of the cordon they pull off their suits, Robin wrenching the mask from his face.

'Christ,' Craig says again. 'Imagine being there when that happened.'

Robin doesn't want to. The idea of watching, as someone bled to death in that way, is horrifying. He can understand why Finn's brain is as scrambled as it is. Killer or not, it would have been traumatising to see. Flailing around the van, blood pumping from his neck.

Being covered in it, soaked in it.

Watching your friend die.

23

By the time Freya and Mina arrive at the homeless shelter, dinner time is in full flow. The dining hall has rows of tables, all the plastic chairs occupied, the chink of cutlery against crockery. A smell reminiscent of school lunches fills the air: overcooked vegetables and roasted meat.

Freya stands at the edge of the room, while Mina makes enquiries. She feels wary eyes on her, instantly able to mark her out as law enforcement. The people at the tables are hunched and shabbily dressed. Few talk, all eat as quickly as they can, shovelling precious food into their mouths.

Mina turns away from the man she's been talking to. A tall, thin bloke – one of the helpers at the shelter – wearing a stained white apron and hairnet.

'Dave here was the one who identified Duncan,' Mina explains.

Dave nods. 'I'm sorry to hear of his passing,' he says. 'Duncan was a good bloke.'

'Can you tell us more about him?' Freya asks.

He shakes his head. 'As I told Detective Constable Desai, I don't know about family or next of kin,' he begins. 'Like most people here, Duncan didn't speak much about his past.'

'Did you know anything about him?'

The man directs them away from the main dining hall, and they move to stand in the quieter corridor.

'I know he was in the army, in his youth. And then inside for a stretch, maybe a few times.' Freya nods; they've already run his background. 'He was trying to turn his life around. Without much success. A lot of the ex-forces guys have the same root problem.'

'Which is?' Freya asks, but she can guess. She's heard it too many times.

'The places they've been to, the things they've seen. It's more than any person should have to cope with. But when they don't have a strong, supportive family to help, or they don't feel they can open up and deal with it, they need to look for other ways to survive. Some turn to drink, drugs. Some turn to violence.'

'Doesn't the army provide support?'

'They do, but they're overloaded. Most are men, I'm afraid. They retreat into themselves, lose the support of their loved ones or just walk away, not wanting to be a burden. Which means they end up on the street. Or in prison, like Thorpe.'

What Dave's saying backs up what Freya has found. Once they had a name, she could find out more about Duncan Thorpe. A stint inside when he was twenty-nine, for manslaughter. Reading between the lines, it sounded like a pub fight gone wrong: local lads squaring up to a group of squaddies, out drinking in a dodgy pub. One ended up dead, after having been on the receiving end of Duncan Thorpe's fist. Out of the army, and into jail.

And it all went downhill from there. Not long after release, he was back in again. Breaking and entering, this time. Nothing since, but it's not hard for Freya to see how Thorpe's life had gone off the rails.

Dave looks back out into the dining hall, thinking. He sighs. 'Duncan came here more often than not. We don't allow alcohol or drug-taking on the premises, so I wouldn't know for sure, but I believe drink was his problem. Plus, I know he experienced flashbacks, traumatic memories. I would often see him wandering the halls here at night, unable to sleep.' His face turns downwards. 'So, I'd guess there was some pretty serious PTSD. Undiagnosed, of course, but when you've seen it so many times...' He shrugs. A caring man, worn down with helplessness. 'When did you say he was found?'

'Wednesday morning. After the storm.'

He nods grimly. 'We were rammed that night. Nobody wanted to be outdoors. We only have so many beds.'

Mina places a reassuring hand on Dave's arm. 'You can't help everyone.'

Dave looks down, his face miserable. 'Yeah, but Duncan was one of the ones that stood a chance. If he'd had the support he needed, he might have been okay.' He looks up, watery eyes meeting Freya's. 'He might still be alive.'

—

Mina and Freya walk out of the shelter, back into the warm spring day.

'All those people,' Mina says as they wander back to the car. 'But for the grace of God, you know?'

Freya nods. They spot a Costa Coffee on the far side of the street and head towards it.

'We get all sorts of shit, day in, day out,' Mina continues. 'No normal person should see the number of dead bodies we have. We've all been called out on deployments we can't forget when we get home. There's a thin line between looking after our mental health so we can continue to do our jobs every day, and ending up like one of those guys.'

They stand in the queue at the coffee shop in silence. Freya thinks about the nights alone when she can't sleep. The images of Amy Miller in her dreams. The guilt of what she did, gnawing at her insides.

'What would you do, Mina, if you felt like that?'

Mina puts in their order, adding a coffee for Josh. She turns back to Freya as she pays. 'Speak to someone. Straight away. The more it festers, the worse it gets.' She takes their drinks, handing one to Freya, and they walk towards the exit. 'I saw a counsellor after that shooting, do you remember?' Freya shakes her head. 'The guy with the shotgun. Blew his head off in front of me when I was a PC.'

They both get into the car.

'Did it help?' Freya asks, fastening her seat belt.

'A bit,' Mina says. She pushes her coffee cup into the mug holder. 'Enough, anyway.'

Mina starts driving, and Freya sips her coffee thoughtfully. That's all well and good, she thinks. But she knows that counsellors are duty-bound to report anything illegal. Talk about what she did to Amy Miller, and that's it. Career over. She might even end up in prison.

But she can't go on like this. Working all the time. She's definitely not getting enough sleep. She remembers Robin when they first met – one look at him and his house and she knew he wasn't functioning well. Overcome by grief and, as she now knows, the knowledge that he had been carrying an enormous load of guilt. What had changed for him since, that he'd managed to pull himself together? Had it been the simple act of confessing to her? The fact that she knew and understood?

She rubs her eyes. Her skin feels dry, paper-thin. She feels pathetic for being like this, not able to cope. And being around Mina makes it harder. She's felt Mina's eyes on her, scrutinising her reactions; she's not the same care-free, chatty woman that Mina left a year ago.

To her dismay, she feels her throat constrict and her eyes grow hot. She swallows, trying to hold in the feelings, but they're bubbling over, and there's nothing she can do. She starts crying. Quietly at first, but then a huge sob bursts out of her.

Mina glances across from the driver's seat, her face dropping in dismay.

'Shit! Freya, what's wrong?'

Mina indicates, pulling the car quickly to the side of the road. She turns in her seat, placing a reassuring hand on Freya's arm as she cries, then digs in her handbag and pulls out a pack of tissues. Freya takes one, laughter mixing with the sobs.

'You're always prepared, aren't you, Mina?' she burbles.

'Two kids under two,' Mina says softly. 'Got a full disaster recovery kit in this bag.' She waits for Freya's tears to subside.

Freya feels the anguish fade and wipes her eyes with the tissue. 'I'm sorry,' she says.

'Don't be silly.' Mina's dark eyes are kind and sympathetic. 'What's going on?'

Freya sniffs and shakes her head. But it's hopeless to pretend with Mina.

'Is it Josh? Did he do something the other night?'

'No! No, Josh's fine.'

'Is it… is it Butler?' Mina asks quietly.

Freya shakes her head again. She knows it is about Robin, of course, but not in the way that Mina's implying.

'No. It's… I'm fine, Mina. I'm sorry.'

'Look at you! You're not fine. What's going on? You can talk to me, you know that.'

Freya trusts Mina. For a moment, she considers it. Unburdening herself of the events eight months ago in that grubby unmarked police car. Telling her all about Jonathan, and Amy Miller, and what she did. She knows she would instantly feel better, but she also knows that she couldn't put that burden on Mina. As a police detective, Mina would be in an impossible position, between the law and her friend, and that can't happen.

Freya shakes her head. 'It's just… it all got a bit much for a moment, that's all.'

Mina looks at her sternly. 'I didn't want to say anything before, but you haven't been your normal self since I've been back. I know we didn't see each other much when I was on mat leave, and that's my fault—'

'No! Mina. Absolutely not—'

'It is. I should have made more of an effort to see you. But I'm here now. You know I'd do anything for you, right, Frey?'

Freya nods gratefully. 'I know. Thank you.'

The phone rings next to them. They look at the screen. *Josh*.

'Oh, for fuck's sake,' Mina grumbles. 'And now his coffee's gone cold, so we won't even be able to placate him with that.'

Freya forces a laugh. 'Let's go.'

Mina starts the engine. She turns to look at her one last time. 'But talk to someone, Freya, please?' she says.

Freya drinks her coffee in silence as they drive the rest of the way to the station. Mina's right. She needs to talk to someone. And there's only one person who will understand.

24

'I know you don't want to hear it, but the evidence is clear.'

DI Jo Craig has acquiesced to Robin's demand to drive, but he's now regretting it – it's only given her more opportunity to talk about the case. She has a file open in her lap in the passenger seat and is flicking through the pages.

'You're right, I don't want to hear it,' Robin mutters.

'The warrant for his medical records finally came through yesterday, and nothing here contradicts what we've found. Blood alcohol was zero when his blood was taken at the hospital, which means nothing, because he'd been in that van for over twelve hours by that point.'

'Any trace of the LSD?'

Craig flicks again. 'No, none. And no sign of two-oxo-three-hydroxy-LSD, which means he hadn't taken any for up to five days.'

Robin's familiar with the long chemical name. He knows that LSD stays in the blood for up to eight hours, so might have worn off while Finn was locked in the van, but the major metabolite of the drug, the two-oxo-whatsit, sticks around for longer in the urine.

So the LSD couldn't explain his confusion or current state. And couldn't be used as a defence for the murder.

'What about wounds on Finn's body?' he asks Craig.

'Nothing. No nicks or scratches. Only a few bruises. But nothing substantial that could be used as an argument for self-defence,' she adds, reading his mind. 'And apart from that, his medical history is unremarkable.' Robin pulls into the hospital car park and switches off the engine. 'See for yourself,' she says, passing him the file.

She climbs out of the car, giving him a look as she goes. 'Hang onto it, I have a copy.'

He watches her walk off across the car park, striding confidently. The beauty of not being attached emotionally to the case, he thinks. Then Freya comes to mind. He wonders how she's getting on with her body in the freezer, working for Josh Smith. Faint jealousy flickers, and he picks up the phone, sending her a quick text. He misses working with her, the to and fro of discussing a case, but he frowns. Baker's warning echoes in his head. He's aware she hasn't been herself this past month or so.

After Jonathan died − and after Amy died − she'd seemed to have picked herself up for a while. Still sad, still grieving, but with a level of relief that he himself had experienced. The case was over. Everything they had done that had broken the law in a myriad of different career-destroying ways was over. Put to bed. And so they'd pootled on. New cases, developing a working relationship with a solid foundation of trust and the secrets between them.

But after Christmas, she was quieter. Less eager to talk to him, to share. They'd spent more time in each other's company, default dinners and nights in front of the TV rather than active arrangements, but she'd retreated into herself. And this last month her work hasn't been up to its usual precision. Things were getting missed, paperwork late to be submitted.

He'll phone her tonight, he resolves, picking up the file in his lap again.

He flicks through the pages of Finn's medical report, and Craig's right, there's nothing interesting. He's rarely been to the GP. An ear infection a year ago. A vaccination when he went abroad. No mental health issues. Nothing that would indicate a predisposition for what Finn was going through now. And no mention of his alcoholism, surprise, surprise.

He gets out of the car and walks towards the hospital. But his pace is slow. He feels the weight of expectation, knowing that Josie will be looking to him to find a way out of this mess. It feels hopeless. He isn't in charge, and although Craig has been giving him access, Robin's sure it's only to the things she wants him to see. The evidence that will convince him that Finn's the killer.

When he gets to the hospital room, everything is quiet. Finn's eyes are closed, Josie is sitting next to his bed, a book in her hand. But she's staring into space, obviously lost in thought.

He knocks quietly on the door to announce his arrival. She jumps slightly, then smiles.

'No change?' he whispers. She shakes her head sadly.

He comes into the room and takes a seat next to her. 'Sandra around? Or Sophie?'

'Sophie had to go to the university. And Sandra's headed home to Devon. She has work. She can't stay here, holding my hand all week.'

Robin nods. He knows the same situation applies to him: he needs to phone Baker, give a time frame for when he'll be back. But he has no idea. How long can this go on for? he thinks. How long should he keep searching?

'What do the doctors say?'

'Nothing new. Still waiting on tests, although god knows what good they're doing. He's worse, if anything. Anterograde amnesia,' she says, checking the notepad next to her. 'And he can't remember what happened. Retro...' She struggles to read her handwriting.

'Retrograde amnesia,' Robin finishes for her.

'Yes. The doctor says he can remember how to do basic tasks, like writing and tying his shoelaces, but he can't form new memories.'

'And they don't know why?'

She shakes her head, tears obvious in her eyes. 'And the doctor says that with the alcohol withdrawal symptoms on top, it's hard to work out what's going on.'

Robin sits down next to her and takes her hand. Finn's alcoholism could be nothing to do with the situation they're in now. In the bed next to them, Finn is starting to stir, his eyes flickering open. He looks over to Robin and blinks myopically; Robin hands him his glasses and he puts them on.

'Rob? Mum?'

'You're in the hospital, Finn. You've been in an accident. Everything's going to be okay,' Josie says softly. She looks at Robin. 'Every time he wakes up, we're back to square one. He can't remember where he is, or what happened.'

'An accident?' Finn asks.

But before either of them can answer, Finn's hands fly to his face and he starts to cry.

Robin sits forward in his chair. 'Finn,' he starts, 'what's the matter?'

He continues to sob. Robin glances through the open door, to the police officer standing guard. He quickly gets up and closes it, then sits close to Finn.

'Do you remember something?' Robin asks. 'About what happened?'

'Finn?' Robin says again.

This time Finn looks at him.

'Finn, what do you remember?'

He stares at him, his pupils unfocused, then down at his shaking hands. Robin notices there are still traces of blood on them, ingrained into the lines of his palms.

'Finn?' he tries again.

'Mum?' Finn says, looking at Josie.

'Yes, sweetie, I'm here.'

'Is he dead?'

Josie glances to Robin, unsure. 'Yes. I'm sorry, love.'

'But he... It's my fault...'

Robin's breath stops in his chest. He knows he shouldn't, but he has to ask.

'What happened, Finn? Why is it your fault?'

Finn starts crying again, and Robin can only just make out what he's saying through the sobs.

'Jacob. Poor Jacob...' Finn whispers.

Robin's confused. Who is Jacob? Robin looks at Josie. She's staring at Finn, her mouth open.

And her face has gone completely white.

25

'What's going on, Josie?' Robin whispers in the hospital corridor. 'Who the hell is Jacob?'

'Keep your voice down, Robin,' Josie replies, with a glance at the police guard. 'He doesn't know what he's saying. He's confused.'

'Finn seemed clear in there,' Robin says. 'What's going on? What's he talking about?'

Josie's face is stern. She looks to Finn, then back to Robin.

'Let's get a cup of coffee.'

–

They walk quickly away from the hospital room, leaving Finn quiet in his bed. After he had said those words, Robin had paused, then tried to get more out of him. But he just shook his head.

'Not another word, Finn. Do you understand me?' Robin said before leaving him, glancing nervously towards the door. 'Not a word, to anyone.'

Finn nodded.

Getting the coffees takes an intolerable amount of time, but at last they are seated in a corner of the bustling canteen.

'Josie?' Robin prompts again. 'What did he mean? Who's Jacob?'

'It's nothing. He's getting mixed up.' Josie sighs, then shakes her head. 'You remember you went to Scout camp every August? You boys must have been about twelve when you started.'

Robin remembers clearly. The smell of damp grass. Cold A-frame canvas tents. Cake at eleven o'clock.

'Yes. And?'

'Jacob was one of the boys there. He was a small kid, blonde?'

Robin frowns. 'He doesn't ring a bell. Finn and I were in separate patrols, so we hung out with different people at camp. But what's that got to do with anything now?'

'Well, he died. I can't believe you don't remember this. Or maybe it was the year you didn't go.'

'Oh, Christ, yes.' A flicker of recognition catches at the edge of Robin's mind. He'd broken his leg the August of 1992. A bad tackle in rugby, and he was in a cast from his toes to his thigh, resulting in a miserable, hot summer. That was the last year of Scout camp, and Finn went alone.

'Don't you remember everyone talking about it?' Josie asks, and Robin shakes his head. The selfishness of a grumpy fourteen-year-old, focusing only on his own plight. 'It was all very tragic.' Josie pauses, drinking her coffee. 'It must have stuck somehow.'

'And that's all there is to it?'

Josie finishes her coffee. 'Yes,' she says. 'That's all it was.' But there's a pause that makes Robin lean forward, trying to catch Josie's eye.

'Josie?'

'It's not important.'

'It *is* important. Finn's in big trouble, and now he's rambling about some dead kid. If there's something else, we need to know. We need to tell DI Craig.'

Josie pauses again, chewing on the inside of her cheek. Then she frowns.

'Josie?' Robin pushes again.

'Oh, Robin, let it go,' she exclaims. 'You remember those camps, there were loads of you boys. Finn didn't even know him. Jacob died. They all had to come home early. That's it.'

'That's it?' Robin repeats.

Josie pushes her coffee cup away. 'Yes.' She looks at Robin sternly. 'Now, are you happy? I need to get back to Finn.'

Josie stands up and walks out of the canteen. Robin stays behind.

He takes a sip of his coffee. It's stone cold.

Is he happy?

No, of course he's not sodding happy. His best friend is in hospital, arrested for murder. He's an alcoholic. And now he's rambling about some dead kid from twenty-nine years ago.

He turns the coffee mug around in his hands, thinking back. What else happened that summer? He remembers the interminable sunshine, the smell of sun cream, the squeals from neighbours in their paddling pools, almost mocking as he sat, sulking, in his cast. Shutting the curtains to stop the sun reflecting off the television as he watched the cricket. He doesn't remember some kid dying, or maybe... does he? Glimmers of memory cut through. A blonde kid, playing football. Flowers and candles and tributes around the pavilion. Mothers talking in low murmurs on street corners. And Finn?

He reaches down and pulls the medical notes that Craig left with him out of his bag. He flicks through, looking for something earlier than adulthood, but there's nothing. Finn's medical records begin the moment he turned eighteen. But there *was* something. Finn didn't start back at school with him that September. Robin's dad had told him that Finn was ill. But with what? His mind's a blank.

Josie's words had been final: there was nothing to Finn's strange proclamation. Nothing to link the death of a kid all those years ago to Simon Sharp. But she had seemed off, her tone dismissive. A denial that was almost over-compensating, hiding a truth she didn't want to share.

They are the closest people Robin has to family, but his intuition still applies. After twenty years spent interviewing people, he's certain he can trust his gut, and he knows one thing for sure.

Josie is lying.

26

Sophie sits stunned at her desk. The colleague she shares an office with – a studious, mousy woman with a fondness for crocheted animals – is fortunately at lectures, thus saving Sophie from having to maintain any semblance of normality.

Her fingers rest in her lap; a cup of herbal tea sits cold in front of her. She runs through their old life in her head, looking for clues of Finn's drinking. These last few months had been different – with Dr Sharp there, he had been busier than ever, more distracted. But Sophie was used to playing second fiddle to his work, and that had always been fine.

She desperately wants a joint. Something to take the edge off how she's feeling. But Robin Butler is still hanging around, and she doesn't trust him not to arrest her. If she gets caught consuming the very substances she's supposed to be researching, she'll have her licence taken away. She'll be thrown out of the university, and then her life really will be over.

There's a soft tap on the door and her PhD supervisor pokes her head round.

'Sophie?' she says. 'I thought I saw your light on. I heard about Finn, I'm sorry. How are you?'

'I'm...' Sophie's not sure how to answer that question. 'I'm doing okay,' she manages after a pause.

'Why don't you take some time off? Be with Finn?'

Sophie's already been to the hospital to see him this morning and sat next to his bed while he slept. When he was awake, he was dull – little movement or thought, like some part of his brain was missing.

She doesn't like to admit it but being around Finn makes it all worse. While she's here, she can pretend her life is normal. That he is at the lab across the road, and they'll go for dinner tonight, maybe out with some friends.

'That's okay. I want to keep busy,' Sophie replies. 'I can handle everything here.'

'But there's that funding application you wanted doing. And the results from the second study to look at, and—'

'I insist,' her supervisor says firmly. 'Take a fortnight off. At least.' She gives a final smile and leaves Sophie alone.

Slowly, Sophie shuts down her computer and puts her stuff in her bag. Then she pauses, paying attention to the twitch at the back of her mind. Being so close to the lab creates a pull, reinforcing her desire to find out what was going on behind those innocuous four walls. What might have caused Finn to be where he is today.

She feels a flare of anger and stands, picking up her bag and striding out of her office. She walks quickly across campus, pace increasing, until she gets to Finn's lab. She tries the handle but it's locked, so she presses the bell, waiting for the answering buzz as the latch is released.

She pushes into the building.

The lab is strangely quiet. For the last few months it's been a hive of activity. Computers whirring, the click of fingers on keys, lively discussion and debate. And Simon Sharp and Finn at the centre of it.

Sophie knew the two of them had their disagreements, but their friendship was built on mutual respect. 'Debate is essential for growth,' Finn once said to her. 'Without challenge, how will we ever improve?'

Finn likes a good dispute. Smiling, he would listen to the person next to him grow more and more furious as he presented the counterargument, one point after another. Or he'd hold a finger up in the air as if to say, hold that thought, then walk away to do research and further reading. His PhD students loved him – even more so once Sharp joined the mix.

She spots Ian Calloway on the far side of the lab and walks over. He's head down over a laptop, an array of electronics scattered around him; he looks up as he hears the sharp clatter of her heels on the tiled floor.

'What was going on, Ian?' she shouts.

His face hardens. 'What are you talking about?'

'With Finn. And Simon.' He stares at her blankly. She grits her teeth. 'Don't tell me that everything was okay here, that there weren't problems. I knew. I saw what it was doing to him.'

Ian's eyes narrow. 'You'd seen him drinking, had you?' he challenges.

She stops, hands in fists. 'No... I...'

'So, you knew he was under pressure. Big fucking deal. Had you seen how he wasn't eating? How he was working through the night, sleeping in his office?'

'Why didn't you stop him? Why didn't you tell me?' she pleads.

'We knew how important this project was to him. It was *everything*,' he stresses, and Sophie knows what he's saying. More important than you. 'But we didn't know he was drinking,' Ian continues, quieter. 'And we didn't know that he was so out of control he would kill Simon.'

'He didn't kill Simon!'

Ian gives her a patronising look. 'Didn't he?' He flicks windows on his laptop and pulls something up. He points at it, turning to Sophie. 'We found this on his computer.'

'Why were you going through Finn's stuff?'

'After the police came and found all the alcohol, we wanted to know exactly what we were facing. So we went through his hard drive. Look.'

Sophie leans down next to Calloway. The screen shows a Word document, its title clear: *Cloud Particle Doppler Spectra from the Updraft of a Mesoscale Convective System*. And the author: Dr S. Sharp.

'This was Finn's research, our research,' Ian says angrily. 'And Sharp was intending to publish it under his name. Finn knew.'

Sophie's mind is reeling. 'But he wouldn't… Finn would have never…' Then she stops. 'You haven't shown this to the police.'

Ian pauses.

'You haven't, Ian! Please say you haven't!'

Ian bows his head. 'I'm sorry, Sophie. But we had to.'

'Who did you send it to?' For the first time Sophie hopes that Robin has been involved. At least he'll be on Finn's side.

'DI Craig, the one in charge.' Ian looks sheepish. 'We gave her a copy of his entire hard drive.'

Sophie turns on her heel and walks quickly away from the lab, angry tears threatening. It was motive, clear motive. But to kill over this? Over some silly weather equipment?

Yet, Sophie knew. That silly weather equipment was everything Finn lived for. And he would have done anything to protect it.

27

At last, Robin's home. He dumps his bag in the hallway, kicking his shoes off into the messy pile. He opens his fridge. He stares inside, trying to get some inspiration for what to cook from a lump of cheese, half a shrivelled pepper and some mouldy mushrooms. He gives up, closing the fridge and walking into the living room.

The place is still a mess. Dust sheets cover his sofa and television. He pulls at a length of wallpaper; it comes away with a satisfying rip. He knows he should get a move on, but he can't be bothered. Perhaps he'll get a man in after all. All that sense of achievement for a job well done just isn't worth the hassle. He glances out of the window. The weather is bright but cool, and he feels the need to get outside, do something to shake off the excess energy.

Robin hasn't been for a run for a few days, and his muscles feel stiff. A few niggles at first, a twinge behind his knee, but after half a mile he gets into his stride. The bassline beats through his headphones, The Prodigy – a good choice given the mood he's in. He needs something fast and noisy to take away the thoughts in his head.

He'd spent the rest of the day at the hospital, sitting silently next to Josie. Robin had watched her like a hawk, but she seemed the same concerned mum she'd been all week. Robin saw no evidence that she was hiding anything; only the strain from being with Finn in hospital was apparent.

And Finn? He wasn't improving. He was still quiet – rarely talking, barely acknowledging Sophie when she arrived later that day, pale-faced and uncommunicative.

There is radio silence from Craig. The policeman on the door had been replaced, but apart from that, there is no movement on the case. It looks like Finn is going to be in hospital for some time, but Robin also knows this only gives Thames Valley Police a chance to collect more evidence against him. In normal circumstances, detectives have twenty-four hours after an arrest to request an extension, release or charge. But the countdown doesn't begin until Finn is judged well enough to be taken into custody, and knowing his state now, it could be a while.

Being on the other side of the fence is infuriating. He has a new-found empathy for relatives.

His watch beeps, marking off two miles, and Robin makes a turn for home. As a kid, he was always sporty – kicking a ball around, getting on the rugby team without a problem – but he had never been into running. He can see why people like it. The soothing repetitive *thud thud* of his feet on concrete, letting his mind wander as he works out the frustrations of the day.

When he couldn't bear it any longer at the hospital, he'd made his excuses and left. Josie looked up as he grabbed his coat.

'See you tomorrow,' she'd said, before turning back to Finn. And he'd nodded, but he now wonders whether he will. How long can he keep on driving up the M3 to be there for them? There's no change in Finn's condition, and he's too far from the hub of the investigation to be any use.

His mind keeps coming back to Finn's words. *It was my fault.* What had he meant? Were his comments about Jacob merely the confused ramblings of a disordered mind or something relevant to the case?

Robin turns the corner into his road and does a final sprint for home. He stops, resting his hands on his hips as he gets his breath back. There's another runner in the distance, coming closer: a woman, lithe and fast. For a moment he thinks it might be Steph and he lifts a hand, before he realises it's someone completely different. She waves back, even though she doesn't know him, and Robin watches her go.

It's strange to think about Steph after all this time. He knows she's been avoiding him, another pathologist attending when one's been needed at his crime scenes. He misses her, and despite wanting to call her, he's respected her need for distance. He knows why they split up – she wanted kids, he didn't – and nothing's changed.

Except now it has. He's done his best not to think about Freya's news about Liv, but he knows he needs to speak to her. What if it is his? Robin's not sure how he'll feel, if that's the case. Co-parenting with Olivia? What a strange thought. And completely terrifying.

Since Robin's sister and her twin two-year-old boys were killed six years ago, Robin's dismissed all thoughts of a family of his own. He simply couldn't bear the idea of losing someone else he loves. But now that it might be forced upon him? He isn't the sort of man to just walk away.

He goes into his house, downs a pint of water, then heads for the shower. After he's dressed, he knows what he needs to do and takes out his laptop, sitting at his kitchen table and logging on to the Police National Computer, looking up Olivia Cross. Using the PNC for personal use is definitely not allowed, but it's related to an old case and he knows he could justify it, if needed. He quickly scribbles down her address, noting it's in a small village on the outskirts of town. A nicer place to live, he thinks to himself. Better schools.

He goes to log off, then stops. His leg twitches nervously; he taps his middle finger on the desk. The PNC is the database for all police activity, covering the whole of the UK, and without thinking about it further, he types in *Finlay Mason*. A list of possible matches comes up, and he selects the one with the correct date of birth.

There's nothing. His address is current, one registered vehicle. No previous convictions. But that's not a surprise.

He does a search for Josie. No record. Then: *Sandra Dean*. Nothing.

He knows Devon and Cornwall Constabulary will have their own local system, so if anything happened in 1992, something might be on there. But he'll need authorisation from a superior officer to access it. Maybe Baker would approve it, but how would he explain the request without potentially getting Finn into more trouble?

Then a memory flashes. Glandular fever. That was it. His dad had said that Finn was ill with glandular fever, and that's why he was late starting back at school that September. He leans back in the chair. He remembers now; it had seemed strange at the time. He'd ignored his dad's instructions to stay away and sneaked round the back of the house, hissing Finn's name. And the face that had appeared at his open window hadn't looked ill. Pale, thin. But not sick enough to be off school for a month.

Robin frowns, sitting at his kitchen table. This isn't helping. But what was he expecting? To remember some key evidence from that time? And of what? That Finn was involved with the murder of some random kid? That Josie covered it up?

It's ridiculous. He's looking for a problem when there isn't one.

He sighs and closes the lid on his laptop. Then he hears the doorbell ring. He gets up and answers it, pleased to see Freya on his doorstep.

But the moment she sees him, she bursts into tears.

28

On the drive there, Freya had rehearsed what she was going to say to Robin, over and over in her head. She was going to stay calm. Explain rationally how she was feeling and why. Then ask for his help.

But the moment she sees his face – his careworn, familiar, hangdog face – she bursts into tears.

He ushers her into the house in dismay, and seats her at his kitchen table.

'What's wrong? What's happened? Is it Smith? What's he done?'

Despite her tears, Freya laughs. 'Why does everyone assume it's Josh? No, it's me. Just me.'

She accepts the offer of a drink and waits while Robin fusses with the kettle and a cup. Eventually, he puts the tea down and sits in front of her.

'Is it something I've done?' he asks.

'No, not at all. How's Finn?' she says, feeling awful for not remembering to ask sooner.

'No change. But don't worry about that. What's going on?'

'It's about…' She pauses. How to explain how she's feeling, when she's not even sure herself? 'It's about Jonathan and Amy and… and what happened.'

He leans back in his seat. 'None of that. None of that,' he stresses again, 'was our fault.'

'I know, I know. It's just...' She starts crying again. 'It was though, wasn't it? If I hadn't drugged Amy, then she wouldn't have died.'

'You don't know that.'

'I do! She wouldn't have fallen and banged her head. I... I feel so fucking awful about it. All the time.

'But it's not just that,' she says quickly, seeing Robin about to speak. 'It's the whole thing. I didn't realise how miserable Jonathan was. I should have noticed... got him out. Helped him. Instead, all I could worry about was me, and the fact that he was still married, and how wronged I was.' She laughs harshly. 'The poor little mistress.'

Robin's forehead furrows. He leans forward towards her. 'That wasn't your fault either, Frey.'

'Oh, but it was, Robin. It was.' She wipes her eyes. 'And now all I can think about is her. I can't sleep. And Amy Miller is the last person I want on my mind.'

'Hmm,' he replies in agreement. He turns the empty mug round in his hands. 'When was the last time you had a break, Freya?' he asks, at last.

'A break?'

'Yeah. A holiday. Time off work.'

She thinks back. Maybe... Easter? But then a manslaughter case came in and they both got called into work. She remembers going to see her parents for the weekend, and it was cold. So—

'Christmas?' she replies.

He shakes his head. 'You didn't have Christmas off. We were both working.'

'We went to the pub on Christmas Eve?'

'A few drinks with your boring skipper doesn't count as a holiday.' He stops again, thinking. 'Come with me down to Devon.'

'Pardon?'

He says it so quietly she thinks she's misheard.

'I'm going back home for a few days. Come with me.'

'What…? We can't… I can't…'

'It's the weekend. Baker won't mind. He'll make sure Smith gives you the time off.'

Freya's struggling to get to grips with what Robin's proposing. It sounds like… It sounds like he's asking her to come on a minibreak with him, but that can't be right, surely? And Baker would never approve that – a sergeant and his DC going for a dirty stay in a hotel? Now why did *that* thought cross her mind? She feels her cheeks reddening in response.

In her silence, Robin carries on talking. 'So, this may sound ridiculous, but Finn said something today. He mentioned some little kid that died when we were fourteen and that it was his fault. And I know it'll be his addled brain talking, but the kid did die, and Finn was there, and…'

His voice trails off and he looks at her. Her brain is slow to catch up, but when she does, she takes a relieved gasp of air.

'You want me to come with you to help investigate!'

'Yes, well, kind of. Off the books, but…' Then he twigs. 'Oh fuck, no, Freya. I wasn't inviting you to come with me because… not like that!'

'Oh, well, good!'

'Separate hotel rooms, I promise.'

'Phew!' Freya says, with an awkward laugh.

Robin looks slightly chagrined. 'Okay, okay, you don't need to be quite so horrified at the thought.'

Freya laughs, properly this time. 'You're just not my type, Sarge.'

She glances across to Robin, grinning. And then an image pops back into her head. The impulsive kiss between them last year. That sudden attraction. Being so very close, almost half-naked with her boss. Weird, awkward, wrong – and barely weeks after Jonathan had died.

Freya feels her face flush and notices Robin look away, no doubt remembering the same thing.

'Fine,' she says, focusing on the here and now. And she realises it's not a bad idea. Even though it's still detective work, of sorts, the thought of being away makes her feel instantly better. 'Clear it with Baker, and I'll come.'

Robin smiles. 'Deal.' Then he looks at her seriously. 'And maybe go and see your GP?'

'And say what?'

'Not the detail you told me. But that you're not sleeping. That you're depressed.'

'I don't want to take any drugs,' Freya says firmly.

'Okay, your choice. But they help me.' He stands, picking his mobile up. 'I'll call Baker,' he says, and walks away towards the living room.

She watches him go, her mouth half-open. For the most part, her boss is tight-lipped, keeping any detail about his personal life to himself. They still haven't talked about what happened last year between him and Steph. He doesn't ever mention any sort of love life, or friends. And then he'll go and do something like this. Share something so private it will catch her off guard and make her think about him differently.

He's a person, like any other. And one she likes being around, very much.

The thought of going on a trip with Robin lifts her spirits. She knows it's going to be a crappy budget hotel.

She knows he'll insist on driving. But, she thinks, it might just be fun.

29

Saturday

The cottage is on a quiet rural street — detached, brick, with four windows evenly spaced across the front. A practical Vauxhall Corsa sits on the gravel driveway. There are two small trees in pots either side of the blue-painted front door.

For a moment, Robin sits in his car and looks at it, unwilling to move. But he needs to know. He gets out and walks slowly towards the door, then raps twice with the shiny silver knocker.

He hears footsteps, then the door's opened.

The woman in front of him smiles.

'DS Robin Butler,' she says. 'I wondered if you'd turn up.'

'Hi, Liv, you're looking...' His gaze drops immediately to the massive bump.

'Fat, yes, I know.' She laughs. She moves out of the way of the door. 'Come in.'

Like the exterior, the inside of the house is neat and clean. Robin remembers her house from before — she's clearly gone up in the world.

'I like the new place,' he remarks.

'Thanks. Drink?'

'No, I won't be staying long.' He hovers in the kitchen doorway, feeling uncomfortable. Now he's here, he's not sure how to say it.

She's watching him closely, a smile playing on her lips. It's clear she knows exactly why he's there.

'How have you been, Robin?' she asks.

'Is it mine?' he blurts out.

'Is what yours?'

'Liv, come on. You know what I'm asking.'

She lowers herself slowly into one of the kitchen chairs. She points to the one next to her and he sits down.

'How, exactly, do you think this baby's yours?' she asks slowly.

'That night I was drunk and you stayed over. You said we didn't sleep together—'

'There you go then.'

He regards her cautiously. 'So you're saying nothing happened.'

'Did it?'

She's toying with him, and he doesn't like it. 'Liv, please. I need you to be honest with me.'

She leans back in her chair and sighs, rubbing the large bump. 'Look. I didn't ask you to come here. I don't want anything from you. So, what's the problem?'

'The problem is, if this is my baby, I don't want to be one of those shitty dads that abandons his kid.'

'So what are you going to do? Propose? Make an honest woman of me?'

'Don't be ridiculous, Liv.'

'So you're going to throw a bit of cash my way, is that it?' She gestures round the room. 'I don't need your money, I'm doing okay. One advantage of my sister dying is that she left behind something more valuable than her

195

shitty, spiteful company. If it wasn't for DC West showing up at my college, you would never have known.'

'So whose is it, Liv?'

'You weren't the only guy around at the time, Robin,' she says, her voice sharp. 'If you remember, I literally had a queue of guys lining up to fuck me. And do a lot more besides.'

'So we did sleep together. Why did you tell me we didn't?'

'Because you were clearly so horrified at the idea.' She shrugs. 'Life is a lot easier when you can live in ignorance. Didn't you prefer it before your pretty little detective told you the news?'

He stays silent. He can't deny it. The idea of having a child, especially one with Liv, was not something he was relishing.

'So get out, Robin,' Liv continues. 'We didn't need you before, and we don't need you now. Me and this little guy will be fine without you.'

'It's a boy?'

Liv sighs. 'Yes. Look, you've done your bit. You're guilt-free, Detective Butler. You turned up at my door and I told you to sod off. So go.'

He stands up, but pauses.

'Go,' she repeats.

He walks out of the house, his head bent. What did he think would happen? That she would fall into his arms, grateful and desperate?

Liv's right, she's doing okay. The house is nice, and by all reports she's carving out a new career for herself.

But he can't just leave. He pulls out his notebook, scribbling his number on one of the pages. He hurries back to her front door, then pushes it through the letter box.

It's up to her now. Out of his hands.

But the thought doesn't provide the relief he was expecting. If anything, the worry is worse.

30

'Ready?'

Freya heaves a large suitcase into the boot of Robin's Volvo, then nods. Robin looks at it dubiously.

'You know we're only going for a few nights, right?'

Freya points to Robin's tiny holdall. 'Unlike you, I'm not planning on wearing the same T-shirt three days straight.'

'I don't know what you mean.'

They get into the car and set off on the journey. It feels strange going with Robin down to where he grew up – but nice. She can relax, knowing he's in charge.

They listen to Radio 2 as the interminable round-abouts of the A31 make way for endless rolling green hills, bordered by high hedges. As they go, Robin explains all the events of the past few days.

'So Finn said it was his fault?' Freya repeats. 'That this boy died?'

'Yes. But Josie's adamant it was an accident. And that Finn barely knew him.' Robin pauses to negotiate a junction. 'The more I think about it, though, the odder it seems. It's the only time in Finn's history where things were a little…' He stops, looking for the right word. 'Off-kilter. Apart from this one,' he adds, grimly.

'And you can't find anything on the internet?'

'It was a long time ago. The newspapers are vague. And the online court registry doesn't go back that far.'

'To the days when you wrote on slates with chalk and only had a skipping rope to play with?'

'Fuck off.' Robin takes his eyes away from the road for a second and smiles. 'I phoned the library. They said all the old coroner court records are on microfiche. We'll have to go down there.'

'How old-school.' She looks out of the window for a second. A huge wall dominates their left-hand side and they pass a statue of a grand stag, looking out majestically across the landscape. She feels like she can breathe again. Last night, for the first time in what seems like forever, she slept a full six hours. More than she'd got in months.

'When was the last time you went home, Robin?'

'It's been a while.' He taps his finger to the song on the radio. 'Nobody's down there any more – only Josie and Sandra. And I've not been in a hurry to relive the memories.'

'Why did you move away?'

'University. Georgia went to Bournemouth Uni, so when it came to deciding where to go, I did the same.' He glances back to Freya with a rueful smile. 'My eighteen-year-old self wouldn't admit it, but I missed her. And Finn was going to Reading, so it seemed like a good fit.'

Robin leans forward and fiddles with the controls on the radio, switching the setting to CD and turning the volume up loud. A tactic to change the conversation, she assumes, but she doesn't mind. Songs blare out from the speakers, tunes Freya only vaguely recognises.

She's heard this stuff before in Robin's car. She leans forward and opens the glovebox, looking at the CDs. Placebo. Garbage. Muse.

'You should think about upgrading to modern-day,' she half shouts, holding the plastic cases out to him. 'Get an iPod at least.'

But Robin's not listening to her, cranking the volume up again on the stereo and singing along to the music. The change in her boss is surprising, his usual hesitant air completely gone as he half shouts, half sings along to the lyrics, almost word-perfect.

'What is this shit?' she laughs over the noise.

'Beastie Boys! You don't know it? Consider this your education, Freya West!'

They continue on to long, straight roads, getting stuck behind lorries and tractors until the dual carriageways provide an opportunity for Robin to put his foot down. The old Volvo rattles along cheerfully; Robin hums along to the music, his fingers tapping the beat on the steering wheel.

They drive through Bridport, then Honiton, then onto the M5, where Freya spots the sign for Exeter Services.

'Here!' she shouts to Robin.

'But we're nearly there.'

'I need to pee!'

He sighs and turns off down the slip road, pulling up in front of the Moto service station.

'Get me a packet of Monster Munch then. Flaming-hot flavour,' he shouts after her as she climbs out of the car. 'And a coffee.'

She raises a hand in acknowledgement and walks into the services.

It feels like a holiday. The long car ride, standing in WHSmith choosing crisps and chocolate, stretching her legs after two hours sitting down. People around her with their families, getting food before continuing their journeys. She joins the lengthy queue for Costa. Work feels like a world away, even though she's here with Robin.

As if reading her thoughts, her phone rings and she looks at it. *Josh Smith*, it says on the screen. She answers it.

'Hi, Josh.'

'Hi.'

There's a slightly awkward pause, like Josh has forgotten what he called to say.

'I… Baker said you were on assignment with Butler.'

Freya hesitates. She wonders what Robin told their DCI. 'Just for a few days,' she replies. 'And it's the weekend. What are you doing at work anyway?'

He laughs, on to more familiar subjects. 'You know the job, nothing stops.'

'Any progress with the freezer?'

'A bit. Fingerprints are back. A whole load of partials, most with no hits, but one match on the system. We're trying to track him down now.'

'That's progress. Are you thinking it's from one of the people who dumped it?'

'Yeah. Although we can't find anything on CCTV.'

'But Thorpe wasn't dead until the night of the storm – Steph confirmed it,' Freya challenges. 'Are you thinking the original dumpers went back to dispose of the body?'

'Yeah. And I know… As hypotheses go, it's not a good one,' Josh admits. 'And we're still trying to locate the vic's next of kin.' He pauses. 'Listen, Freya…'

'Hmm?' She gives the coffee order to the woman behind the counter, only half listening.

Another gap. 'Don't worry. It's fine. See you when you get back.'

Freya says her goodbyes and pockets her phone, as the woman passes over the coffees. She wonders what Josh was about to say, but then dismisses it.

Robin's waiting for her in the car, talking to someone on the phone. She climbs in awkwardly, coffees in hand, and he raises an eyebrow as he talks, his face breaking into a big smile when she pulls the packet of Monster Munch out of her pocket.

He hangs up.

'That was Josie,' he explains. 'The doctors say Finn has a risk of seizures from the alcohol detox. They've prescribed some drugs to help.'

'Shit,' Freya replies. 'But no other change?'

'None.'

'And Josie's happy with our trip to Devon?' Robin ignores the question, opening the packet of crisps and eating one, crumbs dropping messily on his lap. 'You haven't told her, have you?' Freya surmises from his silence.

He shakes his head, his mouth full. He chews. 'Don't want to rock the boat if there's no reason.'

'And where have you told her you've gone?'

'Home. I haven't lied about that. I just said I felt it was time to visit Mum's grave.' He starts the engine again and hands her the packet of Monster Munch to hold. The smell is overpowering, but tempting.

'And she believed you?'

'I think she has bigger things to worry about right now.' He reaches over and takes a crisp.

'I thought you were on a health kick,' she asks.

'What makes you think that?'

'The running? Drinking less coffee? Not getting pissed?'

He looks slightly embarrassed. 'Just thought I should look after myself better.' He grins, then puts one in his mouth. 'But we're on holiday, Frey,' he says, with a spray of crisp crumbs. 'Normal rules don't apply.'

They head off down the motorway again, Robin posting Monster Munch into his mouth at frequent intervals. Freya's phone beeps again, from Josh. A text message this time.

> Hi Freya. What I meant to say earlier was I had a great time with you at the pub on Wednesday, and I'd love to do it again. But without my stupid mates, this time?

She stares at it. Then another beep.

> When this case is over, and it's allowed, do you want to go out with me? xx

'Who's that?' Robin asks.

Freya looks at the texts. She knows Josh would have seen the notification showing that it's been read, but she's not sure how to respond.

'Josh,' she replies. 'About the case.'

Robin nods and goes back to his crisps, taking them off her and balancing them precariously in his lap, one hand on the wheel. There's a fine layer of crumbs down his jumper now, a greasy trail on his fingers.

She looks at the message again, then reaches over and takes the packet, putting the last crisp in her mouth.

'Hey!' Robin protests.

'You've had enough.'

She thinks about Josh. She finds him attractive, when he's not being a dick as her superior officer. She enjoyed the night out, too. But his reputation as a bit of a player precedes him. And to put her heart on the line, go out with someone again? She's not sure she's ready.

So she leaves the message unanswered. And as she looks out of the windscreen, the sign comes into view.

They've arrived in the village of Kingskerswell, Devon. Where Robin and Finn grew up.

31

Robin feels strange as they drive down roads, past houses and landmarks that he knows so well. Past the Sloop Inn on the corner; the primary school he and Finn went to. The football field and the cricket pavilion where he spent his days, and the playpark where he and Finn and the other teenagers spent their evenings, drinking cider. Everything seems odd and familiar, all at once.

He pulls into the car park of the pub and brushes the crisp crumbs off his front.

'Where's the library?' Freya asks, and Robin points to the small low building on the other side of the road. 'It's tiny. Are you sure they'll have what we need?'

'I spoke to them yesterday,' Robin confirms. 'They were going to get them in.'

Sure enough, when they arrive, they're greeted warmly by the librarian on duty: an older lady with short grey hair, a neat cardigan and a necklace made out of colourful over-sized buttons. She smiles tenderly when Robin introduces himself.

'I remember you, Robin Butler,' she says. 'I taught both you and your sister when you were little.'

'You did?' Robin struggles to gain any recognition from her lined face.

'Mrs French.'

'Oh… no.' Robin remembers a serious woman, playing piano in assembly, unsuccessfully trying to teach him how to sing in primary school. 'I'm so sorry,' he tries again. 'Music was not my forte.'

She takes his dismay with good grace. 'You could say that.' She turns to Freya. 'Tone-deaf, this one,' she adds, and Freya laughs. 'Spent most of his time gazing out of the window at the football field. Who could have guessed you'd come here on police business?' Robin ignores the warning glance from Freya; he knows he's pushed the boundaries of the truth. 'I have everything you need. Come through.'

They're shown into a small back-room. Every wall is lined with shelves and piled high with books. Teetering stacks rest on the floor. In the middle of it is a small table, with a large black contraption on top.

'So, the machine's here,' Mrs French says. She flips a switch on the side and the screen jumps into life. 'You know how to work it, right?' Robin nods. 'And microfiche here. I've requested all records from the coroner's court starting from the summer of 1992. Could you be more specific than that? I could help.'

'No, that's fine. This is fantastic, thank you.' Robin's feeling cagey about the reason for their visit. He knows that village gossip is fast to make its rounds and has no wish to become a part of it.

'A cup of tea, then?'

'Yes, please.'

As Mrs French bustles off to make the tea, Robin and Freya sit down at the machine.

'So, how does this work?' Freya asks, and Robin blinks at her.

'You've never used one of these?'

'Not for a while, no. I'm a bit younger than you, you know.'

Robin rolls his eyes. 'So, microfiche is basically pages of a document, but shrunk down in size. And this machine magnifies them.'

Freya opens the large books, where the microfiche have been neatly filed away in rows. She pulls one of the fragile plastic pages out and holds it up to the light. Robin can see the miniature images in black and white. She puts it back and runs her fingers across the dates.

'So what are we looking for?'

'Start with July and we'll go from there.'

'Robin,' Freya says. 'There must have been hundreds of deaths passing through the courts. We can't possibly look through all these pages.'

Mrs French returns with the tea, and Freya gives Robin a cheeky smile.

'Mrs French?'

'Yes, honey?'

'Do you remember a boy dying? An incident at a Scout camp, maybe around summer 1992?'

Mrs French's hands go to her chest. 'Oh yes, such a tragic accident. Jacob Fraser.' She pauses. 'Is that what you're looking into?'

'Yes,' Freya confirms. 'But between you and me, of course. Official police business,' she adds in a low whisper.

'You'll need August then.' Mrs French bends down and selects the right section among the heavy books. 'The bank holiday weekend. Scout camp was always the last week in August, before the schools went back. Not that that poor boy did, of course.'

'Do you remember how he died?' Robin asks.

'I…' She frowns. 'No, sorry. But I remember his parents moved away soon after. Too many bad memories, poor souls. He was their only child.'

There is a long pause, and Robin touches the microfiche, keen to get going. Eventually, Mrs French gets the hint.

'I'll leave you to it, then,' she says.

'See?' Freya whispers triumphantly once she's gone. 'Locals always know the gossip.'

'That'll be round the village before the day is out, I guarantee you,' Robin replies. He sighs, then pulls the first microfiche from the file. 'Let's get started.'

–

Hours later, eyes dry, backs aching, they're still going. Both of them staring at the screen, speed-reading the headings as they flick by. Freya goes to fetch sandwiches, and they take turns to eat in the middle of the room to make sure bits of tuna mayo don't end up on the precious microfiche. Robin finishes his, carefully wiping his hands then shuffling his chair back to where Freya's sitting, head resting on her hands, face barely centimetres from the screen.

He still feels awful that he hadn't realised how bad things have got for her. It seems ridiculous to Robin now – of course Freya would have been traumatised. Of course she'd be upset. After everything he'd done in his past, Amy Miller's death was barely a blip in his numbed, fucked-up brain, but to Freya it must have been a living nightmare.

She seems better today, though, more her usual self. She's smiling again, chatting in her normal way. Out of the detective 'uniform' (the female version seems to be similar to the men's, Robin's noticed: shirts, smart trousers, jackets and the like) she seems more relaxed, wearing a SuperDry hoodie today, jeans and trainers, her hair intricately braided in a French plait.

And he feels better, too. Away from the stifling heat of the hospital, the feeling of helplessness. The drive and the music of his university days have lifted him, as has Freya's easy company.

He leans forward, their shoulders touching. The microfiche scrolls by, page after page, Freya moving the viewer slowly across. Robin grows distracted. Post-carb wooziness. The smell of her shampoo. Weariness from the drive.

'You smell of tuna,' Freya says quietly, her eyes still fixed on the screen.

'You bought the sandwiches.' A pause. Eyes forward. 'Better or worse than the Monster Munch?'

'Are those my only two choices?'

Freya smiles, glancing towards him. Her face close to his. But—

'Wait! Go back,' he says.

He sits up straight, all his attention on the screen. Freya reverses the header into view.

'There. That's him.' Robin reads aloud, 'Fraser, J. Date of birth: January 1981.'

This is the information they're after. Freya carefully lines the page up on the screen and presses the print button. The machine whirs and spits out a blurry copy of the article.

It's dated September 1992. Silently, they both read the details.

Jacob Fraser. Age eleven. Died Wednesday 26 August 1992. Cause of death: cardiac and respiratory failure resulting from a severe anaphylactic reaction. Verdict: accidental.

Freya looks back to Robin. 'What do you remember about this?'

'He wasn't in my year,' Robin says. 'I was at secondary school by then. I think he was in his last year at primary. I remember the talk around the village.'

'Didn't you and Finn discuss it?'

'No, we...' Robin frowns, thinking. Robin was bitter from being forced to miss camp because of his broken leg; he hadn't wanted to discuss anything. 'We were boys,' he replies. 'Typical males. All we talked about was sport. And science, in Finn's case.'

Freya picks up the A4 sheet of fuzzy type from the printer. And she articulates what he's been thinking.

'If Finn did have something to do with this,' she says, 'how?'

32

Freya watches Robin out of the window as he talks on the phone. He paces backwards and forwards on the pavement, his head down, mobile clamped to his ear, trying to get the latest on Finn's case.

This must be taking its toll on him, she thinks. To come back to the village he grew up in, to be faced with the memories of the family he's lost. And to be investigating one of his oldest friends for... for what?

She picks up the report again. The coroner didn't find anything suspicious. A tragedy, yes, but no blame assigned. The Scout leaders did everything right – administered the EpiPen as quickly as they could, called 999 – so if it hadn't been their fault, why would Finn be to blame? He was there, but so were forty other teenagers.

Robin's still on the call, clearly talking to someone he doesn't like; she recognises the downturned mouth, the pinched expression. Robin has never been great at hiding his feelings. No airs. No pretence.

The tiny room is stuffy, the lingering smell of tuna sandwiches unpleasant, so she reaches across and opens the small window in front of her. The fresh breeze is welcome, fluttering the pages of a few books, blowing dust motes into the air.

She can hear the edge of Robin's conversation now.

'...and have you found anything on his hard drive?'
A pause. 'Well, it must have been going somewhere.'
Freya guesses he's talking to DI Craig and sits back at the
microfiche reader.

As she shuts down the machine, removing the paper
from the printer, replacing the dusty cover on the top, she
listens to the low murmur of Robin's voice. She's noticed
his West Country burr is more pronounced, even after just
a few hours here. She wonders if Mrs French is still around
and willing to share more stories of the young Robin
Butler. Ammunition for a gentle piss-take, she thinks. Or
maybe to get out of the more boring admin.

'Are we finished?' Robin says from behind her.

She jumps slightly, as if he could read her mind. 'Yeah.
What did Craig say?'

He sighs, a noise of frustration and annoyance. 'She
won't tell me much, except that they're going to interview
Sophie today. And they've got his hard drive from the
university.'

'What help would the hard drive be?' Freya asks.

'Papers he was working on. Motive,' he says grimly.
'They found the cameras they were using inside the van.
But they weren't recording internally – streaming live via
satellite, so any footage was stored remotely.' He shrugs.
'More secure, I guess.'

'So it could show what happened?'

'Maybe. Except they can't find the file.' He sighs again.
'Anyway. Shall we go and check into the hotel, before
dinner at Sandra's tonight?'

'Yes, good idea.' Freya's knackered. A cup of tea, a
biscuit and a collapse on the bed is what she needs right
now. 'Are you sure you're okay with me coming?'

Robin called Sandra earlier, letting her know they were on their way, and she invited them both to dinner. Freya relishes the thought of a home-cooked meal, but feels like she might be intruding on a long-overdue catch-up.

'Of course,' Robin replies with a smile. 'You'll love Sandra. Just don't let her interrogate you. She'll want to know everything.'

They finish tidying and Freya hands Robin the printouts. He puts them in his bag, both repeating their thanks to Mrs French as they leave.

Freya's looking forward to meeting Sandra. And she knows that with this interrogation, the information's going to be flowing both ways. Perhaps there's still a chance to get that gossip about Robin.

33

Sophie regrets agreeing to this police interview. Even more so that she came alone, without a solicitor. It seemed such an overreaction, to bring a legal representative when she hasn't done anything wrong.

But this room is so formal – the video running, the detectives stern – that she has misgivings about her decision. They've said that she's free to leave at any time, but they made her sign paperwork and the door's closed and she doesn't feel free. Not at all.

She's tired and on edge. She can't sleep. Even her usual yoga and meditation aren't working.

She recognises both detectives from the van. The car park they are now calling the 'crime scene'. She saw Finn that morning, and if anything, he seemed worse. He barely reacted when she entered the room, his features blank. His voice, when he did speak, was flat and deadpan. She told Josie she was coming here this afternoon, and Josie just said, 'Don't make things worse.'

As if she could. As if anything could be worse than this.

The woman detective in charge, Craig, is showing her a photo of a camera.

'Do you recognise this?' Craig asks.

Sophie nods. 'Kind of. Simon's team had loads of cameras over this past week. I assume it's one of those.'

'It's a Sony FS5,' Craig says. Sophie has no idea what that means. 'We recovered it from the van.'

'Isn't that a good thing?' Sophie asks. But from the look on Craig's face, she knows it can't be. Not for Finn.

'Yes, except the memory card transmitted any footage by satellite. To a networked drive we can't locate. Do you know where Finn's laptop is, Sophie?'

'Either at the university or it would have been with him in the van.'

'Is this it?'

The other detective, Grey, pushes another photo across. Sophie recognises the battered old MacBook, stickers plastered on the top. There's a stain of something red across it, which Sophie realises must be Simon's blood.

'Yes, that's Finn's.'

'Did he have any other computers?'

'Only the one at the university. You'd have to speak to Ian to get that.'

Sophie knows full well that Ian's already sent the copy of the hard drive across and wonders why the detectives are being so deliberately obtuse.

'How would you describe Finn's relationship with Simon?'

'Colleagues.'

'Not friends?'

'Well, maybe. Finn doesn't have many close friends.'

'And why's that?' Craig leans forward across the table.

'He's shy. It's hard to get to know him.'

'You managed it.'

'I persisted.'

'What about his colleagues at the university? His PhD students – would Finn go out for drinks with them?'

Sophie isn't sure what Craig is getting at.

'Maybe, sometimes. But Finn said he spent all day with them, so he didn't always want to spend the evening, too.'

'So, Finn spent a lot of time with his colleagues? Would you say they knew him well?'

Sophie stops. 'I don't want to say anything else,' she eventually replies and clamps her lips shut.

'Listen, Sophie,' DI Craig says, sitting back in her chair and putting her arms behind her head. 'I'll level with you. Things aren't looking great for your boyfriend. We're hearing stories of jealousy, of professional rivalry at the university. That Dr Mason was threatened by Dr Sharp and conflict was escalating.'

'Who said that?' She knows exactly who. Ian bloody Calloway.

'I can't say.' Craig pauses. 'You're telling me you never saw any disagreements between Finn and Simon?'

'No!'

'Never?'

The detective knows Sophie's lying, she can feel it. Sophie remembers Finn bitching to her about Simon, but it was no more than the usual disagreements that arise between two exceptionally clever men.

'They had different priorities, that's all,' Sophie says, trying to explain. 'Simon was more interested in the entertainment. Finn knew they had to get the tests right, or the results wouldn't stand up to professional scrutiny. But he would never have hurt Simon.'

'Never?'

'No.'

'Not even if Simon was about to take all the credit?'

So they know about the paper with Sharp's name on it, she thinks. And they've come to the exact same conclusion she had.

As expected, Grey pushes a document across the table towards her. 'This is a printout of a paper found on Simon's laptop. Startlingly similar to one Finn was writing,' Grey says. 'But this only has one name on the top – Sharp's.'

Sophie looks at the printout. 'Simon knew the Doppler was nothing without Finn,' she tries, but she can feel her voice shaking.

'Does it make you angry, Sophie?' Craig asks.

'Yes, but—'

'So how do you think Finn felt when he found out? We found an email from Justin White to Finn. He sent it to him on Tuesday, the day of the storm. Finn knew full well what Sharp was planning. And he went into the van, ready to kill.'

Sophie's hands fly to her mouth. 'He wouldn't. Not Finn.'

Craig's face softens. 'Or maybe he didn't plan it. Perhaps it was a spur of the moment thing, brought on by the stress of testing the equipment and the danger of the storm. Maybe Finn didn't mean to kill Simon. But the fact of the matter is that Sharp is dead, and Finn was the only one there.' She pauses. 'Sophie, look at me.'

Sophie drags her eyes from the paper in front of her, Simon's name at the top.

The detective looks sympathetic. 'Finn's best bet right now is a finding by the court for voluntary manslaughter. The fact that he was an alcoholic and probably under the influence at the time could help him: his lawyers could claim the killing was carried out without specific intent.'

'What does that mean?' Sophie whispers.

'Essentially that he was so drunk he didn't have the state of mind capable of murder,' Craig explains. 'He could plead guilty to manslaughter and his sentence would be much, much less.'

Sophie shakes her head. He would still go to jail. Her kind, sensitive boyfriend would end up in a prison with hardened criminals. He'd never survive.

'But we need your help,' the detective continues. 'You're uniquely positioned as his girlfriend to paint a picture of what Finn was like in the days leading up to the storm. You could make the difference between Finn getting life and him being out within ten years.'

Sophie looks the detective right in the eyes. She will have no part in Finn going to jail. Not for five years, not for ten. Not at all.

'I wish to leave now, DI Craig,' she says clearly. 'Finn did not kill Simon, and I will have no part in your desperate attempt to prove that he did.'

Craig sighs and holds her hands up in defence. 'There's no desperation here, Sophie,' she replies. 'We have more than enough to show he murdered Simon Sharp in cold blood. The threshold test is more than surpassed.'

Sophie stands up. 'I'm leaving.'

'So go, please,' Craig finishes. She gestures to Grey, who stands up to escort Sophie out of the interview room. As he opens the door, Sophie glances back to where Craig is still sitting at the desk. The detective looks relaxed, almost smug.

Sophie knows the police have all they need for Finn to go to prison for murder. But she's not beaten yet.

34

The Premier Inn is large and purple and simple to find. Freya is silent, looking up at the huge building, and with a horrible stomach drop Robin realises his mistake.

'Oh, Freya. Shit. I'm sorry... I didn't think.'

She shrugs. 'It's not like Jonathan died in this one. It's fine. I can't avoid every single Premier Inn just because it's where my boyfriend's body was found.'

'But—' He stops himself, then leans forward to start the engine again. 'We'll find somewhere else.'

'No, we won't. Don't be silly. Besides, I'm knackered.'

'If you're sure.'

'I'm sure.'

They head inside. Check-in is swift, two electronic cards handed their way. Third floor, rooms adjacent.

They head up in the lift and walk along the corridor, following the signs.

'Dinner with Sandra is at half seven. I'll come and get you at quarter past,' Robin says and Freya nods. Then, with a beep and a flash of green light, they're both inside.

Robin goes in and dumps his bag on the bed. He knows Freya hadn't seen the crime scene photos when Jonathan Miller was found, strung up behind the door, but he had, and the room looked just like this one. And probably the room next door. And the one next to that.

He curses himself again for not thinking about it when he booked the hotel. He stands for a moment and listens, but all he can hear is Freya's TV being turned on.

He kicks his shoes off and lies on the bed, staring at the ceiling. They haven't achieved much today; just uncovered more questions and worry. Why was Finn talking about this boy? It was an accident. A horrible one, especially if Finn had been there, but they'd found nothing that linked it to Sharp.

Next to him, his phone rings. It's a number he doesn't know and he hesitates before he answers it.

'Robin? It's Sophie. Sophie Hall.'

Her voice is high-pitched and breathless. Robin inwardly sighs.

'Hi, Sophie,' he says wearily.

'Josie gave me your number. I need to talk to you. I was interviewed by Detective Craig today.'

'And how did that go?' Robin hopes she didn't show up stoned, although from the frantic tone he guesses she could do with some weed right now.

'Fine. I mean, I didn't say anything. But they think Finn did it, Robin. They think he killed Simon.'

Robin frowns. This is hardly news. 'They wouldn't have arrested him if they didn't think that, Sophie. How is Finn?'

'Same. No change.' He hears sniffling at the end of the line and feels sympathy for the girl. This is the man she loves, after all. He should be a bit kinder to her. 'It's just... they mentioned there's some camera footage from inside the van, but they can't find it.'

'I heard that, too.'

'But... but shouldn't they be trying a bit harder to track it down?' Her voice is getting hysterical again. 'Isn't that their job? To find every bit of evidence?'

'I'm sure that's—'

'Can you make sure they are? Phone them, shout at them or something?'

'For a start, my involvement in the investigation is only as an observer. Any evidence recovered by me would be inadmissible in court. Secondly, Craig is a higher rank than me...'

'So?'

'So, she's in charge. That's how it works.' Robin pauses, and he hears her crying again. 'I'll call her,' he says, resigned to his fate. 'See what I can do.'

Sophie hangs up, and he collapses back on the bed with a sigh. Like he can influence Craig. But he'll do as he said, and put another call in. Perhaps he could phone DC Grey. The boy seems far easier to bully.

He glances at the clock. It'll have to wait: he needs to have a shower and change. And he has to admit, he's looking forward to seeing Sandra. Catching up properly for the first time in twenty-two years.

–

He knocks on the door to Freya's room half an hour later, and she answers it. Like him, she's got showered, and her long blonde hair is loose over her shoulders, smelling of something lovely. She's even wearing a dress, a casual, flowing... thing. He doesn't know how to describe it; fashion has never been his forte. Navy blue, with small white flowers. It suits her.

'You look nice,' he manages, after a shocked pause.

'You don't need to sound so surprised. You've made an effort, too,' she says, shutting the door behind her.

'I'm wearing a shirt,' Robin mutters.

'Exactly,' Freya replies. 'For you, out of work, that's practically black tie.'

—

Robin drives the short journey from Newton Abbot back to Kingskerswell and parks at the Co-op. They walk down the road towards the small row of terraced houses where Robin lived his entire childhood. Brick walls, with bay windows and tiny front yards. A small metal fence runs along the front, matching metal gates. Robin points to the one on the left.

'That was ours. We sold it when Dad died.' He points down the row. 'Then Sandra's, then Josie and Finn.'

'Poor Sandra, being sandwiched between the noisy teenagers,' Freya remarks.

'We used to treat her house like a second home. If ever we rowed with our parents, we'd end up at her kitchen table. And if we were all in trouble, we'd all be there, Georgia included.'

'And Sandra never got married?'

'No, I don't know why. It's just the way it was. You don't ask when you're a kid.'

They open the squeaky gate leading to Sandra's front door. Two pretty pots with flowers sit on the concrete of the small yard. Robin rings the doorbell.

The door opens, letting out a waft of tantalising smells, and Robin's stomach rumbles in response.

'Come in, come in,' Sandra says warmly to Robin, then steps back when she sees Freya. 'And who are you?'

'I'm Freya.'

Sandra gives Robin an impressed look. 'When you said your partner was coming, too, I was expecting a bloke. I thought it was your backhanded way of coming out, Robin. Not that there's anything wrong with that,' she adds hastily. 'But this young lady, well!' She gives Freya a warm hug. 'What on earth are you doing with him, my love?'

'No, we're not—'

'She's not my—' they both say at the same time.

Robin finishes the sentence. 'Freya's my colleague. We work together.'

'Oh! That explains it. She's much too pretty for you.'

'Thanks,' Robin replies gruffly, while Freya laughs.

The three of them file through to Sandra's living room. The decor is new and tidy, light blue sofas, undoubtably feminine, with a candle burning on the coffee table. A dining table with four chairs is in the room behind, and a kitchen past that.

'What will you have to drink? I've roasted a chicken.'

They agree on wine. Freya offers to drive and Robin's relieved. He'd fancied more than one tonight. They sit on the comfy sofas, glasses in hand, and talk inevitably turns to Finn and Josie. Sandra's been speaking to Josie every day, but she's worried about how she's coping.

'She's barely sleeping, Robin,' Sandra says. 'All she's ever lived for is that boy, and now he's in trouble.' She shakes her head sadly. 'I'm worried about them both. So how bad is it looking for Finn?'

Robin catches a look from Freya. But there's no point in lying. 'It's not good,' he replies. 'They have a substantial amount of evidence pointing towards Sharp's death being

carried out by Finn.' He sees Sandra about to say something. 'Whether he meant to or not. Finn and Sharp were
the only two in that van. Footage from the outside shows
nobody else arriving after the cameraman left. And with
Finn still in hospital, we're in a catch-22 situation. Nobody
knows what happened, except him. He gets better, and
they'll interview him then charge him. He stays ill, and
we'll never find out.'

There's a long pause while they all take a sip from their
drinks. The wine has gone straight to Robin's head on his
empty stomach, but he appreciates the bit of anaesthesia.

'What happens...' Sandra starts. 'What happens if he
doesn't get better?'

Robin sighs. 'A doctor will need to assess if he's fit to
stand trial. And if not, my best guess is he'll end up in a
secure unit.'

'For how long?'

'For as long as he needs.'

The room plunges into silence again. Sandra isn't as
close to the realities of policing as Robin or Freya, but
she's realised. One way or the other, Finn's in a prison.

His life, as he knew it, is over.

35

Robin's given Freya the headlines from the case against Finn, but hearing him laying it all out for Sandra is sobering. She knows, as well as Robin does, that there is no good news here.

Fortunately, the oven timer rings, disturbing them all from their silence, and Sandra stands up. She shakes her head, as if the physical movement could obliterate the bad feeling in the room.

'Come on, both of you,' she says. 'Let's eat.'

The roast chicken and crisp potatoes are the best meal Freya has eaten in a long time. And, with the delicious food, the mood has changed. Sandra has been happily telling Freya about what it was like living between the Butlers and the Masons. Freya laughing in response, Robin shaking his head, good-natured, as Sandra tells her stories.

'There is nothing about this one I don't know,' she says. 'These walls are paper-thin. Paper!' she exclaims. 'And my bedroom was next to Robin's.'

'Sandra...' Robin says, groaning in embarrassment. 'She doesn't want to hear this.'

'She bloody does,' Freya laughs.

'I'll spare you the worst of it, but let's just say, I knew before his father when Robin Butler lost his virginity.'

Robin jumps up from the table, his hands over his ears. 'Enough, Sandra. Move on!' He gets a new bottle of white wine from the fridge and brings it back to the table.

Freya leans across to Sandra when Robin's back is turned. 'Which was when?' she whispers.

'He must have been, maybe, seventeen? I remember the girl, she was sweet. Carrie, wasn't it, Robin?'

Robin can only groan again in response.

'Used to see them down at the playpark, where all the teenagers hung out, drinking their cider. Hand in hand. What happened to her?'

'No idea,' Robin grunts. 'Didn't care after she dumped me,' he adds pointedly.

'Aw,' Freya says. 'Broke your little heart.'

'She did.' Robin pours himself and Sandra generous glassfuls from the new bottle. 'Finn was happy, though. Meant he could hang out with me again.'

'Never was a popular one with the girls, our Finn,' Sandra explained. 'Too quiet, too awkward.' She laughs again. 'But still got in some spectacular rows with Josie. I would hear it through the walls. Him and Josie on one side, you scrapping with Georgia on the other. Oh,' she says, with a chortle, 'the screaming!'

'Why didn't you have kids?' Freya asks, curious. She knows it's a personal question and she hates it when people ask her, but Sandra doesn't seem to be the sort of woman to mind.

'Just never happened,' Sandra says. 'Didn't meet the right man, and then time passed and I was too old.' She takes a sip from her glass. 'There wasn't the same option to go it alone in those days. Being a single parent was something you did because your partner died, like your dad, Robin, or because the shitbag had left, like Josie. You didn't do it willingly.'

'I'm sorry,' Freya says.

But Sandra smiles. 'Don't be. I have a brilliant life. I have my freedom. A great job. I've travelled, been to places that I would have never been to if I'd had kids. But maybe it would have been nice.' She pauses for a moment, lost in thought. 'Still, I had you lot, didn't I?' She reaches across and ruffles Robin's hair affectionately. 'All the good bits with you kids at my kitchen table, sharing your secrets. I miss your sister, Robin. Georgia called, every week without fail. Did you know that?'

Robin shakes his head, solemn.

'She loved those boys. And she loved you, Robin. She'd tell me your news. How well you were doing at work. What unsuitable woman you were dating.'

He laughs. 'There were many of those.'

'No one now?'

He shakes his head. 'Too busy.'

'Too lazy, more like. You have to make the effort, you know. Beautiful women don't just drop into your lap. You're not getting any younger. Or better-looking.'

'Thanks a lot.'

Freya listens to this warm exchange and resolves to call her own parents. Make the time to go and visit. It's been too long.

The conversation moves on, and Freya watches as Sandra and Robin reminisce. Now that the subject has shifted from his embarrassing teenage encounters, Robin's happy to swap stories. Talking about his parents, his sister. Growing up together in the tiny Devon village. Dinner has finished, and Robin sits back in his chair, wine glass clutched in his hand, smiling more broadly than Freya thinks she has ever seen. It's a different side to him. Relaxed. Himself. She realises just how little about Robin she actually knows.

This guy here teases and jokes. He's more tactile with Sandra than she's seen him with anyone else. And she is with him, at one point leaning over and enveloping him in a big hug. He helps himself to more wine without asking; this is somewhere he undoubtedly feels at home, despite all the years that have passed. His accent is more West Country: the long *a*, the drop of the *h*.

But then, she thinks, he's never been this drunk around her before.

Either his new healthy way of life has lowered his alcohol tolerance or it's the sheer amount of white he and Sandra are sinking, but Freya realises as they finish pudding that he is wasted. Sandra, too. They've moved back into the living room; Freya's offer to wash up is dismissed quickly and Sandra's eyes are half closed. Robin's head lolls to one side.

She looks at the clock – it's nearly eleven p.m.

'Come on, Sarge,' she says, rousing Robin from where he is clearly planning on taking a nap. 'Let's take you home.'

'Are you sure there's nothing going on between you two?' Sandra asks, eyeing them slightly cross-eyed.

'Absolutely,' Freya says. But as she grabs Robin's hand to pull him up from the sofa, his other goes round her waist, steadying himself. And she has to admit, she kind of likes it.

They say their goodbyes, earning another bear hug from Sandra, and they stagger back to the old Volvo. This must be the only way Robin will let her drive, she thinks.

When he's so paralytic that unconsciousness prevents his usual hesitation.

His eyes close again the moment he's strapped in the passenger seat.

'Great,' she mutters. She has no sodding clue where she's going.

But intelligent guesses take her to road signs, and then streets she recognises. Sighing with relief, she pulls up in the car park of the Premier Inn. She nudges her boss, who's started snoring.

'Robin!' she hisses. 'Butler! You stupid twat,' she adds under her breath. She considers leaving him in the car park, but he wakes at the sound of her door opening and the interior light coming on.

'Oh! We're back! Good job,' he mumbles at her, patronising.

He manages a wobbly shuffle into the hotel, then into the lift, and along the corridor. She finds his room key in his back pocket – a more intimate experience than she would have liked – and puts it in his door. He leans in the door frame and looks at her from half-open eyes.

'We make a good team, you and me,' he slurs with a lopsided smile.

'Yes, Robin,' she says, humouring him. 'Now go to bed.'

He leans forward and, to her surprise, gives her a kiss on her cheek. But in his drunkenness he ends up missing slightly, his lips grazing the corner of her mouth.

'Right then,' he says. 'Bedtime.'

And with a loud slam of the door, he's gone.

She looks at the closed door for a second, then shakes her head in disbelief. Just when she thinks she's got the measure of Robin Butler, it turns out she's wrong.

36

Sunday

Robin can remember most of last night. Most. But despite the banging in his head and the desperate need for water, he feels okay. None of the usual haunting regret of having said something ridiculous, although he's pretty sure he did. What made the difference was the company. Sandra had seen it all: the late-night vomiting with Finn, the fights, the teenage acne. And, as it was revealed last night, his early attempts with girls. One night with too much wine wouldn't have fazed her.

And Freya... Well, Freya knows the worst of him. Trevor Stevens, and everything that happened there. The despair, the depths of his depression. And she took it all on, still working with him, day in, day out.

He lies in bed, listening to the hum of the air conditioner, the clatter and slam of doors opening and closing outside. Conversations in the corridor. He picks up his phone: no messages. He sends a quick text to Freya: *Have a lie-in, this is your holiday after all. Will be back later.* Then he adds a smiley face, which feels out of character but necessary.

He has a long shower under surprisingly hot and powerful jets, and gets dressed in the same jeans and T-shirt as yesterday. Out in the corridor, he pauses. There's no noise coming from behind Freya's door, and in the fuzz of his hangover he remembers saying good night. A kiss on the cheek missing, and a slight touch of the lips.

He feels something: a worry that he might have revealed more about himself than he intended. He shakes his head, dismissing it, and leaves the hotel.

–

Robin arrives at the industrial estate in good time and parks outside the self-storage facility. He hasn't been back here since his dad died, when he and Georgia painfully and quickly packed up their father's belongings into boxes so the house could be sold. The intention was always to come back and sort it – a thought that occurs to Robin every month as the direct debit payment goes out. Up until now he hasn't had the inclination.

But being home, speaking to Sandra and fondly remembering his childhood, has made him feel differently. For years he hasn't felt strong enough to dig this stuff out, but now he feels a pull. More than a curiosity; a desire to remember rather than a need to run away.

He heads inside the building. This place impressed him at the time, with the CCTV cameras and the security guard who nods at him as he goes inside. Luckily, the number of the unit has been printed on the key ring or Robin wouldn't have had a clue, looking at the identical orange doors. He puts the key in the padlock, and he's in.

There's more than he remembered. Way more. Boxes are stacked on boxes, then piled on furniture. He recognises their old family dining table – why did they keep it? – chairs lined up down the side. He must, *must* get round to sorting all this stuff out: what a waste of money to keep paying month after month in misplaced nostalgia. Their dad wasn't one for sentimentality; he would only keep what he needed, and the rest went in the bin. That almost went as far as their old childhood drawings, although he remembers their mum intervening. After she died, Robin expects nothing stayed.

Still, there are boxes and boxes here. Robin pulls the closest one towards him, *Mum Ornaments* written on the side in Georgia's recognisable print. He opens it: their mother's china figurines all carefully interred in bubble wrap. Even after her death, they stayed in their glass cabinet — a strange house decoration for a newly single man. But Robin knows their father never found anybody else to spend his life with, and marvels at the love that must have existed between his parents.

Even now, at the age of forty-two, it still seems impossible to Robin that he could find someone and get married. Steph was the closest he'd come to any sort of permanent attachment, and that had been over in less than a week. His thoughts turn to Liv, and the spectre of the baby hanging over him. Christ, to be a father? Was that something he could do?

He remembers his own dad. Gordon Butler was a mechanic by trade, a skill that hasn't been passed down to his son. Robin remembers him always twiddling with something in his hand, a screwdriver never far out of reach. A toy of Robin's that no longer worked. A piece of oily carburettor. A plug that needed rewiring. He left the discipline to Robin's mother, and then, after she died, to Georgia, even though she was only two years older than her brother. He was a quiet man, undemonstrative about his love for his children, but unwavering in his presence.

He never missed a football game or rugby match, and there were many.

Robin realises now how similar he is to his father. The same frown. The same introversion. But loyal to the people he loves, to the last.

Robin sighs and pushes the thought away, then grabs the next box to look through.

-

After a few hours of digging, his headache has got worse, he is desperate for a litre of water and a fry-up, and he is starting to wonder why he came. There is so much crap. Robin is debating paying a company to get rid of it all, when he comes across a box – *PHOTO ALBUMS* is scrawled on the side. He heaves it out and pulls open the tape. There are five identical-looking albums in here, ones he remembers from his childhood. He gently runs his fingers over the blue fake leather cover of the first, tentative about the emotions that might be unleashed should he open it.

He shuts the box again decisively, then pushes it out into the corridor outside the orange door to his unit. He's starting to feel shaky – no food, no coffee in stomach – and has one last look inside before he flicks the light off. He shuts the door, padlocking it closed. He will come back and sort all this shit out, Robin promises himself.

But one step at a time. And he hauls the box of photo albums into his arms and heads back to his car.

37

Sophie still hasn't heard back from Robin. But what did she expect? The man has buggered off to Devon, Josie had told her, and at the one time when Finn needs him the most, so he's hardly going to go out of his way to help.

She's sitting on her sofa, the news playing out in front of her. The media interest has faded now that there's nothing new to report. Finn is still in hospital. Simon Sharp is still dead. She's heard the BBC are going to be putting together a tribute *Storm Chaser* episode for Dr Sharp – some sort of 'best of' compilation to celebrate his life. She knows that will stir up interest again. For a while it was even trending on Twitter: #justiceforSimon. What about justice for Finn? she thinks, tears threatening.

She knows she should go to the hospital, but what would be the point? Her company makes no difference to Finn, and it certainly doesn't help him remember. He just repeats the same old crap, like an annoying broken record. His insane fabricated memories are becoming a respite from his inability to figure out the basics.

So if he can't remember, this missing video footage is his best bet. It's key. She remembers the press coverage at the beginning of the week, cameras flocking round Justin White. If anyone's going to know, Sophie resolves, it's the bloody cameraman.

An hour later, Sophie stands outside the Malmaison hotel. BBC budgets have improved, she thinks, staring up at the posh white-painted walls, the lavish sash windows. This place is *nice*. But how to find out which room Justin White is in?

She pulls her shoulders back and confidently walks into the plush lobby. A smiling, glossy-haired woman greets her warmly from behind the reception desk.

'Sophie Hall, from Reading University, for the meeting with Justin White?' she says, showing her Reading Uni pass. She hopes the woman won't look too closely.

'I wasn't aware there was anything scheduled this morning,' the receptionist says, rictus grin fixed on her face. 'Shall I call?'

'No, no, don't do that,' Sophie says quickly. 'They'll be filming and I don't want to disturb them. I'll just go on up. Room 516, right?' she says, pulling a number out of thin air.

'Oh, no, they were moved to a smaller suite. After...' The woman's face falls. 'You know.'

'I do. Such a tragedy. So...?'

'Mr White is in room 308. Lifts on the right.'

'Thank you.' Sophie smiles warmly and quickly walks to the lifts, her heart beating fast. Calm down, she tells herself as she presses the button for the third floor. What did she think would happen? Escorted out in handcuffs for pretending to be a meteorologist?

The lift pings and she follows the signs to room 308. But once outside, she hesitates. What's she going to say? Still, she knocks. She hears footsteps and the door's opened; Justin White stands in front of her dressed only in his boxers and a T-shirt.

'Sophie,' he says, surprised. 'I thought... I wasn't expecting you.'

'Clearly not.' Sophie doesn't wait for an invitation and pushes past him into the hotel room. It smells of old beer and stale sweat. There are clothes and discarded plates everywhere, the room in darkness. 'What have you been doing in here?' she asks, swishing open the curtains.

Justin winces at the fresh influx of light. 'My best friend died. What do you think I've been doing?'

'Why haven't you gone home?'

'The police asked me to stick around, until... until their investigation is complete.'

'Well, it's not, is it? Where's the footage, Justin?'

'What?' He's still standing in the middle of the floor, barefoot and confused.

'The camera footage from the inside of the van. Where is it?'

He glares at her. 'I don't know. I told the police the same thing. Just... give me a moment.' He picks up a pile of clothing from the nearest chair and goes into the bathroom.

Sophie sighs. While he's gone, she busies herself moving the dirty plates into an orderly pile on one tray, then clears a chair to sit on. There's a knock on the door, and Sophie looks towards the bathroom.

'Answer it,' comes the voice. 'It's room service.'

A smartly dressed man waits on the other side, a selection of plates arranged on the trolley. 'Where do you want it, madam?' he asks, and she points inside.

Sophie hastily clears the table, the breakfast is placed neatly down and the man is dispatched, dirty plates in hand.

Justin emerges from the bathroom, now fully dressed, hair combed and tied back into a ponytail. He sits down in front of the food, and Sophie does the same, opposite him.

It's quite a spread – a full English, toast, croissants, coffee and two mugs. Sophie pours herself a coffee without asking.

'You're not exactly starving then,' she remarks.

'Got to make the most of it while I can,' he mumbles through a mouthful of fried egg. 'Going to be out of a job soon. *Storm Chasers* is hardly going to continue without its star,' he adds bitterly.

'Where's the footage, Justin?' Sophie repeats.

He sighs. 'I don't know. There were two cameras in the van – one mounted in the top-left corner, filming the interior, and a Sony FS5 that Simon would use for close-up interviews.' He puts his fork down and picks up his mug, taking a sip of the black coffee. 'Both cameras upload via satellite to NAS – network attached storage,' he adds in response to Sophie's blank expression. 'And that NAS was set up to back up every hour to a server. In this case, the main BBC one back at Reading Uni.'

'The one in the lab?'

'Right.' Justin reaches over his breakfast to his bag on the floor and pulls out a page of numbers and letters, putting it in front of her. 'This is the read-out from the NAS. It shows that backup was working – see here, that's the name of the BBC server – but there's nothing there.'

'The file's been deleted?' Sophie says, shocked.

Justin frowns. 'That's my best guess, yes. All the data from the Doppler is there, but the folder where the footage should have been stored is empty.'

'What about the original files on the… the network thingy?'

'The NAS. That's gone, too.'

'So who deleted it?'

'I don't know. Could have been anyone with access to the server.'

'It's not very secure, is it?'

'We didn't expect it to record a murder!' Justin's face falls. 'I'm sorry. I didn't mean that. I should have checked it Wednesday morning. But with Finn locked in the van, and the shock of Simon being dead. I just…' He puts his head in his hands. 'Oh, fuck.'

Sophie wants to cry. There was video, something that could have cleared Finn's name, but it's gone.

'Can't someone who knows something about computers recover it?'

'They're trying,' Justin says quietly. 'But they said it's not looking good. Apparently, this person knew what they were doing.'

They both sink into silence. After a moment, Justin seems to regain his appetite and starts buttering a slice of toast. Sophie envies his hunger. All she can feel is a constant gnawing anxiety; the idea of eating makes her feel sick.

Justin takes a bite of his breakfast, and Sophie feels him watching her.

'What?'

'And you're sure…' he starts.

'Sure, what?' Sophie challenges.

Justin swallows. 'You're sure he didn't do it?'

'What? Kill Simon?' Sophie can't believe he's asking her this. 'Of course not.'

'It's…'

'What, Justin? Please share what's on your mind,' she snaps.

He puts his knife down, then leans back in his chair, holding his coffee cup. 'Simon was my best friend. I spent months with him, I knew everything about him. And some of the stories he told me about Finn? Well, they weren't flattering.'

'Like what?'

'Like the story about Simon's penknife. It was a gift from one of his professors, his PhD supervisor, some in-joke between them. You know – that Simon was the only meteorologist you'll ever meet that would know what to do with a penknife?'

'So what?' Sophie's barely tolerating this conversation. It's clear whose side Justin White is on, and it briefly crosses her mind that he might have deleted that footage himself.

'So, Finn was jealous. They'd both worked with that professor, and he had never given Finn anything. The rivalry between Simon and Finn was intense. To the point that I questioned why Simon wanted to work with him.'

'Well, we know why. Because Simon wanted to steal his research.'

'I don't know about that—'

'It's obvious. Simon's name is on the draft paper. You sent it to Finn – the detectives told me. Why would you do that, if it wasn't to show Finn what Simon was doing?'

'I…' He looks down miserably at the remains of his toast. 'I found it by accident. And I felt bad for Finn. Simon was an incredible guy, but I knew he was ruthless, and he'd stomp all over Finn, given half the chance. I thought he'd just have a conversation with Sharp. Clear it up, make sure both their names went on the paper.'

'Well done you,' Sophie says, sarcastically. 'Look what happened next.'

Justin's expression changes. His face contorts, his eyes flash with anger. 'So you agree then, Sophie?' he says, his voice steely. 'Isn't that motive? A man who's been torn up with jealousy towards Simon since their PhD days. Who's harboured a grudge against him for nearly twenty fucking years. A man who sees Simon getting all the recognition and celebrity that he has always been denied discovers that Simon's taking his crowning achievement. His last bid for success.' Justin leans forward. He's so close to Sophie that she can smell the coffee on his breath. 'And you still think he didn't kill him?'

'Piss off,' Sophie hisses. She pushes away from the table and stands up so fast that her chair falls over with a crash. 'You barely know Finn. You have no idea what he's like.'

She turns and walks away quickly, her hand pushing the handle down on the door.

'Do *you*, Sophie?' Justin shouts after her. 'You didn't know he's an alcoholic. You didn't know he was drinking so much that some days his hangovers meant he had to puke in the wastepaper bin. That the only way he could stop his hands from shaking was to top himself up with yet more vodka.'

She turns. 'You knew?' she shouts back. 'Why didn't you say anything?'

'Because we needed him, Sophie! Sharp said everything would be fine. He said he had everything under control. But he didn't, did he? And Finn killed him.'

The tears come thick and fast now. Sophie can't hear any more. She pulls the door open and rushes into the corridor, slamming it shut behind her. She can barely see as she runs out of the hotel, back to her car.

And all the while, the thought runs through her head: is Justin right?

Is he right?

38

Freya wakes by herself – without an alarm, without her phone jerking her awake. She lies in her bed and stretches. She actually feels good. Rested.

She looks at her phone, set to silent. It's past ten; she can't remember having slept this late for ages. The text from Robin makes her smile – she doesn't know when he's ever used an emoji. He must be feeling bad about his state last night. She wonders where he's gone, but forcefully pushes it out of her head. She can't think about Robin all the bloody time. More importantly, what should she do this morning?

She runs a bath and spends far too long lying in the hot water. It's hardly luxury – no bubble bath, no candles, only a bland white bathroom suite – but it's more relaxing than anything she's done for a while. She takes her time blow-drying her hair, sticking on a bit of make-up. What now?

She remembers that Sandra has the morning off and decides to buy some flowers to thank her for the meal last night. Plus, a walk round the village in the sunshine will do her good.

A taxi takes her swiftly to Kingskerswell and drops her on the main road, next to the Co-op. She pops in to buy flowers, then heads to Sandra's house.

The curtains are open in the front window, so Freya decides Sandra must be up and rings the bell. The door opens, and Sandra exclaims happily when Freya presents her with the bouquet of tulips.

'Thank you, my love. Robin not with you?' she asks, glancing behind Freya.

'No, he's on an errand,' Freya replies vaguely.

Sandra escorts her inside. 'Tea, coffee? These are gorgeous, let me find a vase.' Sandra bustles around her kitchen, making the requested cup of tea. 'I have some biscuits here, too. Come, sit. Sit.'

They both take chairs at Sandra's kitchen table, all signs of the dinner last night cleared away. Sandra places two mugs of tea in front of them, plus an already opened packet of chocolate digestives. Freya takes one gratefully.

'So, does your work often take you on trips down to where your boss grew up?' Sandra asks. She has a smile on her face, bluntly asking a question she knows the answer to.

'No,' Freya replies. 'But Robin wanted the company, and I needed a break.'

'Hmm,' Sandra says. 'Sure there's nothing going on between the two of you?'

Freya returns the smile. 'No. Not at all. We're just friends.' But Freya remembers the misjudged kiss last night and can't stop a slight flush making her cheeks turn red.

'You must be a good friend,' Sandra comments, taking another biscuit. 'Robin's fussy about the people he hangs out with. Always has been, even when he was a kid.'

'Tell me about him,' Freya can't resist asking.

Sandra laughs. 'From what I see now, much the same. Always serious, always taking the weight of the world on his shoulders. Had a real sense of right and wrong and fairness, so it made sense that he went into the police force. And he and Finn were as thick as thieves. The two of them were always together, even though they were so different. Robin was sporty, into rugby and football and cricket. Finn was the clever one. But I'd often see them kicking a ball around together or working on their homework. I guess you could say they complemented each other, and that's why they worked so well.' Sandra has that twinkle in her eye again. 'Why do you think you and he work well now?'

Freya dismisses the question. 'Because he's in charge,' she says.

'That's not it at all,' Sandra replies, pouring more tea from the pot. 'I saw you last night. You have a connection. Something very natural. You understand him, and with Robin, that's hard.'

'We've been through a lot together in the past year,' Freya says, and Sandra nods.

'It's nice he has someone looking out for him. I've worried about that boy since Georgia died. You know we got in touch after the funeral?' Freya shakes her head. She'd wondered where Josie and Finn and Sandra had been when Robin had needed them the most. 'We even drove up to see him, Josie and I. But he was having none of it. Said he was fine, even though we knew he wasn't. Looking back, I wish we'd done more,' she says, pensively. She takes a sip of her tea. 'Robin's always been the same: so busy saving everyone he forgets about himself.'

'What do you mean?'

Sandra laughs. 'That boy's biggest strength is his weakness. He did it with Finn when they were kids, and he's doing it again now. His protector. Robin sees someone in trouble, and he has to rush to their aid.' She reaches for another biscuit then holds the packet out to Freya, who takes one. 'A shrink would probably say it comes from his mum dying so young. That he couldn't save her, so he has to try with everyone else.' She shrugs. 'But what do I know about that? My only worry is what happens when he fails.'

She smiles at Freya warmly. 'It's a big relief that he's doing so well now. Being around you must be good for him. Now,' she adds before Freya can interject, 'another cuppa?'

—

After three cups of tea, half a packet of biscuits and a trip to the toilet, Freya eventually pulls herself away from Sandra's cosy kitchen. She's wonderful company, warm and funny, and Freya considers Robin lucky to have grown up around such a woman. Lucky to have had a childhood like this, she thinks, walking out into the village.

She takes a turn up School Road, past a large white corrugated-iron community centre, down past a Scout hut and over a railway bridge. She keeps walking, sun on her face, a spring in her step, until she finds herself outside an old church. She stops, looking at the graves. Some are old; large stone monoliths. Others are new, small, shined granite plaques, marking where ashes must be buried. And sat on a wooden bench is Robin.

His head is bowed, his back hunched, and with a start she realises this must be where his mother is laid to rest. She hesitates. It feels wrong to disturb him, but then her phone beeps in her bag and he turns.

He smiles when he sees her and she lifts her hand in a half-wave, then walks over.

'How did you know I was here?' he asks. His face is drawn but he doesn't look like he's been crying.

She takes a seat next to him. 'I didn't. I was wandering round the village.'

'Not much to see.'

'No. Although you seem to have a lot of community centres.'

Robin laughs. 'We do.'

They sit in silence for a moment, undisturbed except for birdsong and the gentle rustle of wind in the trees. 'It's pretty here,' Freya says.

Robin nods. 'Mum always loved the village. Said there was nowhere else she wanted to be.' He points to a distant grave, and Freya can see fresh flowers have been left by the stone. 'Her ashes are over there.'

'Do you remember her well?' Freya asks. She recalls Sandra's words and knows that Robin's mum died when he was young, cancer of some kind.

'Bits and pieces,' he says, but he doesn't expand, his mouth set in a hard line. Freya senses not to push it.

After a moment, he stands up. 'Come on,' he says. 'Can't sit here all day.'

They head back over the bridge and towards the play-park.

'I was eight when Mum died.' Robin's voice is soft but clear as they walk in the warm spring breeze. 'She'd been ill for a while, and nobody had visited except the nurses and Josie and Sandra. Nobody else gave Dad, Georgia or I the time of day.' Freya glances up at him; his hands are shoved in his pockets, his gaze directed at his feet. She stays quiet, silently urging him to keep talking. 'Then, when she died, suddenly the house was full. People dropping off food, asking me how I was. How did they think I fucking was? My mother had just died.'

They walk another ten paces or so. 'And then Finn turned up. Rugby ball in his hand. And he fucking hated rugby, never wanted to play. He couldn't catch to save his life, probably still can't now.' He laughs, but it's sad, almost reluctant. 'There he was, ready to go.' He stops, and they both look out over the playing field. 'That meant more to me than anything. That Finn knew I didn't want to talk. Didn't want to be around all these people. I just wanted to chuck a ball around and pretend everything was normal.' He shrugs now, and Freya sees him swallowing hard. Then he sighs, a long breath in and out. 'I just want to help him. Like he helped me.'

'You will, Robin,' Freya says gently. She has a sudden urge to take his hand, but she suppresses it, pushing her own hands hard into her coat pockets. He glances at her with a forced smile, then looks out to the open green space.

'Football in the winter, cricket in the summer,' he says. 'That's where they had all the candles and stuff. For Jacob.'

Conversation over then, Freya thinks. 'Robin,' she says instead. He stops. She's been thinking about this, and she wants to share. 'Do you think Josie would have kept anything from that time?'

He pauses. 'Like what?'

'Like diaries, newspaper reports. Anything that might explain Finn's involvement.'

She can see Robin thinking. 'His weather notebooks, maybe. Josie mentioned she still has them.'

'How would they help?'

'He recorded all the measurements from his weather station. He had this home-made thing, cobbled together

247

out of wood and random electronics. Twice a day, he'd write them down, without fail. But when we were older, he wouldn't let me see the notebooks, and I suspected he was also using them as a diary. Thoughts and feelings and the like.'

'Suspected?' Freya asks, with a smile.

Robin returns her expression with a guilty grin. 'I might have sneaked a look. Once or twice.' He pauses, and Freya can see the conflict on his face. A huge part of him probably doesn't want to know, but as a cop, it's a pure bloody-minded urge to find out the truth. She regrets bringing it up.

'It was thirty years ago,' she says. 'There's no way she'd have kept them all. Besides, we can't search Josie's house. We can't get in, for starters.'

Robin's still thinking, his gaze set towards the hill and the row of houses in the distance. 'Josie used to have a broken window lock. Finn and I would use it to get in the back door when he forgot his key.'

'She'd have fixed it by now.'

'Probably,' he says, almost to himself. Then he looks at Freya. 'If she has, that's it. We go home.'

'And if she hasn't?'

Robin leaves the question unanswered. Just starts striding away across the green.

39

They walk back up the hill, up Daccabridge Road, towards the alleyway at the back of the terraced houses. Robin reaches over the fence and unlocks Josie's gate, and the two of them go across the tiny patch of lawn to the back door.

Robin's not sure what propels him towards this disaster. What does he hope to gain from searching Josie's house? For something that might not even exist?

He stands next to Josie's back door, the window to his right. It looks like the same crappy single-pane glazing, but there's no way the lock will still be broken. She must have fixed it by now.

He glances to Freya; she's looking at him uncertainly. Then he puts his palm on the window and pushes it to the right.

At first it doesn't move, but then slowly, surely, it starts to open. He pushes it enough to get his hand through.

'What now?' Freya whispers behind him.

'Now,' Robin says, nerves bunching in his stomach, 'we go in.'

–

Everything is exactly how he remembers. Even the wallpaper is the same. Freya pushes the back door closed behind her, and they stand in the tiny kitchen.

'Where do you think they'll be?' she asks.

He looks around. Coming here feels ridiculous. Josie has never been tidy, but in the intervening years the mess seems to have raged out of control. There is stuff everywhere. Piles of magazines stacked on the floor. Drawers full to the brim, some open slightly, their contents preventing their closure.

'You start down here. I'll take upstairs,' he replies.

'Okay...' Freya says.

He knows what she's thinking, and she's right. They should leave now. Get out of here, go and do something nice. Freya is supposed to be on a break from this shit, after all. But instead, he leaves her staring at the mess and trudges towards the staircase.

Upstairs is no more than two bedrooms and a bathroom. Robin's childhood home was exactly the same, except they'd split the larger bedroom into two, creating precious privacy for both Robin and Georgia.

He pushes the door open into Finn's room, his senses immediately assaulted by reminders from his youth. The room hasn't changed, even down to the same posters of Nirvana and Smashing Pumpkins thumbtacked to the wall. The only difference is the bed is now a double and the smell is distinctly more pleasant.

Robin remembers Finn's obsession with Kurt Cobain, his long-held conviction that the musician's death hadn't been a suicide. Evidence of his single-mindedness was clear even then, although maybe it hinted at the darker side of Finn's psyche. The drinking and depression to come.

He can almost see Finn here, lying face down on his bed, his long limbs hanging off the edge. Reading some book or other while Robin bounced a ball in the doorway, desperate for his company. He never made an effort to find a different friend to hang out with, despite their disparate interests. Why would he? Finn was his best mate. What else mattered?

Looking at the room now, Robin wonders why Josie has never redecorated. Was it a desire to keep a place that felt like home for her only son, to hold onto the past? Or simply a lack of time?

He stops for a moment, thinking. There's no way he and Freya can search the whole house. But equally, seeing this – the level of preservation of Finn's room – Robin has a strong feeling that Josie wouldn't have thrown any of the diaries out. His eyes drift up to the loft hatch over the landing.

He reaches up, opening the small square door and pulling down the ladder. It comes out with a shower of dust. He puts one foot in front of the other on the creaking rungs, then pokes his head through the gap. He gropes around for a light switch, clicking it on.

The light is dim but illuminates enough of the loft for Robin to see. It's small, but the floor is boarded, and he carefully, awkwardly, pulls himself up into the space.

He looks around. There are boxes of many shapes and sizes, most of them close to the opening, where he assumes Josie must have just pushed them in quickly. He opens a few lids. One that clearly contains Christmas decorations and another with some old photo albums. He pulls one of them out: even in the dim light he can see sepia prints, faded shots of a tiny Finn being held by Josie. He stops himself getting distracted and puts it back, but leaves the box close to the entrance.

He shuffles further into the loft, opening and closing the tops of boxes as he goes. Curled-up cables, random crap, old clothes that must have been fancy-dress outfits. And then he sees something that makes him stop.

An A4 dark red folder. Plastic pages inside, gold writing on the cover. The National Record of Achievement: Robin had one, as did every teenager leaving school in the Nineties. It's for the wrong time period, but the folder is stuffed, paper poking out of the plastic pages. Robin picks it up, curious. He opens it: it's full of old certificates and school reports, dates spanning from their first year of secondary to the last. If something else remains from Finn's time at secondary school, it will be in here.

He picks it up, and underneath, there they are. Piles of notebooks, of all shapes and sizes, stacked on top of one another in the box. He selects one: *MAR–AUG 90* written in block capitals on the cover. Organised and meticulous, that was Finn all over. He puts it back, then selects another few, their dates marked clearly on the outside.

He hears Freya shout from downstairs. He takes one last look at the chaos in the loft, then climbs down the ladder, hauling the boxes of notebooks and photo albums with him, the red folder resting on top.

He carries them down to the living room, where Freya is waiting.

'Lunch,' she says grandly, pointing at two sandwiches, a bag of apples and two cans of Diet Coke.

'You risked going out?' Robin replies with a frown. 'Did anyone see you?'

'I went out the back.' She pauses. 'I was hungry. You'd rather I starve?'

He shakes his head, disbelievingly. 'You'd make a shit burglar,' he comments, but reluctantly concedes defeat. His stomach is rumbling, too; it's been a long day already.

'Pass me the cheese one. Since you whinged about the tuna yesterday,' Robin mutters.

They sit down at Josie's dining table; Robin takes a bite of the sandwich, while Freya pulls over the box of notebooks.

'You found them,' she says, rifling through. 'What's in there?' she asks, pointing to the other box from the loft.

He drags it over. 'Photo albums.'

Freya eagerly reaches forward, notebooks forgotten, grabbing an album from the top. She flicks quickly past the ones of Finn as a baby, then stops, a triumphant look on her face. She turns it round.

'Oh, no,' Robin groans. 'What have I done?'

It's a shot of two small boys: identical shorts, matching cheesy grins. One is taller and thinner, the other stocky, with a good distribution of puppy fat on his chubby cheeks.

'That has to be you,' Freya exclaims gleefully.

'Yes,' Robin says, resigned to his fate.

Freya keeps on looking through, occasionally giggling, a huge grin on her face. 'Oh, this makes the breaking and entering worthwhile. Look at you!' She laughs again, pointing to two small grinning faces poking out of carved holes in a big brown cardboard box.

'Don't mock our castle,' Robin says. 'That took us a whole afternoon.'

'How old are you here?'

'Oh, must have been... about five?'

'So you and Finn really did grow up together?'

'Yeah. Sometimes it was the three of us, see?' He points to a shot of him and Finn, next to an older girl. 'Until Georgia would get sick of us boys and find something else to do. We've always been close.'

Robin feels a flash of sadness, knowing that isn't strictly true. Not of late. As adults, they've grown apart, and he wonders how he let that happen. He could blame their different careers, busy lives, his dislike for Sophie, but in reality it's been a case of simply failing to prioritise the time to see his best friend. He makes a fresh resolve to help now; to do everything he can to get Finn out of this mess.

Freya has sensed Robin's change of mood and has put the photo album down, turning to the red folder. She's been filtering through idly with one hand, her half-chewed apple in the other, but now she puts it down, and carefully pulls an official-looking booklet out.

Finn's school report. Dated October 1992 – their first half-term after Jacob's accident. She passes it to Robin.

He flicks though. Attendance record, absence for the first three weeks. Scribbled handwriting from Finn's teachers. A letter: *referral to mental health services*.

While Robin's been reading, Freya's continued looking through the folder.

'Here, look at this,' she says and hands him a piece of paper. An article, clearly torn out of a newspaper. He hands her the school report, then starts to read. *SCOUT CAMP ENDS IN TRAGEDY*, the headline shouts.

> *An eleven-year-old boy has died on the way to hospital after severe anaphylactic shock, an inquest opening heard. Jacob Samuel Fraser was at the annual Scout camp of the 12th troop on Wednesday 26 August, when he started struggling to breathe. An ambulance was called and he was on his way to Torbay A&E when he went into cardiac arrest. He was pronounced dead on arrival.*

> *Jacob was known to have an allergy to bee stings and carried an EpiPen with him at all times. It is not yet known what other precautions had been taken by the Scout leaders to prevent this tragedy.*
>
> *A post-mortem gave the cause of death as cardiac and respiratory failure resulting from a severe anaphylactic reaction.*
>
> *While investigations are ongoing, initial reports state that his death was not suspicious. The coroner adjourned the hearing, and a full inquest will take place in due course.*
>
> *Tributes have been pouring in for the happy and well-liked boy, with an unofficial shrine set up at the cricket pavilion on Kingskerswell village green, near to where Jacob loved to play football.*

Robin stops and puts the newspaper clipping down.

'Why did Josie keep this?' he asks, but Freya just shrugs.

Robin turns his attention to the box of notebooks. He carefully takes them out of the container, creating teetering piles on the table. While he searches, Freya picks up a few, opening them up to random pages.

'You were right: he was using them as a diary,' she says. She shows him an entry.

At the top of the page are the usual weather recordings. *Temp: 18°C, wind speed: 3 m/s, rainfall: 2 mm.* And underneath, a few lines. *School crap, chosen last in PE. Failing in English, got a B- on* Mockingbird *report.* He smiles at that.

'Only Finn would think a B- was failing,' he says. He looks back to the box. 'Oh, here we are,' he says, pulling the notebook out.

JUL–DEC 92 it says in block capitals on the cover. Robin places it in front of him and starts to read, lunch forgotten.

It starts in the same way as the others. The weather was hot that July, temperatures all in excess of thirty degrees, rainfall at zero. Finn's entries are brief, but consistent.

Went to hospital with Rob, he's broken his leg, stupid twat. Now he won't be able to come to camp. Robin snorts. Nice to know he wasn't the only selfish teenager around at the time.

The next day: *Worried about camp. Without Robin there, what??* What, what? Robin thinks. *Perhaps I shouldn't go,* it concludes.

But he had, Robin knows. He flicks ahead to the dates of the Scout camp. The handwriting changes: the weather measurements written in a female script, one Robin recognises as Josie's. She'd clearly been under strict instructions to keep up the hard work while Finn was away.

And then, once he'd returned from camp, it goes back to Finn's. At first, the measurements are written in, but only that. No other comments. And then, there's a gap. Days pass: nothing.

He shows it to Freya. 'What do you make of that?'

'You said he had glandular fever,' she replies. 'Perhaps too ill to check the weather?'

Robin shakes his head. 'No, Finn would have never let it drop. He had flu once, a really bad fever, and he made me go out in the pouring rain to take his notes. He would have made Josie do it.' Robin stares at the empty pages. 'It's like he didn't care.'

Freya slowly looks up from the school report. 'Maybe he was depressed,' she says, her voice low and careful. 'It would fit. He sees the death of a friend – that would be enough to spin anyone out.' She points to the school report. 'He had a referral to mental health services. And from what Sophie's said to you, it's something he struggles with now.'

Robin frowns. 'But Josie said Finn didn't know Jacob,' he replies. 'And, more to the point, why would Josie hide this?' He sighs, closing the notebook with frustration and replacing it in the pile. 'I need a drink,' he says, with finality.

—

They return the house to its previous state, replacing everything perfectly. Robin hesitates over taking the notebook, but concedes that it tells them nothing, and he leaves it with the others.

They walk down the road to the Sloop Inn. Robin has always preferred the Lord Nelson but there's a strong chance he'll be recognised by a local, even after all these years, and he's not in the mood to chat.

The Sloop is a generic chain, bland but functional, and they carry their drinks to the far side. Freya's taken advantage of Robin's hangover and has a large glass of white in front of her. Robin has a lager shandy. He sips it grimly.

'What are you going to do?' Freya asks.

'Christ knows. Probably nothing.' Robin picks up his phone and puts it down again. He wants to call Josie, demand to know what happened, but he needs to approach the topic gently. What he and Freya have been doing is essentially illegal, although Robin's pretty sure that Josie wouldn't press charges. 'What difference does it make?' he asks her. 'Even if Finn was affected by this boy's death, what's it got to do with Simon Sharp? The only assumption Craig will make is that he had some sort of mental-health incident, linked to something that happened when he was a kid. It only strengthens her case.'

'The coroner ruled Jacob's death as accidental. It wasn't anyone's fault,' Freya says gently.

'True.' Robin takes a large gulp of his shandy. 'So why would Finn say it was? And why bring it up now?'

'He's ill, Robin,' Freya replies. 'Who knows what's going on in his head.'

Robin pulls the menu out of the stand on the table. 'Are you hungry?' he asks, desperate to change the subject.

'Starving,' Freya says. 'That sandwich barely touched the sides.'

They choose food: Freya going for fish and chips, Robin for a burger. Freya goes up to the bar to order and comes back with more drinks.

'I saw Steph on Wednesday,' Freya remarks, when she's back at the table. 'She asked about you.'

'How was she?'

'Good,' Freya replies. Robin feels her staring at him. 'What happened between you and her? Why did you split up?'

'Wow.' Robin shakes his head wearily. 'You know how to kick a man when he's down.'

'Thought it might distract you. Are you seeing anyone at the moment?'

'First Sandra last night, now you. No. What makes you think that?'

She shrugs. 'Just wondered what brought on your new lust for life. All this running and stuff.'

'I go for a jog now and then. It's hardly triathlons, like Steph. And where would I meet this mythical woman? The only place I go to is work.'

'Exactly why Steph was so right for you.'

He looks at her, quizzically. 'Why?'

'Shared interest. Mutual ambitions. Same awful working hours.'

'Turns out our ambitions weren't so mutual,' Robin says to his pint. 'Steph wants kids. And soon. That's why we broke up.'

'And you don't?'

'I... well, probably. But after the twins died...' He leaves the sentence unfinished. He knows Freya will understand what he's saying. That after his two-year-old nephews were killed, he couldn't bring himself to be that open, emotionally, again.

'And what about Olivia Cross?'

'I went to see her.'

He can see Freya's surprised. 'And?'

'Neither confirmed nor denied. Jury's still out. It's probably not mine.'

'And if it is?'

'Christ, Freya. What's with the inquisition?' She shrugs and he feels bad for snapping. 'I don't know,' he replies, quieter this time. 'I'll deal with that problem when it comes to it. And yes, I know,' he adds quickly. 'She's due any day.'

Their conversation dissolves into silence, and Robin's glad when their food arrives. They dig in ravenously, Robin covering his burger with a generous dousing of ketchup. Quiet music plays in the pub; people start to arrive as the weekend comes to a close.

'You want to hear something funny?' Freya says, through a mouthful of battered cod.

'Please. Yes.'

'Josh asked me out.'

Robin's head snaps up. 'Josh who? Not Josh Smith?'

Freya nods, mouth full.

'And?'

She swallows. 'By text. I haven't replied.'

'What? You left him hanging?' Robin laughs. 'Savage. What are you going to say?'

'I don't know. I mean, I can't stay like this forever. Jonathan's dead. I have to move on.'

'Move on when you're ready, Freya,' Robin says softly.

'I know.' She takes a bite of a chip. 'But he is fit.'

'Sure. If you like your men tall and boring.'

'With piercing blue eyes.'

Robin turns his gaze skywards. 'Jeez. Just shag him already!' he exclaims, and Freya laughs.

They finish eating in silence. Robin considers Freya's news. So, she might go out with Josh Smith. The thought of this makes him uneasy. But why? He feels unsteady, caught off balance.

But before he can analyse this further, he hears his name bellowed across the pub.

'Robin Matthew Butler!'

The room hushes. Robin recognises the tone. Harsh, angry. Heard far too many times throughout his teenage years. His body recoils with familiar shame.

He turns slowly. Josie is standing in the middle of the pub, hands on hips, face like thunder. Sandra is behind her.

'Robin Butler,' Josie repeats. 'What the hell have you been doing?'

40

Robin feels like he's twelve again. Except this is much worse. There are no chores as punishment, no withdrawal of the television or permission to go to football. Only Josie and Sandra's furious stares, and a pointed finger directing both of them out of the pub. Robin and Freya get up, leaving half-finished drinks.

Out in the car park, Josie lets loose.

'What are you doing, Robin? Going to the library, digging around in things that don't concern you?' Robin stays mute in the face of Josie's fury. 'Ann called me. Ann French?' Robin glances to Freya as if to say, *I told you so.* 'She says you're digging into Jacob Fraser's death. When I said not to! Why would you do that, Robin?'

'I thought it would help Finn,' he tries meekly.

'I *told* you to stay out of it. Why didn't you listen to me? And Sandra says you've been in my house!'

He opens his mouth and closes it again. He looks at the disappointed faces of the two women who thought of him as family. Nothing is going to make this better.

'We're not going to tell anyone,' Freya says next to him. 'That Finn was depressed.'

Josie turns to Freya. 'Bloody right, you're not. It all happened when Finn was a kid. It doesn't matter.'

Robin doesn't like them taking out their anger on her. 'So why is Finn saying what happened to Jacob was his fault?' he directs back at them.

'Because he's ill, Robin! He's sick,' Josie covers her face with her hands, and Sandra puts a protective arm round her.

'It was nothing to do with you, Robin,' Sandra says, as she encourages Josie away. 'Go home. Leave it be.'

He watches them walk slowly to their car, heads bent, Josie's shoulders shaking with emotion.

'Shit,' Robin mutters.

Things couldn't be worse.

41

They drive to the Premier Inn in complete silence. Freya glances Robin's way a few times as they go – his face is hardened, his jaw tight. She can only imagine what he's thinking, and it can't be good.

They park up and walk in through the main doors. In the lift, Freya can't stay quiet any longer.

'Are you okay?'

Robin's head drops. He looks like a chastised schoolboy, cowed and miserable.

'We'll leave first thing,' he replies. The lift tings and the doors open. 'Be ready for nine a.m.'

He walks out ahead of her, towards their rooms, but then outside his door he pauses. Staring at the key in his hand, he says, 'I'm sorry, Freya. This wasn't what you needed.'

Without waiting for a response, he puts the card in his door and goes in.

She watches it close behind him, still standing in the corridor. She's not sure what to do. This mess, it was absolutely Robin's fault, but if it had been her, she wouldn't have acted any differently. Something happened with Finn when he was a teenager, whether it was linked to Sharp's murder or not.

Freya wants to say something to Robin, to make him feel better, but she doesn't know what that is. And he's made it clear that tonight he doesn't want her company.

She takes the key out of her pocket and goes into her room. The two glasses of wine from the pub swill in her system and she boils the kettle, making a cup of tea. Even though it's only just past eight o'clock, she gets changed into her pyjamas – a T-shirt and pair of shorts – and sits under the duvet, propping herself up on her pillow. She picks up the TV remote, but for a moment stops and listens. Last night she could hear Robin next door – the noise from the TV, a plug being pushed into a socket – but tonight there's nothing.

She sighs and puts the television on, selecting a film she's watched a hundred times before.

As she drinks her tea, she flicks through her phone, one eye on the TV. She looks at Instagram. She has a new notification: *joshsmudge started following you*, it says. She clicks on it and Josh's profile loads, his face smiling out from the grid of photos. Some of him with his mates, a few sunsets. Nothing related to work, same with any copper. *Follow back*, the big button entices her, and she clicks it.

Why hasn't she replied to his text? The simple answer is that she doesn't know what to say. She looks at his photos. She enjoyed his company on Wednesday night. It was fun, uncomplicated. Easy. All the things she needs at the moment. But the idea of going on a date with someone – someone who isn't Jonathan – seems alien and strange. So she leaves it unanswered, although she knows that when she goes back to work, it will be the elephant in the room.

The film is predictable, and she debates flicking channels when there's a knock on the door. Barely perceptible, but there. She mutes the television and listens. She hears it again.

She gets up and opens the door.

It's Robin. And he has a big cardboard box in his hand.

Without asking permission, he walks past her into the room and plonks it on the bed. She stares at him, feeling awkward in her pyjamaed state, with no bra and bare legs. Like her, he's got changed — tracksuit bottoms, T-shirt, bare feet — but he doesn't seem to register the inappropriateness of their attire.

'I found this,' he announces, pointing to the box. 'I went to my storage locker this morning. These are our old photo albums.'

'Okay...'

'Some baby shots, you know. The usual stuff. But I found this.'

He holds out a blue leather-bound album.

'From 1992.'

Robin perches on the edge of her bed and opens the album as Freya sits beside him. The only light in the room comes from the lamp by her bedside and the television, a flickering glow on their faces. Actors talk to each other on the screen, mute but persistent.

'Look, here...' He points to one photo. She leans closer to see what he's indicating.

It's an old photo, showing boys in green jumpers, and Freya recognises the Scout uniform.

'See, there's me,' Robin says, pointing to a small figure on one side. 'In Owl Patrol.'

'Okay...'

'There's Jacob Fraser. And there's Finn.' He points again. 'They were in the same patrol. He did know him. They would have done everything together at that Scout camp. Slept in the same tent. Eaten at the same table. And here—' He holds out the school report from earlier. 'I borrowed this, had a read. All the teachers say that Finn was quiet that first term. More withdrawn than usual.'

Freya looks from the photo back to Robin. 'So?' she asks, slowly. 'This fits with what we said before, that he was depressed. Why does it matter?'

'Because Josie lied! I know what Finn was like, as a teenager,' Robin says. 'He so wanted to be liked. I didn't care what the other kids said about me, but Finn? He was desperate to fit in.' He looks at her, his face dark. 'What if... what if he was feeling like that again? With Simon Sharp.'

Freya stares at him. 'So, what?' she says, quietly. 'Finn killed him out of jealousy?' She pauses. 'But this only adds weight to Craig's case.'

Robin sits up, running his hands down his face. 'Oh, fuck, I know. But what happened in that van, Freya? Who else could have killed Simon?'

'I don't know,' Freya replies, exasperated. They're just going round in circles. She sighs. 'Do you want tea?' she asks after a pause.

He nods, quieter now, detecting her tone. 'Yeah, please,' he replies.

She gets up, again aware of how she's dressed. To put clothes on feels like she would only be drawing attention to the fact, but before she decides what to do, it seems he notices.

'Shit, Freya. I'm sorry.' His cheeks flush slightly, and his gaze averts decisively to the floor. 'This is so wrong. I shouldn't have knocked on your door.'

But his awkwardness only amuses her now. She grabs a hoodie from her chair and puts it on. 'It's fine,' she laughs. 'What's a late-night hotel visit between friends?'

He smiles. 'Fuck, still.'

She puts the kettle on, and his gaze turns to the television screen.

'I used to watch this film when I was little,' Robin comments.

'Me too.' Freya sits next to him, perched on the edge of the bed. 'Listen,' she says. 'Whatever happened when Finn was fourteen doesn't matter. Depressed or not, Finn did not murder Simon Sharp. You know that.' She smiles and he looks at her for a second. 'There's nothing more you can do. Leave this alone. And leave Finn's case to Craig's team.'

He doesn't answer, so deep in thought, and Freya wonders if he's even listening.

'Robin? Please? Leave it be.'

At last, he nods. She makes the tea, takes the school report out of his hands and swaps it for the mug. She puts the album back in the box, then takes her own tea and sits cross-legged on the bed.

She flicks the sound back on on the television, and both sets of eyes go to the screen. The film has moved on, but she knows the story from repeated viewings, almost able to repeat the lines back to herself.

She scoots back in the bed, leaning up against the headboard. After a moment, he does the same. They watch the film, and the clock ticks round. They share a joke, reminisce about a particular scene, but never touch, never make eye contact.

And when the credits roll and she reaches over to turn the TV off, she notices he's fallen asleep, slumped where he's sat. She can barely hear him breathing, but his eyes are closed, his face relaxed. He's dozed off maybe half a dozen times on her sofa, but here, on a bed, it feels strange.

He moves slightly in his sleep. She debates waking him – she should, she knows – then decides against it. It's kind of nice with him there. She's missed the company; the feeling of a body next to her as long dark nights close in. She knows Robin is the wrong person, but any ship in a storm, she thinks, as she gently climbs under the duvet.

Robin's still lying on top of the covers, his weight strange next to her. Then, as tiredness overtakes any awkwardness, she falls asleep next to him.

–

When she wakes, light is trickling in through the gaps in the curtains. For a moment she wonders where she is, then remembers and looks at Robin. He's rolled over in the night and is now on his front, his face mashed into the pillow. His features are relaxed. His cheeks have a malleable look to them, his mouth open slightly.

It's a face she's come to know well over the last nine months, but never in such an intimate way. His face has a worn quality to it, crinkles around his eyes, frown lines between, even when he's asleep. He looks better with a bit of stubble, she thinks. Wonky ears, bump in the middle of his nose, not obviously attractive in the same way that Josh is, but handsome, yes. He stirs and she looks away quickly.

She picks up her phone: it's early, only just five a.m. She's still tired, but desperate for the toilet.

She sits up, trying not to disturb him, and swings her legs out of the bed. She walks quietly to the bathroom.

But as she goes to close the door, she can't help one last look back. His feet are bare, the soft underside visible. And before she knows what she is doing, she gently runs her finger down it.

He flinches, and she takes an intake of breath, jumping away and into the bathroom.

But that tiny bit of soft skin. She couldn't resist.

Part 3

42

Monday

Robin wakes with a jolt, then sits up slowly, scratching the underside of his foot. He looks around. It's not his room, and he realises with a flash of embarrassment that he's in Freya's bed. Quickly, before she comes out of the bathroom, he grabs the box of photo albums and scurries back next door.

Even though it's far too early, he can't get back to sleep. After about an hour, he gives up and makes himself a coffee. BBC *Breakfast* has started and he watches, eyes half-open, liking the distraction of the usual depressing news. Government ineffective, businesses incompetent. Death, destruction, murder. So, it's not just him then.

Josie's disapproval is seared into his mind. He wishes he could do something to put it right, but he knows things have gone way past that. And still, the undesirable fact is that he wants to know what happened. Why would Finn say that anything to do with Jacob was his fault if it isn't true? Is Josie protecting Finn? And what does it have to do with Simon bloody Sharp?

He rubs his eyes, gets up and makes another coffee, then has a shower. When he's dressed, he sends a quick text to Freya – *Are you up?* – but gets no response. He puts his shoes on and leaves the hotel.

The massive Tesco across the road is open, and he wastes half an hour buying random food for breakfast, plus two coffees from the shop next door. Then, back at the Premier Inn, he knocks on her door.

She answers, up and dressed, and takes the coffee eagerly.

'I'm sorry for falling asleep in your room,' Robin gabbles immediately. He offers the plastic tray of pink-sprinkled doughnuts as an apology.

'You're forgiven,' she smiles, selecting one. 'Although I'm starting to take it personally. Is my company really that dull?'

She perches on the edge of the bed, eating the doughnut delicately, holding it between two fingers. He sits on the chair, doing the same, but with less success.

'I promise, it's nothing to do with you,' he replies.

But actually, it is.

When he's with Freya, he relaxes. There is none of his usual worry: the social awkwardness he has around others. She's seen him at his worst, all pretence gone – so his unconscious lets him sleep. He realises with a start that she's probably the only person, apart from Liam, with whom he feels this way.

She finishes the doughnut, then sips her coffee. He notices that her case is already packed; next door, his is the same. He offers her another doughnut.

She shakes her head. 'Let's keep them for the journey,' she replies.

–

This time, the 120-mile drive from Devon to Hampshire is quiet. Robin is more solemn; the holiday feeling has gone.

Going home hasn't been nearly as bad as he imagined – confrontation with Josie aside – and he resolves anew to return and sort that dratted storage unit out. The box of photo albums lurks in the boot.

They pass Exeter Services and hit the A35 without event. Freya looks out of the window, softly singing to a song on Radio 2 that Robin's never heard before.

'Freya?' Robin says, and she turns. 'This wasn't exactly the break you were after, was it?' She looks at him blankly. 'I mean,' he continues, 'you needed some time off, and all I did was drag you into more bloody police work.'

She smiles. 'It's fine. It didn't feel like work. I feel better.' He looks at her doubtfully. 'I do, I promise! Not, you know, one hundred per cent, but it was a break. Time away from the station, from everything that reminds me of Jon. I will go and see the doctor,' she adds, quieter now. 'But being away with you, having dinner with Sandra and…' She pauses for a moment. 'It felt good. That's all. I'm just sorry it didn't end as you wanted it to.'

'I'm not sure how I wanted it to end,' Robin says. 'I wanted to help Finn. And look how that turned out.'

His phone interrupts them, ringing loudly over the speaker. Robin answers it and DCI Neal Baker's voice booms around the car.

'Butler, where are you? Are you headed back?'

Using his surname can only mean it's police business. Robin answers accordingly. 'Yes, guv. We're on our way now.'

'We? You and West? Good. Come straight to the station. West can continue the freezer investigation with Smith. You come to my office.'

'What's it concerning, boss?' Robin asks, feeling the drag of bad news.

'Just come here straight away, you hear me?'

'Message received, guv. ETA about an hour and a half.'

Baker hangs up and Robin glances to Freya. 'That can't be good,' he says.

And for the first time, he wishes for roadworks on the A31. Anything to hold off the feeling of impending doom.

43

Despite the fact that Robin's been in the car for three hours straight, he does exactly as he's told and heads directly to Baker's office.

DCI Neal Baker is sat at his desk, a grim expression on his face. He points to the chair in front of him and Robin sits down.

'So,' he begins. 'DI Craig's been in touch.'

'And?' Robin almost holds his breath. But what news is he hoping for? Finn's either been assessed fit to interview and has been charged with Sharp's murder or he's still desperately sick in hospital. Turns out it's neither.

'She wants you to leave her alone.'

Robin sits back in the chair with a frustrated sigh. 'I've been away all weekend. What more does she want?'

'She wants to get on with her job, Robin. And she's fed up with you questioning her every move.'

'I haven't been—'

'You have. And you know it.' Baker's tone is softer this time. 'Listen, to appease me she sent across the file and I had a good read last night. Everything tallies. The PM results, the blood spatter from the scene, the testimony from the camera crew and the lab. If it were me investigating, I'd have come to the same conclusion.'

'Is the camera footage still missing?' Robin asks.

'Yes – and that's a problem. And the fingerprint analysis from the knife is contradictory.' Robin goes to say something but Baker stops him. 'Even without that, Rob, there's a whole load of evidence that says he did it. Look, here.' He pulls the file out from underneath another on his desk. 'Read it. And you'll see it doesn't look good.'

He holds it out; Robin takes it.

'I'll give you one more day, Robin. Then you'll either be off on compassionate leave, supporting the family, or I expect you back at work. You can take over this freezer death from Smith, because he's getting bloody nowhere.'

'Thanks, guv,' Robin says, and leaves.

The door closes. Around Robin, the police station is busy with its usual bustle. He envies the coppers, with their enthusiasm and purpose. He looks at the file in his hand. It's bulky, which is always a bad sign.

He sighs. Baker's right, Craig's right – even Josie's right. He needs to leave it alone. But first, he thinks, I'll make sure. And he heads home to have a read.

44

Josh does a double-take when she walks into the incident room, then blushes in a way that Freya finds pleasing.

Mina throws her hands in the air and exclaims, 'Thank god you're back. I can't deal with Captain America by myself any longer.'

Freya laughs and sinks down into the chair next to them. 'Been having fun then?'

'She's exaggerating,' Josh protests. 'I'm not that bad.'

Mina gives him the side-eye. 'It's a good job he's pretty.' Josh blushes again. 'So how was your trip?' she asks.

'Fine.' Freya changes the subject. 'Do you want coffee?'

Mina holds her mug out eagerly and Freya makes her way to the kitchen. She notices Josh trailing behind, then glances back as they both go inside.

'Listen, Freya,' he begins, hesitantly. 'I'm sorry about that text. I shouldn't have asked you out. It was a spontaneous thing, and I sent it and then you didn't reply and then I realised how bloody inappropriate it was.' Freya lets him talk, and he gabbles on, staring at his empty mug. 'I'm your sergeant—'

'Temporarily,' Freya interrupts.

'Yeah, but still. I shouldn't have put you in that position. I realise now you wanted to say no and you didn't know how, and...' He trails off, then manages to meet her eyes for a second.

Freya smiles. 'It was fine. It wasn't that at all.'

'It wasn't?'

'No.' Freya takes his mug out of his hand and washes it with the other two in the sink. She's playing for time, debating whether to tell him. She can feel Josh's eyes on the back of her neck.

'I'd like to go out with you—' she starts.

'You would?'

She turns for a second, smiling at the big grin on his face. And she realises that now she's said it that she would. Very much. 'Yes. But it's complicated.' She spoons instant coffee into their mugs. 'I was involved with this guy, a while back. It ended badly.'

'I know all about bad break-ups…' Josh starts, but she cuts him off.

'He died.'

'Oh.' Josh's face falls. 'I'm sorry.'

Freya dismisses his comment with a shrug, then pours the boiling water into the mugs. She points to the fridge that Josh's standing awkwardly in front of. 'Milk?'

'Right, yes.' He hands it to her and she pours it in.

'I just need a bit more time.' She stirs the coffees, then throws the spoon into the sink. She passes him his mug. 'If that's okay?'

'Yes. Of course.'

They walk back to Mina, who's watching them with curiosity. Freya avoids her unsaid question quickly: 'Made any progress on our freezer man?' she asks. 'Duncan Thorpe?'

'Christ, if only,' Mina says. 'Every lead comes to a dead end. The guys who dumped the freezer have an alibi around time of death—'

'And bugger-all motive,' adds Josh.

'Bottles and fag butts in the bus shelter have four different DNA profiles and a variety of fingerprints, but no hits on the system. Although some do match the prints found on the freezer. Plus, the lab found fibres on the vic that don't match his clothes.'

Freya raises an eyebrow. 'Our trio of troublemakers?'

'Maybe,' Josh agrees. 'But not enough grounds for a warrant to confirm. CCTV is a complete loss – nobody was out in the storm.'

'And there is no dashcam footage, no cashpoint cameras, no witnesses, no trace round the freezer or foot-wear marks.' Mina leans back in her chair. 'If you want to kill someone, it seems the middle of a storm is the best time.'

'Are we even sure he was killed?' Freya asks.

They shrug in unison. 'Official COD is suffocation,' Josh says.

Mina looks pointedly towards Josh. 'Tell her,' she pushes. Then she looks at Freya. 'Josh has a theory.'

'It's stupid.'

'So share,' Freya says.

'And we have no way to prove it.'

'Why not?'

'The only way we can is to get hold of the freezer and replicate the conditions. And the lab said no.'

Freya looks from Mina to Josh and back again. 'Would the same type of freezer work?'

Josh looks at her, interested.

'Because,' Freya continues, 'I have that exact one in my house.'

45

It's not good, and Robin knows it; DI Jo Craig's investigation into the murder of Dr Simon Sharp is solid. He's been sitting at his kitchen table for two hours now, reviewing her file, paper and documents laid out in front of him.

Interview transcripts, crime scene photos, the full report from the post-mortem – it's all here. The PM concludes cause of death was exsanguination from the knife wound on his neck. The blood spatter in the van tallies. The interview with the cameraman talks about the argument – even Finn's own PhD student Ian Calloway agrees that the relationship between the two of them was strained. Finn's hard drive contains a paper written by Sharp, taking full credit for the radar they were testing that night. And Finn himself was a mess. Not looking after himself, drinking more than should be humanly possible. Even experimenting with LSD, although there was none in his blood that day.

But despite all this, Robin still can't believe that Finn would resort to murder. Even if they had argued, even if he was drunk – to take a knife and slit someone's throat? It's ridiculous.

He looks at the photos of the crime scene again. He remembers it from that day, and from the subsequent visit with Craig. Blood everywhere. Mess and papers strewn around. A few plates lying discarded on the side. A window, shut, with a line of blood across it.

He flicks through the reports in front of him and picks up the lab results on the knife. Blood from Simon Sharp, as would have been expected. But the next finding wasn't so clear. The only fingerprints found on the knife came from Sharp.

He squints at the photos, showing the location of the prints. One on the handle, and a thumbprint on the blade. But nothing from Finn. That doesn't make sense, surely? As Baker said, it's contradictory to the arrest. How could Finn have killed him without putting a single print on the knife?

Robin pushes the photos to one side and picks up a memory stick, sent along with the file. He puts it into the side of his laptop and it whirs for a moment, loading.

The memory stick contains three videos, and Robin clicks on the first. It's footage, professionally filmed, from outside the van. Finn is standing next to Simon Sharp, looking nervous next to the confident Sharp, watching him intently as he talks. Simon's doing an introduction to the programme, talking about what they're there to do and the storm they're expecting that night. He's clear and charismatic, everything Robin has come to expect from watching the previous episodes of his show. Robin feels a pang of sadness for the man. For the potential he had, before it was wiped out.

Sharp introduces Finn, who then talks for a moment about the equipment they're testing. Once he's on a subject he knows, Finn's manner changes. He looks directly into the camera, his face alive, his voice full of enthusiasm. They cut, and the video ends. The time: 21:46.

He moves on to the next, and it's dull. Robin can see it's footage from the outside of the van during the storm. He glances down at the report that DC Grey put together describing the video, listing the events seen on screen. Everything ties up with the reports from that night. The rain begins. At 00:32 Justin White leaves, then the wind intensifies and the storm escalates. It's chaos out there; Robin can see the weather conditions that Justin had described in his interview: the wind, flashes of lightning, furious rain, all beating down on the car park. It's bedlam. The weather subsides, gently, steadily. Then nothing happens until 03:38 when Justin White returns and calls the police.

So far, so expected.

But the last video makes a lump catch in Robin's throat.

It's a more informal film, recorded on a handheld camera. It's just Finn and Sharp in the van, sat by the table, the night dark, the storm beginning. Sharp is smiling, holding a large bottle of champagne. The camera is placed down next to them and Finn comes into shot, holding out a mug to be filled by Sharp. The two put their arms round each other and smile into the camera, chinking their mugs together in celebration. This is the Finn that Robin knew. Enjoying the moment, the pinnacle of his professional career. And these two are happy. There is no animosity between them, no reluctance. On this video, they look like good friends.

Robin looks at the timestamp: 01:05. Just before the eye of the storm hit. He shakes his head. So in the two hours after this video was taken, Sharp was killed.

He glances at the time – it's way past visiting hours at the hospital now, and Robin feels the guilt. He knows he should have gone there to check on Finn, but he was avoiding Josie. He needs to apologise, but he hasn't yet mustered the energy. And he can't take another show-down. Or at the very least, her disappointed silence.

He shuts the laptop lid angrily, and as he does so, he hears a knock on the door. He gets up and answers it, smiling when he sees his brother-in-law.

Liam sighs when he sees him. 'Why don't you answer your bloody phone, Robin?'

'Sorry, I've been busy. But if I'd known you'd come round looking like this...'

Robin moves out of the way, as Liam pushes past him into the hallway, dragging a large racing bike behind him. He's head-to-toe in bright orange Lycra, a bike helmet on his head. Liam's walking oddly, and once the bike is leaning against the wall, he sits down at the bottom of the stairs to take off his cleats.

'You're not allowed to take the piss,' Liam replies, taking a swig of water from the bottle attached to his bike. 'I wouldn't have to come out here if you just spoke to me once in a while.'

'Don't you have a car?' Robin tilts his head to one side and appraises his brother-in-law with a wince. 'Christ, Liam, I can see what you had for breakfast.'

'Piss off. Now fetch me a towel, before I freeze to death.'

Robin does as he's told and goes upstairs to his bath-room. When he comes back downstairs again, Liam's sitting at his kitchen table, looking at a crime scene photo with interest. Robin throws the towel to him and Liam wipes the sweat off his face.

'Is this what you've been working on?' he asks.

'Yeah. Although not work, as such.' Robin explains the case as best he can, talking about Finn and all the evidence against him.

'I'm sorry, mate,' Liam replies. 'But it looks like you've done everything you can for your friend.'

'I know,' Robin replies, grimly.

'And how was Devon?'

'Unchanged.'

'You should have said, I would have come, too. It must have been hard to go there alone.'

'Freya came with me.'

'Oh, okay.' There's a long pause, and Robin feels Liam looking at him.

'Nothing like that,' he replies.

'No? Oh, okay. I guess, I just hoped...'

Robin smiles. 'You did, did you?'

'Christ, I'm turning into Georgia.' Liam takes a long breath in, then leans back on Robin's chair. 'All she ever did was worry about you. "Do you think Robin's okay? Do you think that new girlfriend is right for him? Do you think we should invite him round for dinner?" It used to drive me mad, Rob.' He laughs. 'And now I'm doing it.'

Robin returns Liam's smile. 'I'm fine. Honestly. And I promise there's nothing going on between Freya and I.'

'You can hardly blame me for thinking there is. She's the only person you talk about.'

'That's not true,' Robin responds automatically, but then he realises Liam's probably right. Who else does he see every day?

But Liam's gone quiet. He's staring at the tabletop, his face downcast, his eyebrows knitted together.

'Are you okay, Liam?' Robin asks.

'Yeah... Look, I need to talk to you.'

Robin senses the mood change. The familiar sinking sensation in his stomach grows. Whatever Liam has to say, Robin knows it's not good.

'Go on,' he says cautiously.

'I wanted to tell you first. Before you found out any other way.'

'Okay...'

'It's just...' Liam takes a long breath in. 'I've been seeing someone,' he says quickly. 'And it's not serious. But I think it could be. And I didn't want you to think... or... I don't know. But I wanted to tell you.'

Robin is surprised. But not shocked. And his overwhelming feeling is joy: he's pleased for Liam.

He leans forward across the table towards his brother-in-law. 'Mate, it's been nearly six years since Georgia and the twins died,' he says softly. 'You deserve some happiness.'

'It's not about replacing them. Nobody could ever take their place.' Liam's still staring miserably at his hands. 'I wasn't even looking. But she's in my cycling club, she does triathlons and she's... I don't know.' He looks up and meets Robin's gaze. 'She's nice. I like her.'

Robin thinks about Steph. These women and their triathlons. Then he has a sudden worry. 'What's her name?'

Liam frowns a little, his eyes sharp. 'Lizzie. Why?'

'No reason,' Robin replies with relief. 'Listen, Liam. I knew you were going to meet someone one day. And I'm glad you guys have so much in common. Because if she still likes you after seeing you in this get-up, then, well...' Robin smiles.

'Piss off,' Liam says again, and the awkwardness is gone. 'You sure you don't mind?'

'Not at all. But thank you for telling me. Do you want to stay for dinner?'

'No, no, I should go. Need to finish this ride before it gets dark.' Liam wipes his face again with the towel, then folds it into careful quarters. He stands up and Robin follows him.

He opens the front door, as Liam puts his shoes on and wheels the bike back into the street. 'Oh, shit!' Robin says, catching a glimpse of his car. 'I still have Freya's suitcase in the boot.'

Liam fastens his helmet with a loud click. 'Better go and drop that off to her then.'

'Nah, she can do without it until tomorrow.'

'Sure?' Liam raises his eyebrows then gets on his bike. 'Perhaps she can help you with some closure on your case.'

Robin watches as Liam cycles off down the road, his lean figure streamlined and elegant on his bike. He tries to imagine his own stocky build in Lycra, and fails. No, cycling is definitely not for him.

He looks back into his house, at the case file strewn on the table. Then, without further thought, he grabs his keys and phone, and heads off to Freya's.

46

There are more cars than usual outside Freya's house, as Robin pulls in: her pastel-blue Fiat 500 and two others. He sees a light on, and hears voices and laughter, as he rings the doorbell.

Freya answers with a smile and a quick thank you, then heads straight back inside. Robin follows her, plonking her suitcase down in the hallway and walking through to the kitchen.

All the lights are on, and Josh Smith is there. Robin watches them. They're standing in front of her chest freezer. The lid is open, and the appliance is humming loudly, desperately trying to keep cold.

'What's going on?' he asks, and they turn. Josh looks sheepish.

He nods a greeting. 'Sarge,' he says, despite the fact they're off duty. 'It was her idea,' he adds quickly.

'I don't want to know,' Robin replies. Freya and Josh start playing rock-paper-scissors, and Robin watches them curiously as he flips the kettle on, before going into the living room. Mina is sitting on the sofa, silent, a mug of tea in her hand. Robin slumps down next to her, then gives her an awkward sideways hug.

'It's been too long, Mina,' Robin says. 'Surprised to see you here, though.'

'Don't consider me part of their hare-brained scheme,' Mina replies, going back to slowly sipping her tea. 'I'm just here for the peace and quiet, and to pretend my sergeant's keeping me late at work.'

Robin nods. 'Fair enough.' There's an explosion of laughter from the kitchen. 'What *are* they doing?'

'Josh has a theory that the man got into the freezer alone, without help. Freya's trying to prove it's not possible.'

'Josh thinks it's an accident? Interesting,' Robin says, almost to himself. He smiles at another burst of laughter from Freya. He's enjoying hearing it, wondering how long it's been since he's heard her laugh like that. 'Has she been okay this afternoon?' he asks quietly.

'Freya?' Mina looks towards the kitchen. 'She was quieter than usual last week and got upset at something on Friday. She seems more herself since the weekend.' Mina stares at Robin. 'Anything we should know?'

'It's not like that, Mina.' Why is everyone so convinced that he and Freya are together? Robin thinks. First Liam, now Mina.

'No?'

'No, never.'

Mina nods, seemingly satisfied with his denial.

'But keep an eye on her, will you?' Robin continues. 'She doesn't tell me everything. It would be good to know someone else is looking out for her.'

'Always,' Mina replies.

The two of them sit in silence for a moment, listening to the chatter in the other room.

'Mina,' Robin starts. 'Do you mind if I ask you a personal question?'

Mina turns towards him, an interested look on her face. 'Fire away.'

'Do you like being a mum?'

Mina raises an eyebrow but pauses, giving his question due consideration. 'Some days, no. When the little sods won't sleep, when you spend hours preparing a dinner they refuse to eat. When they turn every nice, civilised social occasion into absolute chaos.' She smiles thoughtfully. 'But when they nestle their heads into your chest or put a chubby warm hand in yours. When they're actually quiet and asleep. When you see them change, and grow into their own little personalities. Then yes. Those are the moments that are worth it.' She looks at Robin with curiosity. 'Why?'

'Just... just think maybe I've reached that age,' he replies.

She gives a sharp bark of laughter. 'Let's not kid ourselves, Butler. You're way past that age. How old are you now?'

'Forty-three next month.'

Mina finishes the last swig of her tea. 'Good job you're a bloke,' she says to her mug.

Noise starts up again in the kitchen: Josh talking quickly, Freya giggling.

'What are they up to?' Mina says, getting to her feet. She grabs Robin's hand and pulls him off the sofa. The two of them go to the kitchen and stand in the doorway.

Freya is standing next to the freezer, which is now shut.

'Push!' Freya shouts at the closed lid. 'Push harder.'

'Is Josh...' Robin starts, as the lid pops open and Josh stands up, putting his arms out in a triumphant salute. He is wearing clothes that Robin recognises as Freya's — an old T-shirt and tracksuit bottoms, far too small for him — and

Robin bitchily enjoys the normally pristine Josh looking such a state.

'See,' Josh crows. 'It is possible. And it's way harder to get out of there than I thought it would be.'

'So, what?' Robin asks, looking from them to the freezer. 'Your theory is he got in that freezer by himself, then couldn't get out and suffocated?'

'Yes, why not?' Josh replies. 'He would have been looking for somewhere dry, and with those teenagers in the bus shelter, he had nowhere else to go.'

'But an old freezer?' Robin looks doubtful, and Freya points at him.

'See? I'm not the only one who thinks your theory is bullshit.'

'It was blowing a full-on gale. He's cold, wet. Probably not thinking straight. How do you know what you'd do in such circumstances?'

Robin raises his hands in defeat. 'Okay, okay. You have a point. But it's a theory, Josh, that's all. How do you prove it?'

The three of them look towards Robin, and he realises how effortless it is for him to take charge. 'Sorry,' he mutters. 'Your case, Josh. Whatever you think.'

Josh nods and stands up a bit straighter. 'I'll go and get changed,' he says, and heads off.

Robin watches him go. Despite his initial misgivings, Josh Smith doesn't seem like a bad bloke. Sure, he has an air of arrogance and confidence that Robin is suspicious of, but Freya seems to like him. She's still laughing with Mina, returning her slowly thawing food back to her freezer, putting her kitchen to rights. She has a slight flush on her cheeks.

Being here, throwing theories around, challenging, testing the DCs, Robin realises how much he misses being at work. Being back to his usual job. A case that doesn't involve his oldest friend. Where he can immerse himself in the evidence and the theories and the team-work. Everything with Finn is exhausting. All the pieces that don't fit. He just wants it to be over.

But he knows that despite Craig's best efforts to prove to him that Finn is guilty, he can't believe it. He picks up a bag of peas and replaces it in the freezer. And Josh's theory comes back to him.

He stands up straight and takes a sharp intake of breath. He pulls his mobile out of his pocket and dials a number, not caring now about keeping his distance.

'Steph?' he says as she answers. 'I need you to look at a body for me. I need a second opinion on Dr Simon Sharp.'

47

Tuesday

Sophie's up early; she knows what she has to do. She stands, nervously, at the door, hand poised to knock. She debated bringing croissants or coffee, but rejected the idea quickly. She doesn't want to be too obvious.

She knocks loudly, twice. She feels her stomach knot and forces a smile on her face.

A man opens the door and blinks at her, confused.

'Sophie?' he says. 'What are you doing here?'

'Oh, I'm so pleased you're in, Col,' she says, deliberately shortening his name. She knew he would be there. It's Tuesday, nine a.m. Colin is a man with a strict routine. 'I need your help.'

He flushes slightly and shows her into the room. It's crowded, with rows of computers, piles of monitors and keyboards in cardboard boxes, wires trailing. Other faces pop up from behind their computers, meerkats curious at the strange arrival to their territory. The smell is a mix of Lynx body spray and barely suppressed BO.

Colin points to the seat next to his desk. She sits down and looks at the monitor. On the screen are rows and rows of incomprehensible code.

'What can I do for you?'

'So,' she begins. 'One of the students I'm supervising on the BSc has managed to delete a file.' Sophie smiles, a hand on his arm. Flirting gently. 'An important one.'

Colin nods sagely. 'Do you want me to recover the file?'

'Can you do that?'

'Maybe.' He shrugs. 'If the backup's still there.'

'Oh, that would be incredible, thank you,' Sophie gushes.

Colin blushes again. 'What server are we looking at?'

'BBC-READ-VID-DR07,' Sophie says, carefully spelling out the name of the BBC server from the piece of paper that Justin White showed her on Sunday.

Colin nods and turns to his computer. She waits as he starts work, staring intently at the screen as he types. Lego R2-D2 and C-3PO figures stand guard, Blu-Tacked to the top of his monitor.

Sophie knows Colin from freshers' week; they were in halls together all those years ago. She'd liked him instantly. He was studious but fun, with a fondness for Star Wars and flaming sambucas. She'd bumped into him again in the first year of her PhD and discovered that he was back at Reading, now in the IT department. And a man who knows computers is always useful. Laptops fail, files are lost, operating systems crash.

And videos are deleted.

'So,' Colin says, not shifting his gaze from the screen. 'You're in luck. I can log on remotely, so we don't need to go to the server room.'

A row of windows and file names appears on the screen.

'What are we looking for?' he asks.

Sophie frowns. 'Start with any video files recorded last Tuesday night.'

Colin turns, his hand paused on the mouse. 'The night of the storm?' he asks slowly.

Sophie nods.

It's clear Colin has realised she's lying. There's a long pause. Everything is completely silent, bar the tap of keyboards. And then: 'Did you know,' he says, quietly, his eyes back on his screen, 'that Lego released a special edition Snowspeeder in 2019, to coincide with the twentieth anniversary of Lego Star Wars?'

'Did they?' Sophie replies, innocently.

'Hmm. And it's a retired product. So you can't get it from shops. But I found one on eBay. New and sealed in its box. One of a kind.' He lifts his eyes for a second, meeting Sophie's gaze. 'Would you like to see it?'

Sophie suppresses a smile. 'Sure,' she replies. 'Send me the link.'

He nods, picks up his phone and taps quickly. Then goes back to his computer.

Sophie's phone beeps. She opens it up. Seventy-six bloody quid. For a Lego set. But it's worth it. For Finn.

Colin's still moving between windows, typing commands into the search function.

'The police were in,' he says, under his breath. 'Spoke to Jimmy.' He points to the office on the far side. 'My boss.'

Sophie pauses. 'And?'

'He couldn't find the video files. Whoever got in before us did a good job. Backups gone, too.'

Sophie holds out her phone to Colin. 'So why have I just ordered a Battle of Hoth Snowspeeder?' she hisses.

But he smiles. 'For the event log.'

She turns quickly. 'You can see who logged in and when?' He nods. 'And why don't the police have that already?'

'Because Jimmy's a dickhead and didn't give it to them, and the police didn't think to ask.'

He starts typing something incomprehensible to Sophie, his fingers flying over the keys.

'It was the nineteenth last Wednesday, right?' he asks, without looking up.

She cranes forward towards the blue screen and the line of code.

```
Get-EventLog security | Where-Object
{$_.TimeGenerated -gt '05/19/2021'} | Where-Object
{($_.InstanceID -eq 4634) -or ($_.InstanceID -eq
4624)} | Select-Object
Index,TimeGenerated,InstanceID,Message |
Add-Content C:\Downloads.txt
```

He presses return with a flourish. Immediately, the screen fills with data. What looks like numbers, times, dates. Her eyes scroll the list, until she sees what she's looking for.

She looks at the username. And she knows who deleted the file.

48

After Robin disappeared from her house last night with barely a goodbye, and Josh and Mina left, Freya found that, once again, she struggled to sleep. But this time it was the man in the freezer giving her pause.

She doesn't know why Josh's theory bothers her so much. It is plausible. Tragic, yes, but possible, that he climbed in and suffocated. After all, there are laws around dumping freezers for that reason: kids have died in that exact way. But that was children. Was a fully grown man really so weak that he couldn't force his way out?

And the fingerprints on the freezer are an anomaly. Who do they belong to? Connor? The boys? Someone else entirely? She lies back against her pillow in frustration.

As the light starts to trickle in, signalling morning, Freya gives up and goes into work. There is nobody else in the car park, the incident room empty as she sits down at her desk just past seven a.m. She puts her coffee and almond croissant down, boots up her computer, then pulls up the photos of the freezer.

The fingerprints cluster over the top and round the handle. Freya theorises it was the trio of boys: had they been messing around with it and didn't want to own up to the cops? Or had they been involved? And what about Connor Vardy?

There was something about Connor's interview that Freya found odd. The normal level of nerves was there, but there was something else. A shiftiness. A desperation to get away. The fresh bruise on his cheek.

She remembers Robin's words about Finn: *he so wanted to be liked. Desperate to fit in.*

Freya needs to know more. She logs on to the police databases and starts to find out all she can about Connor Vardy.

–

Two hours later, Josh arrives, a tray of coffees in his hand. He's startled to see her there, already so engrossed in her work, and hands her one of the cups. She takes it gratefully. He shrugs his jacket off, then sits down next to her.

'What are you looking at?'

'Background for Connor Vardy,' she replies.

'Anything interesting?'

She's gone through both the RMS and the PNC with a fine-tooth comb, then looked up records for his mother and grandfather. She's called children's services, the National Probation Service. Carried out internet searches. Called on every resource at her disposal. And she lays it all out for Josh.

'So, as a kid, he was on the watch list with children's services, never in school for longer than a few days at a time. His mother was a mess – warnings for shoplifting, drunk and disorderly, the lot.'

'When did she die?' Josh asks.

'2015, and, as you know, Connor went to live with his grandad. And at that point his life turns around. He starts getting good grades. College says he's a good kid, could go far.'

Josh squints at the screen. 'So, what's your point?'

Freya sits back in her seat, clutching her coffee. 'He knows these boys. And I think he has more information than he's letting on about that night. Let's get him in, in a proper interview room.'

'We can't arrest him, we have no grounds,' Josh replies.

'Fine. Voluntarily then. But let's make sure it's recorded, lay it all on thick. Make him sweat.'

'He'll say the same as he did before.'

Freya smiles. 'Let me try? Please?' she begs. 'I have an idea.'

49

Up close, the previously handsome face of Dr Simon Sharp couldn't look worse; six days in cold storage hasn't done him any favours. His skin is grey and peeling, sunken into his cheekbones. His eyes stare glassily at the ceiling.

Steph's influence has worked wonders. The coroner agreed to the second opinion and the body was transferred down that morning. The forensic pathologist herself has just finished undoing the good work of the previous doctor, unpicking the thick stitches holding Sharp's abdomen together.

'It's going to take me a few hours yet,' Steph repeats. 'You should go.'

'I'll wait,' Robin insists.

Her shoulders slump. He knows Steph's not enjoying his company. The last time they were in the same room together was over nine months ago, and she was unceremoniously telling him to get out of her house. Not her fault, he knows.

He takes a seat on the far side of the mortuary and watches her at work. Even fully dressed in her PPE, she cuts an impressive figure – her body full of energy, fit from the triathlons she races at the weekend. They would never have worked as a couple, Robin tells himself. Even with his new-found love of running, she is too good for him.

He hears Steph sigh loudly behind her mask.

'Have you found something?' he asks.

'It's not that.' She pauses again, scalpel in hand, then selects a pair of tweezers from the tray, looking closely at Sharp's neck. 'I hate this awkwardness between us, Rob.'

He looks up quickly.

'There's no reason why we can't be friends,' she continues, almost talking to the corpse. 'And I know it's down to me that we're not, I told you not to call. But this. This is shit.' She pauses and Robin stays silent, unsure of what to say. 'And I miss you,' she finishes quietly.

'I miss you too.'

She looks up, peering at him over her mask. 'Do you?'

He nods. 'I'm so sorry everything ended like that.'

She shrugs in reply and goes back to her consideration of the body. 'Everything here is as I expected. Do you want to see?'

She points to the gown and masks; Robin suits up and stands next to her.

She uses the tweezers to pull back the lacerated skin on his neck, showing the mess underneath. 'See here,' she says, pointing with a gloved finger. 'Tiny nick to his carotid. Would have made a hell of a mess. Wound consistent with the penknife found at the scene.'

'Anything else?'

'I'll keep looking.'

Robin moves away and sits back on his chair.

'How's your friend?' Steph asks.

Robin sighs. He still hasn't been to the hospital to see Finn, although he phoned the ward that morning for an update. 'Very confused. His short-term memory's fucked, and he can't remember what happened. The doctor said he's been coming out with some ridiculous stuff about the storm, almost like he's making up stories to compensate for the parts he can't remember.'

Steph pauses. 'They've done blood tests, right?'

'I think so. He's having trouble walking, although the doctor says it's hard to work out what symptoms are related to the night of the storm and what's from alcohol withdrawal.'

'He was an alcoholic?' Steph repeats.

'Apparently so,' Robin replies. 'I had no idea. Some friend I am.'

Steph turns round to face him, scalpel in hand, when his phone rings. 'Sorry,' he says, and pulls it out to answer it.

He doesn't recognise the number, and when he answers, the voice is hysterical and female.

'Robin, please, I need your help.'

She's breathless and frantic, barely understandable through her panic.

'Who's this?' he asks.

'Please. The baby. It's early. It's coming. I…' There's a long, protracted scream at the other end of the phone.

'Liv? Shit.' Robin jumps to his feet. 'I'm sorry, I have to go,' he shouts at Steph, as he heads out of the mortuary. 'Where are you? Are you at home?'

The screaming stops, and the panting resumes. 'No, the hospital. Labour ward. Please, Robin. I'm scared.'

'I'm on my way.'

Robin doesn't hesitate. He runs into the main body of the hospital, then grabs the arm of the first person in scrubs that he sees.

'The labour ward? Where is it?' he asks.

303

The man smiles indulgently. 'First floor, maternity unit. Florence Portal House. That way,' he points.

Robin sets off at a run.

50

The contractions started in the middle of the night. At first, they were no more than strong period pains, a dull ache in her stomach, but they woke Liv, her heart beating faster in response. She waited, lying there in the dark, and for a while there was nothing. She closed her eyes. Then another came. She glanced at the clock, memorising the time. It was too early. It couldn't be happening. Not now.

But when her waters broke at five a.m., there was no kidding herself any more.

She put in a call to her midwife, calmly telling her what was happening.

'Contractions are ten minutes apart,' she said. The midwife was gentle and reassuring.

'You're a long way off yet, love. Keep walking around, get some food. Call me back when they're every five minutes.'

Liv kept track, diligently monitoring the time. She paced her kitchen, waiting until the next contraction came and she couldn't do anything but stand, leaning against the counter, trying to breathe the way she was told to.

I can do this, she repeated, like a mantra. *I can.* She knows she's been through a lot worse, but this is new. The fear: it's not just for her, but for the tiny boy inside.

She has no birth partner. She'd debated it, in the early days, but who could she have asked? Even if they had been good candidates for the job, her mother and her sister were both dead. She has friends, but nobody she could ask to do *this*. Nobody she would trust by her side.

No. She would do it alone. She'd survived this far. She would do it again.

But the pain was growing. She tried watching some television but she was restless, unable to concentrate. She sat on the sodding gym ball, like someone recommended, but it was no good. Nothing helped. She managed some food, eating toast in small, manageable bites as the wave of the contractions became longer and harder. Her hand hovered close to her phone. Desperate to call her midwife. Wanting to be close to the doctors and nurses who could make sure everything was okay.

Then, when the last cramp caused her to grit her teeth and cry out, she made the call.

'Now,' the midwife confirmed. 'Come in now.'

The taxi driver didn't waste any time. He didn't want this woman giving birth in his cab. He helped her through the double doors, carrying her bag, holding her arm in the corridor as she doubled over, her legs weak.

The midwife took over. Taking her blood pressure, strap round her tummy to monitor the baby's heartbeat. A steady feed to the machine next to her. She lay on the bed, the canister of gas and air reassuring by her side, determined not to use it.

'There's no award for tolerating the pain, love,' her midwife said. But not yet, Liv thought. Not until it gets really bad.

And it did. Worse than she imagined. Floods of agony that rolled down from the top of her belly to the bottom. Clenching her fists, she counted as she tried to breathe, but nothing helped, until she sucked on the gas desperately.

She felt sick; she couldn't eat. She tried walking up and down the room, but her legs felt wobbly. She was forced to lie on the bed. The face of the midwife changed from supportive understanding to concern. Doctors arrived, standing over the heart-rate printout with stern faces. They introduced themselves, explained what was going on, but she couldn't remember what they said. Only that her labour wasn't progressing the way it should. That the baby was stuck.

The midwife came and stood next to her bed. 'Honey,' she said slowly, her voice measured with controlled calm. 'Is there anyone you can call? Anyone?'

Her determination faded. She was tired, dizzy, confused. She wanted someone here. Someone who could take charge. Who could deal with panic, and stress, and hard decisions.

And Liv thought of Robin.

51

Robin explains who he's here for and they hurry him through to her room. Liv's on the bed, on her side, her hair damp, her face contorted in pain. There's a midwife next to her, and he pauses in the doorway for a moment, frozen by the unfamiliarity of the scene.

Liv looks at him through half-closed eyes.

'I'm sorry, Robin. I didn't want... I didn't think...'

He reaches out and takes her hand. It's sweaty and hot. 'It's fine, Liv. Don't worry.' He turns to the midwife next to him. 'What's going on?'

'Liv's in established labour, but we're concerned. Things aren't progressing as they should, and from the ultrasound, we believe the baby's turned and is now in a breech position.'

'Can she give birth like that?' Robin asks.

'It's possible. But he seems to be in distress. If his heart rate drops again, we'll have to go for an emergency C-section. We'd rather take her in now. Manage the situation before anything gets worse.'

Liv turns to him. 'I don't want that. I want to give birth naturally,' she says. But even Robin can see she's weak, barely holding onto the reality of what's happening around her.

'Liv,' Robin says, holding her hand tightly between both of his. 'The main thing is we get that little boy out,

308

and he's healthy and happy. And that you're okay.' He reaches over and moves a strand of sweaty hair out of her eyes. 'You know that, don't you?'

She pauses. Then she nods slowly.

Things happen quickly. A rush of more people in scrubs, paperwork, needles and discussion. A cannula is inserted into Liv's hand. Robin is hurried away to get changed.

Nobody has asked who he is. They must have assumed he's the father – something he doesn't try to correct. He's caught in a tide of people who know what they're doing. Procedures honed to a fine art. Doctors and nurses in a perfect choreography of movement.

He's shown back to Liv's side. She's in an operating theatre now, blue drapes blocking their view of anything below her chest. She seems calmer but holds his hand tightly as he sits next to the bed. She even manages a smile at his get-up: full scrubs, his hair covered.

A doctor sits by her side, monitoring numbers and read-outs on the screens. The anaesthetist, Robin assumes. A team of people are on the other side of the drapes, a surgeon in the middle, scalpel in hand.

Robin leans forward to Liv. 'Are you okay?'

'Hmm.' She closes her eyes and Robin can see she's breathing out slowly through her mouth. The doctor asks a few questions – basic stuff: her name, date of birth – and she answers. He ducks back behind the blue screen. Robin feels helpless in the face of all this proficiency, not knowing what on earth is going on. There are murmurs, movement, an exchange of equipment. Not long passes, maybe five minutes, and then Robin hears a tiny cry.

Liv opens her eyes at the noise. 'He's out?' she gasps.

A masked face appears. The eyes smile. 'He's out. And he's fine. A strong, healthy little boy.'

Robin feels a flutter of excitement. And the exact moment he's ready to be a father is the moment he realises he isn't one.

The tiny baby is held in the surgeon's hands; blood and goop and all manner of indescribable body fluids cover the boy. He's screaming reassuringly loudly.

Robin watches as the baby is handed quickly to a midwife, who attends to him for a moment with another doctor. Liv's eyes stay on him the whole time, watching as he's swaddled up, a tiny yellow woollen hat placed on his head, before being passed round to her. He's bundled up with Liv, skin against skin.

Liv looks down at the boy and manages a groggy smile.

'He's gorgeous, Liv,' Robin whispers. And he means it.

The baby's eyes are brown, framed by long eyelashes. Full cheeks, a fuzz of black hair – and a complexion at least three shades darker than Robin's.

Liv looks from the baby across to Robin. She still seems out of it, hazy on a variety of drugs and her own endorphins.

'I'm sorry, Robin,' she says.

He's not sure what she's apologising for. Making him think the baby was his, bringing him here out of the blue? But whatever it is, he doesn't care. After all the chaos of the past week – the worry around Finn, the uncertainty with Jacob's death, even the fragile state of Freya – he needed something good. A miracle, a new life. A future with promise and good intentions.

Some things do end well after all, he thinks.

52

Freya and Josh sit on one side of the table, Connor Vardy on the other. The duty solicitor sits by his side: a man about Freya's age, tall and slim to the point of skinny, in a smart navy suit. Alex Reynolds – Freya's met him before. He's fair and measured; discreet, unlike some. He makes notes on a yellow legal pad.

'My client would like to hear what you have to say,' the solicitor begins. 'Against my advice, I should add.'

Connor fidgets, picking at the corner of one of his nails, staring resolutely at the tabletop; a piece of skin is separated from Connor's cuticle and dropped onto the shiny surface.

'You're free to leave at any time,' the solicitor directs to Connor. 'This is a voluntary interview.'

Connor nods.

'Are you sure you don't want a drink?' Freya asks him. 'Water? Coke?'

'No, I'm fine, thank you,' Connor mumbles.

They've signed the correct paperwork and they're ready to begin. Josh leans back in his seat, waiting for Freya to start. This morning, she's running the show.

'Connor,' Freya begins. He doesn't look up. 'We wanted to talk to you again about what happened the night of the storm.'

'My client has told you already,' Reynolds replies. Freya glares. I thought you were one of the nice ones, she thinks.

'Yes, you did,' she says, directing her response to Connor. 'But we've found out some things since then that we wanted to get your views on.'

Freya opens the file in front of her and pulls out a photo. It's a young man in army uniform, smartly posed against a formal backdrop. She turns it round and puts it in front of Connor.

'This is Lance Corporal Duncan Thorpe,' Freya says. Connor glances at the photo. 'This was the man found dead in the freezer.'

Connor looks up again, and this time studies the photo properly. His jaw clenches, then his eyes slide away.

'If you don't mind,' Freya says softly, 'I'd like to tell you a little bit about him.' She doesn't need her notes; she knows it off by heart. After she finished researching Connor and his family, she moved back to Duncan Thorpe. And she tells him everything she found out.

'Duncan was born in 1966, so he was just fifty-five when he died. He joined the army at eighteen and served until 1995, when he was involved in a dispute in a pub. Someone died and Duncan went to prison, where he stayed until 2006. Unfortunately, when he got out, he found it hard to hold down a job. He went back inside for a few years, and in 2017 he found himself homeless. Then, last Wednesday, your friend Barry found him dead in the freezer.'

'Why are you telling me this?' Connor says. 'I don't know how he got there.'

'A victim's past is irrelevant here, DC West,' the solicitor adds.

Freya takes a sip from the glass of water in front of her, biding her time. She ignores the lawyer. 'But I think you do know, Connor,' she says at last. 'I think you know more than you're telling us. And I think you're covering for your friends.'

'They're not my friends.' Connor knows exactly who Freya is talking about.

'Maybe not. But you're covering for them. And I don't understand why.' Freya leans forward slightly. 'We spoke to the college and to Barry, and they say the same thing.' Connor looks up sharply. 'That you're a clever kid and you've got a good future ahead of you.'

'That's bollocks,' Connor mumbles.

'Barry says your grandad would have been proud of the man you've become.'

Connor stares at her. 'You know nothing about me or my grandad.' He looks to Reynolds. 'Can they do this?' he asks him. 'Can they ask me this stuff?'

'Get to your point, Detective,' the solicitor replies.

'I know a bit about your grandad, Connor,' Freya continues. 'I know that after your mum died, he took you in. I know that he was a respected man in his community. That he raised money for charity. And I also know that he went to prison. For aggravated burglary, in 1999.'

'So what?' Connor's stance changes, defensive for his grandfather.

Freya takes a deep breath in. This is their last chance, and she knows it could all go wrong.

'I've done my research, Connor. There wasn't much difference between your grandad and Duncan Thorpe. They were both in the armed forces. They both wound up in prison. But in your grandad's case, when he got out, he turned his life around. He was good with his hands, like you. He worked with charities that assisted ex-offenders, trying to give other men like himself a second chance. Your grandad was at HMP Winchester at the same time as Duncan Thorpe. He might even have met him. And if he'd known about his plight, I bet he'd have done anything to help him.'

She stops. Connor is bending down so close to the table, his forehead is almost touching his hands. Then she realises he's crying.

'My client needs a break,' Reynolds interjects.

She glances nervously across to Josh. He gives her a barely perceptible nod. Carry on, he's saying.

'Connor?' Freya almost whispers. 'Please. Tell us.'

He shakes his head, still not looking at her. 'I can't.'

'Please, Connor. You can.'

'Detective. My client—'

'They'll destroy me.'

The room falls silent. Even the solicitor is quiet, hand paused on his pen.

'Who?' Freya asks. 'Mark, Tyler and Lee?'

Connor nods. Then he looks up at Freya, tears streaming down his cheeks. 'They made Grandad's life a misery. They'd sit outside his house until the early morning, drinking and shouting. When I came to live with him, it got worse. Dog shit through his letter box, graffitied our house. You name it. They said—' He stops abruptly.

'What did they say? You tell us, and we can put them away. For good.' Freya pauses, leaning forward, her face close to his. 'This is manslaughter, Connor. Murder, if we can prove it. Potential life in prison. This isn't criminal damage or trespass. This is serious.'

'Connor, you don't have to answer that,' Reynolds snaps. 'My client isn't under arrest.'

Josh sits up straight. 'You keep quiet and it's not good for you either, Connor,' he says. Freya glances at him as if to say, careful now. Overplay the bad cop and the solicitor will whisk him out of here in seconds. 'Even if you didn't do it, that's still conspiracy. Assisting at least.'

'I can't, I can't.'

'Connor, you can.' Freya takes over again. 'You're stronger than you think. You're a survivor. Even now, you're living alone, looking after yourself. Going to college, getting a qualification. Carving out a life you can be proud of. What would your grandad tell you to do, Connor?'

Josh places a hand on her arm and she sits back in her seat. The solicitor scowls. She knows there's nothing else they can say; they've played all their cards. The boy still has his head on his hands, but his crying has lessened.

Then he mumbles something, but she misses it.

'Say that again, Connor?' she asks.

He sits up, wiping his eyes with the sleeve of his sweat-shirt. 'They did it,' he says. 'They forced that guy into the freezer.' He starts to cry again but his words are clear: 'And I did nothing to stop them.'

53

Once Connor starts talking, he can't stop.

His solicitor tries to interject, but he carries on, words falling from his mouth, unabated. He tells the detectives how he came across the three boys drinking in the bus shelter on his way home from the railway. At first he kept walking, his head down as they jeered, throwing bottles his way, feeling the glass shatter at his feet. But then he slowed.

'Play with us, Vardy,' one of them mocked. 'Come on, join in.' He paused. Although he hated these boys, the pull of belonging was too much. He'd always envied their tight gang, their in-jokes, their laughter and fun. He'd never had friends.

'You want a drink?'

He turned. Mark Black was holding a bottle out to him. It was dark and the storm was gathering force, wind pulling at his coat. He knew he needed to get home, but what was waiting for him there? An empty fridge. Another can of watery baked beans.

He walked back to the bus shelter. At first he feared a trick, but Mark jiggled the bottle again, the vodka sloshing in the bottom. He reached forward and took it. Mark nodded.

'Chill out, Vardy,' he said. 'It might do you some good.'

He took a swig, then Mark pushed the bottle up again into his mouth, forcing him to take another. The vodka was harsh but warming. The boys laughed, but in a different way, an approving way, then handed him an open can of beer.

For the next hour he sat with them. Listened to their laughing and joking as he drank can after can. It started to rain, but they were dry in the bus shelter. He took a proffered cigarette, even though he didn't smoke, and felt himself get woozy and light-headed.

'Truth or dare time,' Mark said.

'I'll go first,' Tyler replied. 'Dare.'

'Moon the next car that comes down the road.'

'Fucking easy,' Tyler said with disdain. He walked to the edge of the pavement, hood up against the rain, then pulled down his trousers as a car approached. The car sped past, throwing up a cascade of water as it drove through a puddle. Tyler laughed and rejoined them in the bus shelter.

'You next, Lee.'

'Dare.'

'Chicken with the next one. The next car.'

Lee gave him a cocky stare. 'As you wish.'

Connor's heart was in his mouth as Lee stood in the middle of the road. Lit in the approaching car's headlights, he stood squarely in front of it. A loud beep, a squeal of brakes, then Lee leapt out of the way, laughing.

They got worse from there. Down this can in one. Smash the window in the bus stop. Set fire to the bin. Nothing stopped them. Connor's turn – take a punch in the face. Nothing he hadn't experienced in the past – and Lee's blow was feeble, barely bruising his cheek. He rubbed it as he sat down, enjoying the gleeful cheers from the boys.

He felt accepted. He was one of them.

The storm was fiercer now. The wind whipped the trees into a frenzy, rain so hard it blew into the shelter, soaking their clothes. And then Connor saw him. He'd seen him around, the homeless guy. Sometimes, during the quiet moments, the man would make his way up to the railway station and Barry would welcome him into the café, sitting him down with a sausage sandwich and a cup of tea. He was always quiet, always polite. Connor couldn't believe he was out in this weather.

He passed the bus shelter where they were all sat, and Mark shouted to him.

'We in your house, mate?' he taunted. 'Come and say hello.'

The man went to turn, but Mark walked out and took him by the hand.

'Hey, mate,' he said, pulling harder. 'Let's find you a bed for the night.'

The homeless guy tried to pull away, but Mark held fast. 'Come on, guys,' he directed to Connor and the other two. 'It's my dare. And I say we find this guy somewhere to sleep.'

Tyler and Lee leapt to their feet, and the three of them pulled their hoods up, surrounding the homeless guy. They pushed and cajoled the man across the road and up the track leading to the station.

Connor watched them, unsure. This was more than a bare bum towards a car. He had a bad feeling about it all.

Then Mark called back. 'Come on, Connor. You're one of us now.'

And Connor followed them.

With an increasing sense of horror, he saw the freezer in the lay-by, the white almost glowing against the darkness. It had been there since Sunday night; Barry had cursed loudly when it had been dumped. And through the darkness and the pouring rain, Connor watched.

He did nothing as they dragged the man towards it.

He did nothing as Mark opened the lid.

He did nothing as he listened to the man protest, his shouts of anger, almost drowned out by the cackle and the laughter from the boys.

He did nothing as they forced the man inside, closed and sat on the lid, drumming their feet against the sides. Tyler stood up and danced a mocking jig on the top, the rain soaking him to the skin.

He did nothing as the rain fell and the wind howled.

And the man suffocated inside.

—

Once the boys grew bored, they climbed off the freezer and opened the lid. And he was dead.

Connor could tell that even Mark Black was shocked. The colour drained out of his face. Hushed, they looked at the dead man, curled up at the bottom of that chest freezer. Still and silent.

'What the fuck are we going to do?' Lee stuttered. Connor could see he was on the edge of tears.

Mark turned. 'Nothing,' he shouted. 'We do nothing.' He glanced around. They were alone, in the middle of the deserted track. 'We go back to mine, play Xbox, make sure my mum and dad clock us.' He turned to Connor. 'You go home. But you say nothing, you hear me?'

The three boys crowded round him. Mark prodded a hard finger into the centre of Connor's chest.

'You keep quiet, Vardy. Because if you don't... if you don't...' His features were hard. Resolute. 'If you don't, we'll go to your grandad's grave and we'll dig him up. We'll dig him up and lay out his rotten, stinking corpse for all the world to see.'

Connor felt vomit rise in his stomach.

'You hear me?' Mark repeated. 'You were as much a part of this as we were. Agree, you bastard.'

Connor nodded, mute.

'Right. Now let's go.'

Connor watched them walk back down the track, then turn left towards where he knew Mark lived. He stared down at the freezer. What could he do? Call the police and he'd be fucked.

He did nothing.

Until now. Now he talks until his mouth is dry, the story is told and the detectives in front of him are pale and unblinking.

54

Freya and Josh emerge stunned from the interview room. After Connor had finished talking, Josh did the only thing he could be expected to do.

'I'm sorry, Connor,' Josh said. And Connor looked down at the table, resigned for what was to come. 'But I am arresting you for the false imprisonment of Duncan Thorpe...'

Freya listened as he finished the caution. A caution he'd already received at the beginning of the voluntary interview, but one which had to be repeated.

Josh and Freya stand in the corridor. The solicitor joins them, looking back to where Connor has been escorted away to be booked into custody. Face cast down, silent.

'Are you going to arrest him for murder?' Reynolds asks.

Josh frowns. 'Maybe, Alex. And let the CPS decide the charge later.'

The solicitor puts his notes into his rucksack and heaves it onto his shoulder. 'Well, keep me informed.' He tilts his head at the detectives. 'Wasn't expecting that one when I got the call this morning,' he comments ruefully. 'Some days are just full of surprises.'

Freya and Josh watch him leave. There is no doubt about the case now: the other three boys will be arrested, their fingerprints and DNA taken, and Freya knows they'll be a match to the exhibits collected from the crime scene and the bus shelter. Whether the three plead guilty or not doesn't matter. Even now, Freya knows they probably have enough for the CPS to agree to charge.

Freya looks in the direction of the custody suite. 'That poor boy,' she murmurs.

'Not even a boy,' Josh replies. He sighs. 'He's eighteen, an adult. Same as the other three.'

'Yeah, but that's it. Their lives are over.'

Josh nods grimly. He knows what Freya is saying, why she feels so down, despite the fact that they have got justice for Duncan Thorpe.

Connor Vardy was someone with potential. He'd survived a shit childhood. He'd survived his mother dying, and his grandfather dying. He had support around him from Barry at the railway, and the tutors at college. Yet, on one walk home, the desire to be wanted, to be part of a group, had overtaken all common sense.

'You don't need me for the moment, do you?' Freya asks. She needs a breath of fresh air; she wants to get away from the station for a while.

Josh nods. 'Go ahead. Mina and I can take over for a bit. I'll call you when the other three have been brought in.'

Freya goes back to the office, grabs her bag and heads out. She walks down to the car park, then phones Robin. He answers on the second ring, but his voice sounds slow and distracted.

'You okay?' she asks. She can hear traffic noise in the background.

'Yeah, good. Just had a weird day. Where are you?'

'On a break. At the station.'

'Do you want to come and meet me?'

He tells her where he is and hangs up. She squints at the phone in confusion, then gets into her car.

–

Traffic is light, and the day is sunny and warm. She parks in the centre of town then walks up pedestrianised streets until the huge, dominating sight of Winchester Cathedral comes into view.

Robin isn't the only one taking his break in the cathedral grounds. Groups of teenagers sit on the grass, sandwiches and drinks in hand. There is a feeling of fun in the air, of summer being just around the corner. She spots Robin on the far side, sitting on the grass, his legs out in front of him. His face is pointed up to the sun; his eyes are closed. He's smiling slightly and has such an air of relaxation about him that it almost doesn't seem like her boss at all.

He opens an eye as she comes closer, then sits up properly, crossing his legs. She collapses down next to him on the grass.

'Are you okay?' she asks tentatively.

'Yeah. Why?'

'You seem... Are you on drugs?'

He laughs. 'No. It's just been an odd day.'

And he tells her about Liv, and the labour ward, and the baby being born, while her mouth drops open in surprise.

'So, it's not yours?' she manages at last.

'Definitely not.'

'Are you...' She's not sure how he might feel about the news. 'Relieved?' she tries.

'I don't know what I am. It's one less thing to worry about, that's for sure. But the idea of it all wasn't so bad in the end.' He turns to her. 'And how's your case coming on?'

She talks about Connor and the confession, his face creasing in sympathy as she tells the story.

'It's just so depressing,' she finishes. 'All so fucking unnecessary. That the guy would be homeless in the middle of the storm. That three nasty teenagers would think it fun to force him into a freezer. That he would die as a result.'

'You can't change any of that, Freya,' Robin says. 'You can only do your job.'

'But it's all so senseless. Same with Jon.' Freya stops. She hadn't meant to get onto this subject, but sitting here, with Robin, it feels good to let it out. 'Why did he have to die?'

Robin looks across at the massive cathedral, the shrine to a supposedly benevolent god that created a world where these injustices happened. 'I don't believe in any of this stuff,' he says. 'In God, or his plan, or that we have a destiny we can't control.' He picks a daisy from the grass and rolls it around in his fingers. 'I asked the same question when Georgia and the twins died.' He looks sideways at her for a moment. 'And I couldn't find any answers. Not straightforward ones, anyway. We just have to carry on, living our lives in a way that would make the people that loved us proud.'

Freya remembers her own words to Connor, merely hours before. He hadn't made his grandfather proud, had he? Not in the end. But he'd owned up to what he'd done, and maybe that was a start.

'Robin,' she begins. 'About what happened with Amy.' He looks across at her, the usual frown back on his face. 'Is it over?'

'I think so, Frey. Yes.'

'Okay.' Next to them a pigeon looks for crumbs; a peal of laughter from a toddler echoes round the cathedral grounds. 'What are you going to do about Finn?' she asks at last.

He sighs. He lies back again in the grass, his hands behind his head. He stares up at the sky. 'I really don't know,' he replies. Then he closes his eyes.

Freya stays sitting. The sun is warm, and a gentle breeze blows across the grass. It's hard to imagine the storm from a week ago, given the beautiful weather now. She looks at Robin. He's wearing jeans and a navy-blue polo shirt pulled up slightly around his waist, exposing a thin strip of skin. His eyes are still closed, and she thinks about that odd night in the Premier Inn. What was that? What is *this*?

Normal DCs don't sit in parks with their sergeants. They don't go on trips to Devon; they don't have heart-to-heart conversations about love, and life, and God. But then, normal DCs and DSs don't have the secrets that they have between them.

She pulls a daisy out of the grass, makes a hole in its stem with her nail, then threads another through it. She repeats it, until there are five or six in a line. The action is soothing, a meaningless pursuit from her childhood.

But the calm can't last for long. Robin's phone rings; he awkwardly pulls it out of his pocket, then answers it.

'Steph?' he says, pushing himself up to a sitting position with a grunt. 'What have you found?'

Steph? Freya thinks. When did he start talking to Steph again? Freya watches as Robin listens, then he gets to his feet.

'I'm on my way,' he says, finishing the call.

'I have to go to Reading,' he tells Freya and she realises that she doesn't want to go back to the station. To listen to three horrible teenagers bluff and deny and *no comment* their way through their interviews.

'I'm coming, too,' she replies.

55

Any love for the universe that Robin might have fostered from his experience with Liv is lost as he battles the traffic up the A33 towards Reading.

The dual carriageway is crowded, all the traffic lights against them. Robin arrives in the Royal Berkshire car park with his patience tested to the limit.

Freya follows wordlessly behind him as he walks quickly towards Finn's private room. Even from a distance, he can see a crowd of people in the corridor, recognising familiar figures as he gets closer.

DI Craig and DC Grey stand on one side, silent and grim-faced. On the other, Sandra is talking to Josie, her hand resting reassuringly on her arm. They all turn as they see Robin and Freya approaching.

Robin introduces Freya to the pair from Thames Valley Police, and Craig gestures to an empty room to the side. Josie watches the four coppers leave, her face questioning.

'What's going on? Where's Steph?' Robin asks once the door is closed.

'I was going to ask you the same thing, Butler,' Craig snaps. 'It's bad enough that you felt the coroner needed a second opinion and went behind my back to get it without keeping me waiting for the results.'

'She's with the coroner,' Freya says quietly, looking at her phone. Craig turns to her sharply. 'Dr Harper,' she continues, showing them the screen with Steph's message. 'She says she wanted to update him first.'

Craig throws her hands up in the air with exasperation. 'So I'm supposed to hang around here, waiting for something that could potentially destroy my entire case?'

'If your evidence is as strong as you think it is, then there shouldn't be a problem, should there?' Robin retorts.

'My evidence is fine. You've got the file, haven't you?'

Robin is aware that Craig has been extraordinarily accommodating of him throughout this investigation, polite despite the pressure she must have been under and her senior rank. But he also knows that this is his friend's freedom at stake. Her desire for results cannot be what's important here, especially when the evidence is not as cut and dried as it should be.

'Yes,' Robin replies. 'And both you and I know there are holes.'

'Like what?'

'Like the fact that the knife only has Sharp's prints on it? How did Finn kill him without touching the murder weapon?'

'Perhaps he was wearing gloves.'

'Gloves you've not been able to find? And while we're on the subject of missing evidence, how about that camera footage?'

'We're still working on that.'

'Not very hard, by the sounds of it.'

'Okay, fine. Then who killed him, Butler?' Craig is furious, her face red and blotchy. 'Who?'

Robin is silent. He has no way to answer that question and she knows it.

'It's easy to question someone else's investigation,' Craig continues. 'But harder to find a solution when it's your neck on the line.' She winces slightly at her turn of phrase. 'That man in there,' Craig says, regaining her composure with an angry finger towards the door, 'was the only person in the van with Sharp. He had motive. He had opportunity. And the alcohol and drug abuse only show a man falling apart under the pressure from his significantly more successful, popular colleague. And you're saying he didn't kill him? Come on! Even you must admit you're being swayed by your personal relationship.'

A gentle knock on the door interrupts her and they all turn.

'What?' Craig shouts.

The door opens and Sophie's standing there. Robin feels his jaw clench.

'DI Craig,' Sophie begins. 'I've been trying to get hold of you.'

'I know. I got your messages. We can speak later.'

'No.' Sophie walks decisively into the room and shuts the door behind her. 'We need to talk now. It's about the footage from the night of the storm.'

All four police officers turn towards Sophie. She nervously digs in her bag and pulls out a sheet of paper. She holds it towards Craig.

'What's this?' Craig asks.

Robin cranes his neck to try and see. It looks like a computer printout from a spreadsheet. Lines of text in columns.

'It's the event log from the BBC server at the university,' Sophie says, and Robin feels a ripple of apprehension. 'Where the video was stored.'

'Why do you have this?' Robin asks Sophie. 'And, more to the point,' he turns to Craig, 'why don't you?'

'Our digital team checked that server,' she snaps. 'There was nothing there of use. The video files have gone.'

'Yes,' Sophie says, waggling the page in her face. 'But this says who logged on and when. Don't you want to know *who* deleted them?'

Craig snatches the page from Sophie's hand.

'And?' Robin asks impatiently.

Craig looks up from the paper. She hands it to Robin, who scans the text. A login for CALLOI occurs first thing Wednesday morning. Then nobody else until WHITEJ logs on, on Wednesday night.

'Ian Calloway,' Sophie says smugly. 'Have you spoken to him?'

'Not since his statement last week,' Craig replies. 'But it makes sense he would delete the files. He's Finn's friend. He's got rid of proof of the murder.'

'That's one theory,' Robin says. 'Sophie,' he asks, turning to her. 'With Sharp dead and Finn in prison, who would get proprietary rights to the Doppler?'

'Well, the university, essentially. They own everything.'

'So there's no money as motive—' Craig begins, but Sophie interrupts her.

'That doesn't matter. You don't work in academia for money. You do it for professional recognition, to be at the top of your field. And someone would have to publish the findings. Take the glory. And that would probably be Ian now.'

Sophie frowns. 'I've never liked Ian. I thought he was jealous of Finn, but Finn always said I was being silly. But when I saw him last week, it felt like he was enjoying all this. Enjoying the fact that, with Finn out of the way, he was in charge.'

Robin smiles weakly at Sophie. He was wrong about her. She is passionate and impulsive, but that has worked in their favour in this case. She came through for Finn, which was more than he's achieved.

But it's too late. 'So Calloway deleted the videos,' Robin sighs.

'No,' Sophie says, frustrated. 'This is what I've been trying to tell you. This shows he didn't just delete the files.'

She leans over and points to a line on the piece of paper, the server log that Robin's still holding.

19/05/21 09:25:54, Copied, it says, then a letter: an external drive.

And below it: *19/05/21 09:25:58, Deleted*.

Sophie looks up at Robin. 'He copied them first,' she says. 'He might still have them.'

Robin turns quickly to Craig. The look on her face is something between humiliation and anger. She's screwed up, and she knows it.

But she turns to her DC, galvanised into action.

'Grey,' she shouts. 'Get hold of Calloway. Arrest him. Now!'

56

The hospital ward is noisy and overheated. Liv's body feels broken – the incision across the bottom of her belly throbs with pain whenever she moves – but Liv has never been happier. Her baby lies next to her in the plastic wheeled cot, wrapped up tightly in a blue blanket. Every now and again she leans over and looks at him, to check he's still there and this is real.

He screams, of course. He cries all the time, his eyes screwed shut, his mouth open, tiny fists pumping in anger. And when he does, she awkwardly picks him up, wincing from the pain in her tummy, and pushes him against her breast. It didn't work at first, but the midwife showed her how to latch him on and now he has the hang of it, feeding happily as her milk starts to come in.

The nurses come round occasionally, but for the most part she's alone. She watches the other mothers in their beds, as visitors arrive. The dads, the proud grandparents, bringing presents and cooing over the newborns. They seem like a different species, these families, but Liv doesn't allow herself the luxury of self-pity; she never has.

But she does let herself think about Robin.

She's had a message from him. A simple: *How are you?* She hasn't replied; she doesn't know what to say. She feels bad for misleading him about the baby. But when he turned up that day, she couldn't resist implying they'd slept together. That tiny bit of control was too much of a temptation.

And now she feels embarrassed, letting her guard down when she was in labour, letting him see her at her most vulnerable. She doesn't like it. She feels beholden to him, like she owes him something, and that's the feeling she dislikes more than anything.

But she'd liked daydreaming about Robin as the father. A nice man. A decent man. Unlike the real father: one of the bouncers at the club, a married dickhead with kids of his own that she slept with once without a condom when she needed the extra cash. Robin is nothing like him. Instinctively she knows Robin is someone that can be relied on to do the right thing, although the memory stick and the CCTV footage come back into her mind.

What was he doing there, that day with Trevor Stevens? Why was her sister so keen for her to have a copy? But after everything that has happened over the last few days, she doesn't like the idea of holding onto it. She hates the thought that she could be responsible for something bad happening to Robin.

Liv hears a small snuffle from the cot next to her, and she looks over. He's stirring, her boy's arms and legs moving in the blanket. His face changes to the already familiar disgruntled expression. She still hasn't decided on a name; nothing seems right for this tiny miracle at her side.

She's not sure what will happen from here. They've said that they can go home soon. Maybe tomorrow. It worries her slightly. She hasn't the foggiest idea how to look after a baby, and she has no fallback if things go wrong. But in her heart, she knows she'll be okay. She always is.

She doesn't want a man in her life; she doesn't want Robin Butler. She's happy with the way things are. Her and her baby boy.

Just them.

57

Ian Calloway is not a man used to the inside of police cells. Freya can already see the rings of sweat under his arms, his hands visibly shaking, as he sits opposite DI Craig and DC Grey in the police interview room.

Craig acted quickly, sending Grey to the lab and getting straight on the phone to her DCS. The arrest was swift, charges of perverting the course of justice and wasting police time more than enough to search the lab and his computer. The digital team are working hard now, trying to locate the missing videos.

Freya and Robin have been confined to the room next door, watching the scene via a computer screen. Freya heard the exchange between Craig and Robin – the latter annoyed to be kept at a distance – but now, as she sees the expression on her boss's face, she knows Craig was right. There is no way Robin could control his anger sat in front of this man.

Freya herself feels the frustration. The knowledge that this man had willingly made a difficult situation worse. Hiding the evidence that showed what happened that night in the van.

Calloway's asked for a lawyer, and the duty solicitor is sitting by his side. But, looking on, Freya knows how this interview's going to go.

'Mr Calloway,' Craig begins. 'I'm not going to keep you long.'

Freya sees Ian's head tilt up, a hopeful expression on his face.

'We have all the evidence we need to charge you,' Craig continues, and Freya enjoys watching his optimism fade. 'We just need to clear a few things up first.'

'I'm so sorry, I… I didn't think…' Ian starts, until his solicitor silences him.

A faint smile appears on Craig's face. 'What did you do, Mr Calloway?' she asks.

'I'm so sorry.' The solicitor goes to stop Calloway again, but he shakes his head. 'I need to tell them,' he mumbles, and the solicitor sits back in his seat, defeated. Ian turns to Craig. 'I worked so hard for those guys,' he says. 'For Finn and Dr Sharp. I put my whole life on hold, getting that sodding radar up and running. And then, the night of the storm, as we're having a glass of champagne before we all head out to the van, Finn pulls me to one side and says that my name's not going on the paper. Says that there was a potential problem with the authorship, but he and Simon have had a chat, and it would be just the two of them now. Something to do with diluting the credit if there were more names listed.'

'And you were angry?'

'I was furious. I had an argument with Finn and he made me stay behind at the university. I should have been out there, in the van with them. Making a name for myself. I should have been on TV!' he exclaims loudly. 'But Finn wouldn't let me, even after everything I've done for him.'

'Craig's not having to work hard on this one,' Freya whispers to Robin. 'He's going to confess to murdering his granny, if she's not careful.'

Robin smiles tightly and turns back to the screen. Freya can see Robin is stressed – she would be, too. She knows he's keen to get eyes on the tape, but half of her is worried about what the video might show. What if it's exactly as Craig believes – Finn murdering Sharp? What then?

'So you saw your opportunity,' Craig prompts Calloway.

'You had your man,' Ian says. 'You knew what he'd done – he was locked in the van with the body. And I thought that with Sharp dead and Finn in prison, I could finish analysing the output from the storm and publish it myself. With Sharp's name, too, of course.'

'Of course,' Craig says sarcastically. 'So why steal the video? You could have done that anyway.'

Ian pauses. 'I didn't want anything to muddy the waters.'

'Muddy the waters? How?'

Robin and Freya lean closer to the screen, as Ian continues talking. 'The film – it's not what you'd expect. It's…' He shakes his head. 'Watch it for yourself, you'll see.'

And, as if on cue, there's a knock on the door. Grey opens it and pokes his head round into the corridor.

'We have it,' Grey says, coming back into the room, breathless and eager. 'We have the video.'

58

The four of them crowd round the monitor in an empty interview room, as the harassed techie gets the video running.

'So, I'll scroll to after Justin White leaves, when something actually happens,' he says, and Robin watches as the video fast-forwards. 'I'm sorry to say,' he continues, 'but the camera angle isn't great. It was positioned at the back of the van, facing forward, so you have quite a big black spot.'

'But you see the murder?' Craig asks him.

The techie hesitates. 'See for yourself,' he replies, stepping backwards.

The video plays. He's right: the camera captures the monitors and equipment at the front of the van, but the entire back third is out of shot. The table, where Sharp was found, can only just be seen. But the quality is good and in colour: Finn and Sharp clear as they go about their work.

At first the film is boring. Both scientists sit in front of screens, watching an array of data. Occasionally, they talk; there's no audio, but they seem to be smiling, their manner relaxed. The timestamp clicks round and Robin notices the camera start to shake slightly. It's 01:10, the time the eye of the storm hit. The lights flicker; flashes of lightning burst outside the window. Both men seem happy – big grins on their faces, hands waving excitedly. At one point Sharp reaches over and enthusiastically hugs a smiling Finn.

Robin glances at Craig. She's concentrating hard, her elbows on the desk, her chin resting on her hands. Robin knows this could be it. The moment that could free Finn – or put him away for good.

On screen, Finn has moved out of shot to the back of the van. He re-emerges a few minutes later, two plates with sandwiches in hand, and he passes one to Sharp. The two men sit back down in front of the monitors; the storm continues to thunder around them.

But then things start to change. Sharp stands up; his hands go to his throat. He seems to be choking, and Finn stands up next to him, thumping him twice on the back. Sharp's shaking his head, and then he moves forward, ducking out of shot. Time ticks by. Only Finn can be seen, his face shocked, his eyes wide behind his glasses. He's clearly panicking.

The two men have to crouch slightly in the small van; Robin remembers the cramped space, the feeling of claustrophobia that must have only worsened under stress. Robin watches as Finn's hands flap; he walks to the monitors, then back again. He picks his mobile phone up, tries to make a call, throwing it down in frustration. Then he runs forward quickly, going out of shot.

'Where have they gone?' Robin snaps to the digital technician. 'Why can't we see them?'

The techie looks apologetic. 'That's what I meant, Sarge. The black spot.'

'And there's no other camera?'

'No. There was a little Sony they used for filming earlier, but nothing else that captures this.'

'Butler,' Craig says. 'Look.'

The two men are still out of shot, but occasionally something comes into view at the edge of the screen. The top of a head. An arm. And then, at one point, the two men together, seemingly fighting. They tussle together in the restricted space, then disappear.

Robin can only guess at what's going on. Something happened to Simon and the two men got into a fight. But it's not murder, Robin thinks. It's not—

His hands go to his mouth. He stares at the screen, shocked. Robin has seen some things in his time – horrific, scary, violent acts – but this scene renders him speechless.

Sharp has come back into the main part of the van. And the video shows the sickening action in high-resolution, full-colour definition.

Sharp's staggering, his hands clamped to his neck. He's flailing about, twisting and turning in panic, head, limbs, hands bumping against the sides of the vehicle. And the blood. The blood is everywhere.

It pushes out from between his fingers, spurts erupting in a fountain of red, hitting the walls and the window. He turns, his mouth open, gasping, his face puce, eyes bulging. And still the blood flows.

Sharp drops to his knees on the metal floor. The blood has completely soaked his shirt now; his hands and arms are covered with it. He looks back, to where Finn must have been standing. His mouth opens and closes a few times, and then he falls. His body lies where Robin remembers it, half under the table, legs bent under him.

Robin looks at Freya, stunned. Her mouth is open, her eyes unblinking: an expression he knows must be echoed on his own face.

They look back to the video. A blood pool expands around the body. Finn walks back into shot. One step, then another. Slowly, his gaze fixed on the motionless Simon Sharp on the floor, Finn shuffles past, his back to the wall, keeping as far away from the body as possible. He paces for a moment, bloody footprints in his wake. Then he sits down. His knees go up to his chest, his arms wrap around them. Still staring.

'He stays like that until about half three,' the techie says.

'Then what?' Craig asks, her voice no more than a whisper.

'Then he panics. He gets up and locks the door. Starts screaming and shouting. Until you guys arrive.'

'Shit,' Robin mutters.

Craig looks at him. Her voice is faint. 'I'm sorry, Butler.'

And he nods. There is nothing else to say. The video is clear. There was nobody else in that van.

Finn killed Sharp. And everyone knows it.

Even Robin.

59

The air stills. Everyone is silent. Even though Craig has her man, nobody, not even the most hardened police officer, likes to watch someone die.

'Poor guy,' Grey whispers, his hands over his mouth.

Robin can't sit there any more. He gets up and walks out into the corridor. It's empty, nobody around, and he stands for a moment.

He has no idea what to do. He's failed everyone. He's a terrible friend. He didn't even know Finn was an alcoholic, and he certainly hasn't been around for him over the last few years. Josie was relying on him to save her son and he hasn't done that, only made matters worse.

He hears a door open and close, and glances over. Freya's standing next to him, her face sympathetic.

'You okay?' she asks.

'Hmm,' is all he can bring himself to say.

'I'm sorry.'

He nods, then stares up at the ceiling, taking a long breath in. 'What do I do now, Freya?'

'You tell Josie the truth. And we apologise for breaking into her house.'

Robin manages a laugh. 'Yeah. That wasn't the best decision I've ever made. Sorry for dragging you into it.'

'Ah, never mind,' Freya says. 'You make life interesting, Butler, I'll give you that.' She puts a hand on his arm for a moment and rubs it. 'Come on, mate, let's get out of here.'

But before they make it far, his phone rings and he pulls it out of his pocket.

'Steph?' he says. 'It's okay. We have the video. We know what happened.'

'You do?' she replies. Her voice sounds surprised. 'You've seen it all?'

'Well, no...'

'Then you don't have a clue. Get DI Craig and come to the Royal Berks,' she finishes. 'I'll see you in ten.'

–

When they arrive, Steph is waiting for the four of them in the corridor outside Finn's room. She has a thin file in her hand; she passes a copy of the report inside to Craig and then another to Robin. She points to the empty hospital room across the way and the four of them go obediently in.

'Sorry you've had to come all this way,' Robin says to Steph. She looks good, Robin thinks, now she's out of her pathology PPE. Her hair is a bit longer, tied up in a high ponytail. He likes it like that. He really has missed her, he realises with a sting.

Steph gives a tired shrug. 'What else have I got to do, Butler,' she replies, 'but respond to your every demand?' Despite her words, her tone is light and her eyes meet Robin's with a smile.

'What exactly is going on, Dr Harper?' Craig says sharply. 'I have a case to wrap up.'

'I'm sorry, I won't keep you long. The coroner wanted me to share my findings with you directly to avoid any confusion.'

Robin recognises her tone – it's the patient, measured voice she uses when she's on the stand, giving vital information to juries.

'I don't know what you've been watching on the video,' Steph continues, 'but I think I can shed some light on what happened that night.'

'And let me guess: you have a different cause of death?' Craig asks.

'No, no,' Steph replies. 'Cause of death is exactly right. Exsanguination from an incision to the carotid artery. Sharp bled out in minutes.'

'So why are we here?' Craig snaps, exasperated.

Robin is confused, too, and opens the file. He watches as Steph sits down on the empty hospital bed. She's taking her time, wanting to get the message across in the right way.

'While my findings don't contradict those from the first post-mortem, it's my more detailed enquiries that I want to share. As doctors, we're as guilty as anyone of confirmation bias: so blinded by the obvious that we don't look any further. To the other smaller details that might also be pertinent to the case.' Steph opens the folder in her hand. 'So, with this in mind, I did a full and comprehensive review of Simon Sharp's body, and I found a few other interesting features.'

The whole room is silent, all four police officers waiting for Steph to speak.

'On first examination,' she continues, 'I noticed a large amount of laryngeal and pulmonary oedema. Fluid in the tissues of the neck and damage to the lungs,' she adds, and Robin knows she must be hugely simplifying what she's found. 'Plus, obstruction to his airway caused by oedema and mucous plugging.' She looks at them all.

'When Simon Sharp died, he was having massive problems breathing, and that's if he was managing to do so at all.'

Robin remembers the staggering around on the video, Simon looking like he was choking.

Craig scowls at Steph. 'So would I, if I had a knife wound to my neck.'

Steph shakes her head. 'No, I believe this was prior to the exsanguination. To confirm my hypothesis, I tested his blood: he had raised levels of mast cell tryptase.'

Robin watches as Steph takes in their blank faces. 'Just before Simon Sharp died, he was experiencing anaphylactic shock.'

'An allergic reaction?' Craig stutters. 'To what?'

'I went back over his medical records. Simon Sharp had an allergy to peanuts. And looking at his stomach contents, he was eating something that looked like a sandwich before he died.'

'We know he did,' Robin replies. 'We saw it on the video.' He grabs his bag, pulling the file out and rifling through the pages. He pulls out a crime scene photo and puts it in front of them; two plates lying on the side. 'See here. But surely he would have known that, and been careful? Carried an EpiPen or similar?'

'Not all allergy sufferers carry an EpiPen,' Steph replies. 'And he might not have realised how serious it was. Severity can change over time. Even a tiny amount could induce a reaction.'

Craig glances down at the photo, then looks up, frustrated. 'But so what? A nut allergy doesn't cause a knife wound to the neck. Or,' she barks, annoyed, 'are we saying that Mr Peanut went after him with the penknife, too?'

'What if he did it himself?'

Freya's been silent up to now, leaning against a wall on the far side, listening intently to Steph.

'Don't be so stupid,' Craig scoffs.

'No, hear me out,' Freya says. She stands up straight and addresses the room. 'They're stranded in that van, alone, storm raging outside. Simon can feel his throat closing, realising he's struggling to breathe. Finn's worse than useless in a crisis' – Robin nods – 'and he remembers he has a penknife in his pocket. And he knows how to do an emergency...' She tails off, looking to Steph. 'He called it a crike?'

'Cricothyrotomy,' Steph says, supplying the correct term.

'That's ridiculous,' Craig blusters.

'Is it?' Freya faces her, standing her ground. 'He's done it before, live on TV. And it worked then, the guy survived. He's the sort of bloke that believes he can do anything. He drives into tornadoes for a living. He has the arrogance, the Type A personality. So he tries to pierce his own windpipe. Tries to find a way so he can live. And it goes wrong.'

Freya stops. Robin looks at the faces around the room. Craig looks doubtful, Grey disgusted. He knows he himself can't yet get on board with the idea that Simon Sharp slit his own throat.

But they hadn't seen the actual act on the video. It's possible.

Steph's looking down, studying the photos from her post-mortem, laying them out on the bed in front of her.

'Finn's left-handed, right?' Steph says to Robin. He nods. 'And Sharp was right-handed?'

Craig agrees.

346

'So, look here. The cut clearly starts from the middle of the neck, then round to the right-hand side, nicking the carotid.' She pushes a photograph forward, skin loose over a neck wound. 'Which my colleague assumed was caused by someone left-handed, but which could equally have been caused by Sharp.' She squints at the photo. 'And these shallower cuts here, at the front of the neck, are hesitation marks. Again, in the first post-mortem they were said to have been done by a reluctant assailant, but they would fit better with Freya's theory. That he made a few aborted attempts first, before desperation took over.'

The room plunges into silence. Everyone deep in thought. Robin can guess what Craig's thinking. A defence lawyer presents this to a jury, however ridiculous it sounds, and it might create reasonable doubt. And it fits with the footage on the video. As a theory, it's bonkers, but it's possible.

Robin's finding it hard to believe it himself. It makes him feel slightly sick – the idea that someone could stick a penknife in their own throat so they could survive. But, as he well knows, people do strange things when they're pushed to the edge.

And the tussle. The fingertip bruises on Simon Sharp's arms. Finn had been trying to stop him.

A quiet knock interrupts the stunned silence, and Josie puts her head round the door.

'Robin,' she says. 'Finn's asking for you.'

60

Robin follows Josie out.

'Listen, Josie—' he starts, but she stops him, her hand in the air.

'No, Robin. I can't be dealing with you now.'

'I just wanted to apologise—' Robin tries again, but there's a shout from Finn's room.

'Not now,' Josie repeats and leaves him, going in to see Finn. Robin follows, chastened.

Finn's sitting up in bed, his glasses on. It's the first time Robin's seen him in days, and he looks healthier: his cheeks have a pink hue, his hair washed and brushed. He smiles as Robin comes into the room.

'Rob! It's been ages!'

'I know, I—' Robin begins, but Finn cuts him off.

'I haven't seen you since that night we went out, you know, when we got wasted.'

Robin's uncertain what he's talking about and glances to Josie.

'Don't worry about me being in hospital, Rob. Honestly,' Finn continues. 'Doctors say they'll have my appendix out in no time. Routine op.'

Josie pulls Robin to one side. He's aware that Steph and Freya have come into the room behind him and are watching the exchange with interest.

'He's been like this since the weekend,' Josie whispers. 'He keeps on coming up with these random explanations about why he's in hospital. Like he can't remember and he's making something up to cope with it.'

'Has he done this for other situations?' Steph's been listening to Josie and now joins them. 'Other questions he's been asked and can't answer?'

'Yes. Constantly.'

Steph frowns. 'Do you mind…?'

Josie nods and gestures towards the bed. Steph approaches Finn.

'Finn?' she says. 'My name is Dr Steph Harper. Do you mind if I examine you?'

'Go for it,' Finn agrees. 'I remember you from last week.'

Robin, Josie and Freya stand back and watch as Steph examines Finn. She looks into his eyes, asks him to stand up, get out of bed and try to walk. His movements are uncoordinated, his shuffling slow, with a wide gait.

'What day is it, Finn? What date?' she asks.

'December, nearly Christmas.'

'How old are you?'

'I was born in February 1978.'

'So that makes you…?'

'Forty-two.'

Josie glances at Robin. Finn's missed a birthday – he was forty-three in February.

'And where are you?'

'Hospital, clearly,' he laughs. 'Doc says I'll be out in a few days.'

Steph turns back to Robin. 'When he came in, was he muddled, disorientated?'

'Yes, he was the same when he was in the van. Didn't know where he was, couldn't remember what happened.'

'And he's an alcoholic?' she adds bluntly.

Robin nods.

Her head dips slightly. 'I need to speak to his doctor,' she mutters and walks quickly out of the room.

Robin watches her go, confused, then follows after her. Steph has paused, talking to a nurse in the corridor, who runs to a phone and makes a call.

'What are you thinking, Steph?'

She's still deep in thought. 'When did Finn come in?'

'Last Wednesday.'

'So, nearly a week ago?'

But Robin doesn't have time to answer her question, as a man joins them in the corridor.

'Dr Harper? I'm Dr Blackstone, Finn's doctor. I'm just doing my rounds. You want to speak to me?'

The man towers over Steph, not looking too happy at being summoned.

'I'm sorry for calling you, but I was here with DS Butler,' she begins, gesturing to Robin, who doesn't even get a nod. 'And I had some observations about Finn.'

'Right...' Dr Blackstone's holding Finn's chart in his hand and is quickly reading the pages, not looking at Steph.

'He came in with symptoms of disorientation, memory loss—'

'Both anterograde and retrograde, yes.'

'Changes to his eyes and vision, ataxia, confusion, exaggerated storytelling and confabulation?'

'Correct. Plus, symptoms arising from his alcohol withdrawal: shaking, anxiety, nausea, sweating. The usual.'

'What were his thiamine and B1 levels when he was admitted?'

Dr Blackstone stares at Steph for a moment, then his eyes slowly drop to the chart. His fingers flick between the pages.

'That can't be right,' he says under his breath.

'Dr Blackstone?' Steph prompts.

Robin watches as his face turns pale and he meets Steph's gaze. 'We didn't test for vitamin B when he was brought in through the ED. It's not part of the baseline bloods. You have to specifically request it.'

'And you didn't?'

'No.' He clears his throat, awkwardly. 'We didn't know about the alcoholism until later, and we didn't suspect...' His voice tails off as he stares at the chart again.

'What's going on?' Robin asks, but Steph ignores him.

'What did his MRI show?' she asks.

'Some damage in the dorsal medial thalamus and the mammillary bodies, but nothing significant. Shit,' he mutters under his breath, then turns to the nearest nurse. 'Please get Finn Mason started on thiamine. Now.' The nurse rushes off and Blackstone turns back to Steph. 'We'll get the lab to run the tests ASAP.'

'Steph?' Robin repeats. 'What's going on?'

'I'll go and speak to his family,' Blackstone says quietly, and leaves Robin and Steph in the corridor.

Steph turns to Robin. Her face is serious; he can tell immediately that it's not good.

'There's a condition called Wernicke's encephalopathy, and it's caused by a lack of vitamin B, in particular thiamine. It's found most commonly in people suffering from malnutrition, often resulting from alcoholism.'

'But Finn's not malnourished,' Robin begins, then he stops. He remembers Sophie's words about Finn not eating properly, knows his own worry when he first saw his friend's gaunt appearance.

'It might have resulted from as little as two to three weeks of unbalanced nutrition. Coupled with Finn's drinking and probable vomiting, it's likely this has occurred.'

'What does it mean?' Robin asks. 'You can treat it, right?'

'Caught early, yes. But Wernicke's in alcoholics is commonly associated with another condition called Korsakoff's syndrome, and given Finn's amnesia… I'm sorry, Robin. But if he has Korsakoff's he may have some permanent damage to his brain.'

Robin's hands go to his mouth and he leans back against the wall, stunned. 'They said it was psychological,' he manages after a pause. 'That all Finn needed was time.'

'Sadly, in this case, time was the one thing Finn didn't have,' Steph says. 'They'll know more once they've done some more tests. A repeat MRI will show the extent of the possible damage to Finn's brain. And you never know, he might respond to the thiamine.'

'But he might not,' Robin says.

Steph places a reassuring hand on his arm, then leans forward and wraps her arms round him. Robin leans into the hug, resting his chin on the top of her head, his eyes closed.

'No,' Steph says, from Robin's chest. 'He might not.'

61

Potentially irreversible brain damage. Might never be able to form new memories. Freya feels like an intruder as she listens to the pale-faced doctor explain the situation to Josie and Sophie.

All from a lack of vitamin B? Freya can barely comprehend how things have gone so wrong. Missed because nobody thought to ask for the right blood tests. A nurse arrives with a bag of fluids in her hand and hurriedly links it up to Finn's cannula. A new MRI needs to be scheduled; calls made to a neurologist. Clinical psychology, occupational therapy – everything seems to be happening now.

The doctor leaves and Josie slumps at Finn's side, holding his hand. Finn is sitting up in bed; to Freya, he doesn't seem to have understood. He's inattentive, apathetic to what's going on around him. Sophie's moved backwards against the wall, pale, standing with her hands over her face. Then she turns and walks out, past Freya.

Freya hesitates for a second, then follows her. She doesn't know Sophie, only what Robin's told her, but she shouldn't be alone.

Sophie heads quickly through the first double doors out, then keeps walking until she's a good distance from the hospital. Freya wonders if she's leaving, until she stops at a bench and sits down, digging in her bag, pulling out a hand-rolled cigarette and lighting it.

'Hi, Sophie?' Freya says tentatively. 'Do you mind if I join you?'

Sophie looks uncertain, then nods. She takes a drag from her cigarette and blows it out in one long plume.

'I'm Freya. I work with Robin.'

'You...' Sophie's face falls. 'Oh shit,' she mutters, and Freya, noticing the sweet smell of weed in the air, realises that the hand-rolled cigarette is a joint.

But Freya holds up her hands. 'Look, if you don't tell anyone, I won't.'

'Thank you,' Sophie says, then she starts to cry, bent forward, hands over her face.

Freya takes the joint out of her hand before she sets her hair on fire and lays it delicately on a corner of the bench. Then she reaches over and puts an arm round Sophie. She knows what it's like to have your life tipped upside down in a matter of seconds. Sophie may not have lost Finn, but right now he's not the man she loves, and might not be again.

After a while, Sophie's tears abate and she sniffs, wiping her eyes. 'I didn't think this could get any worse,' she says. 'I assumed it was all repressed memories. Like you see on TV. One day he'd remember what happened in a big flash, and I'd have my Finn back.'

'I'm sorry,' Freya replies, although she knows her words are pathetic. Nothing will make things better.

'What do I do now?' Sophie says, looking at Freya with wide eyes. 'What if he's like this forever? What if this' – she points angrily back to the hospital – 'is it?'

'Give it time, Sophie. You don't need to make any decisions now. See what the doctors say once they've run their latest tests.'

Sophie nods, sniffing again, as Freya's phone starts to ring. She pulls it out of her pocket with a final squeeze of Sophie's shoulder, and watches as Sophie reaches for her joint, putting it back between her lips.

'And don't let Robin see that,' Freya says with a smile, as she moves away. 'Josh? How's it going?'

'Ugh.' An exasperated sigh comes from the other end. 'Solicitors everywhere. All three have lawyered up. But they're not wriggling out of this one. Vardy's made a formal statement, CCTV confirms the time the boys went home, and the fingerprints have all come back as a match on the freezer and on the bottles and cans in the bus shelter.'

'Anything on the DNA on the fag butts?' Freya asks. She realises how much she likes speaking to Josh, his Geordie accent soft and lilting.

'Not yet. And we're waiting for fibres taken from their clothing to match to the ones found on the victim's body. But even without that, CPS have given us the green light to charge.' He pauses. 'Where are you? I can hear traffic.'

'Outside the Royal Berkshire Hospital.'

'Reading? What are you doing there?'

'I'm with Butler. Helping out with his friend.'

'Oh, okay.' Another pause. 'Do you want us to hold off so you can be the one to charge them? It was your insight, Freya, that got us where we are now.'

She smiles. 'Don't be daft, you did the hard work. You take the glory. Just let me know how it goes.'

Josh laughs at the other end of the phone. 'I will. Are you back tomorrow?'

'I should think so.'

'I'll look forward to it. See you, Freya.'

She ends the call and looks at her phone for a second. Despite the stories round the station, he seems like a nice guy. Maybe, just maybe…

She sighs, then heads back into the hospital. She thinks about Jonathan – what would he say? Go for it, probably. And a relationship with Josh, what would that be like? They'd have to follow the proper procedure, since they work together. Notify Baker, or whoever needed to know, and—

Christ, why is she thinking about this now?

She's reached the corridor outside Finn's room. The door is open, and inside she can see Robin talking to his friend, while Josie is sitting watching them, her mouth downturned. What a terrible situation for her, Freya thinks, not knowing whether her son is going to get better. Another victim of that awful night.

Robin gives Finn an awkward hug, then turns to Josie. But she shakes her head at Robin and he walks away, towards where Freya is waiting.

'Here you are,' Robin says. He's trying to keep his tone light, but she recognises the usual signs. His forehead is furrowed, head tilted slightly down, jaw tight. There's no doubt Robin's upset. 'Shall we go?'

He starts walking towards the exit and, without a word, she follows.

62

Robin can feel Freya watching him closely, as they get in his car and start the journey home. But he knows that if he starts to talk, he'll crumple, and he can't do that now. He can't.

He's still struggling to process what they found on the video and what Steph told them from her post-mortem. Robin knows Craig's gone away to discuss the case with her superiors, and he wonders what conclusion they'll come to.

So, Simon Sharp was allergic to nuts. Steph said they can run further tests to confirm that, as well as the resulting anaphylactic shock. But Robin's finding it hard to come to terms with the idea that he might have slit his own throat. And that Finn saw it all? What a horrific thought.

Robin can't imagine how terrifying that would have been: to be trapped in the middle of that raging storm, watching as your friend bled out in front of you. No mobile phone signal, no way of getting help, as Simon Sharp collapsed and died.

It all makes sense now: Finn's words in the hospital. *It was my fault.* They know from the video that Finn handed Sharp the sandwich that killed him. And the allergic reaction must have stirred something up in Finn's disturbed

357

consciousness, remembering Jacob Fraser all those years ago.

'Did Steph say any more about Finn's prognosis?' Freya asks. Her voice is hesitant and gentle.

Robin shakes his head. 'They won't know any more until the morning.'

'Oh. And how are things with Josie?'

'You saw her, Freya,' he replies, sharper than he intended. 'She hates me. And I don't blame her.'

'She needs time.'

Robin clenches his jaw. He's fucked up so many times this week, but his relationship with Josie is probably the worst. He feels the familiar tightening of his throat and he stares, determinedly, at the road. He will not cry. He won't.

'I should have known Finn was drinking,' Robin mutters.

He hears Freya turn in the seat next to him. 'Sophie didn't even know, Robin. Or Josie.'

'But I should have noticed he was struggling. I should have been a better friend.'

'Robin,' Freya says softly. 'If even his girlfriend and his mother hadn't realised what was going on, why should you?'

'I hadn't seen him since February. What sort of a friend was I?'

'Rob, I have friends I haven't seen for years—'

'But your supposed best friend?' he interrupts.

'I've only seen Mina's new baby once,' Freya says. 'Sometimes that's just the way life is. You've had a lot going on. You have a busy job.' She pauses. 'You can't be blamed for Finn being sick.'

'But brain damage, Freya? Fucking permanent brain damage?' He stops, forcing himself to take a long breath in. He clears his throat before he speaks again. 'What a mess.'

'I know,' Freya murmurs in reply.

They don't say anything else for the rest of the journey. Freya puts the radio on and Robin's glad of the music filling the deathly silence. And he's grateful to Freya, too, for just being there.

They stop outside the multistorey car park, where Freya left her car earlier that afternoon, and she undoes her seat belt. Sitting in the cathedral grounds seems like a long time ago to Robin; so much has come to pass since then.

Freya opens the car door.

'Sure you don't want to come back to mine?' she asks.

'No, no. I'll be fine.' He forces a smile, and she gets out of his car. He doesn't particularly want to be alone, but he also doesn't want to inflict his company on Freya. She must have had enough of him over the past few days.

And as he drives to his house, he realises he hasn't asked about her, or her case. Have those kids been charged with murder? He knows it was because of her unique slant that they've got that kid to confess. She is an incredible detective, and he never acknowledges that fact.

He gets home, parks up and lets himself into his house. The living room is still a state, denuded walls looking back at him accusingly. He will finish it himself, he decides anew. Even if it takes months.

He places his bag on the table and reaches inside, pulling out a memory stick. DC Grey gave it to him as he left the hospital.

'It's not relevant to the case,' he said. 'But I thought you'd want to see it.'

Robin had looked at it, confused, but before he could ask any more, Grey had been called away.

He makes a cup of tea now and fires up his laptop, putting the memory stick in the side. The computer loads a single video file, and Robin clicks it open.

The inside of the van comes into view. The timestamp in the corner reads 00:54; before the storm. Only Finn is in shot, sitting next to the table. Sharp is holding the camera close to his face; Finn looks embarrassed.

'So, tell me about Sophie,' Sharp asks.

'What's there to say?' Finn replies, trying to push the camera away.

'How did a nerdy old scientist like you get someone as lovely as her?'

Finn laughs. 'No idea. But I'm a lucky man.' He pauses. 'I'm going to ask her to marry me.'

'No!' The camera shakes, as Simon leans forward and gives Finn a hug. 'Good for you, mate.'

'I've no idea if she'll say yes.'

'Course she will. So, tell me about her. How did you meet?'

Robin listens, mug of tea in hand, as Finn talks about Sophie, a shy smile on his face. It's clear how much he loves her; Robin had no idea things were this serious between them.

'Robin doesn't like her, though,' Finn finishes, and Robin feels the familiar flash of guilt.

'Robin?'

'My best mate,' Finn replies. 'And I can't blame him. Both Sophie and I behaved like wankers when we saw him last.'

'So call him. If he's your best mate, he won't care. Buy him a beer and all will be forgiven. Anyway,' Sharp says from out of shot. 'I thought I was your best mate. I'm offended.'

'Piss off,' Finn says, laughing. 'I've known Robin my entire life. We grew up together.'

'That must be nice. To have someone who knows you that well.'

'It is.' Finn's expression is thoughtful. 'I know that whatever happens, Robin will have my back. Plus he's a cop, so, you know. He can arrest people and stuff.'

Sharp laughs. 'Always handy in an emergency.'

'Yeah. I haven't been there for him as much as I should have, though. His...' Finn pauses, and Robin knows he's thinking about Georgia and the twins. 'He's been through a hard time these past few years. I've been a shitty friend.'

'So call him,' Sharp says. 'It's never too late.'

Finn nods, then glances up as a loud crack of thunder echoes round the van. 'Shit, that was a big one,' he laughs. 'Turn this shit off, we need to get sorted.'

The camera jerks for a second, then the video goes black.

Robin stares at the screen. He feels his vision blur, his breathing halt in his chest. Hearing those thoughts, from Finn's own mouth, was almost too much to bear. His best friend – the person who knew him better than anyone else – knew he'd have done anything for him.

But Sharp had been wrong. It was too late.

Robin can't hold back any longer. The events of the past week – the murder, going home, Finn's diagnosis, even Freya's struggle – all come back in a rush; the facade he's worked so hard to maintain crashes down in an instant.

He's alone. It doesn't matter now. His face crumples and the tears come. He puts his head in his hands and his shoulders shake, as he starts to cry.

It's too much. It's all been too much.

63

Wednesday

Robin arrives in the doorway of Finn's room at the same time as Dr Blackstone, and from the expression on the doctor's face, Robin knows what he's going to say. Although he didn't think it possible, the doctor looks greyer today: all colour gone from his face, his lips leached of blood. Josie's waiting already, thin and pale. To Robin's surprise, she reaches out to take his hand as Dr Blackstone starts to speak.

'I'm afraid there's been no change in Finn's condition overnight,' he says. Robin feels Josie's grip tighten. 'The thiamine has restored Finn's vitamin B levels to normal, but unfortunately it looks like the damage has already been done. The MRI shows considerable lesions on Finn's brain, destruction to regions of the cerebellum – the area that coordinates muscular activity, hence his trouble walking – and some damage in the dorsal medial thalamus. I'm sorry, but his amnesia isn't going to significantly improve.'

'What about his short-term memory?' Robin asks.

The doctor shakes his head, grimly. 'It's unlikely Finn will be able to form new memories. I'm sorry.'

'And if you'd caught this earlier?'

There's a pause that says it all. 'It's possible,' Blackstone replies, 'that with early treatment of thiamine the Wernicke's might not have progressed to Korsakoff's; or the severity of Finn's symptoms might have been reduced. But nothing would have been guaranteed. The outcome might have been the same as we see today.'

'But it could have helped,' Robin challenges.

'Yes,' the doctor admits. 'It could have.'

There's a long silence. In the gap, Robin's vaguely aware of the background noise of the hospital: people going about their usual business, carrying on with their lives, while in this stifling, overheated room Finn's future has been destroyed.

'So there's nothing you can do?' Josie asks, her voice little more than a whisper.

'We've referred him to the clinical psychology team – they've been doing amazing things in rehabilitation. And we'll make sure Finn's transferred to a long-term therapy unit as soon as possible. He'll be more comfortable there.'

'And why didn't you spot this before?' Robin asks, unable to help the edge of anger creeping into his voice.

The doctor stares at him. 'We should have,' he begins. He clears his throat loudly. 'But with Finn's alcohol withdrawal and the benzodiazepines he was prescribed masking the symptoms, it got missed. It's a tricky one to diagnose.' The pager on his waist beeps, and Robin notices a look of relief cross his face. 'I'm sorry, I have to go,' he says, and leaves.

Robin stands in the corridor with Josie. He feels stunned. Josie looks into the room at her son, asleep in his bed.

'What do I do now?' she says, then starts to cry. Robin pulls her close in a hug and holds her tight.

'One day at a time,' he says, as she sobs into his chest.

After a while, her crying abates, and she pulls away from him, wiping her eyes with a tissue.

Robin gives her a sympathetic look. 'You hungry?' he asks. 'You look like you haven't eaten in days.'

She nods.

'Come on, I'll buy you breakfast.'

–

They walk in silence towards the hospital canteen, the two of them at a ceasefire – a necessity, given the circumstances. Robin's afraid to talk or to mention their argument. Slowly, they make their way down the queue, Josie picking up toast and butter and marmalade, Robin grabbing coffee for them both.

He pays and they take a seat on the far side of the room.

It's busy, just past ten a.m., people needing sustenance to get on with their day. Robin looks around while Josie eats: nurses, doctors, some patients in dressing gowns sitting at the tables.

'You want any of this?' Josie asks, pushing a slice of toast across to him. 'I don't seem to have much appetite nowadays.'

Robin takes it. No point letting food go to waste.

'Do you remember when you were teenagers? Can't have been more than fifteen or sixteen,' Josie says. 'And you'd both appear on a Sunday morning, completely hung-over but trying desperately to pretend you weren't.'

Robin smiles. 'We thought we hid it so well.'

'And you'd have slept in Finn's room on the floor, for some reason, rather than walking two doors down to your own house.'

'Georgia always gave me hell for getting pissed. You were more understanding.'

'So that was it.' Josie smiles at him. 'I owe you an explanation, Robin. About what happened with Finn that summer at Scout camp.'

'No, no, not at all. I'm so sorry I didn't listen to you. I'm sorry I searched your loft.'

She manages a laugh. 'I never thought *that* would happen. A police detective breaking into my house.' Josie takes a sip of her coffee, then places it down on the table, staring into it. 'Honestly? I thought that if you knew what happened, it would make the situation worse.' She shrugs. 'Guess it doesn't matter now. He's no longer under arrest, did you know?'

'I wondered. I noticed the room guard had gone.'

'Yes, this morning. DI Craig came by. She said that in light of the new evidence they were going to recommend a verdict of accidental death. That Simon had done it to himself.'

'That's something,' Robin replies.

'Hmm.' Josie thinks for a second. 'Finn was there, you know. When Jacob Fraser died. He saw it all.'

'What happened, Josie?' Robin asks quietly.

'I don't think they ever knew. Jacob was allergic to bee stings, but he carried an EpiPen and all the Scout leaders knew how to use it. But they were in the middle of nowhere, and the EpiPen didn't work. That poor kid was done for even before the ambulance arrived.'

Robin's coffee has gone cold, but he drinks the last dregs anyway, waiting for her to continue.

'There was no love lost between Finn and Jacob. Jake was one of the popular kids, even though he was a few years younger than Finn, and he made Finn's life a misery at that camp.'

Robin frowns. 'He did?'

'Yeah, without you there, Finn was fair game. He was always a target for bullies, but they didn't dare if you were around. I know you punched a few for him over the years,' she says, with a smile. 'Finn and Jake got in a fight the day before, and Finn said he wished him dead. So, when Jake died...'

'He couldn't possibly have thought it was his fault?'

'No, but he took it badly. You know Finn. Delicate soul. He didn't like the thought that Jake had died and he couldn't make amends. He did nothing but cry for weeks, wouldn't eat, didn't go out. Didn't want to go to the funeral. He missed the start of school, do you remember?'

Robin nods. 'You said he had glandular fever.'

'It was as good an explanation as any. I took him to a counsellor, but it didn't make any difference. And then you started writing him these silly notes, putting them through the door because you said he was infectious. It made him laugh. And your cast came off, and you wanted to play football and wouldn't take no for an answer.'

'I was a selfish dick, even then,' Robin replies, ruefully.

'No, it was good for him. It got him out of the house. There was you, with your limp after your broken leg. And him, all pale and skinny. You made quite a pair.'

'And that's it?' Robin asks. 'That's all there was to it?'

Josie nods. 'I thought that if DI Craig knew Finn had depression in his past, it would be one more black mark against his name. I should have told you. It was ridiculous.'

'It's fine. I should have left it be. I'm sorry,' Robin apologises.

Josie nods, then her mouth turns down and she looks like she's going to cry again. 'What are we going to do, Robin?' she says.

Robin sighs. 'Exactly what the doctor said. Get him settled in this therapy unit. Make sure he sees the right people. And you never know what might happen.'

The two of them walk slowly back to Finn's room, arm in arm. When they get there, Sophie's by Finn's bedside, talking quietly to him. They both look up when Josie and Robin arrive.

'Rob!' Finn says, all smiles. 'Haven't seen you in ages.'

Robin returns the grin. 'I know, Finn. It's been too long. Listen, I've got to head off. Work is calling. Sophie,' he says, 'can I have a word?'

Sophie looks surprised and gets up. They walk out into the corridor.

'Have you spoken to the doctor?' Robin asks.

Sophie nods. 'Yeah.' Her hand goes to her mouth and she stares at the floor. Robin wonders what she's going to do. Would she stick around, stay by Finn's side, given his prognosis?

Instead of asking, he pulls the memory stick out of his pocket. He hands it to her, her face confused. 'It's footage from the night of the storm,' he says. 'It's Finn, and he's talking about you. I thought you might want to see it.'

Sophie stares at it for a moment, then looks up at him. 'Thank you,' she says. He nods, then goes to walk back into the room. 'Robin?' she calls after him, and he turns. 'Are you going to be around more?' she asks.

'Yeah,' he replies. 'As much as Finn and Josie need me.'

'I'll see you soon then,' she replies.

Robin says goodbye to Finn and Josie, then starts to walk out. As he goes, his phone rings and he answers it.

'Butler,' says Craig at the other end. 'Are you at the hospital?'

'Just leaving now.'

'We've closed the investigation against Finn. No further action.'

'I heard.'

'It was the right decision. Given everything that's happened. And we charged Ian Calloway with perverting the course of justice. Did you hear we found the spare camera at his house?'

'No?' Robin's interested, but not surprised.

'Yeah. Taken out of the boot of Justin White's car the night of the storm. So he was trying to sabotage Mason and Sharp from the outset.' Craig pauses. 'Listen, I wanted to say thank you, for your help on the case.'

Robin laughs. 'You're kidding me.'

'No.' Craig sighs loudly at the other end of the phone. 'You were a pain in my arse, but you're a good detective. I wish I had your tenacity.' She pauses. 'What made you think to order the second opinion on the PM?'

Robin remembers the night with Freya and Josh and the freezer. 'It was something Freya said. They were testing an assumption that a death they were working on could have been an accident.'

Plus, Finn's bizarre tangent to Jacob Fraser's death. Robin had wondered: could the circumstances round Simon's death have been similar?

'Well, thanks,' Craig says again. 'And I like your DC, too. I like the way she thinks.'

'You can't have her,' Robin says quickly.

Craig chuckles. 'Tell her to call me when she gets sick of you. See you around, DS Butler,' she finishes. 'I just hope that next time we're on the same side.'

Robin hangs up. He's at his car now and climbs behind the wheel, before he makes another call.

'Freya,' he says when she answers. 'I'm on my way in. You got anything for me to do?'

Freya laughs, and Robin finds himself grinning. He's looking forward to seeing her, to getting back to his own nick, being around people he knows and enjoys working with.

'I've got some paperwork here you can help me with,' she says. 'And Josh mentioned something about a B and E that needs attention.'

'Fine, anything,' he replies. 'See you at lunchtime.'

'I'll get you a sandwich.'

'That would be good. Tuna?'

'Piss off.'

And with that, Robin starts the engine and drives home with a smile.

64

Sophie can't stand it any more. The repetitive speech, the constant reminding, the stuff he makes up. This shell, this destroyed husk – this isn't the man she loves. He looks like him, has the same voice and the same mannerisms. But everything else? It's gone.

The man in the bed is a stranger.

She heads off to the toilet, but when she's finished there, she realises she can't bear to go back. Stumbling, she walks quickly away from the hospital, out to the car park, then drives home. Her vision blurs, her hands shake. She can't do this, she can't.

Finn has his mother. He has his doctors, his therapists and the army of other experts who have been in to talk to them today. He doesn't need her. Half the time he doesn't even remember her. He asks, confused, 'How long have we been together?' He won't miss her when she's gone.

With trembling fingers, she puts her key in the door and closes it behind her. He should have died, she thinks, then hates herself for the very thought of it. But it would have been better. She could have grieved properly, then moved on with her life. Rather than this – this nothing.

She lies on her bed and, furious with the world, she punches her fists into her pillow. Nobody understands. It's hard to explain what's happened, what Finn's like now. People just think he's forgotten what happened in the

371

storm. Like that's a good thing, that he won't be cursed with the memory and the trauma of Sharp dying that night. But he doesn't remember anything. What he had for breakfast that day. Christ, he can't even remember if he *has* had breakfast.

Nobody asks about her. Nobody wonders if *she's* okay. It's about Finn, and she knows that's how it will be from now on. Her whole life will revolve around this lookalike; she will go from being his equal to being his nurse. Is that what she wants from her future?

She feels so alone. Already, she's felt the difference from the people she thought were her friends. A few have been there for her, but some have backed away. Not knowing what to say, what to do.

She rolls over on the bed, then winces, feeling something hard in her pocket against her hip. She pulls it out – it's the memory stick Robin gave her. She squints at it. What could this possibly show her that Robin thought was so important?

But curiosity pulls, and she gets up from the bed and fetches her laptop. Slowly, the video loads.

'So, tell me about Sophie,' a voice from behind the camera speaks: Simon.

'What's there to say?' Finn replies, trying to push the camera away.

Sophie looks at her boyfriend on the screen. This is the man she knew. Embarrassed at being filmed. Nervous, pushing his glasses back up his nose with his middle finger. The slight awkward hunch of his back. And shit, she misses this guy, so, so much.

'How did a nerdy old scientist like you get someone as lovely as her?'

Finn laughs. 'No idea. But I'm a lucky man.' He pauses. 'I'm going to ask her to marry me.'

Sophie watches as Simon leans forward and gives Finn a hug. 'Good for you, mate,' he says.

'I've no idea if she'll say yes.' Even after all the time they've been together, Sophie's surprised by his lack of confidence. Of course she would have said yes. Yes, a million times over.

She pauses the video and gets up, fetching the little velvet box from Finn's suitcase. She takes the diamond ring from its cushion and puts it on her finger for the first time. It fits perfectly, and she looks at it for a second, the stone sparkling in the light.

She presses play again.

'Course she will,' Simon says. 'So, tell me about her. How did you meet?'

'University, where else?' Finn replies. 'She asked me out.'

'Why doesn't that surprise me.' Simon laughs.

'And at first I couldn't work out what she was suggesting. Sophie was – still is!' Finn corrects himself. 'This incredible woman. She's smart, beautiful – you've met her,' he directs to Simon behind the camera. 'Much too good for me.'

'Much,' Simon confirms.

'And she was asking me out. I couldn't believe it. I still can't believe it. Every morning I wake up next to her and can't work out how I got so lucky.'

'I'm pleased for you, mate. But yeah, get her to marry you before she twigs what a loser you are.'

'Exactly.' Finn smiles and looks into the camera. Sophie feels like he's looking right at her, and she starts to cry, her vision blurring. 'My luck can't hold out forever.'

She hears Finn start to talk about Robin, but tunes it out. She can't stand the irony. That this was almost the exact moment his alcoholism caught up with him and his body failed. That Sharp ate the wrong sandwich and died.

And now he's in hospital and nothing will ever be the same again.

She wants to be with Finn. To feel his arms around her, his steady breathing in her hair. And then she thinks, but she can. He's not dead. He's still here.

Simon's loved ones can't say the same. He's gone for good. The news reports that his funeral will be held soon. For the people that loved Simon, that's it.

But Finn's still alive.

Sophie feels a bitter sting of self-hate. She's been so selfish. So blinkered. Inside, he's the same man she fell in love with. They'll find some way of getting him back – to a new normal. Treatments, therapy, drugs, whatever. The brain is an incredible organ, it can repair. Neurons can form new paths.

It might be hard, but so what? It's nothing she can't cope with.

She sits up on her bed, clicking away from the video and opening a new internet browser. She's used to reading medical research and scientific papers. If help is out there, she'll find it, and she'll get it for Finn.

She looks at the engagement ring on her finger. And, determination renewed, she starts to read.

65

The day of the funeral is bright, the sky a clear blue, the sun warm on Freya's face. She stands quietly by the freshly dug grave – Robin by her side, then Mina, then Josh.

Everyone is silent as the coffin is brought out on the shoulders of pall-bearers. In perfect synchronicity, they set the coffin down, then stand back with a formal bow.

The vicar starts talking, and Freya watches the others at the graveside. Thorpe's sister is here, his only family: a thin, pale woman who's been estranged from him for years, for reasons she hasn't talked about. There's Dave, the volunteer from the homeless shelter, and two men with him who Freya assumes must be people who knew Duncan from there.

And the four of them.

Freya wanted to be there, and the others agreed. Duncan Thorpe had little family. He was alone when he died, but he shouldn't be alone at his burial.

The last of the exhibits have come back from the lab. The DNA found on the fag butts and the bottles in the bus shelter is a match to all of the boys, Connor Vardy included. But the only fibres found on Thorpe's body come from Mark Black's jacket, seen on CCTV and seized from his house. The partial fingerprints on the freezer match Black and Garratt. Lee Cernis gave a full confession; a boy with a better solicitor and more sense than the other two.

Freya's attention is diverted back to the graveside, as the vicar concludes his eulogy. The coffin is lowered into the ground. With a final solemn nod, it's over, and the crowd starts to disperse.

'I'm going to head off,' Robin says. 'I'll see you at the station later?'

'Sure,' Freya agrees. She reaches up and straightens his tie, come loose in his characteristically scruffy manner. 'Have you got a present?'

'Of course, who do you think I am?' Robin says with a smile.

He heads off with his usual slow lope, and Freya watches him go. They've been working together again over these past couple of weeks, and it's been nice. Back to their usual routine: two coffees in the morning, each taking it in turns to buy for the other. They've been on a sexual assault case, and despite the grim nature of the investigation, she's been enjoying herself.

In the brief lulls at work, she catches Robin watching her, his quiet concern for her warming. She's even spent a Saturday with him, paintbrush in hand, helping to sort out the mess he'd made of his living room.

It was a strange day. Robin in tracksuit bottoms and an old Foo Fighters T-shirt. Music playing on the radio, the windows open, a cool breeze blowing through. Despite him being her boss, she felt relaxed around him, taking the piss out of his singing, pulling him up on his frankly horrible efforts at painting. At the end of the day, he offered to cook dinner, but she refused. Somehow it felt wrong. Too intimate. More like a date. And that wasn't what this was.

It wasn't.

Josh, on the other hand... He's on the opposite side of the graveyard, talking to Thorpe's sister. He's looking nice today, dressed in a black suit and tie, a white shirt underneath. It flatters his dark hair and brings out the blue in his eyes.

Mina is standing next to her, watching her with a barely disguised smirk.

'What?' Freya says.

'I can tell you want to.'

'Shut up, Mina.'

'What's stopping you?'

'I... I don't know,' Freya replies, and she realises she really doesn't. Jonathan's death doesn't loom so large nowadays.

She's even been to the doctor. The woman GP listened for far longer than their allotted eight minutes' appointment time as Freya talked through the sanitised version of the problem – the death of her boyfriend, unable to sleep, working too hard, struggling to cope. She was handed a prescription for Zopiclone and told to book another appointment after a fortnight. It was no more than Freya expected, but actually just the act of talking about it helped. She's cut back at work to her normal contracted hours, and spent evenings at home, catching up on Netflix. She's even been on a night out with the girls, reluctantly enjoying herself in a hot and noisy bar over too many cocktails.

Perhaps she is ready.

Josh comes over to stand with the two of them, then looks confused at Mina's expression.

'What?' he asks, smiling.

'I'm going to go,' Mina says. 'Leave you two to it.'

'To what?' Josh says, puzzled.

'Josh,' Freya starts. 'Can you answer something for me?'

'Anything.'

'I heard a rumour that the reason you and Elise split up was because you slept with someone one month after you arrived here.'

'Bloody police station gossip.' Josh shakes his head in disbelief. 'Half true.'

'Which half?'

They start walking slowly away from the graveyard, down the neat gravel path towards their cars.

'Yes, I slept with someone a month after I got here. But Elise and I had already split up by then.'

'Promise?'

'Promise.'

They stop next to Freya's car. Josh reaches up and pulls the tie away from his neck, then undoes the top button of his shirt. The action makes something flip in Freya's stomach. Something she hasn't felt for a while.

'Why?' he says with a slight smile.

'Just wondering.'

'Why?' he asks again. He's close to her now, and Freya can smell his aftershave, something she could definitely get used to.

Maybe it's the simple act of standing in a graveyard, reminding her that life is short. Or maybe it's Sandra's words from a few weeks before: don't leave it too late. But Freya decides to take the leap.

'Does that offer still stand?' she asks. She's desperately trying to play it cool, but she can't help the smile creeping onto her face.

'Which one?' But his expression betrays his mock innocence.

'You know exactly which one.'

'Are you asking me out, Freya West?'

'Yes. Now stop taking the piss or I'll change my mind.'

He laughs. 'There is nothing I would like more,' he replies.

Freya feels her face flush and quickly gets into her car, leaving him standing in the car park. She closes the door and starts the engine. Through the window, she can see Josh watching her, his hands in his pockets, a big grin on his face.

What have I let myself in for? she thinks to herself. But she can't help but smile.

66

Robin stands outside the blue-painted front door and presses the bell. He has a present in his hand, wrapped in light yellow paper. It has teddy bears on it. Inside the house, he can hear the faint sound of a baby crying.

The door opens and Liv stands there, the chubby baby in her arms screaming blue murder.

'Come in, come in,' she says, and goes back into the living room, slumping onto the sofa.

He follows her through, moving a pile of baby clothes off one of the chairs and sitting down. Liv's normally pristine house is a complete mess, every surface covered, discarded glasses and mugs strewn around.

'How are you doing, Liv?' Robin asks over the noise of the screaming.

Liv herself is equally dishevelled, hair tied roughly back from her face, a line of something white and curdling down her shoulder. But she smiles widely, her eyes bright.

'Fucking knackered,' she replies. 'This one feeds on the hour, every hour. Doesn't care whether it's night-time or not.' She reaches up and undoes her top, then expertly pushes the baby towards her breast. Robin tries hard to focus on her face. 'But we're good, aren't we, Lucas?'

'Lucas? That's a lovely name,' Robin replies. He offers his present. 'I got you something. Or rather, for Lucas.'

'Thank you. I'll open it later, if you don't mind. Got my hands full.'

'Course.'

They sit in silence for a moment, the baby sucking happily on Liv's breast. Robin debates making his excuses. He's not sure why he's here, except for the fact that Liv had texted him, inviting him over.

'Robin,' she begins. 'I wanted to thank you. For everything you did when he was born.'

Inwardly, Robin sighs with relief. Liv has always been unpredictable. But this? This is fine.

'I… I don't know,' she continues. 'I panicked. I don't know what I would have done without you there.'

'I didn't mind, Liv. It was quite an experience.'

'I bet!' she laughs. 'When you woke up that morning, you hadn't expected to watch someone be cut open and a baby pulled out.'

'A lot of things I'd never expected have happened recently. Seeing Lucas here being born is probably the best.'

'Well, good.' Then a look passes across Liv's face that he can't interpret. 'Listen. There's something you should know.'

'What?' he asks, warily.

Liv points to the bookshelf at the side of the room. 'Over there, in the small blue pot.'

Robin gets up slowly and goes across. He looks to where she's pointing and finds a light blue ceramic jar.

'Inside,' Liv says.

He picks it up and tips the contents into his palm. His stomach drops. It's a black memory stick. He's seen one like this before. He turns slowly, holding it between two fingers.

'Take it,' Liv says.

'What's on it?' But he knows. Of course he knows.

Amy had one just like it. With footage from the CCTV of the garage. Footage proving he met with Trevor Stevens mere minutes before he had his fatal car crash.

'Amy gave it to me,' Liv confirms. 'The night she died.'

Lucas has finished feeding and she holds the drowsy baby in one arm, while re-dressing herself with the other. It's such a surreal conversation to have in these circumstances. Death, murder – and newborn babies.

'And what have you done with it?' Robin asks quietly.

'Nothing,' Liv replies. She winds Lucas, then deftly swaddles him in a blanket and places him in the carrycot on the floor, before sitting carefully back down on the sofa. 'And I don't intend to. This is Amy's shit, not mine. Having it in my house feels dirty. I don't want it any more.'

Robin carefully puts it in his pocket. 'There's no other copy?'

'Not as far as I know.'

'Thank you, Liv.'

But Liv shakes her head. 'Robin, I don't know what you did, or what went on between you and Trevor, and I don't want to know. You and I have spent a bit of time together over the last year or so, and I pride myself on having a good sense about people. And I think you're one of the good ones.' Robin shakes his head, but stays quiet. 'You did the right thing for Jonathan. And you did the right thing for me. That's all the evidence I need. Okay?'

Robin nods slowly. 'Okay.'

Liv smiles. 'Now make me a cup of tea, will you? I'm gasping.'

It's late by the time Robin leaves. The sky is getting dark, night closing in. He's stayed with Liv far longer than he intended, taking brief childcare duties while she had a shower (although Lucas slept the whole time, so Robin didn't have to do anything), then tidying up the mess in her kitchen.

They talked, a bit. Liv mainly gushing about her baby, Robin about the twins. It felt good. Therapeutic even, to see her doing so well.

There's no doubt in his mind now that he wants to be a father. The pride he heard in Liv's voice, the hope, the new joy in her life. He doesn't fear it now, more a worry he might miss out. Because who is he possibly going to meet? he thinks. You don't leap straight to parenthood. You go on dates, like the look of someone, fall in love, move in together. Sandra was right – women don't just drop into your lap. You have to make the effort.

But it won't be with Liv. Robin leaves her house with no doubt in his mind that that's it. There's nothing between them, and there never will be. She doesn't want it and nor does he.

For a moment he sits in his car outside her house, wondering where to go next. It's late; Freya must have finished at work by now, and he realises how much he's looked forward to seeing her every day. Her easy smile, her gentle teasing, making him laugh.

Robin knows it takes a lot for him to feel truly at ease with someone, and this past fortnight he's felt at his best being with her again. She's the first person he sees every day, the last person he speaks to at night. Never anything untoward, never anything his DCI would disapprove of, but still. It's there.

He picks up his phone and texts her.

> Took longer than expected with Liv. You
> still at work?

He waits. Three dots rotate on the screen and he smiles, imagining her texting, the concentration on her face.

It beeps.

> Left hours ago! At pub.

He replies.

> What pub?

A slight pause.

> O'Neill's.

He starts the engine of his car and heads back. He's not usually one to socialise with work colleagues, but today he fancies it. To be around people, have a pint and listen to the conversation. He hopes Mina will be there; he wants to catch up properly about her kids. And to see Freya.

He parks up at home, then starts walking towards the pub. The atmosphere in town is buzzing. It's a Friday night, and people are out in the streets, enjoying dinner on the tables outside on the High Street, listening to the buskers next to the Buttercross. He crosses the road quickly and walks up to O'Neill's.

The pub is full; Robin can hear the chatter of conversation and laughter before he's even opened the door. And then he sees her. Through the large glass window, he watches Freya as she stands next to a high table, a glass of wine in her hand. Her long blonde hair is loose, and she's laughing; Robin realises in a sharp moment of clarity how beautiful she is.

He places one hand on the door handle. And then he notices who she's with. Josh Smith is standing next to her. He's in the same white shirt from the funeral, tie now discarded, collar open wide at the neck. But on Josh this casual look seems classy, attractive, when Robin knows on him it would just look a mess. Josh leans forward and says something into Freya's ear. She laughs in reply, then puts her hand on his arm.

Robin pauses. This is more than two workmates out for a drink. This is something else. He remembers Josh asking her out when they were away in Devon, and her coy response. She likes him, he can tell.

He taps his middle finger on the door handle, thinking. Freya deserves this. A man like Josh, who can make her happy. Someone attractive and fun and quick to smile. Uncomplicated; exactly everything Robin isn't. He looks at Freya. At the line he shouldn't cross.

And Robin Butler turns and walks slowly home.

Acknowledgements

Finn's story has been on my mind for years, so a big thank you to Louise Cullen at Canelo for letting me write it. Your guiding hand on the manuscript made it the altogether better novel it is today. Thank you also to Francesca Riccardi, Siân Heap, Claudine Sagoe, Jenny Page, Nicola Piggott and Iain Millar; they are an incredible bunch at Canelo.

Thank you to Ed Wilson, for steering me through the crazy, and to Hélène Butler and the rest of the team at Johnson and Alcock.

This book pulled on more experts than ever before, and I couldn't have written it without their guidance:

Thank you to the usual suspects – to Dr Matt Evans for all things medical, and PC Dan Roberts for all things police. (Matt, I'm sorry, there really was quite a bit with this one.) On the meteorology side, thank you to Dr Alec Bennett, Dr Marie Bennett and Professor Giles Harrison. To Dr Sam Batstone, thank you for providing the solution to what was wrong with Finn and for everything related to WKS. Thank you to Steph Fox for your help (and graphic photographs) on the blood spatter scene.

Thank you to Anne Roberts and Maria and Isaac for the guided tour of Kingskerswell, and to Shake, Damian Sciberras and Ed Kernahan for the technical guidance on cameras. Thank you to Aidan Riley and Robin Nash for everything Navy, and Ali Burns for everything TA (even though the whole plot line got cut, sorry.) For the valuable information on servers and IT, thank you to Sophie Harper and Simon Ricketts. Thank you to Charlie Roberts for spotting the gaping plot hole that everyone else missed, just in the nick of time. And finally, thank you to Susan Scarr and Laura Stevenson.

As always, all mistakes, deliberate or otherwise, are down to me and me alone.

Last but not least, thank you to Chris and Ben. And let's not forget Max, who has destroyed my peace and quiet in ways only a small black spaniel knows how.

Do you love crime fiction and are always on the lookout for brilliant authors?

Canelo Crime is home to some of the most exciting novels around. Thousands of readers are already enjoying our compulsive stories. Are you ready to find your new favourite writer?

Find out more and sign up to our newsletter at canelocrime.com